Illusions of More

A Novel

by

Janiece Hopper

Sage Lane
Woodinville, WA

Published by Sage Lane
Woodinville, WA

Illusion of More is a work of fiction. All names, characters, places, occurrences, objects, and assessments are products of the author's imagination or used fictitiously.

ISBN 13: 978-0-9814777-3-2

Dedicated
to
American public school teachers
and the work of The Writers' Lair

Prologue

Stay away from the river.
The old ones say
the diamond on top is really the tear
drop
of La Llorona.
Stay away from the river.
Do not dip a toe.
The depths
seize
whatever you reach with.
The ghost of the mother who
drowned
her own
binds
with a black shawl.
Stay far away.
Too many forget.
Sometimes, the river
will
rise.

Chapter One

"My reading is dead!" Pilar gasped. The little girl held the fourth grade reading book, rigid as a stillborn, across her open palms as if pleading with the pretty *gringa* teacher to take the burden away. Wrenched from her mother's tongue, she was reeling from an abrupt entry into the United States. I was right there with her when Ms. O'Mara took the textbook away, shrouding its disposal with a typewritten page. I'd been smuggled in with Pilar, buried just below her memory. In old countries, folktales tell of ghosts. Sometimes in new countries, the dead can tell tales of folks. It's possible in places like Purewater.

"Oh honey!" In English, the sweetness of the hive is a term of endearment and Sienna O'Mara's voice was as soothing as *meil* on a raw throat. She looked into Pilar's eyes and assured her, "You can read this. *Tú puedes leerlo. Esta es tu cuenta.*"

The auburn streaks in the teacher's long hair glinted like summer night lightning illuminating desert sky. Sienna knelt, tilting her head close to Pilar's as if she didn't know or didn't care that the girl's aunt had been picking nits just days before. Her breath smelled of cinnamon—of celebrations in Mexico. As she pointed to Pilar's words, gun shots exploded in the distance.

A disembodied voice, lanced with panic, flooded the room. "This is a lockdown!"

The jarring squeal of sirens racing down First Street echoed

1

through the thinly insulated walls of the modular classroom. Eyes widened as children clasped hands.

"This is a lockdown!" Principal Hayes repeated through the intercom. "Teachers, you know what to do."

Sienna strode toward the heavy metal door and used the hex key on top of the fire extinguisher to lock it from the inside. She pulled a yellow plastic flashlight from a backpack hanging nearby. The expired batteries gave barely enough light to guide everyone toward the middle of the portable where bookcases created a hallway of sorts. "Come over here!" she commanded. Her voice was calm and filled with authority.

"*Venga!*" a girl named Cassandra grabbed Pilar's hand and pulled. Abuzz with terror, children burrowed like bees into the deepest cells of a hive. Sienna gestured for them to sink onto the floor with their backs against the shelves.

The sirens grew louder. "Are the bad guys here?" Javier tensed. "Are they going to get us?"

"We are safe," Sienna replied.

He glanced from side to side. "What if they break in?"

"I'll fight them," she promised.

"Do you do karate?"

She shook her head. "No. Yoga."

Kids looked at each other, questioningly.

Javier drew a ragged breath. "I'll help you," he promised.

"*Yo tambien,*" Miguel said.

"That's very nice of both of you," Sienna replied, "but I can handle the bad guys all by myself."

Que machisma! The children relaxed. Huddled together, they managed grim smiles, all except Pilar. She was terrified, as rigid as a skeleton buried in Sonoran sand. A wailing squad car skidded into the school parking lot. It shut off its siren, but the officer's radio spouted terse jumbled codes. After weeks of skirting the law, Pilar was surrounded, certain *la policia* were coming to get her now. Her story lay forgotten, on the edge of a battered student desk.

Pilar was a newcomer in a small town in one of the northernmost parts of the United States. She'd been sent from a village that hadn't made it onto any map of Mexico that could be found in *Los Estados Unidos*. Pilar and her older half-brother, Esteban, lived with their godparents, Ramon and Lucia Vega, in a tiny riverside apartment perched over *Casita Rio,* the only Mexican restaurant in Purewater. *Casita Rio* was thriving in Purewater, but Pilar was not. When she was in her homeroom class, she spent a lot of time looking at pictures in the *Reading Fare* textbook and failing to "follow along" as her *gringo* classmates read paragraphs aloud. Tracking words she had never heard spoken, let alone seen in print, was impossible. Her classroom teacher frowned as if Pilar continually lost her place on purpose.

Sienna O'Mara worked with small groups of kids who didn't know very much English. The children told Pilar that although *la maestra de inglés* wore no ring, she was in love with a man whose picture was on the back of a teacher book. This seemed like a perfectly feasible romance. After all, someone's older sister kept a crinkled tabloid image of *El Fuego's* lead singer taped to the inside of the kitchen cabinet to reward herself for putting dishes away.

The children told Pilar that Sienna had a son named Matt and that he already knew how to drive. They discussed the teacher's dangling earrings and the jeans she wore with petite rhinestones embroidered on the back pockets. They told Pilar that she was smart and that she'd gone to college. "So she can sit on desks whenever she wants." Sienna had promised them all that if they grew up and went to college they could come back to Moore Elementary School and sit on any desk, including hers, if they wanted to.

She never told the English learners that special opportunity was a long shot on two levels. Not many English learners finished high school in Purewater, let alone went onto the university. And if they did, she might not be around when they came back. Funding for her position was always precarious, granted more or less begrudgingly, depending on which of the Hadley sisters was on the school board.

When standardized achievement test scores become the primary measure of a student or a teacher, readers are taught they need to know who did what to whom and why right away, but, Sienna O'Mara was patient. She held the tension of not knowing long enough to do the story Pilar dropped into her lap justice. The living may say she was a teacher who went too far, but for the dead, for *Los Muertos,* the jury is still out.

Chapter Two

The crime that led to the lockdown started early in the day. While a *gringo* going by the name B.J. Baldwin posted a help wanted ad on the Internet, Pilar cried over her breakfast at the table in the snug kitchen of *Casita Rio*.

"She can't understand the teacher," Lucia said. *"No entiende la maestra."*

Ramon frowned at the tears rippling on the *leche* in the child's glass cereal bowl. He seemed on the verge of tears himself. "Five days a week is hard to get used to, isn't it, *mija*?" In Mexico, Pilar had only had school a few times a month. "Do you want to stay home?" he asked. "Do you want a job making *mole*?"

It was early autumn and already cold outside. Working with her godparents in *Casita Rio*'s snug kitchen sounded far more appealing to Pilar than shuffling through the dense fog rising off the river to face the incessant English and bewildering worksheets piling up in her desk at Moore Elementary. There were more students in her new school than there had been people of all ages back home in Redención and the only Spanish her harried American teacher, Mrs. Nancy Albright, seemed to know was *"Apurate!"* Hurry up!" Pilar gazed at Lucia through weary eyes and wet lashes. Couldn't her *madrina* see how much happier she'd be if she quit going to Moore Elementary School and just stayed home?

"Ah!" Lucia sighed as if she fully understood the allure of

grating cocoa, but she scolded her husband. "Ramon, she didn't come to this country to study *mole*. Here, school is regular. She can go through all the grades." With the hem of her apron, Lucia dabbed at Pilar's cheek. "Stop this, *mija*! Your banana will be too salty."

Esteban burst through the curtain between the kitchen and dining area of the restaurant. He stopped short in dismay. His little sister's tears frightened him in ways the border patrol did not.

Pilar drew back from Lucia's makeshift hanky. She did not want to trouble Esteban. At seventeen, he was working full-time at *Casita Rio*, chopping vegetables and washing dishes and Pilar knew her brother well enough to know Esteban did not want to be confined to a kitchen. He'd been working since they'd arrived and Ramon and Lucia were not actually able to pay him for his labor. It was enough that they'd taken the undocumented children in at all. Pilar knew the four of them were doing their best to adjust. Indeed after only three weeks in Purewater, Esteban had already found his true love. Now, he wanted to buy a new outfit, one without frayed edges and frying stains to wear to Dulce Gantala's *quinceanera*.

Ramon glanced at the paper, still quivering in Esteban's grip. "*Qué es esto?*"

"*Trabajo!*" Esteban exclaimed. Someone had brought a print-out of Baldwin's Internet ad to post on *Casita Rio*'s community bulletin board. They did this because few new immigrants had access to online technology.

By the time Pilar lugged her faded Goodwill backpack from the apartment to Moore Elementary School, Baldwin had thirty-one applicants for the landscaping job he'd posted. The same number of men had applied as there were kids in Nancy Albright's fourth grade class and Esteban was one of them. He'd used the restaurant's telephone to call. When Baldwin answered, he asked if Esteban was able to hack thorny blackberry vines for ten hours straight. Imagine asking a young man from a village teeming with *machismo* if he were strong or skilled enough to do anything!

Esteban didn't say that he had practically been born brandishing a machete in his hand. He simply replied, "I can work hard all day."

"*Bueno!*" Baldwin said. "You must come in uniform, a black

sweatshirt, jeans, and work boots." He told Esteban all of this in poorly articulated Spanish lifted from what he'd typed into Google translator at the public library. He was clever, leaving no record of his plot on his personal computer. "Oh," Baldwin added casually as if he hadn't also planned this bit, "Don't forget a ski cap, black. It's colder than a *bruja's* tit out there."

Although Baldwin knew nothing about witches, he seemed like *un jefe bueno* to Esteban. He seemed like a boss who could help him get what he wanted, a dance with Dulce at her fifteenth birthday party. The event was still months away. He'd have time to save up his earnings. He nodded with the receiver still to his ear, grinning, giving Ramon what he'd already learned was an American affirmative, a thumbs-up.

When the call ended, Esteban swept through the empty dining area of the restaurant, checking the creases of the booths where what was in patron's pockets sometimes fell out. And with the combination of coins he found there jingling in his pocket, Esteban dashed to Bonny Deals, covering the five blocks and crossing the busy highway quickly to buy a hat. Work boots cost more money than Pilar's grandma in Mexico had ever had at one time in her whole life! He didn't have enough for them. He hoped *el jefe* would not notice that he was wearing the pair of battered athletic shoes that Ramon had given him upon their arrival in Purewater, he and Pilar still wearing cheap flip-flops the coyote picked up for them at a Wal-Mart somewhere in Arizona.

Esteban followed older men desperately casting their caps down on the checkout counter, each rationalizing the purchase whether he got the job or not. They moved through the express lane, paying cash while, one aisle over, the manicured stay-at-home moms from up on Teagan Hill who owned the gardens the men wanted to work in, waited to slide their debit cards through the machine. They chatted with their toddlers about the diapers, juice boxes, coloring books, and other luxuries like new towels moving down the conveyer belt. And while they stood there, effortlessly teaching their offspring hundreds of English words, Pilar sat in school painstakingly copying the directions from a *Reading Fare* worksheet onto the lines meant for the answers to the questions because she did not know what else to do.

After lunch recess, Pilar hurried to her English Learner's class, while thirty-one men waited in thirty-one different locations within a ten block radius of the school. Esteban stood where Baldwin had told him to, just outside the front door of the public library, right by the book drop. And Baldwin, wearing the exact same uniform he had prescribed for all his applicants, strode into the Bank of U.S. to hand a note to the teller. She went to the vault and returned with two large canvas bags. Only when she handed them to him did anyone in the building realize the institution was being robbed. A teenager in the next line met her eyes.

"Robbery?" he mouthed.

The teller nodded, pressing the panic button under the till. As Baldwin sprinted out of the building through double glass doors, Matt O'Mara tossed his deposit onto the counter. "I'm going after him."

He darted after the thief the very instant Chief Goodwin got the call, spurring Purewater police to action. Chief Goodwin's secretary called the school district's central office and the operator there called Moore's principal because the bank was only a block away from the elementary school and there was no telling what the crook would do next. Within two minutes of the holdup, Deedee Hayes came on the intercom, announcing, "This is a lockdown!"

As Pilar cowered in the eerie shadows of bookcases, her ELL teacher's son dashed after Baldwin. Matt stopped momentarily, suddenly remembering he'd parked in a fifteen-minute-only stall. Would they tow his car? Even if they didn't, he'd be late for his Civics class. He heard his Tae Kwon Do instructor's voice in his head, telling him he was overthinking.

Matt's split second of indecision had given Baldwin enough of a head start to dash across First Street and into an alley where a tan SUV waited between the liquor store and laundromat. Baldwin tossed the money bags in. He pulled his black sweatshirt off over his head and jumped into the driver's side. The vehicle backfired twice as he gunned the engine and sped behind Purewater businesses.

Matt sprinted after Baldwin so he could report which side street the crook turned up on his way to the highway. He was surprised when the vehicle turned toward the river instead. Matt ran faster, never thinking about the possibility of getting shot until a flying pebble from the gravel road struck his upper lip. Stung, he stopped. He realized that if the bandit were armed, it would be wise to act as if he were giving up, but once the SUV disappeared behind a copse of alders, Matt slipped into the woods.

He picked through red-fringed cedar trees and bushes drooping with over-ripe blackberries until he came upon the SUV. The driver's side door hung open. Matt was stunned to catch a glimpse of Baldwin riding an inner tube down the frothy Purewater River. Nearly gaping with incredulity, Matt reached for his cell phone.

It wasn't in his pocket. He'd left it on the seat in his car back at the bank. Ignoring the blackberry thorns that sliced his hands and at his ears, Matt dashed out of the wooded zone. Sprinting toward First Street, he saw police lights flashing ahead. He was very close to the public library. As he reached the parking lot, he recognized Officer Stroup with his gun pointed at a familiar kid.

Breathlessly, Matt shouted, "That's not the crook!" Panting, he pointed a bloodied finger, "He's...he's on the river."

Keeping his weapon drawn, Stroup tried to make sense of Matt's report.

"He didn't do it," Matt gasped. "I was at the bank and I saw the robbery." Still panting, he gestured at Esteban whose eyes were wide with terror. "Besides, I know him."

Esteban was so frightened it took him several heartbeats to realize that Matt was the kid he'd sat next to in chemistry for the three days he'd tried American high school. Esteban had no idea how to read English and there had been no such thing as science in Redención.

"Hey, professor," the teacher had said, looking at Matt as if he were somehow more able than she to facilitate a newcomer's understanding, "help him. The unit test is in two weeks." Matt had tried really hard, but just because his mom was an ELL teacher didn't mean he could say much more than *"Me llamo Matt"* and *"Buenas dias."* He certainly didn't know how to explain molecular chemistry in a foreign language. Esteban dropped out long before the high school ELL teacher had time to test him to verify that he needed help learning English.

Since then, the two young men had seen each other in the alley behind the dojang a few times. *Casita Rio* was right next to Master In-Su's. Sometimes, when Matt walked to his car before or after class, he glanced in the open back door of the restaurant to see Esteban and Pilar enshrouded in steam, unloading the dishwasher together. Sometimes, when Esteban took the trash out, he glanced in the open back door of the dojang to see Matt doing push-ups. They never talked when they crossed paths, like the time they both took recycling out one Saturday morning. They simply nodded in recognition of each other's humanity. Now Esteban looked from Matt to the police officer. Could *el gringo* help him? Would he? And why would he bother, if it meant getting involved with *la policia*?

"Matt!" Officer Stroup exclaimed. "Are you the kid from the bank?" Stroup, a few local police officers including Chief Goodwin and the fire chief studied with Master In-Su. Matt sparred regularly with all of them.

"I chased the crook to the river," Matt explained. "And the guy jumped in an inner tube and floated away. His SUV is still down there."

Stroup was even more incredulous than Matt had been. Nevertheless he lowered his gun and radioed the information in. As sirens heading south filled the air, he questioned Esteban about his clothing. Esteban was silent, panicking about what would happen to his little sister if he was taken away.

"He doesn't know much English, sir," Matt said.

"Ask him why he's wearing that outfit. Same as the robber."

Matt looked down at his own clothes. "Uh, sir, I'm wearing the same as the robber, 'cept for the ski cap and shoes."

Stroup glanced at Matt's always grungy sneakers, now made more so, caked as they were with bits of mud and woodsy debris and chuckled. From his radio, they heard "Confirmation. Suspect under South Side Bridge on a black inner tube."

10

"Sorry, kid." With a curt nod to Esteban, Stroup leapt into his car and sped off with the siren blaring. Two blocks south, in front of the dentist's office, he saw another man dressed in jeans, a black sweatshirt, and ski cap. By the end of the day, the seven policemen in Purewater had apprehended twenty-seven, identically-dressed men standing in different locations all around town. They were all hauled down to the station for questioning. The ones who had no legal documentation were sent to a detention center, marked for deportation. Luckily, Esteban was not one of them.

He did not know what to say to Matt except an awkward *"Gracias."* Before Matt could reply, *"De nada,"* Esteban turned away and bolted back to *Casita Rio.* He spent an hour trembling on his knees among mite-laced *escobas.* Broomstick bristles poked at him while he prayed in a closet. Then, under self-imposed house arrest, he imprisoned himself in the kitchen, dicing chiles for the rest of the day. Lucia gave him red onions to chop as well, an excuse to provoke the warm tears she knew the tightly drawn skin on his thin face needed to remind him he was still alive.

Matt returned to the bank, wondering if there would be a ticket on his windshield. The bank manager had no interest in pressing charges for a parking violation. Instead, Mr. Penn thrust antiseptic hand wipes, Band-Aids, and the plate of chocolate chip cookies from the drive-up window into Matt's sweaty palms. By the time he'd eaten a cookie, Moore Elementary had been given the all-clear.

The robbery cost the kids in Sienna's class precious learning time. She only got to see each of her groups for thirty minutes a day and it was already time for her fourth graders to leave.

"Venga!" Cassandra pulled on Pilar's hand to no avail. Pilar was still petrified. Back up against binders full of standardized test preparatory material, she could do nothing except sit like a brittle bush, desiccating at the foot of a giant saguaro.

Sienna looked every child in the eye to see if any of them were still even a little bit scared before she let them burst out into the fresh air where the yard duty whistles seemed engaged in a vigorous call and response with the faint sirens receding in the south. Then, she got her stainless steel commuter mug from the corner of her desk and returned to sit on the floor beside Pilar. The tea she'd made during lunch was still warm, but not nearly as hot as she liked it. Star anise and licorice wafted in the air as she took the lid off. She wanted to reheat her drink in the staff room and find out why there had been a lockdown, yet in the immediate aftermath of the robbery, she just sat with a frightened little girl. She just sat, silent and strong, sipping lukewarm tea.

Ten minutes later, when the bell rang, she said, "I'm going to call Mrs. Albright to ask if you can stay here until you are ready to go back to class. Okay?"

Pilar did not, could not answer. She watched Sienna look up the extension and dial.

"Nancy," she said. "This is Sienna. I've got Pilar out in the portable. The lockdown was scary for her, so I'm going to let her stay with me for a while." Sienna frowned. "*Reading Fare* test? Seriously?" She paused and said, "No administrator is going to expect you to make her take it. She's a newcomer. It's not appropriate. No! I'm not saying we should dumb anything down, but she just got here." As the voice on the line continued, she bit her upper lip hard and raised her eyes to the ceiling. Finally, Sienna said, "She's upset. I'll send her back when she's ready." She hung up to sit with Pilar some more.

After a while, Sienna said, "Those sirens were so loud. *Muy ruido!*" She touched her ears and grimaced. "*Me duele el ojeas.*" She put her hand on her heart. "*Y mi corazon? Y tu?*" She searched Pilar's face and, finding what she was after, declared, "*Pilar es fuerte!* Pilar is strong." The teacher's proclamation seemed to be a form of fibrillation. Pilar was released from the rigidity of terror with a jolt. "*Venga!*" Sienna said, as if raising the dead. The girl stood.

Sienna led Pilar to a small table near the larger kidney-shaped one where she usually met with groups and gave her a piece of plain paper and two plastic boxes. The first was filled with *un arco de iris*, a rainbow of colored pencils. The second was filled with crayons in a wide range of human skin and hair colors. "*Hacer que necesitas,*" she whispered softly. "Make what you need."

Pilar didn't really know what to do with a blank page. The only kids who had time to draw in class were the ones who finished their work early and, of course, Pilar never could. During the grueling trip to America, she had been allowed to color. She had two coloring books—one of classic nursery rhymes and another filled with sketches of *las sirenas*, mermaids. On the hot, black rubber floor of a rust-coated van, she filled in lines that had already been drawn, taking care that the cooler centers of the softening crayons did not snap as the bright wax bled through her fingers.

Pilar had always understood that the journey to America was both necessary and forbidden. She obeyed instructions to dive under stacks of brightly woven *frazadas* if she ever felt even the slightest downshifting of speed. There was no danger of her missing it. The 1982 Dodge brakes squeaked with any pressure, so the instant she heard them applied to the van, Pilar burrowed under a sea of blankets, imagining that each one represented another wave of the ocean. She pretended to be a mermaid, safe in a clamshell *cama*, while men with big guns opened all the doors, drank up all the water, took the coyote's cash, and kicked his tires.

Make what you need? As Pilar pulled the box of multicultural people colors toward her, she began to forget the sirens, the police, and her ELL teacher poised to yoga-fight bad guys.

Sienna's cell phone vibrated. Pilar glanced up. Sienna smiled at her reassuringly as she took the device from her purse and answered. "Yes." Her smile disappeared. "He did what? Has anyone seen him since?" Sienna cut the call short. Her hands shook as she speed-dialed and listened.

She paced the portable like a *puma*, trapped on a plateau by a flash flood in the surrounding canyon. The tic in her tight jaw mirrored the agitated twitch of a wildcat's tail. Cords of tension rose in her neck. The color drained from her cheeks.

If Pilar hadn't been in such need of soothing herself, she might have noticed the teacher paling two shades lighter than her normal tone. Instead, the girl found a crayon that generally matched her teacher's complexion and filled in an oval face, the outline of a woman's torso, and then surprising herself, picked up a green crayon to give her figure the tail of a mermaid. She selected burnt sienna and made her mermaid's hair long and wavy. Pilar let the rich color undulate all the way down to the end of the mermaid's jade fins.

With trembling hands, Sienna set her phone down and took a *Reading Fare* textbook, identical to the one she had relieved Pilar of, from the ledge of the whiteboard. She moved a piece of red construction paper sticking up out of it to a new place so that it looked as if they'd read the day's designated pages, despite having a lockdown.

Her phone buzzed. She snatched it up again. "Hello? I've been trying to call him. His car? The police? Oh, I see. Thank you so much for calling me." She dropped her phone back onto the table with a clatter and rubbed her temples vigorously with her fingertips.

Matt strolled into the portable. Sienna lunged toward him. With the puma soothed, she stopped her frantic approach. "Are you okay?"

"Of course," he said. "Why wouldn't I be?"

Her emerald eyes grew moist with affection as she took in his lean frame, familiar black sweatshirt, jeans, and beat-up old shoes. Her love for him warmed the room. Pilar gasped as she saw pink hearts alight from her teacher's solar plexus and flutter toward Matt like butterflies. Eagerly, she picked up a pink pencil.

"Mr. Penn called and told me you went after the robber." Sienna grasped her hair at the nape of her neck as if she would gather it into a ponytail, even though she didn't have a rubber band.

"I did," Matt said, "The fool escaped down river on an inner tube. I think they must have caught him by now." He ran his hand through his short, spiky hair. "I was freaking out about getting a parking ticket."

"It wouldn't stick after everyone realized you were trying to help." Sienna paused, tilting her head back, releasing her hair and the tension in her jaw. Then, unable to stop herself, she blurted, "By doing something insane!"

Matt stiffened.

"And dangerous! Did he have a gun?"

Matt shrugged.

"You could have been killed," she insisted. "You should have let the police handle it. They have training."

"What training do you need to run?" Matt snorted. "He would have made a clean getaway if I hadn't chased him."

"I'm not talking about running!" Sienna snapped. "I'm talking about the approach!"

Matt rolled his eyes. "You're the one who says I move like a ninja when we're hiking."

"Matt, you are infinitely more precious than money. I hate that you put yourself in danger for it."

"I didn't put myself in danger for money, Mom. I just did the right thing. Justice is important. Someone has to step in when something bad goes down. People can't just sit around and wait for the officials to show up to take care of everything." Impatient with her worry, he nonetheless softened. "It's a crime to rob a bank, Mom."

"I know," she sighed.

"It's a federal offense."

"Why weren't you in class?"

"My civics teacher is sick and they couldn't find a sub to cover class. They told us to go to study hall. I'm all caught up so the aide said I could go to work early. I went to the bank on my way."

"Did anyone go after the robber with you?"

"Nope. No one else there could have kept up. Besides, the guy was driving."

"While you were running?" Sienna scowled.

First graders spilled into the portable, interrupting the interrogation, disrupting her angst. "Okay," she said, comforted by the sight of her students' happy faces. "All's well that ends well and I'm proud of you." She smiled at Matt. "I want to hug you."

Pilar looked up to see Matt take a tiny step backward and she wondered why.

Sienna crossed her arms over her chest. "Do you need anything?" she asked. *Que necesitas?*

"Just milk. We're out. I can get some on my way home if you'll pay me back."

Sienna nodded, as a first grader threw his arms around her waist and squeezed.Matt smiled approvingly at the little kid embracing his

mom. Pink hearts seemed to flood the portable. Several framed
Pilar's mermaid on the page. Pilar grinned. She had done exactly
what Sienna told her to do. *Hacer que necesitas.* Make what you need.

Chapter Three

Baldwin was caught on film by a group of teenagers from one of Purewater's alternative high schools. For all his careful planning, for all his calculations about the ferocity of the current, it had never occurred to Baldwin that a dozen students would be near the South Bridge collecting water samples during his getaway. Their vans had been parked and unloaded in two different locations along the Purewater so the northernmost kids saw the guy with two bulging bags on his lap first and texted their observations to the group farther south. They'd all been taught to document what they saw out in the field so by the time Baldwin floated past the second group, their cameras were ready.

After police requisitioned all the smart phones containing images of Baldwin, they discovered something odd. Two large black neoprene bags had been on his thighs while he passed the first group. When he spun by the second, only one remained. Analysis showed that remaining sack was only slightly larger than one of the original bags taken from the vault. Baldwin had definitely not shoved one bag inside of the other to consolidate. Thus, the report surmised that Baldwin had lost half his loot, yet managed to vanish with three hundred and fifty thousand dollars.

With a group of teenagers tweeting that three hundred and fifty thousand dollars, had fallen into the river somewhere between the public library and the South Bridge, it wasn't long before crowds of people gathered along the Purewater. Many met behind *Casita Rio* and Master In Su's studio. Once the immigrants among them realized local, state, and federal officials would be canvassing the town searching for Baldwin, they hurried home to get their papers and to warn family members and friends without the precious documents to lie low.

When Pilar got home from school, Esteban, with red-rimmed eyes and the wide blade of a glistening knife in his trembling hand, had just finished scraping a mountain of onions and *chiles* into a pot. Lucia was slicing cheese into smaller more manageable blocks so he could move on to grating. The mermaid Ms. O'Mara had allowed her to create had reminded Pilar of the coloring books their coyote had given her during the journey to America so she took them, a blanket, and the hot quesadilla Lucia gave her for her after-school snack under the table. With one of Esteban's sour-smelling shoelaces snaking beside her, Pilar colored a lamb, the one that followed the Mary of English nursery rhymes to school.

In Redención, their village in the Mexican state of Clemencia, there had been no sheep, but Pilar's *abuela* had kept goats. The billy, *Diablo*, stalked the children on the days when the school was open. On the mornings that they got to attend, the teacher clapped her hands briskly and the students filed inside the low concrete building where classes were held. *Diablo* scrambled up onto the flat roof. When the first lessons were over and Pilar's friends and cousins gleefully raced outdoors to play, he leapt off the structure to head-butt them from behind.

When he did that, Pilar would hit him on the head as hard as she could with the *béisball* stick. Unfortunately, Diablo delighted in this, repeating his naughty behavior with a gleam in his dilating eyes. Pilar had spent a good many recesses beating her grandmother's goat. She had been strong, in her own eyes and in the eyes of the other children.

Sienna had been right; the ELL teacher uncannily correct. Pilar was strong. She was *muy fuerte*, yet after the day's events at Moore, she felt fragile. She wanted her mother with an overwhelming intensity. She missed her grandmother, her whole village, even that nasty *chivo*. And so, even though Mary's little lamb looked a lot cuddlier in the coloring book than grandma's e*stúpido* buck had ever been in the flesh, Pilar shaded Mary's sheep black.

She'd been under the table so long that by the time Ramon rushed into the kitchen, Esteban and Lucia had both forgotten she was there. Ramon steered Lucia by the shoulders to the back door, opening it in time to see Officer Stroup staking a bright yellow police barrier along the riverbank.

In that sweet moment of reuniting with Ramon after an afternoon of worrying about Esteban, a breeze blew in through the back door. A strand of Lucia's long, black hair escaped the single braid cascading down her back as her husband told her the news. Though her figure was full, she was barely five foot tall. Wearily, she leaned back into her husband's chest, letting him support her weight for awhile. Her navy canvas shoes were too small. She'd bought them because they'd been pleasingly cheap. Her chafed ankles and aching soles never let her forget the bargain she'd made. Although, she did her best to keep the unglued linoleum that masked the concrete floor of the kitchen clean, it wasn't capable of reciprocating her care with a cushioning response. Bouncing on the balls of her feet to stretch her spasming calves, Lucia watched the activity in wonder, repeating what Ramon told her in questioning disbelief. "The money could be someplace right outside our back door?"

From her hiding place, Pilar dreamed of finding a lot of *dinero*. First, she would buy Lucia and Ramon a washing machine and dryer so Lucia wouldn't have to miss a single episode of her favorite *novella*, hauling dirty clothes and cleaning rags to the laundromat where the defunct T.V. was missing an essential electrical cable. Then, she'd ask Ramon to help her send to Mexico for a basalt stone table and rolling pin so Lucia could roast, peel, and roll her own cocoa beans instead of buying bricks of wholesale chocolate, which while easier, just didn't make her *mole* as fine as what she'd made in Redención. After that, Pilar would buy Esteban two new American outfits. And, for herself, she'd maybe get some bright flowers in clay pots like the ones she'd seen at Bonny Deals to put all around the apartment. That would remind her of home. Oh! And she'd splurge on some American jasmine shampoo like Ms. O'Mara's. Pilar smiled at the thought of smelling like her teacher. Of being her teacher's twin. Of being *gemelas*.

Ramon said, "With that much money, we could hire *un abogodo* and get Raul out of the detention center so he can find out what happened back home. We could send him to Redención with armed guards."

"With that much *dinero*," Lucia said, "we could bring the rest of the *familia aqui*." As steam from the mole simmering on the stove wafted out of the open door to assimilate with river mist, she gasped, "And we could find *una curandera* for the children."

Ramon slid his hands from her shoulders down her arms and squeezed as if to make his point sink into her skin. "*La chica* did not see what happened. She was in the chicken coop."

"*Ella tiene susto.*" Lucia insisted. "Her soul is buried under the ground. *Pilar necesita una limpia.*"

"*Qué?*" Pilar poked her head from beneath the table. She'd caught her name, and nothing else. Her godparents spun around. Lucia's shushing fingers were already upon Ramon's lips.

"*Qué? Queso.*" Esteban teased, sprinkling cheese onto his little sister's head.

The *cotija añejo* fell, spackling her dark hair like white stars in the Redención sky where there was no light pollution. Pilar flopped over onto her back, letting Esteban drop bits of heaven into her mouth. Ramon picked some out of the bowl and fed it to Lucia. She did the same for him. With a taste of family after a horrifying day among strangers, Pilar laughed somewhere between happy and hysterical. She did not know Esteban had spent most of the afternoon in the closet. She did not know her big brother had *susto* too.

Chapter Four

A few days later, Pilar awoke in her bed, which was really a chaise lounge cushion that Ramon had found in the summer clearance bin at Bonny Deals. The scents of feast day wafted into her corner of the living room. Sage smoke. Spicy carnation. Rolling to her side, Pilar's sleepy eyes focused on Lucia kneeling before the window that overlooked First Street. White paint bubbled and crackled upon its splintered windowsill. Yet, a candle and an old beer bottle holding red and white flowers had turned it into a sacred altar. With a fine-tip, permanent black marker, Lucia had drawn a diminutive image of *La Sirena*, Redención's patron saint of protection, on the glass. *La Sirena*? Pilar had forgotten all about her, or had she?

As her godmother bowed her head in prayer, appealing to *La Sirena* in a mixture of dialect and Spanish, Pilar thought of the mermaid she'd drawn. The picture was pinned to the corkboard just above Sienna's desk in the ELL classroom. In the joined palms of her hands, Lucia cradled something, something formed from dough made in her own kitchen. Of course, Pilar thought, there is no petition clay to be had in America. With salt and flour, a candle, and a pen, Lucia had done exactly what Ms. O'Mara had told Pilar to do. *Hacer que necessitas.*

Pilar sat up. If she went to school, she could see the ELL teacher again. Crawling from beneath the heavy woven blanket the coyote had given her, she joined Lucia at the altar, noticing the fallen head of a scarlet carnation splayed upon the floor. In Mexico, they'd all gone—sisters, cousins, aunts, to trade coins for the ample bunches of calla lilies and red carnations that vendors hawked along the trail to *La Sirena's* shrine. Now, in the United States, with treasure-seekers trolling the banks of the Purewater behind their home, Lucia and Pilar recalled and longed for the relief that lit up the faces of those who laid their blooms, their worries, and small clay figures representing their deepest desires before the little statue of *La Sirena*.

***

Pilar stood, small and silent, beside the entrance to the cafeteria, watching Sienna take her spot for bus duty. Longing to go to her English teacher for a warm *"Hola!"* and a friendly hug, the girl clutched the red flower that had fallen from Lucia's altar. She'd brought it for Sienna but found herself confounded. Walkers weren't allowed in the buses' designated unloading zone. She couldn't get to Sienna, so she watched her closely, waiting for the teacher to notice her. Of course, Sienna had already seen Pilar and wished she could call the girl over to chat while she waited for the buses, but she couldn't start a precedent like that. It would be chaos if all the walkers were allowed in the unloading zone.

It was the Feast Day of *La Sirena* in Redención. In Purewater, it was the day to redistribute teaching staff based on a complex formula involving student count and budget codes. And so it was that Jolie Fox, Purewater District's newly hired school librarian, was unceremoniously re-assigned to Moore Elementary School. Pilar and Sienna both watched the elegant woman approaching the school from the staff parking lot.

With her dark hair pulled into a simple knot at the nape of her neck, Jolie looked like a librarian. Still, Sienna quickly matched the stranger wearing a simple green sweater dress, black leggings, and boots with the photo on her ID badge. Years earlier, Sienna had loved being Moore's school librarian. Back then the district hadn't funded a full-time, full-benefits library position. She'd been happy with part-time work when she was still married, when her salary was simply supplemental. She wouldn't change places now. She loved ELL. Still a tiny twinge of jealously sparked beneath the warm welcome she gave Jolie.

Jolie seemed nervous. Her uneasy gaze alighted on the pillar behind Sienna where a swipe of gray paint arced over Sienna's head. The ugly splotch, blotting out once sunny saffron paint, was as high as an adult could stretch. Anxiety flickered across Jolie's face. "What exactly," she blurted, "does it mean to say we are a school in improvement?"

"It's a euphemism," Sienna explained. "For failing."

"At renovation?" Jolie had been overwhelmed by the unexpected directive to pack up her things and move. She'd been alarmed by the personnel director's unwillingness to discuss the problems at her new assignment with her. Now that someone actually seemed ready to answer her questions about Moore's issues, she felt the odd urge to slow down the revelations.

Sienna laughed. She knew it was easier to acclimate to the most obvious flaws first. "Say goodbye to the light," she said. "The facilities improvement committee has decided it's time to take things more seriously around here. It's time to upgrade—to Drainpipe Gray."

"It's a little dreary."

Sienna nodded and shrugged. Jolie would meet the custodian, Captain Swabby, soon enough. Mic Schwab had gotten his nickname from telling students that the skull and crossbones tattooed on his bicep were left over from his pirate days when he ordered anyone who misbehaved to swab the deck. He often threatened the naughty boys with starting his favorite discipline plan up again. The mop tattooed on his opposite bicep came much later, after he'd retired from the Navy, found the Lord, and got clean. Now, somewhere in his late fifties, he was a muscular man, squat with long arms and an even longer grey ponytail.

Captain Swabby would have been willing to climb a ladder, would have liked to paint a whole pole at once, the whole school, for that matter, but school districts weren't like Spanish galleons filled with gold, nor were they run like military ships. The budget was tight. And, there were other restrictions. He could only paint for a limited amount of time per day, otherwise, the district would have to contract out and collect bids from professional painters. This was not feasible.

Though he didn't get his way when it came to the repainting process, Captain Swabby was a powerful man. He kept all repair and cleaning supplies locked away. His key ring, with the circumference of a handcuff, was always looped around his belt. Banging against his thigh, it made him sound like a warden as he strode up and down the halls. At Moore, teachers had to beg for rolls of paper towels and wait for him to refill bottles of disinfectant so they could wipe down their sinks and clean the surfaces children sneezed upon. He certainly didn't have time for that degree of cleaning.

Sienna said, "We're failing because our reading scores are so low."

"Why?"

"Because in the past three years," Sienna explained, "the percentage of our kids who qualify for ELL because they speak another language at home has drastically increased."

"What do they speak? Spanish?"

"Mostly. Hmong, some Chinese, Indian, Arabic, and Ukrainian."

Jolie's realtor had advised her to avoid the Moore area if she decided to buy a home in the Purewater School District because of Moore's failing status. She'd tried to tell him that a neighborhood school's state standardized test scores didn't matter to her now that her daughter was in college, but he'd urged her to think about resale value. She'd actually laughed when he'd first mentioned the high-stakes WASTE. The realtor hadn't seemed to notice anything funny about the acronym.

"Do ELL kids take the WASTE?"

Sienna nodded.

"In English?"

"Yes. And the WASTE is challenging even for the kids up at Teagan Hill who have been speaking English their whole lives."

"How long does it take for kids to learn English?"

"Well, every child is different," Sienna explained. "For most of them, it takes a few months to a year before they can get by on the playground, at the store, at the doctor's office." Her eyes roved over to Pilar. "The truth is that it really takes several years of intentional English development to acquire the language needed to perform like a native speaker on the WASTE."

"Several?" Jolie's surprise was evident. "So… close to half of the kids here just don't have the language proficiency they need to keep the whole school from being labeled failing."

"That's right." Sienna said grimly.

"Well," Jolie scoffed, "Why don't Chase Haight and his GOTCHA reporters get that?"

As if a six-eyed, brown recluse spider had suddenly fallen from the facade overhead, both women froze. Like a venomous creature on an invisible drop line, comments that Chase Haight, a media mogul, had made on national radio about the incompetency of public school teachers hung in the air between them. Purewater's school board president, Brenda Hadley, had quoted him extensively on Facebook. Both of them seemed determined to make public school teachers public enemy number one. Brenda had been elected to the school board because she'd convinced the community that there was no excuse for Moore's low test scores.

Sienna shrugged again. There was a lot she could say about the subject, but the first school buses were pulling into the lot. There would be very little time to talk to another adult until the end of the day.

"Well, thanks," Jolie said. "I asked around at Teagan Hill. No one could explain why this school is so bad." She blushed. "You know, what I mean."

"Hi, Ms. Fox!" a blonde girl, school board president Brenda Hadley's own granddaughter, interrupted. "I've got all my library books!"

"Good for you!" Jolie exclaimed as Laurali, hunching forward beneath the weight of her Hello Kitty backpack, stopped, grinning. She clearly expected to be praised. Jolie appeared confused. "What are you doing down here? You are supposed to be up at Teagan Hill."

"I ride the shuttle up. Grandma told Daddy that this school

sucks. She made him sign the papers so I could go to the better one. She wanted my uncle to make my cousin come too, but my aunt is alternative." Laurali rolled her eyes, clearly repeating what her grandmother had said, "Plus, she's willful."

The rest of what Laurali might have said about her aunt was swallowed up by a throng of children descending from the arriving buses. Over the heads and hum of children, Jolie and Sienna exchanged an amused glance. It seemed now as if the words *alternative* and *willful* fluttered between them, like a butterfly, trying to avoid the recluse's web.

As Jolie went to meet the principal, Sienna greeted children. "Good morning! Welcome to school!"

A boy, doused in man's aftershave with hope in his brown eyes, stepped close. "Do we have ELL today?" he whispered. His friend leaned in, "Can we read our stories?" A girl stopped in front of Sienna, whipped a poem out of her pocket and read it on the spot. Another pulled a new dollar store notebook out of her backpack. "See, Ms. O'Mara! I got this in case I want to write on the bus."

Still standing alone by the cafeteria, Pilar watched as the enthusiasm for storytelling swirled around Sienna. Then, some girls begged Sienna to show them the picture of her favorite author— Doctor Andy Dalhstrom. Jostling to stare at the screen of her cell phone, they batted their eyelashes, giggling at the publicity photo from his publisher's website. The silver flecks in his blonde hair were barely noticeable, but he was obviously much older than the heartthrobs they searched for on the public library computers.

"He's smart. Right, Teacher?" Alondra asked.

"Yes. He's very smart."

"Is he ever gonna do a concert?"

"Probably not," Sienna said. Her eyebrows arched in amusement. "He gives talks. People call them lectures."

Nodding sagely, the girls hurried toward Pilar, stepping out of the designated unloading zone and sweeping her into the cafeteria for a free breakfast and a fascinating discussion about the distinctions between Miss, Ms., and Mrs. that seemed so important when dealing with teachers. That Ms. O'Mara was a Ms. in a building where all the other teachers were Mrs. was such a mystery to them. Pilar pushed the carnation into her pocket. Her fingers would smell spicy all morning. Sadly, the flower would shrivel before she had access to Sienna to present it.

As Sienna greeted poor children disembarking from public school buses, she thought of the Statue of Liberty and suddenly on the Feast Day of *La Sirena*, the *New Colossus* scrolled through her mind. *Give me your tired, your poor, your huddled masses yearning to breathe free. The wretched refuse of your teeming shore. Send these, the homeless, tempest-tossed to me. I lift my lamp beside the golden door.*

As a hungry child hurrying to a free breakfast jostled her arm, Sienna lifted her stainless steel mug high. More air brakes hissed. The golden door of Bus 27 opened.

A voice at her elbow quipped. "I just don't get it."

Sienna looked down at the waist-high *gringo* barging into her beatific vision of herself hailing yet another wave of children onto hallowed ground. "You just don't get what?"

He gestured up toward her steaming cup, held aloft as the masses milled around them. "Why you need that." He shook his blonde head accusingly. "Every single morning!"

Who was this kid to question her caffeine habit? Sienna thought of a few questions she might ask him. Is that grape jelly matting your hair? Is that spaghetti sauce smeared across your cheek? Instead she replied, "How else do they light up the Statue of Liberty?"

He chuckled fondly. Second grade patriotism is so pure. Every day they say the Pledge of Allegiance. Every day they sing, *This Land is Your Land*. *Gringo* studied her face shrewdly for a moment and then announced, "I went to the dollar store." Solemnly, he quickly cast her as a customs officer and, compelled to declare, pulled the flap of his jacket aside, revealing a handful of red, white, and blue marbles hidden in his inner coat pocket. Contraband! It was not Toys From Home Day. He forged on, playing the odds she'd excuse his transgression if he had an educational purpose behind it. "What's the chance of me picking a white one?"

"Is this a probability question?" Sienna raised her eyebrows, clearly impressed. The kid had her pegged.

He nodded, waiting for her answer.

"I'd say about half."

He looked surprised. Obviously, he hadn't worked it out for himself yet. "You know," he cautioned. "You gotta be careful. Not to lose your marbles." He zipped up his coat, telling her the school rule, as if she didn't already know it. "You aren't supposed to have them here."

Sienna nodded, considering his words. Somewhere along the line, maybe in the staff lounge, she'd heard gossip that this child's difficulties stemmed from being born addicted to a mind-altering drug. He was very small for his age. His mom had made great strides in life and was in recovery. And, at least today, he wasn't carrying his lunch from home in the usual bag, emblazoned with a sex toy shop's logo. Apparently, Sienna thought hopefully, things were looking up for his little family.

Gringo was, however, still wearing fleece footed pajamas under his coat and a pair of rubber boots acquired from Goodwill. Both were at least two sizes too large. And it was not Pajama Day. This was not appropriate for a fourth grader. With a sticky cowlick spiraling above his scalp, he looked rather like a Doctor Seuss character. Yes! Sienna thought. Cindy Lou in *The Grinch Who Stole Christmas*. She wondered if *Gringo* had ever read about the Grinch. "Jonathan," she said, attempting to broach the dress code gently, "I see you are wearing jammies to school."

"It's my uniform," he told her. In response to her inquiring expression, he went on. "I'm a sleepwalker or," he shrugged, "a dreamer. I can't decide." He saluted, flashing wide gaps between his crooked front teeth and clomped to the cafeteria.

Chapter Five

Not long after the Feast Day of *La Sirena*, one of Pilar's new classmates, Lupe, read the final draft of a story to Sienna. The crinkled newsprint between her fingers was dog-eared from erasures, but Lupe's ability to give breath and life to text was not dead, like Pilar's stillborn had been. Lupe had a thriving Reading Baby and was enchanted with her new life as a reader. She delivered her personal narrative, reading her own words with pride.

"*Fantástico!*" Sienna declared. "*Muy Bueno!*" She waited long enough for her pleasure to induce a little pride. Once Lupe was beaming broadly, Sienna created a small space between her thumb and index finger, asking, "May I ask the author just one little question?"

Lupe nodded graciously. The silver-lined earrings her brother had just brought her from Mexico City glinted in the glare of the fluorescent light overhead. Dual images of the Virgin of Guadalupe shimmered on either side of her round, brown cheeks.

"Did you ask your mom about the name of the store? Is it really called the Swami?"

All of the students looked up from the stories they were writing. Beneath a handmade banner emblazoned with the words, *The Writers' Lair,* they nodded. They were in perfect solidarity with Lupe over the name of everyone's favorite place to shop.

"Sorry, kiddos," Sienna said. "I just want to be sure." Her voice grew hushed as if they were in a church speaking of *los milagros*, of miracles. "Lupe is about to publish."

Cassandra leaned toward Pilar as Sienna went on, describing all the things Lupe had done well. With pepperoni from the cafeteria's pizza still on her breath, Cassandra tried to help the newcomer understand what Sienna was praising, but she didn't know the Spanish words for *sequence, events,* or for any of the punctuation marks. Cassandra simply repeated Sienna's English, not even recognizing that she wasn't interpreting. Still, as if she were Pilar's big sister teaching the baby of the family an important skill, she smiled encouragingly, revealing several shiny silver teeth. Pilar found herself wondering how the mermaid she had drawn would look with a silver tooth. There had been a silver crayon in the box. She could have used it when Sienna gave her the supplies to *hacer que necesita.* Pilar looked up at her mermaid, still hanging over the teacher's desk, and decided she was perfect just the way she was.

Sienna went on. "Lupe has a very good story here. I just don't want her to do all the hard work of copying her story onto our fancy paper if something isn't quite right."

In America, schools have Xerox 98 paper, bright white like most American teeth. Sienna copied black lines on the paper to guide the formation of her students' letters like braces straighten those pearly whites. She copied the lines on the paper late at night, after the office closed. Parents of students up at Teagan Hill Elementary groaned about orthodontist's bills while Moore Elementary teachers were repeatedly chided at staff meetings for using too much toner. Sienna listened, but she still insisted upon rewarding her young authors with specially-designated "publishing" paper.

"I've never heard of Swami," Sienna revealed. "Of course, I'm not much of a shopper. In fact, *mi hijo,* Matt, used to tell people his clothes came from UPS. " As if it were time for the students to stop tricking her, she asked, "Do they really sell nachos at a store called the Swami?"

Pilar nodded with all the rest, ignorant of what she was agreeing with. She just wanted Sienna to hurry up to finish with Lupe and come kneel beside her. Instead, Sienna gestured for all the kids to crowd around her computer. Pilar rushed the open spaces between moving children, wiggling her way up to Sienna until she was close enough to catch a whiff of that glorious jasmine shampoo. Once, she'd spent an hour sniffing hair products at the One Dollar Store trying to match it, but Lucia would explain. "You won't find it here. *Las maestras no compran aqui*. The teachers don't shop in places like this. They are rich. *Son ricas*."

Selecting Google images, Sienna typed *Swami* into the search bar. Pictures of an angry punk band with spiky purple hair and several peaceful Yogis sustaining various mudras appeared. She typed the words *Swap Meet* into the search bar and one of the first hits was a white wooden sign stenciled with bold red block letters. SWAP MEET TODAY.

"That's it!" Lupe exclaimed.

"Yes! Yes!" the other children chorused, breaking into rapid Spanish. None of them had enough vocabulary to say it all in English. They examined the other pictures the search produced, people strolling among booths, looking at car parts, jewelry, and toys. Sienna nodded encouragingly, noting her students' inconsistent pronouns and code-switching, the going back and forth between languages. A girl spoke of her mother buying a hairbrush. One boy told how his uncle got a grill to make *carne asada*.

With a twinkle in her eyes, Sienna said, "In English, we call a place like this a swap meet." She emphasized the final sound in the two words so they could hear she wasn't saying Swami.

Alondra rolled her eyes. Javier slapped his forehead and they all giggled. It was just another mistake, like so many they were accustomed to making, and it was okay in ELL. But they all knew, outside The *Writers' Lair*, in the regular classroom, it could have been another instance in which it was wiser to limit what one said to the few words one really knew.

Sienna appealed to Lupe. "May we change Swami to swap meet?"

Lupe shrugged.

"If you use swap meet all your readers will know what you mean."

Lupe shrugged again. The other kids had already known what

she'd meant. Dimples formed in her cheeks as she grinned. "Okay." She tossed her glossy black braids behind her shoulder and zipped her hot pink Hannah Montana jacket over the Blessed Mother pendant her brother had bought to match her shimmering earrings. Her eye roved to the clock. "I fix tomorrow," she promised. Sienna grinned well aware that Lupe was giving in to the teacher's crazy request so that she wouldn't miss a single second of recess.

While Sienna took the slick *Reading Fare* student book off the ledge of the whiteboard and moved the red bookmark a few pages, the kids slid their writing projects into their ELL folders and dropped it all into the assigned basket on their way out the door. Only Pilar stayed behind, standing by Sienna's desk. Sienna knew Pilar needed a lot more help with English than she was getting. She could also see the girl needed help with her shoelaces. Lucia hadn't let her get Velcro, insisting she learn to tie, so Pilar was forced to struggle with English syntax and first world shoestrings all at the same time. She bent to untangle a knot.

Sienna clicked to close Google images. Instead of disappearing, a large Swami from her first hit assumed full screen. Swathed in pure white silk, the holy man winked at the teacher, as if he were Skyping from a remote temple in a faraway land. Sienna gasped. Ever alert for danger, Pilar stood suddenly, letting her attempted loop unravel.

Sienna read the caption scrolling beneath the image, as if hearing her own voice would help her make sense of the technological glitch. "*Swami* means one with the Self. A Swami is dedicated to the pursuit of the divine inner Self." Sienna ran her finger under Lupe's title articulating, "The Swami." She gave Pilar an encouragingly smile. "Read it."

Pilar put her finger right where Sienna's had been. "The Swami," she mumbled, attempting to mimic. She wasn't really reading yet, but she laughed in delight because holding Lupe's vital Reading Baby was a sweet, borrowed pleasure.

Sienna laughed too. Like the Mary's Little Lamb that Pilar colored black in honor of the diabolical goat who'd made her strong, a Swami was definitely against "the rules" at school. Slipping in through unvoiced spaces, through a back door left open by two fortuitously dropped final consonants, the Swami followed the children to school. He came because a teacher who knew that everyone needs to laugh and play in the swap meet of learning a new language was going to need him.

Chapter Six

Sienna's chat with Jonathan, the marble-smuggling *gringo*, had given her an idea for her Halloween costume. On the last day of October, she dressed as the Statue of Liberty. With weak autumn sunlight radiating from her tin foil crown, she went to bus duty and welcomed a whole host of characters. Superheroes burst through the swinging doors of the school buses as if they were exiting Clark Kent's obsolete telephone booth ready to save the world. Fairies floated past, their green tulle wings sparkling with incandescent glitter. Princesses, clad in pink satin gowns and crowned with diamond tiaras, wandered by. A few friendly witches waggled long black fingernails waving hello. Pilar's friend, Alondra, disguised as Dorothy on her way to Oz, stopped to let Sienna peek at the plush pup stuffed in an old Easter basket. "I'm off to meet the weezard." She sang with a heavy Mexican accent as she skipped away, her ruby red shoes slapping on flat, gray concrete. Next, Iron Man flexed his muscles, confessing, "I wanted to be Mario from the video game, but it was forty bucks!"

"I like Iron Man," Sienna assured him. "You look great." He gave her a thumbs up. "So do you, Liberty." And then he was off, chasing a trio of powdered-faced vampires, undaunted by the polymer fangs cutting into artificially bloody lips.

Even though it was Halloween, there was no suppressing the system's mandated data monster. His end-of-the-month appetite had to be fed, so Nancy Albright had to give her class the Unit Two

Reading Fare test. Kids were supposed to read two full pages of small print and answer eight multiple choice comprehension questions. And then they had to do that much again! Another story of equal length and with the same number of questions followed the first. There were also six skills pages, two each about phonics, grammar, and vocabulary. After that, they were supposed to write an essay comparing how the characters in the two separate stories at the beginning of the exam were alike and how they were different. That's what Pilar was expected to do, too. But she didn't even understand the directions telling her so.

Pilar swallowed hard, her eyes darting around the classroom. Kids moved their lips silently, ostensibly reading. Some feigned ease, too zealously marking answers. The only sounds in the room were the clack of the teacher's keyboard as Nancy furiously typed an email and the nervous clicking together of Alondra's ruby shoes. One, two, three! The EL's weren't familiar with the classic message Glinda the Good Witch had given Dorothy Gale in the magical land of Oz, but they all felt the truth of it in Alondra's heels as they skipped word after word they didn't know. "There's no place like home."

Nancy must have felt Pilar's desperate eyes upon her because she met them momentarily and then screwed her lips together in a disapproving kiss of the air before she hit the send button. Mortified, Pilar stared back down at her test and found herself lip synching words she couldn't read in all sorts of crazy ways. After a few seconds, she turned the page and began the pantomime all over again.

After a really long time, Nancy came to look at her lack of work. "You have to do this." Although the teacher wore a soft, black sweater appliqued with over-sized candy corn, she sounded just like a *Federale* ordering a villager to empty his pockets. Her face remained impassive as she commenced a humiliating shakedown. She pushed a single student desk out into the hall, leaving a trail of spilled contents in its wake. Indicating for Pilar to bring a chair, she said, "Finish out here." When Pilar carried the seat to where her teacher pointed, Nancy went back into the classroom and closed the door on the girl.

In the coolness of isolation, Pilar's face smarted as if she'd just spent too much time out in the desert sun, but the burning sensation she felt came from a smoldering internal mixture of shame infused with rage. Internally, her intestines twisted violently, bloating with hatred for English and for America. From behind the door to the self-contained Special Education classroom directly across the hallway, an anguished child screamed the very English words Pilar wished to say. "I WANT TO GO HOME!" Pilar's heart skipped staccato, like a machine gun. The other child was clearly in distress. What were they doing to him or her in there? Would she be next? Her legs trembled as she crouched over her vital internal organs. She scanned the space, searching for the closest exit.

Then, she saw Sienna, dressed as the Statue of Liberty, sitting on a hard, child-sized chair at a small table in the hall with Miguel, a second grader who lived in the apartment over Master In-Su's Dojang.

Miguel's teacher, Mrs. Tammy Lewis, stepped outside of her classroom. Clearly annoyed by the noise, she asked, "What's happening in Special Day?" Sienna shrugged as Tammy loomed over her. The odd, oversized mouse ears on her head cast a strange shadow across the eyeliner whiskers she'd drawn on her cheeks. She scanned Miguel's blank paper, wrinkling her pink snub nose, as if smelling something too foul for even a rat to consider. The kid across the hall screamed again and Pilar imagined running all the way to her grandmother's crooked house in Mexico although, at the moment, she'd gladly settle for *Casita Rio* and the comfort of godparents.

"Miguel is doing great," Sienna told Tammy, adding *"muy bien,"* for the boy's benefit.

Tammy wrinkled her nose, doubtfully. "But will he be done in five minutes?"

"Tammy!" Sienna cajoled. "We're dabbling in poetry here."

"Oh come on, Sienna!" Tammy snapped. "He doesn't have to win *a prize*."

"A boy needs time to capture the essence of his Mom." Sienna said.

"Oh brother! I just want to know what he's thankful for, so I can get the November bulletin board up. You know how Deedee is." Tammy spun around yelling "Hey! Batman! Stop that!"

While Miguel wondered if his teacher wanted him to write about his brother and struggled to speak about his mother, another wail filled the air. "I WANT TO GO HOME!" Sienna ignored the screams, focusing on Miguel's restarts and stammering, "Ah!" she finally exclaimed. "Your mom works in a greenhouse!"

"No. No. Ms. It's white." Miguel's eyes were wide with panic.

Sienna flipped a notebook open and hastily sketched a picture. "Does it look like this?"

"*Si.*"

"With plants and flowers inside?"

"*Si.*"

"There are different names for a place like this. We usually call it a *greenhouse*."

"*Pero es blanca!*" he trembled.

"Well, it's a house for green plants," she said gently. "Right?" She waited for him to nod and explained, "That's why we call it a *greenhouse*."

A loud crash came from within Special Day. A chair hit the door on the inside, jostling it in its frame. "I WANT TO GO HOME!"

Tears welled in Miguel's dark, almond-shaped eyes and sweat beaded upon his forehead. Ms. O'Mara offered him another word. "We could also call it a *hothouse*."

"Yeah," he nodded. "I go in and *mi*...my head gets..." He had no words for what happened to him, was happening to him, but he got his meaning across by wiping the perspiration from his brow.

"You get sweaty in there."

He nodded, relieved to get another label, one he could use for his every day experience. "Sw...sweaty."

"People sweat when they get hot." Or, Sienna thought, they are nervous, afraid of being judged too slow, stupid, found lacking, shamed.

Nearby, Pilar had gone sweaty, too. Licking her lips, she tasted salt. It drew her back down into the awareness of her—of her own body. Sweat. She had sweated a lot on the way to America, cowering in the back of the coyote's van, hiding under blankets on the way to the border. A person who perspired that much needed salt. There had been a big block of it, swiped from a rich man's cattle field. Esteban had used a tire iron to break it into very tiny pieces to suck on. It had been nasty, but at least it made them feel as if they had some provisions. When the journey finally ended and they arrived at *Casita Rio* where Lucia had a huge meal waiting, it had felt like crossing over into heaven. Sitting out in the hall now with a kid screaming behind closed doors made Pilar recall the captivity of her flight to the new country and made her want to run. It would be better to be in the kitchen with Lucia instead of being held accountable for finishing a paper she'd couldn't read. It would be much better to be working on the day's big project at home, filling hollow plastic skull-shaped molds with sweet paste. The only reason Pilar didn't high-tail it out of there was because she knew kids weren't supposed to run in the hall and she didn't want her beloved Ms. O'Mara to see her breaking the rule.

Sienna was asking Miguel, "Are you thankful because your mom works in a hothouse?"

Miguel nodded.

"Do you like plants? *Te gusta plantas y flores?*"

He nodded, relieved she'd exhausted the English synonyms for greenhouse. "*Me gusta porque cuando le dan dinero, ella puede comprar comida.*"

"*Claro!*" She nodded. "My *hijo* Matt likes to eat, too." She wrote on the elliptical piece of orange construction paper that Tammy had given them to serve as an oversized turkey feather. She ran her finger under each word, showing him how to read, "I am thankful my mom works in a hothouse. It is good she has a job. I like to eat." Miguel chortled and then he read it, haltingly to himself.

His face lit up just like the Swami's had when he appeared to fill Sienna' entire computer screen in *The Writers' Lair*. Miguel recognized his unique and familiar Self, represented by foreign words.

Tammy opened the door abruptly. "Done yet?" The sense of the

Swami vanished. Tammy scanned the paper feather. "That doesn't make much sense."

"Of course it does," Sienna said soothingly. "And he can read it all by himself."

"Well," Tammy snapped, "let's just see how he does on the *Reading Fare* unit test."

Another chair ricocheted off the metal door. "I WANT TO GO HOME!"

Tammy whirled around. The velour tail pinned to the hem of her blank tunic hit the door frame with a threatening thwack. "Come on, Miguel."

Miguel hesitated, whispering. *"Es la maestra un raton?"*

"Si," Sienna said, without suppressing the mischievous glint in her eye. Tammy's dig about winning a poetry prize was hard to overlook. "But here, we say she is a *mouse.*" Miguel darted into the classroom, keeping his distance from his teacher and her disturbing appendage.

Now inconsolable weeping flowed out of Special Day. Pilar imagined the tears would soon seep out from beneath the well-rattled door and flood the hallway. She hoped that Sienna would come to her, that they could ride the waves of sadness away to somewhere safe and peaceful together. Instead, Cassandra appeared at her side, silently gliding out of their classroom with Nancy Albright's hall pass in her hand.

"No entiendo." Pilar lamented, indicating her blank test.

In an old First Communion dress rigged up with gold wire wings, Cassandra was an angel of mercy on a mission. She smiled benevolently. "I came to help you. I know all the answers."

Pilar grinned gratefully, feeling even more relief as Sienna approached.

"Hi girls!" Sienna's whole body stiffened at the sight of the *Reading Fare* test. Nevertheless, her tone of voice remained relaxed. "What are you two doing out here?"

"I help her," Cassandra explained. "So she can do art."

"You aren't really supposed to help on a test," Sienna spoke gently. Then as if on second thought she said, "But since Pilar doesn't understand the language its written in, I'd say it's okay." Uncomfortably, because she was a teacher, she added, "just for today." She knew it would take years of todays before it would be fair or reasonable to expect Pilar to take a test like that by herself.

Cassandra held out her hand for Pilar's clammy pencil. With her garland halo quivering above her crown as if she were receiving direct transmissions from Heaven, she bubbled in the first answer.

"Oh!" Sienna chuckled softly. "You can't do it for her. You have to tell her what to do."

Cassandra nodded. After a moment's thought, she explained in Spanish. "Pray. Pray to Mary, Jesus, and Joseph." She pointed to the test. "Look at number 1. One is always for Mary. Ask her if the answer is A, B, C, or D. Now, feel your left foot. Which toe tickles? If is your big toe, the answer is 1, if it's the next toe the answer is 2, like that. Don't do your little toe. It's just a baby. It knows nothing. It's not fair to ask. Then, look at question number 2. Two is for Jesus. Ask him. Feel your toes. Do you understand?"

Pilar nodded, but her faith had been sorely tested during the past several months. Even her most earnest prayers had gone unanswered.

"Three is for Joseph," Cassandra said. "Then, go back to Mary. Mary, Jesus, Joseph. Get it?"

Pilar nodded. It did seem like a good plan.

"Do you always take tests like this?" Sienna asked.

"I just started doing it this year," Cassandra sighed, "Fourth grade is really hard."

"Do you get good scores?"

Cassandra shrugged. "Mary, Jesus, and Joseph get busy. People always distract them, trying to tell them stuff, asking for help. Sometimes the answers they want to give me get mixed up with the ones they are giving other people." She lifted her hands up into the air and laughed a little. "Who cares? Commuting with them is good."

Sienna nodded, the English teacher in her noted Cassandra's mispronunciation of the multisyllabic word *communication* while the poet within caught a glimpse of the girl gliding over some purgatorial HOV lane, the supportive breath of psyche beneath her angel wings as she shuttled between the Holy Family's home in Heaven and school in Purewater. "Does it matter what kind of shoes you wear when you take a test?"

"Flip-flops are the best, but we aren't supposed to wear them to school."

"I WANNA GO HOME!"

"Start with Our Lady," Cassandra urged Pilar.

Pilar bowed her head, made her request. As the slender red second hand ticked around the clock overhead, blood rushed into her third *dedo*! She gasped, eagerly bubbling "c" for the first question. Then she slowed, filling the circle in thickly, darkly, enjoying the throbbing in her toe, luxuriating in the sensation of having an answer.

"I WANNA GO HOME!"

Mrs. Albright burst out of the classroom, stopping short at the sight of Pilar filling in the correct answer. "Good," she said, grimly, adding, "I'm so glad the Statue of Liberty is here to see what you are capable of when the bar is set high enough."

Sienna arched her eyebrows, and was about to speak when Nancy cut her off, cocking her head at Special Day. The candy corn earrings that matched her sweater swung from her earlobes. "Did I hear someone screaming?"

"Yes," Sienna replied. Her voice highly modulated. "We need to talk about this testing, Nancy. Multiple choice at the frustration level can't reveal what a child knows."

Nancy cut her off. "It's best if these kids know what is expected of them right from the beginning. You were right there when the *Reading Fare* trainer said we sabotage their futures if we protect them from grade level expectations in the present."

The principal, Deedee Hayes, accompanied by an unknown blonde woman came through the doors leading into the fourth grade wing of the school. "Oh, shoot!" Nancy hissed, her eyes darting to her October bulletin board. "We haven't even started November yet." She glared at Sienna for several long seconds and then, as if she had no more time to spend with a teacher as dimwitted as Sienna O'Mara, clapped her hands briskly. "Okay, girls! Time to move

41

along. Cassandra! Get back inside! Pilar, you have five more minutes to finish that test!"

Cassandra waved her pass in the air.

"Why haven't you gone already?" Nancy was clearly exasperated.

Cassandra said, "I was talking."

Nancy scowled. "Hallways are supposed to be quiet so people can work."

"We were working," Sienna said. "Being able to speak and listen in a new language are essential for reading and understanding it."

Nancy stared past Sienna, watching the woman with the clipboard back out the main door. Her eyes widened as Deedee began to walk her way. "Just hurry up!" she hissed. She stepped back into her classroom, quickly shutting the door behind her.

Cassandra did not hurry to the bathroom. She stayed right where she was, standing with Sienna and Pilar, watching *la jefa*. Moore's principal always wore well over a thousand dollars per day in designer clothing, department store shoes, and jewelry.

"Wow!" Deedee exclaimed, striding toward them, grinning broadly at Sienna. "I love your costume! It's amazing what you can do with a little aluminum foil." She gestured toward Sienna's grey wool clogs less enthusiastically. "And I guess those work."

Sienna opened her mouth to speak, but Deedee went on. "I was up at HQ and got a text that there's a problem in Special Day. I don't know what are they calling me for. We just hired another two-hour teacher's aide."

Sienna didn't know what to say. Before she could manage a reply, Deedee asked. "Do you know how much money that guy dropped in the river a couple of weeks ago?" She tapped her elegant chin with the tutti-fruity polished tip of a perfectly manicured fingernail. "Three hundred and fifty thousand bucks!" She shook her head wistfully. "If I could get my hands on that, I'd put it all in my retirement account."

With a poker face, Sienna put her hand on Cassandra's shoulder and gently nudged the girl toward the bathroom. "Are you planning to retire?"

"Not until I turn this school around."

Pilar muttered. "Jesus! *Ayudame!*" Help me!

"I'm committed to my mission." Deedee said. "It's not much fun though. Everyone is so uptight nowadays. Gee whiz! Do you know there's a petition going around town against that cute little shop downtown? What's it called?" She snapped her fingers, obviously expecting Sienna to supply the answer. When she did not, Deedee tried, "Lover's Lane? Lover's Loot? I can't remember. Anyway, people are all hot and bothered about the lace-up lingerie in the front window."

Sienna jutted her head toward the children.

"Oh!" Deedee drew in a sharp breath? "Do they understand everything I'm saying?"

"The angel probably does."

"Good." Deedee nodded approvingly. "We've got to get these kids moving along. The requirements are only going to get tougher." She glanced back from where she'd come as if half expecting to see the woman with the clipboard still standing where they'd been talking. "Still, all we really need," she continued, "are high expectations. From now on, I expect Moore Elementary students to earn above average test scores on the WASTE and someday very soon I expect to be the toast of the realtors' luncheon for exponentially increasing home values in Moore's attendance zone, even if the real estate market is sour."

Sienna touched Cassandra's shoulder, applying gentle pressure, trying to push her toward the bathroom but *la chica* dug her telegraphic *dedos* into the ground. "It would be great if the real estate market improved," Sienna agreed. "But there's a problem with the new curriculum, Deedee. The ELL kids are having a really hard time with *Reading Fare.*"

Confusion and then annoyance flickered over Deedee's face. "Of course they are having a hard time!" she snapped. "It is a challenging program and we're just starting out with it." She blinked several times and then, as if getting a hold of herself again, smiled broadly. "But just you wait! Once they get in the swing of it, our scores will skyrocket! We'd deserve a big wad of incentive... if there were ever a chance of getting a perk in the public sector! Don't worry, Sienna! If we were running a corporation and got the results this new adoption is going to give us, we would get as much as Baldwin stole from the bank for a holiday bonus! As it stands, they're telling us to get those results just to keep the funding we do have coming in."

"I took the *Reading Fare* test," Cassandra blurted. "And it was easy."

Deedee nodded effusively. "Good! Good!"

"She has a very interesting approach," Sienna said. "Maybe we could talk…"

"I just pray," Cassandra confessed, giddy in the glow of Deedee's glee.

Deedee clasped the child's hands in her own. "I always prayed in school too!"

Sienna cleared her throat. "And Cassandra just taught Pilar to do it, too. That's how she got the right answer."

"Success breeds success!" Deedee beamed.

Cassandra flashed a broad smile. Pilar thought the way her silver tooth contrasted with her golden wings was beautiful.

Deedee let go of Cassandra's hands to pat Sienna's shoulder. "You're a walking social studies lesson. And you look great to boot." As if remembering something tantalizing, she asked, "How is your boyfriend?" She framed the air, making quotation marks with her fingers as she uttered the final word.

Sienna didn't want to talk about Andy with her boss. "Deedee," she said reasonably, "you probably should go into Special Day. It sounded like furniture being thrown."

"Okay." Deedee looked disappointed. "Girl talk, later." She began to turn toward Special Day, but stopped short. "Hey, you don't work with Jonathan, do you? Cute kid. Blonde with blue eyes. Bad breath. Stinks to high heaven."

Sienna shook her head.

"Not ELL, is he?" Once more Deedee was disappointed in Sienna's response to her questioning. "No one ever washes his clothes. Of course, his dad has spent time in jail…and you know Mom is too busy keeping up with her boyfriends. The kid's in my office right now because he keeps bringing marbles to school and it's not even Toys-From-Home Day. I wish you could work with him...make him understand. Is there a possibility he could be...what?" Again, she snapped her fingers a few times. "Ukrainian?"

Sienna's mouth dropped and Deedee returned to what she clearly really wanted to talk about. "You need to fill me in on your romance. I feel responsible for it, you know? I mean, I literally put that hunk in your hands." She went on plaintively. "All I ever do is attend boring meetings and out of tune band concerts. I never get to see my husband anymore. Besides, I've been married *forever*. I have to live the...erotic life...vicariously." With a titter and a wave, Deedee turned, leaving the same way she'd come, completely forgetting to go into Special Day.

Sienna looked ruefully at Cassandra. "Didn't you have to go to the bathroom?"

"No. I just needed a break." The little girl sounded desperate just like *los hombres* at the bar in *Casita Rio* who told Ramon, "*Necessito un cerveza.*" Sienna nodded, sympathetically, just like Pilar's *padrino* did when he poured the beer, minimizing the froth forming at the head.

Cassandra and Pilar walked back into their classroom together. The angel and her initiate. Seething with frustration, Nancy took Pilar's incomplete test. "Maybe you would have finished," she said sharply, "If you weren't out there just talking with Ms. O'Mara."

Chapter Seven

Cold air nipped at Sienna's hands, her chin, and the tip of her nose. She pulled her white down comforter up and over her head to, as her mother Bridget would say when donning a hat, keep the fire inside. It was the first of November. She may have been shivering from the chill in the early morning air, but since it was also All Saint's Day, *las brujas* in Redención would have said she was shuddering because the filmy veil between the living and the dead was parting. They would have said it was because the spirits were queuing up, ready to push through as if the boundaries between those with bodies and those without them were as pliable as fan palm, rustling in the desert.

Yet, upon waking, the only significance Sienna assigned to the day was that it was the one on which she permitted herself to reprogram the thermostat. Setting it to sixty-five degrees Fahrenheit until the first of April would cause her to cringe every time she got a bill from the power company, but it would make it easier to drag herself out of bed each workday if it weren't quite so icy in the master bedroom. A misnomer, of course. There was no master.

Sienna recalled more of Bridget's maternal advice, imparted during her divorce from Matt's father. "All you ever really need is a hot water bottle and a thick pair of socks." Since Sienna's husband had been globe-trotting on business so much for so long before their split, Sienna already knew there was truth in those words. She was also actually appreciative that, because there was no master, she could toss and turn and sprawl and tug blankets at will, especially on those nights when worrying about work kept her awake. But a hot-blooded man would have been lovely to lie beside at that moment.

Ugh! She rolled over in bed, remembering. Didn't Deedee realize that referring to an employee's *erotic* life was inappropriate? Maybe she was simply using the word *erotic* incorrectly. What an ELL teacher I am! Sienna thought. Actually, Deedee seemed woefully ignorant of many words that mattered, *newcomer* for one and *language acquisition* for another. Sienna thought of how Miguel's face had lit up when she'd given him the term *hothouse*. A poet's appreciation for *Swami*, for *swap meet* coursed through her. Not a single word in *Reading Fare* was inherently more important than the ones the kids wanted to learn to share their own experiences and record whatever realities they chose to, maybe even needed to, reveal.

Sienna rolled over again. Why on earth would Deedee expect her to engage in "girl talk" about her quote, unquote boyfriend, while dismissing Sienna's professional insight? Why indeed, when Deedee herself, had wheedled money out of the Purewater school board to take a team of Moore teachers to Washington, D.C.? Not only that, Deedee had gone into the conference bookstore and generously purchased the keynote speaker's latest book *Cognitive Collisions* for everyone she'd brought to the conference. Is that what she'd meant when she said she'd put Andy in Sienna's hands? Sure, Deedee had handed a copy of his book to each staff member as they slipped into their seats for Andy's opening session, but she'd had nothing to do with the relationship that sprang up between them after that.

It was three hours ahead in Maryland. He'd definitely be up. Sienna got out of bed, made tea, and Skyped her boyfriend. Sitting in a lotus pose, with her laptop in a position least likely to reveal the faint smile lines age was beginning to etch upon her face, she sipped Saturday morning Darjeeling as they exchanged greetings, small talk and fuzzy grins. Andy had just returned from his regular run through Rock Creek Park. Despite the poor resolution on her outmoded screen, he was still adorable, even with a terrycloth sweatband around his brow.

Before long, their conversation turned to work. Sienna said, "*Reading Fare* is not a good fit for children who don't know very much English."

"I looked into it," Andy said, stretching his hamstrings. "*Reading Fare* is not an intervention program. Never was. Never will be."

"The publisher claims to have consulted with Greshem." Sienna said, referring to an ELL expert whose name was listed in the credits in the teacher's manual.

Andy scoffed. "Yeah. I had a drink with Greshem not long ago. He said Pica's not the same company it used to be. The new CEO, the heir to the throne, has some ironic first name like Julius. Made me think of Julius Caesar. Of course, Greshem was glad to get the consulting fee. But, in truth, he's disgusted with what they've done. He said Pica used to hire editors with educational backgrounds. Now they just tack some ridiculous, no-brainer blurbs in the bottom margins of their teacher editions and claim the curriculum has ELL and intervention components. If Purewater wanted to buy something scripted, they should have bought a real intervention program for your school to use."

Sienna sighed. "Someone somewhere says we are dumbing it down if we don't give all the kids the exact same level of instruction."

"Then why the hell did Deedee waste all that money bringing your staff to the conference this summer?" Andy asked, truly perplexed. "Didn't I bend over backwards to contrast *Brown v. The Board of Education* with *Lau v. Nichols*?"

"Yes," Sienna said soothingly. He had done an exemplary job explaining how the United States Supreme Court ended segregation for black students with *Brown v. The Board of Education* and then in *Lau v. Nichols* recognized the need to create access to comprehensible curriculum and instruction for English learners. Andy had gone to great lengths to explain how equal could be a violation of civil rights. While he'd emphasized how holding students who are learning English to the same levels of performance as children who already know English is not fair, Deedee had been texting about the evening's dinner reservations. Nancy Albright had snuck out to the drug store for a pair of nail scissors. Upon her return, she'd whispered, "It's so much fun to be able to do an errand in the middle of the day."

Andy seemed dismayed, "I thought I was clear that using the exact same teaching materials and tests is actually a regression to the sink or swim methods that *Lau v. Nichols* sought to ameliorate."

"You were clear about all that," Sienna said, "but we're regressing. It's sink or swim at Moore. I don't know why we're doing something we already know won't work, especially when we already know something else that will. Kids need to know enough English to be able to tell their own stories before they can read and understand someone else's!"

"Using *Reading Fair* with English Learners is as discriminatory and illegal as not letting certain segments of a population participate in school at all." Andy pulled his headband off with a husky growl. His hair stood on end like a lion's mane.

"I know," Sienna said, thrilling to how committed to social justice he could be even in his late forties, after achieving success in his profession. Well, in a way, social justice was his field.

It had been delightful for her to sit in the grand conference hall with a brand new book on her lap and watch as Andy stepped to the microphone. Recognizing him as an old college acquaintance was as delicious as the Butterscotch Blondie the two of them would share later that evening. She'd forgotten his name over the years but, as Andrew Dahlstrom began to speak, she remembered him sitting in the back of her children's literature class. He'd only made it to midterms. Their class, all women after he left, took his exodus as a sad and irritating commentary on the state of public education. He'd dropped the credential program because he realized he could earn as much or more driving for UPS than a classroom teacher with a decade of experience would see on her paycheck. Plus, he could start pulling that kind of money in immediately without waiting to finish his certification, find a job, and work for ten years first. Clearly though, Andy had found his way back into education, back to where his heart was.

As he signed her book, he'd asked Sienna if she'd ever taken a children's literature class. Yes. Grinning, he went on. Had she ever created a board game based on the *Ugly Duckling*? Ha! She'd be tarred and feathered like *Brer Rabbit*, if she did something that creative with students at Moore now. Amazed and flattered that he'd remembered her, Sienna had laughed.

Deedee had immediately invited him to accompany her staff to what, coincidentally, turned out to be his favorite restaurant. By All Saints' Day, Sienna and Andy had been dating via the Internet for almost two months. Sienna said. "Brenda Hadley's school board campaign slogan was "Impressive Expectations." *Reading Fare* has been adopted to fulfill them. People in Purewater just don't understand what English Learners need."

"Impressive expectations remind me of Dickens. Of *Great Expectations*."

"Yeah," Sienna said. "I don't get why Deedee and Nancy Albright seem so determined to dole out such indigestible gruel and sugarcoat it, by calling it high expectations."

"You are so poetic." Andy cupped his hands. "Please, sir," he begged, pathetically, "can I have some more?"

"Sorry Oliver," Sienna said.

"The name's Oliver," Andy said. "Oliver Twist."

Now, she leaned closer to the computer screen. "*Reading Fare* pretends to be nourishing, but it's not. The publisher promises results, but the curriculum is actually unnecessarily confusing and disempowering for at-risk kids. I'm going to have to find a way to make Deedee listen to me."

"Yep. And you should start wearing a tee-shirt that says eschew obfuscation. I'll pick one up for you at the university bookstore tomorrow, so you can wear it to work."

"I don't think anyone on my staff will know what it means."

"Then I'll get you hired out here," he said.

"Wouldn't that be a conflict of interest?"

"Who could blame me for wanting to talk shop with and kiss the same woman? Honestly, Sienna, I feel like an infatuated college kid these days. I can't concentrate on grading midterms."

"Am *I* distracting you?" Sienna couldn't help giggling. She knew she was batting her eyelashes at a laptop, yet she still couldn't stop herself.

She remembered how after Deedee and the other teachers finally went up to their rooms, they'd hugged. It had begun as a friendly farewell embrace, but the smell of his aftershave had been inviting for her and he was intoxicated by the jasmine scent of her shampoo. Struck by desire, they'd kissed instead of backing out of each other's arms. Every prism in the chandelier above them had twinkled, as if the lamp were drawing the luminosity from every other source in the ornate room to bathe them in a singular spectral light.

"Mmmm!" Sienna had purred.

"Mmmm," he'd echoed. "Can we try that again?"

They did. "In fairy tales," she'd murmured, "things come in threes," and their lips met once more.

Now, with the memory of those magical kisses boomeranging against their respective screens, Sienna said, "Ten days seems like a long time."

"I wish I were there right now!" Andy said. "What are you going to do today?"

Sienna had been unsure of her plans until the answer slipped right off her tongue, "I'm going to the swap meet." Sienna paused. Andy had seemed serious about the shirt. "And I wear a medium."

***

Purewater's swap meet was held at the fairgrounds near the South Side bridge, but Sienna parked her car further north at the trailhead where B.J. Baldwin had abandoned his vehicle. She loved her daily weekday walk up on Teagan Hill where she lived, but she branched out, hiking a different route on the weekends.

Western red cedar and deciduous trees boasting plum, crimson, and marigold leaves lined the riverside trail as Sienna set off at a brisk pace, all the while imagining her son chasing a criminal. Matt would be at the dojang all morning. Maybe she could stop on her way back to the car to buy him a taco at *Casita Rio* for lunch. The food was always good there and she could count on seeing at least one, if not several, of her students whenever she stopped in.

Lost in her thoughts, Sienna gradually realized there was a surprising number of teenagers along the river for so early on a Saturday morning. Many were sharing binoculars, peering into and across the river. She decided either the local Audubon or Save Our Fish associations were hosting some sort of youth event.

A girl wearing a form-fitting jacket and lounging on a huge granite rock bordering the river caught Sienna's attention. It was Dulce Gantala, a former student. She had to be close to fifteen by now. Her maroon hoodie must have been chosen to match her long, manicured fingernails and her glossy lipstick because it certainly wasn't anywhere bulky enough to keep her warm on such a chilly morning.

Dulce had first enrolled at Moore as a fourth grader. Back then, she'd worn her shiny black hair in two braids. Now, if she'd wanted to, she could easily tuck her free-flowing locks into the back pockets of her low-slung, skin tight jeans. She'd grown up, but Sienna still recognized her. She did not know the striking, shirtless young man who stood ankle-deep in the river beside Dulce. He had dark brown skin and jet black hair. The ragged hems of his worn jeans were rolled up to his knees as he maneuvered the splintered handle of a shovel with his bare hands. The water was frigid. He had to be freezing. Still, Sienna could sense the red hot attraction between the kids. It was palpable, sweet and, disturbing.

"Dulce?" Sienna called, hoping that by initiating conversation she could somehow remind this clearly smitten teenager that she had once wanted to go to college to become a teacher—that once upon a time she'd wanted to come back to Moore and sit on Sienna's desk.

"Oh!" Dulce exclaimed, happily as she recognized the woman who'd taught her English. "I miss you so much!"

"I miss you, too." Sienna smiled at her and at the boy, inviting him into the conversation. He nodded at her pleasantly, but did not speak. Evidently, he did not know much English.

"Why are so many kids down here today?" Sienna asked.

"Because of the bank robber," Dulce explained. "People think they can find the money."

Amused by the treasure hunt, Sienna asked, "How long have you two been out here?"

"A few hours. We started early because Esteban has to go to work soon." Dulce's tone was tinged with pride. Jobs were coveted in the immigrant community.

"What will you do with the money if you find it?"

Dulce shrugged. "At least go out for ice cream. Esteban almost got arrested when the police were chasing the robber. Lucky for him, nothing bad happened. A kid came out of the woods and saved him. He says it was *un milagro.*"

Sienna had been so concerned about Matt getting hurt in the chase. Now, she realized how his quick action had saved another mother's boy from a terrible fate. Thank goodness, they'd both been safe.

"Poor Esteban," Dulce confided. "He was really scared. He and his little sister just got here. Do you have a new girl named Pilar?"

"*Pilar es su hermana*?" Sienna asked the boy. He nodded and she introduced herself.

"*Senora O'Mara*!" He grinned, telling her in Spanish how much Pilar enjoyed her class.

Sienna began to respond, but Dulce interrupted. "People with no papers are scared," she said urgently. "You won't tell the police about all the people in Purewater without them, will you, Ms. O'Mara?"

Sienna looked Dulce in the eyes. "I don't care about papers."

Dulce's eyes rolled upward with relief. She had no idea that the United States Supreme Court had decided *Plyler v. Doe* back in the eighties, freeing a teacher from any concerns about the citizenship of her students and their families. "Kids wanted to come out here last night to look for the money instead of going trick-or-treating, but some of the parents were worried about us getting taken by *La Migra* or falling in the water." She scoffed, "All the grandmas started talking about ghosts."

As Dulce translated this for Esteban, a panicked expression flashed across his face. A stream of rapid, agitated speech followed. All that Sienna could manage to understand was "*Pilar no debe escucharlas."* Pilar should not hear of this. She did not doubt his desire to protect his little sister from something scary, but Sienna sensed that Esteban was reacting against a phantom from his own past as well.

Dulce recognized it, too. She spoke to him soothingly in Spanish. "Ms. O'Mara," she said quickly, "can you please explain the science to Pilar? Just tell her the river moves too fast and she should stay away. And can you tell her, there's no such thing as ghosts? Teachers always say that anyway. I mean, if there's a ghost in a story, they always say there's no such thing."

"I could go over river safety." If the whole town were embarking on a treasure hunt, it would be a good idea for teachers to address it, but Sienna found herself surprisingly uneasy at refuting the ghost story the grandmas were telling. Why? She wondered. Was it because as a poet she already knew there are often consequences for dismissing what exists in other realms?

As Dulce comforted Esteban, a ray of sunlight grazed the rocks overturned by the boy's bankside digging. One of the wet stones flashed silver. For a moment it seemed as if he'd actually unearthed a miner's nugget. Sienna scooped it up. The stone was round. Like a candle, it had a concave surface. Instead of containing melted wax, it held a thimble-sized pool of water. While she considered the illuminated rock, Dulce opened her arms and Esteban waded right into them.

When Sienna said goodbye, the teenagers didn't seem to hear her. She continued her walk south, suspecting neither Mr. or Mrs. Gantala had any idea that their beautiful daughter was out with this handsome and fragile young man. Dulce's father worked at the local tire shop and her mother behind the deli counter at Bonny Deals. Documentation had never seemed to be an issue for the Gantala clan.

Sienna caught herself assuming that Dulce would want to date "up." Elementary kids almost always embraced newcomers, but she knew more established teens were sometimes hesitant to befriend them and could even be harsh and judgmental of those who reminded them of their own vulnerability in the mainstream. As she dried the rock and slipped it into her fleece pocket, Sienna wished she could just "explain the science" and remind Dulce and Esteban to be careful around the raging river of first love, but that wasn't her job, was it?

Chapter Eight

Mariachi music and the scent of nacho cheese spiced with jalapeños floated through the air. As she reached the fairgrounds, Sienna realized her students had been telling the truth about the swap meet all along. They really did sell Nachos there, right next to a booth where tissue-paper piñatas dangled from overhead cables.

Nearby, a battered folding table boasted giant marigolds outgrowing their tiny seedling trays. A second table sagged under the weight of white plastic pails filled with the very last dahlias and sunflowers of the season. Mrs. Yang, the grandmother of several of Sienna's Hmong students, plucked blooms from various buckets, snipped their stems, and deftly created lavish bouquets. Her granddaughter Bao, one of Sienna's favorite second graders, stood ready to wrap them in brown paper and rubber bands. This may have been a swap meet, but Grandma Yang's sign was clear. She had zero interest in trading. She expected cash.

Wearing a T-shirt that promoted a brewery, Ian Hadley, Brenda's son and Laurali's dad, appeared. Ian was an overweight, red-faced man. He was with his brother, Mark, who was much lankier and wore a red bandana tied around his forehead. They lugged an old engine past the flower stall.

"Hey!" Ian Hadley said, "I bet a bunch of flowers could save both of us from some grief tonight." The men set their load on the asphalt in front of Grandma Yang.

His brother read the price list. "Ten bucks to enjoy this baby without nagging?" He patted the top of a metallic cylinder affectionately as if were the downy head of a toddler clinging to his leg. "Sounds like a good deal to me!"

"Good deal. These thirty in the store." Grandma Yang waved her hand over the ready-made arrangements.

Sienna was almost sure that was most of the English the elderly woman knew, but her price was right. If Sienna hadn't had to hike back to her car at the other end of Purewater, she would have definitely bought a bouquet for herself. Ian reached into his back pocket for his wallet.

Sienna turned her attention to the other treasures the swap meet offered. Several folding tables were piled high with car parts and farm equipment. Other tables were covered with chipped dishes and used baby clothes. She noted a group of children with black hair, of stair-step heights, standing around a spread of old toys and tattered books. She recognized some of the books. Darn it! What were they doing here? She'd culled them from Moore's library back when she'd been the school librarian. Some were culturally offensive, particularly to Native Americans. Others were overtly sexist.

During the first big influx of English Language Learners into Purewater, Sienna ordered brightly illustrated Mexican folktales. She'd put an order in on the morning the Gantala kids and their cousins enrolled. She'd stayed late to process the books as soon as they'd arrived to get them on the shelves as quickly as possible. She'd wanted the kids to feel that their culture was welcome in the school.

Bao was suddenly at her side, presenting her with a red dahlia. She was a quiet child, more reserved than most of Sienna's other students.

"Thank you." Sienna said warmly, knowing Bao would have been embarrassed by any more profuse appreciation.

Upon hearing her familiar voice behind them, the children at the table turned. Cassandra, Lupe, and Pilar stared at Sienna.

"Why you here?" Cassandra finally blurted, breaking through the awestruck silence of seeing a teacher outside of school.

"I wanted to meet you at the Swami!" Sienna winked at the girls.

"Swap Meet!" They cried, bouncing on the balls of their feet. "It's called a swap meet!"

Sienna laughed. "Oh excuse me. I meant to say that."

"*Hola Maestra!*" Cassandra's mother joined them quickly, clearly mortified to see her daughter jumping up and down and shouting at the teacher. She had a sleeping baby in the sling she wore beneath the woolen shawl over her shoulders and she balanced a tray of leggy marigolds in her hands.

Sienna admired the baby, putting Mrs. Fuentes at ease. Mrs. Fuentes could not resist asking the question that the ELL parents asked Sienna more than any other. "*Cómo se comporta?*" How is my daughter's behavior?

"*Ella es muy buena.*"

"*Y la lectura?* It is good now?"

It still bothered Sienna to remember the parent-teacher conference Nancy called shortly after school began in September. Through the interpreter, she'd told a worried Mrs. Fuentes that Cassandra was supposed to read ninety-three words per minute on a fourth grade passage that she had never seen or heard before, but that she could only read twenty-eight. Basically, since fourth grade was considered the make-it-or-break-it-year for literacy, Cassandra had to start reading three times faster than she currently did within the next few months or she would never catch up in school. Mrs. Fuentes swallowed hard. She couldn't read in English or in Spanish.

"Let's look at this another way," Sienna broke in using her own halting Spanish. "My fluency score in Spanish is about sixty on text I've practiced a few times. And it's a lot slower if I'm working to understand what I'm reading."

Nancy shook her head. "Let's keep to the point. Fluency is our first priority. The National Reading Commission told Congress fluency comes first!"

Mrs. Fuentes wrung her hands when the interpreter told her that Congress was involved in her daughter's reading problem. Sienna tried to explain, "The idea is that if a child can read at the target speed, reading has become so automatic that she's no longer having to think about sounding out or recognizing words. When kids read with fluency, they can concentrate on what the words mean. Putting fluency first doesn't work out very well for people who don't know the language they are reading, because they can't be sure if they are sounding out correctly. They don't know if the words they read are actually words in the unknown language. They have no way of telling if what they read makes any sense or not. There's just no feedback loop if people can word-call in a language they don't know. That's why I teach English by having kids write their own personal stories. They already know everything that happened and what the people in them were thinking and feeling, so their brains can focus on the words they need to learn to tell about that."

"Cassandra is required to reach ninety words per minute by Christmas," Nancy said firmly. "You need to help her at home."

"Okay." Mrs. Fuentes agreed.

As she left, Nancy told Sienna, "I've got the rest of my conferences covered. Please don't waste your time coming to any more of them."

Now, at the swap meet, Mrs. Fuentes reported that Cassandra was always writing little *cuentas*, stories at home and she was reading them to her younger siblings. She thanked Sienna for working with Cassandra in *The Writers' Lair* and led her daughter away.

Sienna carried the red dahlia past displays of used cutlery and secondhand kitchenware. Bao, Lupe, and Pilar escorted her, heads held high. They made their way toward a tent at the end of the lot where Sienna assumed a trio of grinning musicians wearing silver-studded charro outfits, shiny leather boots, and wide-brimmed hats strummed classic guitars inside. And on the way, she began to notice pots of marigolds everywhere – splashes of radiant yellow and bold oranges seemed to rush forward, shimmering in the foreground of her consciousness. Some of the flowers were banked against the curb so a woman could tie her child's shoe. Others were sunk into the faded canopies of strollers so *las abuelitas* could rummage through piles of multi-colored Christmas lights. Packs of top-heavy, leggy marigolds were precariously wedged between piles of used clothing so they wouldn't tip over as middle-aged men held shirts up against their bulky midriffs to approximate the fit.

The mariachi band paused. Sienna barely registered the silence because all the marigolds were reminding her that while today was All Saints Day, tomorrow would be The Day of the Dead and she was wondering if she should celebrate it in the Writers Lair. A sudden explosion of rap startled her. What spewed from an old Honda Civic's radio was jarring; the lyrics disturbing. The children at her side did not seem affected by the switch in genre, but the faces of the happy adults around her suddenly grew grim at the inciting chant, "Dust the cops off." *Imbécile!* The Mexicans all thought instantly. Everyone knew that the local police and federal agents were still combing the surrounding area, looking for traces of the bank robber. They could be upon them all within moments.

The two Hadley men who'd just bought bouquets from Grandma Yang were parked directly behind the offending car. They were arguing about how to pack the engine they'd just gotten at the swap meet into the old Citation they'd driven to the event. The Citation was already full of automobile debris. The sudden noise turned irritation about the lack of space to instant outrage. It was fine to be serenaded by Mexican music while combing the swap meet. It was another thing, altogether, to have their eardrums assaulted while trying to cram their prize in the car, while resisting the fear that it might not fit. Fury at what was clearly gangbanger music invading their town, flashed in their eyes.

In the car ahead of their Citation, Sienna saw a young man with lowered lids and pale skin, slouching behind a chipped windshield. His head bobbed with the heavy beat. He seemed completely oblivious to the fact that he was forcing the community to listen to a piece they resented hearing. Ian Hadley stepped forward—a tire iron in his hand. Sienna's heart leapt to her throat. There was violence in the music. There was violence in the air.

Suddenly, the side door of a weathered Dodge Galleon parked at an angle next to the Mariachi tent slid open. A broad shouldered man in cowboy boots, faded jeans and a plain black T-shirt ducked his head out. Scanning the scene, he stepped down from the van, running his hand through his spiky black hair and then over the scant beard on his chin. Roused, like a father from a Sunday nap to snake a clogged toilet, he strode purposefully toward the pulsating Civic.

"Gaul?" Pilar gasped, grabbing Sienna's hand.

Lifting a muscular, deeply tanned forearm, the man Pilar called Gaul thumped on the window. The kid inside did not hear. The motion of Gaul's arm caught his attention. He rolled the window down, "*Qué?*" Insolence glittered in his basalt eyes.

Gaul mouthed something only the juvenile could see. The kid shrugged, rolled up his window, and started his car. Gaul tapped the window again. The offending music stopped. Gaul stepped aside. Gaul watched the car disappear. Then he turned to Ian Hadley.

Gaul's dark eyes traveled to the iron rod in Ian's grip. He gestured toward the oversized engine and the too small car. "Do you need some help there?" Ian shrugged, sheepishly. Gaul stepped forward quickly, expertly directing the men on how to rearrange their junk so that the new acquisition would fit.

Lupe and Bao wandered a little closer to the Citation. Overcrowded vehicles and homes were part of their daily lives and they knew there was value in observing this man's technique. Pilar watched too, but not like a girl watching a man help other men solve a puzzle. Still clinging to Sienna, she'd ossified, much like she had during the lockdown.

"*El conoce?*" Sienna asked.

"*No se,*" Pilar said with a dazed expression.

"You don't know if you know him?" Well, Sienna thought, of course, a child in Pilar's situation could get confused. Of course, Pilar would experience bouts of disorientation in a new country. Sienna wished the school district could still fund a school counselor for situations like this, especially one who could speak a variety of different languages.

Ian Hadley and his brother-in-law left the swap meet using the cylinders of their newly acquired engine as vases. As the men drove away, the bright faces of sunflowers, red dahlias, and a few giant marigolds bobbled in the back window of Ian's Citation.

The children went to play with the flower stand's discarded

stems and stray buds. Sienna watched them for a moment, listening to the multi-lingual dialogue of their game, remembering how she once played with her mother's fuchsias. As a little girl, she'd spent hours in Bridget's San Jose, California garden, pretending that each blossom was a fairy. Wearing pink tutus and raspberry tights on their stamen legs, Sienna's fuchsia fairies had leapt from the hanging basket tower to the ground, intent upon enchanting the toads that lived under landscaping rocks. Matt had never been interested in playing with flowers. He'd always liked tossing rocks into Teagan Creek.

Sienna wandered over to the Mariachi tent, vaguely disappointed to discover there was no band—just a boom box and long tables piled high with bright Zapotec blankets and folk art inside. She looked over tin hearts, hand-painted terra cotta tiles, carvings of *los santos*, and free-standing niches that could be installed in corners of the home, creating instant altars for honoring the saints. Some items looked worn, authentically vintage: others newly varnished.

Like Grandma Yang's flowers, these were for sale. Sienna read the business card attached to a stunning serape. *Arte para la Gente.* She noted the price tag. Suddenly, Gaul was by her side. He smelled of sage and patchouli as he said, "This was handmade in Clemencia."

Clemencia sounded familiar. Sienna thought maybe that was where Pilar had come from, though she'd only had time for a brief glance at the girl's records before creating her ELL file in moments stolen between teaching, testing, and preparing for lessons.

"Do you like it?" Gaul picked up the serape.

"It's beautiful."

"Would you like to try it on?" He asked, pushing it toward her. He sounded friendly. There was no pressure in his tone.

"I wouldn't really wear something like this," she confessed, taking it from him. It's weight felt reassuring, like a guaranteed shield against the bite of winter, but she wouldn't pay that much for something she wouldn't wear very often. In Purewater, the only ethnic dressers were the Pakistani mom of a fifth grade boy and the Iraqi aunt of four girls. In fact, if Sienna wore a serape with such a bold pattern, people would assume it was because she was an ELL teacher trying too hard to make a statement. So, she smiled ruefully, glad she'd had a chance to see his wares before Gaul realized there was no market for them in Purewater and took them away.

"This serape is woven from ixtle, a traditional fiber that comes from the maguey plant." Gaul seemed to expect her to know the significance of that fact. Seeing that she did not, he explained, "It's made from the same material as Juan Diego's cloak was."

"Juan Diego?"

"The *indio* who saw Our Lady of Guadalupe," he spoke as if he were gently chiding her to remember a story she should know well. "They met in December. It was the dead of winter and she gave him an armload of blooming roses. She told him to wrap them in his cloak to prove to the bishop that she was real."

Sienna thought of the jewelry Lupe had worn on the day the Swami joined *The Writers' Lair*. "Ah, yes. I do know that story."

"Put it on," Gaul urged. As she hesitated, he took the serape from her. "May I?" Barely waiting for her nod, he draped the holy material over her shoulders. "And the dyes in this one are from completely natural sources."

Sienna admired how cleanly the black and red stripes were delineated from the white sections. She found herself wondering if the colors would run when she washed it.

"The red comes from the crushing of female beetles."

Beneath the serape, Sienna suddenly went cold. For a woman who serenely bought and wore fleece made from recycled soda pop bottles, crushing a living cochineal to dye yarn seemed archaic and cruel. Still, she didn't want to appear squeamish or unappreciative of traditional art, so she left the serape on. The fringe fluttered as her hand swept over the carvings of dancing skeletons displayed near her. "I love all of this. It's really wonderful."

Gaul arched his eyebrows slightly with the playfulness of a man happily accepting a compliment from *una mujer bonita*. "Thank you." It didn't matter to him whether she bought or not. "I am Gaul Santiago."

She told him her name, that she taught English in town and,

remembering Pilar's odd reaction to him, had second thoughts about disclosing such personal information. She cocked her head slightly, considering him carefully. Maybe he was a fraud. If he really owned a gallery in Santa Fe, why would he be traveling so far north in a vehicle which by all appearances was apt to leave him stranded on the side of the road? Maybe the serape had actually been made in China. Gaul was good-looking. He was probably a revving-down Don Juan, an expert in weaving lies.

Gaul nodded as if he recognized her initial, almost obligatory distrust and forgave her for it. "I buy and sell arts and crafts so people in Mexico can feed their children. I think it's great that you teach the kids who can get here what they need to know to make a living in the United States."

"Well, that's one way to look at it," Sienna said. "But I want to teach so kids can reach their full human potential."

As if she'd lost his attention, Gaul's eyes traveled around the swap meet, toward the empty space where he'd just helped Ian Hadley rearrange his car and back to Grandma Yang's flower stand. Under the table bedecked with marigolds, the little girls were exchanging discarded flowers and trading words in three, maybe four languages. "Are any of them your students?"

"They are." Sienna claimed the girls more like a proud *tía* than a school teacher all the while hoping that Pilar wouldn't get confused about which new words she learned were Hmong and which were English. Would she think red and say *liab*?

Sienna shifted slightly under the serape. "I think the girl in pink is from *Clemencia*. It must be a very creative place. She's an artist in the making."

"Is she working with sculpture?"

Sienna was taken aback. At Moore, worksheets reigned supreme. Deedee had scolded the first grade teacher, Mavis Penn, for letting children practice letters formation with salt dough. Sculpture was definitely not part of the curriculum. "Just crayon on construction paper," she said, almost guiltily.

"Very good! I'll bid on her work!"

Suddenly, something about his enthusiasm felt authentic, good, and true. Sienna imagined him taking Pilar's mermaid away. She was surprised by the small wave of anxiety that washed over her at the thought. "I couldn't bear to give it away."

He reached for the serape. It seemed to tear away from Sienna like an adhesive bandage pulling at tender hair follicles. And it was at that moment she realized that wearing something dyed with bug's blood wasn't what had bothered her, it was the phrase—the crushing of female—that had chilled her.

He refolded the wrap carefully, but his mind was on something else. Finally, he said, "I may be wrong about this, but if you are that little girl's teacher, I think maybe you should have something from her homeland. Will you wait just a moment while I get it?"

Sienna nodded uncertainly. Her house payment was probably, at this very moment, being transferred out of her checking account to pay the lender, leaving just enough for a month's worth of groceries and gas. Just because he wanted her to have something, didn't mean she had to buy it.

He hesitated for a moment clearly still considering and then disappeared into his van, leaving Sienna to ponder a set of ornate wooden crucifixes.

Gaul returned, bearing a painted terracotta woman. She was about twelve inches tall. Her neck was long and thin. Her forehead was wide. Her hair was painted black. She wore a yellow gown and a miniature *rebozo*, a baby-carrying sling, was strapped across her shoulder, but there was no baby in it. A vertical fissure ran from her brow to her bare feet. Gaul traced it lightly with his finger. "There has been a lot of trouble in the state of Redención lately," he said as if political unrest were directly responsible for the schism in the clay. "I...I... knew this was a precious piece when I snatched it. It's a little different from the artist's other work."

Snatched? Sienna was alarmed. Did he steal and profit from the disempowered indigenous?

"I couldn't find her. Redención was empty, essentially."

Empty? Essentially? Sienna's heart lurched. Like Pilar and Esteban, Gaul had seen something terrible. Sienna was overwhelmed by sadness.

65

"It feels right to give this lady to you because I can see you know what needs to be done for the children."

No one ever spoke to her about her work like that. Tears sprang to Sienna's eyes as he placed the statue in her hands.

"The place this clay comes from is a well-guarded secret." Gaul told her. "The clay is special, especially when used for *calaveras*."

Calaveras? As she held the figurine, a distracting tingling began in her fingers. It felt pleasant, yet wondering if she were beginning an allergic reaction of some kind to the paint or clay, kept her from accessing the English definition of the Spanish word in her mind. What were *calaveras* again?

"From what I could glean, the clay itself comes from soil moistened by a hot spring in an underground aquifer," Gaul went on. "The people call it *matriz*. They say it's given by *La Madre Ardiendo*, the volcano that determines the destiny of Redención."

Sienna's arm had begun tingling. She heard Gaul say *La Madre Ardiendo*, but in her head, a woman's voice whispered "*La Mujer de Tierra*." Gaul peered intently into her eyes. "You are right. The clay should only be handled by a Woman of the Earth."

Sienna was confused. Why was she tingling? How had Gaul heard what she hadn't said? How had he heard the voice in her head?

"Tell me," he said slowly, "What did that little girl draw in your class?"

"A mermaid."

"A mermaid?" He frowned thoughtfully. "What does she look like?"

"She has long hair."

"Like yours?"

Sienna shrugged, shaking off his unnerving intensity. "Maybe." Just because he'd given her a gift, just because he'd read her mind, didn't make her hair any of his business.

"Pardon me," Gaul stepped back a little and Sienna realized she'd been holding her breath.

"I was just thinking about how much she must adore you," he said. "How much you must inspire her."

He seemed sincere. Sienna decided he was a decent man. She lifted *La Mujer de Tierra* slightly. The tingling made her arm tremble slightly. "And I'll keep this on my desk to inspire me."

After thanking Gaul again, Sienna stopped at Grandma Yang's booth. Dulce and Esteban had come for Pilar. Sienna impulsively bought a mixed tray of bright yellow, orange, and red marigolds. It wasn't a particularly practical decision because she would have to carry the flowers all the way back to her car. Her fanny pack was already crammed with her wallet and keys. It wasn't quite long enough to lay *La Mujer de Tierra* in so she zipped the figure standing upright inside, facing outward. "Like a joey," Bao remarked with a shy, grin, delighted to remember the name of a baby kangaroo.

As Grandma Yang made change, Sienna rubbed her relieved arm, realizing she probably wasn't allergic to the clay or the paint on the figurine. She thought the tingling she felt while holding the statue could have been because she probably pinched a nerve in her neck from sitting on student chairs out in the hall. She remembered Miguel trying to write about his mom with Tammy agitatedly hovering overhead. She watched Pilar, Esteban, and Dulce walking the river trail back toward downtown Purewater. Where was Pilar's mom? Sienna realized she knew nothing about her.

Moments later from inside his van, Gaul watched Sienna head the same way. It was too late to question his decision to give her *La Mujer de Tierra*. It was too late for him to regret his loss of the lady. He told himself the statue was only valuable if it would be used and it could only be used by a woman who was sensitive to its power and believed that it had value. He'd done the best he could with what was left.

Chapter Nine

As Sienna left the swap meet, she met Jolie strolling arm-in-arm with Purewater's police chief, Captain Wolfgang Goodwin. His nickname was Wolf. He greeted Sienna with, "Matt flipped me again." He rubbed his lower back. "God, he's getting good."

"Sorry." Sienna frowned sympathetically, although she couldn't help feeling a small tinge of relief that her son could probably protect himself in certain kinds of danger.

"Dispatch reported some commotion down here." Wolf said. "Did you see anything?"

"Commotion?" Sienna shook her head. "Related to the bank robbery?"

"No. That's up to the Feds now. This call was about music. Did you hear it?"

"Oh! That only lasted for a minute. Who would have called the police so quickly?"

"Probably one of Brenda Hadley's people. She was against the city issuing a permit for a swap meet right from the get-go. Rebecca is in office right now, so it went through."

"Brenda and Rebecca Hadley are sisters," Sienna explained to Jolie. "Part of the Purewater dynasty. They switch back and forth between city government and the school board. I think they were born to personify the pendulum swing in politics and embody the Reading Wars."

Wolf furrowed his brow. He had no idea what the Reading Wars were, but he knew Purewater politics. "I guess I should warn you that I could get called away from a date for an overturned dumpster on a moment's notice. I suspect today's calls will mostly be about smashed pumpkins."

"I'll take my chances," Jolie said. "I've always got a stack of novels ready to play second fiddle."

"A foreign film works for me." Sienna said.

"I'm partial to a football."

"As *second* fiddle?" Jolie asked.

Wolf winked at her. "That all depends on who's playing first."

Sienna was happy to see Wolf flirting. They'd always been friendly, but never dated. They'd always assumed that it wasn't a good idea for a woman to date her son's sparring buddy. As Wolf would confess much, much later, it was at that moment he realized that if he had the money that Baldwin had lost in the river, he'd wine and dine Jolie until it felt appropriate to surprise her with a diamond engagement ring and two tickets for a first-class honeymoon cruise.

Unaware of all this, Jolie gestured toward Sienna's marigolds. "Aren't we bound to get frost soon?"

"These are for my portable. Tomorrow is *El Día de los Muertos*."

Jolie and Wolf both looked puzzled.

Sienna explained. "It's a Latino holiday to honor the dead. There's a book about it in the library that I bought when I was still the librarian at Moore right before I started teaching ELL."

"I didn't know you used to be Moore's librarian," Jolie said. "We should talk as soon I get through the Veteran's Day assembly. Right before I left last night, Deedee said she wanted me to organize the whole thing, including having the high school band and all the flag girls march past Moore to kick it off."

For a moment, Sienna imagined Deedee in the lead, waving a *Reading Fare* banner. "You can't pull that off by next week! There are too many logistical issues."

"She insists it's essential for poor kids to see a parade. I reminded her there's a good chance it will be pouring rain. And..." Jolie paused uncomfortably.

"What?"

"She snapped." Jolie said. "Really. She stomped her feet and shouted 'I'm sick of everyone around here raining on my parade!'"

"She must have been taking a lot of heat for allowing Halloween."

"But think about all the flack she'd get if something goes wrong with six hundred kids on the sidewalk in bad weather."

"Not gonna happen," Wolf said. "Too late to file the paperwork. We can't just shut First Street down because Deedee Hayes gets another crazy idea." His blue eyes twinkled as he jutted his chin toward Sienna. "I never pegged you for a swap meet kind of girl. Shouldn't you be out in the woods hugging a tree or writing a poem?"

"You're profiling, Wolf. One of my students wrote about coming here and I wanted to check it out."

"And now they've got you celebrating The Day of the Dead, too?"

"It's the fastest growing holiday in Purewater, Captain. You should probably keep that in mind." She winked at the new couple before her. "You two have fun. Don't forget to ice your back later, Wolf. I'm off to see if my black belt will let me buy him a taco."

***

On All Saints Day, Pilar ate *empanadas* for lunch and then climbed on a stool to stir the *mole* simmering in the black cast iron pot on the stove. She didn't have a food handler's permit and couldn't risk being seen, so when she helped at the café, Pilar kept herself hidden behind the heavy canvas curtain between the kitchen and the dining area. That afternoon she was tempted by a plate of *calaveras de azucar*.

Lucia had made sugar skulls the day before. While Pilar was at school, learning to pray for the best multiple choice answers on a test, Lucia and Ramon had discussed serving *calaveras* in the restaurant on *El Día de Los Muertos*. Ramon had held a skull up, considering all the orifices. "This not a Chinese cookie."

Lucia sighed. "Americans love good fortune. They sure don't

70

want to stare death in the eye socket." With that, they scrapped the whole idea. Now, the best craniums were upstairs on the altar. The misshapen ones had been behind for snacking.

Esteban was working in the kitchen after the swap meet, chopping lettuce, and Dulce stood much closer to him than anyone should stand next to a man wielding a knife. When Lucia noticed this, she studied Dulce, as if she were lifting the layers of the girl's skin and peeking beneath them, as if she could see how Dulce's spine shimmied like a fishing rod with a bite on its hook. Lucia had been the same way with Ramon at that age so when Dulce begged to stay and help, Lucia thought it wise to give them both a little breathing room. She asked Dulce about school and when the girl confessed to having homework, Lucia urged her to go, kindly inviting her to return for a cooking lesson when the café wasn't quite so busy.

Dulce's thanks were profuse. Pilar guessed Dulce loved Esteban enough to want to grate cheese instead of doing a research paper. She probably also wanted to learn how to make the best *mole* in the state. Maybe she wanted to land herself a job at *Casita Rio* as soon as Ramon and Lucia could afford to pay her. On the way back from the swap meet, Dulce told Esteban and Pilar that if she had the money Baldwin lost, she would have a fancy quinceanera and then move her parents and five siblings out of the two bedroom apartment they rented in the South Side complex to buy a four bedroom, two bath house with a yard for all of them to live in. She'd invite her aunt and uncle and cousins to move in, too.

After Dulce left, Pilar popped a whole *calavera* into her mouth and continued to stir the *mole*. She loved the way the mixture swirled around the spoon as it began to bubble in the cauldron. Over the drone of the kitchen fan, the staccato thwack of Esteban's blade on the cutting board, and the hum of happy diners coming from the front of the restaurant, an argument from the alley behind wafted through the open kitchen window.

"I'll pay for it." Sienna insisted. "Do you want chicken or beef? Corn or flour tortilla?" Pilar knew her teacher was talking to her son. It made her realize that Lucia sounded a lot like that. Perhaps Lucia got away with talking to customers like she was their mother was proof that her food was truly delicious or that, on some level, people like being to be cajoled to eat.

"Mom," Matt said, "you aren't supposed to eat right after you work out."

"Did Master In-Su tell you that?" She sounded indignant or disappointed. "Is that a Korean thing?"

"I'm just not hungry."

"I can eat when I'm not hungry!"

"Mom!" Matt barked, as if to snap her out of something. "You don't believe in force feeding."

"Right," she said, instantly sounding more like herself. "I'm going in for lunch. If you change your mind, please come join me."

With that, wild with excitement, Pilar dropped the spoon in the *mole*. She burst out of the kitchen, sprinting through the tables toward the yellow tiled foyer, intent on being there to greet her teacher the instant she walked through the front door, but Pilar lost her footing and slid smack into the belly of a man waiting to be seated. As Gaul Santiago caught his breath and steadied her, Sienna stepped through the doorway behind him. "I know you! I know you!" Pilar shouted exuberantly as if she hadn't seen the teacher just twenty minutes earlier. Evidently, the *calavera* had made her too hyper and too loud.

At first, Lucia was shocked to see Pilar excited about anything. Then she was terrified, waiting for people to complain about children being in the kitchen. The chiles on the plate she held suspended under a patron's nose made his eyes water. Ramon was troubled, too—about something else. He rushed to Gaul, barking at Pilar, *"Disculparse chica!* You do not know him. You have never seen this man before. This is my old friend from New Mexico."

With the same sensation she'd felt when livestock salt pickled her dehydrated tongue, Pilar snapped into the required ignorance. "I'm sorry," she said looking at the men with a mixture of fear and pluck. *"Estoy hablando de mi maestra."*

Sienna hoped Pilar would not get in trouble on her account.

"Sorry! Sorry!" Ramon mumbled to everyone and to no one in particular. The only response was a customer's request for more salsa and another pitcher of water.

Gaul's eyes were very kind as he spoke softly to Pilar. "*No te preoccupas.*" He turned and smiled at Sienna. Amusement at seeing *La Mujer de Tierra* peeking out from the bag at her hip, flickered across his face. "We meet again."

Sienna could do little more than nod to acknowledge being at the same place at the same time for the second time that day. Ramon nearly flung a basket of warm tortilla chips and a tray of little black pots, miniature caldrons de *brujas*, heaping with sour cream, salsa, and guacamole on a table for her. With a smile, he pulled out a chair, gestured for her to sit. As soon as she did, he rushed forward, clasped Gaul by the arm, and scurried him back into the kitchen.

Lucia followed the men with studied nonchalance. Given her fears about the health department, she surprised Pilar by calling over her shoulder for her to give "the lady" a menu. Later, Lucia would be mortified for not recognizing, let alone greeting, the ELL teacher more graciously. Sienna did not mind. Clearly an important reunion was taking place.

Sienna already knew she wanted a taco, but she took the menu from Pilar to let her play waitress and to practice her own reading in Spanish. She sat there, softly mouthing the foreign words aloud just like the ELL kids in Pilar's classroom did when they read English. Pilar watched mystified. Mrs. Albright said kids had to keep their mouths closed when they read. Ms. O'Mara was doing it wrong, too.

Nonetheless, with her "below standard" style, Sienna read the paragraph about how Ramon and Lucia began their business with a taco truck. They'd made their rounds each day to the many tulip fields in the valley and sold tacos to hungry harvesters.

"It gets easier for me to read this every time I eat here," Sienna told Pilar. "It is good to read the same thing over and over again." Then, she ordered the original, "Taco de Tulip."

Pilar scurried to the kitchen. Lucia didn't seem to mind her coming and going now. Lucia quickly dished up Sienna's plate, straining to hear what Ramon and Gaul were saying in rapid Spanish.

"More," Pilar insisted, as if encouraging her *madrina* to stuff the white flour tortilla as full of food as her heart was with admiration for her teacher. As Lucia drizzled another spoonful of mole sauce over Sienna's meal, Pilar snatched a tiny *calavera de azucar* and popped it into her own mouth.

Lucia was so keen to talk to the men that she handed Sienna's plate to Pilar. With the candy skull melting on her tongue, the proud young waitress hurried out to her favorite customer.

She stopped short as she approached her teacher's table. A casual observer would have thought Sienna was just admiring her new purchases. But the marigolds and the achingly, somehow familiar statuette she'd set across from her—as if they were girlfriends having lunch—filled Pilar with a complex mixture of emotion. The child's hand wobbled as she served her teacher. Like lava from the mouth of the volcanic *La Madre Ardiendo*, bits of the overfilled taco slid over the rim of the plate. The chicken, drenched in chocolate and spice, the sharp cheese, and the freshest lettuce from Lucia's kitchen flowed to the feet of *La Mujer de Tierra*. Ashamed of her clumsiness, Pilar winced, gulping the last remains of one sweet skull.

"*No te preocupas.*" Sienna smiled reassuringly. Using *una cuchara,* she scooped up a huge dollop of guacamole, playfully plopping it right on top of the spillage. To the clay lady, she said, "*Pilar y yo, le damos lo mejor de esta mesa.* We give you the best from this table."

Sienna might as well have bought Juan Diego's knock-off serape and started wearing it to work and around town. By graciously turning Pilar's anxious trembling into an ad hoc celebration of *El Día de los Muertos*—into an *ofrenda,* she became an ELL teacher who opened a border. All that was left was the crossing.

Chapter Ten

Early Monday morning, Sienna slipped Pilar's mermaid picture and a color printout of last week's Swami into cheap black metal and plexi-glass frames. She hung the two representations on the wall behind her desk and placed *La Mujer de Tierra* and an ebony pot of marigolds on top of the bookcase directly below the portraits. Her decorating done, she dashed to bus duty where Miss Whitfield, arriving for the day, informed her she would not be sending any of her first graders to ELL. They hadn't finished their *Reading Fare* tests before Friday's dismissal. There was no arguing about whether they could attend ELL or not. She needed to record their scores.

With unexpected free time, Sienna decided to give Miguel Pena extra attention. He'd been brave, promising to help her fend off the bad guys during the lockdown, but he hadn't been very productive yet in *The Writers' Lair*. When Sienna entered Nancy Albright's classroom all of the students were at their desks with their math books open—to double-faced pages chock full of story problems.

In the back row, Pilar's head was bent over the text so that it looked as if she were studying. Really she was playing some sort of blinking game with herself. Left eye, right eye. Sienna wondered if the child might be developing a nervous tic.

Nancy was reading quickly, "If they each had forty-eight party favors, how many bags did they get?"

On her way to Miguel, Sienna knelt beside Cassandra,

whispering "Where are your glasses?" Cassandra reached in and pulled a sequined case out of her desk. Sienna recognized it from the swap meet.

"Party favors," Nancy reiterated. "Party favors are the little prizes you get at parties."

Sienna tapped beneath the word *favors* and Cassandra slid her finger beneath Sienna's. Cassandra was proud of her hot pink nails. On Sunday, Dulce Gantala had come over to the Fuentes apartment to visit with Cassandra's big sister. All the girls had painted their nails and chattered about Esteban. That had been such a fun party! Cassandra smiled at Sienna. Her round lenses made her look like a wise little owl.

Miguel was bewildered and interrupted Nancy. "But favors are not little prizes."

"They *are* little prizes," Nancy said with her eye on the clock instead of the child's face. "Just take my word for it, Miguel." It bothered Nancy immensely to have the ELL teacher hovering, wanting to take someone away from her lesson. It was math time after all. Not ELL. The pacing guide was brutal. She couldn't even afford the time it took to acknowledge Sienna's presence in the room. "Now, how many party favors does each kid get?"

Cassandra bowed her head, pressing her heels into the floor, toes upward imploring Mary, Jesus, and Joseph. Miguel's mind was not on division, nor was he invoking any form of divine intervention. His brow knit in overt consternation, while he muttered, rehearsing his next stab at rebellion. He opened his mouth wide.

Sienna said, "Come with me, Miguel." The exact moment a kid's limited English proficiency throws a classroom teacher off her lesson plan is the exact moment she is most willing to relinquish a student to an ELL instructor. And, indeed, Nancy finally gave Sienna a curt nod.

In the hallway, Sienna compared party and wedding favors with the favors Miguel did to help others and kindly explained, "Miguel, this is just another time when different things have the same name in English."

Anger lurked in the crease of his knitted brow. "Why didn't Mrs.

Albright tell us that at the beginning of math instead of forcing me to say my confusing."

Sienna had never heard him question adults before. She'd never seen him surly. She did not offer him the noun *confusion* to replace his misused adjective. "I guess she wanted to focus on the math lesson."

"I can't!"

"What?"

"Focus on the math when I didn't know what she was talking about. She said to take her word, but I didn't know what it was."

"She was thinking that you could have solved the problem even if you didn't really know what party favors were. Could you have done the math if it were *sopapillas* instead of party favors?"

"Why do a math problem to find out how much of something I got if I don't know what my something is?"

"I guess it's to practice for when you do know what the something is."

"Why can't I practice with stuff I know?" He looked a little wild-eyed. "This keeps happening. I'm *ahogarse* by words."

Miguel was on the verge of noticing how often his very reasonable questions and legitimate observations were "drowned out" in school. Concerned, Sienna edited his story, giving Miguel a new word for the setting, *yard*, so he could write about the favor he'd done for his grandma. He'd trimmed the bushes because as he explained, "She doesn't want her yard to be a safari," and Sienna let the last word stand for jungle.

After that, Sienna went to Tammy Lewis' classroom, scanning the new November bulletin board in the hallway. Just as she'd feared, little Miguel Ortega's poem about his mom working in the hothouse was not displayed alongside all the others in which children expressed gratitude for cuddly puppies, playful kittens, and computer games.

"I'm getting another boy from Mexico," Tammy told her grimly. "They just sent him over to the clinic to get his shots, but the uncle who enrolled him has to go to work so he'll be bringing him back afterwards? Can you test him?"

It wasn't very nice to give the placement WELTS to a child on his first day in an America, but Sienna did have to turn the month's ELL count into the district office by 8:00 the next morning. If the new boy did qualify for ELL services the state would, theoretically, give the district a few extra dollars for the month of November. Or was that the Feds? Who knew? Even though Purewater relied on local levies to pay for her position, she knew the money—wherever it came—from was needed. She wondered if the new boy would have a reaction to the shots and if itch, pain, or swelling would affect his test performance. Oh well, she thought, newcomers always welcomed an opportunity to leave the overwhelming classroom and go to a quieter place with a gentle teacher who spoke a little Spanish or was at ease with the silence between people who spoke different languages. "I can test him if you send him over after last recess."

***

The fourth graders were delighted by the marigolds, calling them *Flores del Muertos*, flowers of the dead. They were awestruck by *La Mujer de Tierra* whose presence transformed the teacher's bookcase into an altar very much like the ones their mothers, aunts, or grandmothers kept in the little niches of their crowded homes. After church on Sunday, Lupe had drawn a detailed picture of Purewater's swap meet to go with her story. Sienna taped the picture on the wall right next to the framed portrait of the Swami. She gestured at them, grinning and asked, "These are not the same thing, are they?" All the kids laughed. It was fun to have an inside English joke in *The Writers' Lair*. The group discussed possible titles for the three pieces of art before moving onto the day's assignment.

Ancestry was one of the fourth grade's weekly *Reading Fare* vocabulary words. Sienna knew that having the kids draw pictures of *abuelos y abuelas* would generate lots of descriptive language and interesting narratives. The work on grandparents was well underway when Hothouse Miguel brought Valentin, Tammy's new boy, to the portable.

Clearly, Tammy had forgotten the plan to test him after recess.

78

Sienna couldn't administer a placement test while she was teaching a group, but she didn't have the heart to send Valentin back to class. He was obviously in a daze after his first hour at Moore Elementary School. After his shots, he'd had ten minutes in class before heading into a bewildering cafeteria where he had seconds to choose from a buffet of unfamiliar foods. He wasn't sure where to sit or how to eat what he'd grabbed. Then, he had been shooed outside for fifteen minutes of recess and then practically herded back to the shouting teacher's room. Now, with the few bites of the salty hotdog he'd gulped triggering an uncomfortable thirst, he rubbed the blindingly white bandage covering the injection site as if his arm really did hurt. Sienna decided it would be kinder to let him acclimate in *The Writers' Lair* instead of sending him back to Tammy's class before giving him the WELTS.

Sienna thanked Miguel and introduced herself to Valentin, quickly realizing that his Spanish was not very well developed. She guessed he spoke an indigenous language. She decided to grab his enrollment paperwork during recess to see where he'd come from and how much schooling he'd had there.

Miguel gazed longingly around *The Writers' Lair*. "I can stay— here help him?"

"Sorry, no," Sienna said. "I wish you could, Miguel." She sighed regretfully. *Pobrecito*.

Miguel shuffled to the door while Sienna seated Valentin between Cassandra and Lupe. Sienna knew the girls would automatically assume the roles of big sister and she'd observe how they talked to him to get clues about his language, but Pilar was the one to lean forward and speak in dialect. Valentin's face lit up as he responded with a long stream of excited speech. Pilar replied eagerly. Meanwhile, Miguel lingered. His spine pressed against the horizontal bar which would release the door.

Sienna ignored him for as long as she thought he could get away with being gone before Tammy chewed him out for dawdling. "Is that silly latch stuck again?" she asked.

"I fix it," Miguel said and he left, beginning his long, slow shuffle to the main building.

During class, Cassandra had drawn her grandpa, a stick man surrounded by chickens and her picture triggered lots of conversation and new vocabulary, *hen, rooster, chicks, coop, henhouse, lay, set, crow, cluck, scratch, peck.* Fortunately, by the time the talk turned to *spurs* and *razor blades* part of underground cockfighting scene in Purewater, it was time for recess.

Valentin and Pilar were still talking earnestly. Although Sienna didn't know the language, she recognized the questioning intonation in their conversation and she invited the children to stay in during recess. She gestured for them to sit at the smaller side table so they could continue talking and she could prepare the big table for her next class.

They'd just moved when they all heard pounding feet ascending the metal ramp outside. The door burst open and Deedee and Nancy marched through it, like a sheriff and deputy coming to break up a saloon brawl in a vintage Western. Instead of brandishing a pistol, Nancy waved a *Reading Fare* test in the air.

Deedee stopped short. The scene in the portable was not what Nancy's frantic calls and emails intimated. "Nice flowers!" She inhaled deeply. "Particularly since I've just come from Special Day. The shit is hitting the fan in there." She shuddered. "Literally. Behaviorally disordered kids in diapers is a disaster!" She gazed and gestured toward Lupe's colorful rendition of Saturday's swap meet. "I love how cheerful it looks in here."

Nancy snorted impatiently. "We're not running an art gallery. Letting kids color is not teaching them to read." She waved Pilar's *Reading Fare* test at Deedee. "All students are expected to take the unit test and, as you can see, Pilar didn't do what was expected."

"She can't read it," Sienna said.

"You have to give these kids the opportunity to try." Nancy snapped.

Deedee glanced at the exam and passed it to Sienna. "She did the first question. You can see she got it right."

The paper trembled in Sienna's hand like a diamondback's rattle. She tried to modulate her voice. "This is at her frustrational level."

"I know you have a heart for these kids, Sienna." Deedee said.

"And for how hard they struggle, but we can't deny them access to our rich grade level material just because they speak a different language."

"She shouldn't have to take this test," Sienna said, "Even *Reading Fare's* own placement criteria says that it has no value if the child can't read."

"Well, even if she doesn't understand what she's reading, we need her test scores to know how she compares with the other fourth graders." Nancy broke in. "We need to put the data on spreadsheets so we can rank every kid."

"Rank them?" Sienna asked. "Why? You already know most of the ELL kids are at the bottom. We should be teaching them instead of testing them. What's the value of giving them tests before we have a chance to teach?"

"So we know if they need more help."

"We already know they need more help. I'm trying to give it to them."

"Not the right kind." Nancy snorted.

"I think if the newcomers know how far behind they are right from the get-go," Deedee said, "it will motivate them to study for their WASTE."

"Or demoralize them!" As Sienna's nostrils flared, the scent of marigolds filled her sinus cavity. "There's actually very little diagnostic information or motivation in a zero."

"But the curriculum tells us what skills they need if they miss a question on the test." Nancy said.

"The curriculum assumes that the kids already know the thousands of basic English words they need before they can even approach the skills the curriculum assigns to each question."

"I think you are being too specific," Deedee said.

Sienna clenched her jaw. Being specific mattered…*swap meet, hothouse, party favors*.

"And you are sabotaging our future test scores by coddling these kids." Nancy glared at Sienna. "You can't just do your own thing. You have to follow the curriculum."

Soundlessly, still sitting side by side, Valentin and Pilar watched as Nancy cast *El Ojo Malo*—the Evil Eye at Sienna. Flabbergasted, Sienna looked to the bookcase full of educational texts and the glossy paperback with the handsome author photo facing out.

"Don't you remember Lau v. Nichols?"

Deedee furrowed her perfectly plucked eyebrows. "That Chinese kid in Mavis' class?"

"No," Sienna said. "It was the 1974 Supreme Court Case that established English Language programs to address this very issue. Giving kids who don't understand English the same books, worksheets, and tests as we give kids who do, isn't giving them equal access to an education. It's not an equal opportunity when they can't understand the language of instruction or assessment."

"Oh, your boyfriend was talking about that." Deedee smiled indulgently.

"No matter who talks about it, it's cruel to the children and to the teachers who care about them. And it's educationally unsound."

"Sienna!" Deedee chided. "I live on triple shot espresso. I don't have time for love or theory."

"What about civil rights? What about the human need to find meaning in life? Deedee!"

"These kids are lucky you care so much about them," Deedee said, "but no one is coming to Purewater to investigate their civil rights or see if they have discovered the meaning of life. They get a lot better here on our taxpayers' dime than most kids in the world ever get. And, if we don't get our test scores up in the next few years, someone will come to investigate *us* and we'll all be out of a job."

Nancy nodded. "It's so embarrassing when they print our test scores in the paper."

"Look," Sienna said levelly, "all we have to do is create conditions where the kids get excited about language and literacy and..."

"You can't just go around doing whatever *you* want," Nancy shrieked.

"I'm helping kids build relationships with literacy!" Sienna replied.

"Relationships?" Deedee asked. "With literacy?"

Nancy shook her head scornfully. "You just need to have fidelity!"

"Fidelity?" Sienna asked.

"Yes!" Nancy said. "Fidelity to *Reading Fare.*"

Sienna wrinkled her nose with disgust. "That sounds like a chastity belt!" Who, in the vast field of contemporary educational reform had the *cojones* to command *fidelity* in a profession filled with highly qualified, underpaid women?

"I'm taking about fidelity to implementation!" Nancy strode over to the copy of *Reading Fare* perched on the ledge of the white board and opened it to the scarlet bookmark Sienna had left tucked into it the day the Swami came. "Ah ha!" she exclaimed. "Deedee, Sienna may say she cares about the kids, but look! She's cheating on the basal! We're supposed to be two chapters ahead of this by now."

Clearly, Nancy was not well. Sienna looked to her supervisor for help, but it wasn't forthcoming. Deedee seemed to be in a trance.

Tears stung Sienna's eyes. If they wouldn't honor what was obvious in their daily work with kids and, if they didn't think Supreme Court rulings applied to them, why would they give any credence to what she said? This wasn't just frustrating for her and the children. It wasn't just potentially illegal. It was dangerous. They were erasing so much—compassion, common sense, court rulings—and inviting a very particular cruelty into the school. Sienna shuddered, as if cold fingers were squeezing the nape of her neck.

Pilar and Valentin had joined hands, clearly poised to flee. Sienna wondered how Deedee and Nancy could act as if these children could not understand this adrenaline-boosting battle, but still expect them to read and comprehend complex material in small print and a foreign language.

"And now I have to go *teach.*" Nancy strode out as if she were the only one who ever did any real work in the building.

"The truth is," Deedee gestured toward *The Writers' Lair* banner, "these kinds of kids don't need all this."

"They do need it!" Sienna said. "And what is all this about fidelity? Fidelity! My foot! I never made a vow to *Reading Fare.* This adoption is like a shotgun wedding for an arranged marriage."

"Calm down, Sienna. You're just too passionate for your own good. Life isn't all Butterscotch Blondie with ice cream and a hot professor on top."

Sienna glanced at Pilar and Valentin, petrified in their seats. Clay children, *Niños de tierra*. "If we were physicians," she crumpled Pilar's test in her fist. "This would be malpractice."

Deedee's eyes narrowed. "How dare you say your way is better?"

Sienna imagined the school officials up at the district headquarters. They all had brass name plates displayed on their desks, right next to the pictures of their own children. "Whose way is this?"

"Don't ask questions like that!" Deedee ran her tongue up the front of her teeth, making a disapproving, sucking noise.

"*Who* wants *us* to do this to, what did you call them? These kinds of kids?"

"You know," Deedee said, "You really aren't the right fit for Moore Elementary. I suggest you begin looking for a job somewhere else. Maybe at a fancy prep school. Until then, do what I say. Try a little fidelity to our students' success."

Chapter Eleven

On *El Día de los Muertos,* Pilar was thrilled when Sienna passed a concave river stone around the table in *The Writers' Lair,* encouraging the child who held the "talking rock" to suggest a name for her mermaid picture. Pilar listened to their ideas, thrilled to have her work taken so seriously. Ultimately, she chose the most beautiful name she knew. *Maritza.* Sienna called her drawing, *The Maritza.* Lupe decided to call her scene *Meet Me at the Swamp Meet.*

After that, Pilar went to work on the class project, drawing the *casita,* the little house where her *abuela* lived and worked in Redención. With the volcanic *La Madre Ardiendo* towering in the background, she drew that nasty *Diablo,* dogs, and the host of squawking chickens that tried to stake their claim indoors by laying eggs in the clay pots *abuelita* made for the market. Sienna hastily wrote English words next to many things in Pilar's picture. She printed and repeated roof for *el techo,* door for *la puerta,* window for *la ventana.* The canal outside, she labeled *canal.* Pilar giggled, delighted to learn that a word in English could be so close to one she already knew in Spanish. It was like a buy-one-get-one-free candy! Then Pilar learned her grandmother's hair was gray hair, *pelo gris.* Grandma wore its length tied back in a scarf, *un pañuelo.* She wore a skirt, *una falda,* and a blouse, *una blusa.* Those words were very close. More *dulce gratis.* What was even sweeter for Pilar was after Sienna read the words to and with her several times, Pilar could read them as well!

The air was redolent with *flor de los muertos*. *La Mujer de Tierra* stood on Sienna's bookcase. Her *rebozo* was empty, but the guacamole offering Sienna had made at *Casita Rio* still stained her feet. On the other side of the veil, between the Living and the Dead, Pilar's ancestors waited for her to remember. Sienna was there. She would help with the grief.

Then, Valentin came through the door. The ancestors decided to wait a moment. Like a sleeper waking from a dream, the old language surfaced in the deepest part of Pilar's brain and she began to speak to him. During recess, she sat knee-to-knee with him at the small table, pointing to the canal on her paper, whispering in the language *de los abuelitas*. "Do you know *Canal del Luto*?"

Valetin nodded, swallowing hard, too shell-shocked and inexperienced to realize how unusual it was for someone in Purewater to be aware of, let alone speak, in the dialect they shared.

Pilar spoke urgently, "Do you have your family?"

He shook his head. "Only my uncle. He works on a Llama farm." Valentin was also too green to know that, in Purewater, llamas were a rich person's hobby, not beasts of burden.

"No mother?"

He shook his head.

Pilar pushed some crayons his way. "Do you know how to color?"

"A little," he said. "I learned on my way to America."

"That is good. In Ms. O'Mara's class, you can make what you need. Make who you need."

As the scent of *La Flor de los Muertos* wound its way through their olfactory cells, Valentin reached into his sweatshirt and pulled out two small *calaveras*, graced with lint and pocket dust. He gave one to Pilar. Both children popped the sugar skulls into their mouths. As the heads dissolved on their tongues like communion wafers, the connective tissue between the two hemispheres in Pilar's brain became permeable. She was about to remember. Beneath the gaze of La Mujer de Tierra, she was about to remember. Her ancestors were about to come through.

But instead, Mrs. Albright and *la jefa* burst into the room. There was shouting. Pilar froze. There were tears in Ms. O'Mara's eyes. On the day of the year when the veils were thin, at the moment the spirit world was ready to send *una muerta* through, Deedee Hayes came to the altar in *The Writers' Lair*, insisting upon the omniscience of a very particular type of *Muerta*.

The body of Pilar responded to the tension of it all with a flood of gastric acid and mucus.

Valentin was at her side. "We are still alive," he whispered. "You are okay." Even though his own first day at Moore was traumatic, he gently patted Pilar between the shoulder blades. When she looked up, wiping her mouth on the back of her sleeve, he showed her the concave talking rock. "And we have the Awka."

***

I remember the splat against the green plastic liner of the trash bin as I was delivered into the new world. My amniotic fluid was laced with sticky granulated vomit. From below Pilar's chin, I watched Valentin rest a comforting hand on her upper back while he waved the rock under her nose, like smelling salts.

Like my living children had once slumbered in my womb, I'd been curled in Pilar's cultural memory and smuggled into a foreign country. I might have lain there in her mind, dormant, indefinitely — disintegrating before sprouting. On *El Día de los Muertos*, Pilar might have remembered her own mother. She might have learned some of the words she needed to talk about what happened. Instead, Deedee Hayes intercepted, making a cold-hearted demand for an entirely different spirit.

Sienna carried the trash can to the door and set my New World spawning bed outside. I ascended quickly, merging with the mist rising off the Purewater. Unseen, but seeing all, I could peer into the classrooms of Moore Elementary and into all the shops on First Street. I saw Lucia grating more cacao in the kitchen at *Casita Rio*. I saw Master In-Su and Chief Goodwin working out at the dojang next door. I saw into the Hadley homes. I heard the sisters arguing about the school levy with one another on the telephone, watched them shaking their fists at one another through the dining room windows of their neighboring river front homes.

I looked through the decaying roof of the school district's headquarters and watched administrators huddle around a computer screen, staring in dismay at Moore's fourth grade WASTE scores. Meanwhile, on the other side of the very wall that the computer was plugged into, middle school kids who cut class uncapped over-sized permanent markers. I watched them scrawl graffiti all over the superintendent's dumpster.

Over in the largest of Purewater's apartment complexes, I watched a drug deal go down in the parking lot. Next door to where Cassandra and the other Fuentes lived, a silent man named Mr. Guzman hit his silent wife and the only noise that came from that unit sounded like someone beating the dust from a hanging rug.

And I could not only see all the people. In the boundless, multi-lingual, unfeeling sort of omniscience Deedee demanded, I knew their histories and their past and present ways of thinking. It didn't matter if the unemployed trolling the riverbank thought in English, Spanish, Hmong, or Chinese. I understood every form of "I hope I find the money."

Inside the portable, Sienna offered Pilar a drink of water, the chance to rinse the taste of vomit from her mouth. Then, succumbing to *la jefa*, she gave Pilar the crumpled *Reading Fare* exam. Resisting *la jefa*, she set a timer for five minutes, gently telling Pilar to do whatever she could.

Valentin placed the "talking rock" between Pilar and himself, as if it were something to share. Sienna rewarded him with an approving smile. She boiled water with the electric pot she wasn't really allowed to have in the portable and while her tea steeped, she watched Pilar pray for answers and mark incorrect ones on her paper. Trauma and psychic labor had worn the girl out down to every last toe.

Sienna turned to the Swami's portrait wondering, "Why are our true selves being forced out of this school?"

The Swami smiled benevolently at her. Then acting like the good ELL teacher she was, he repeated back what she'd just said, adding a small correction she didn't yet know she needed. *"True selves are being forced out in this school."*

Meanwhile, after her fiasco in Special Day, Deedee simply couldn't endure witnessing any more bodily extrusion that day. She fled the instant Pilar began to gag so she caught up to Nancy quickly.

Nancy said, "It is going to be better for everyone, even for Sienna herself, if we're all practicing fidelity. She just can't see it now because she's distracted by her Ivy League boyfriend and all his big ideas. I heard she's flying back to D.C. to visit him this weekend."

"Oh, I know all that," Deedee said, airily. "I think she's just trying to use all that civil rights rhetoric to put what she likes to do above the prescribed curriculum."

Neither of them noticed *todos los muertos* on the playground. Neither of them noticed the ghostly remains of deformed and starved Reading Babies scuttling among the fallen autumn leaves or limply littering their path, like so many unwanted Chinese baby girls left in empty fields to mewl and starve. They walked on, eager to forget Sienna's unpleasant gravitas.

"So," Deedee asked, "will the drill team be wearing their hair up or down?"

"We spent half an hour arguing about it last night," Nancy sighed. "I can't talk about it now. It's time to get to get my class from P.E."

Deedee laid a detaining hand on Nancy's arm. "When I was in high school, we all grew our hair out to the same length." Images of the locker room full of black and blue poly-china silk flags leaning against aqua cinderblock came to her. She could smell the aerosol, hear the girls in lacy bras and nude tone tights chattering away. "We got to state championship."

"Well, at this point we are just going to douse the girls in hairspray, even if they complain about headaches. Bobby pins slide out during the performances and distract the judges." Nancy realized she'd forgotten to write her objectives for the next lesson on the board. "I hope Sienna corrects Pilar's *Reading Fare* test for me when Pilar finishes. It's the least she can do. It takes forever to correct those, let alone enter the data into the program to see why a kid got the wrong answer."

Deedee watched Nancy hurry into the gym. She didn't really want to face the third grade boys who had spent recess in her office, accused of writing the F word on the bathroom walls. She sure didn't want to call all the Life Skill's parents to inform them of the potential biohazards inherent in the earlier incident. She just wanted to stand there, listening to the American flag rippling on the pole in the middle of the courtyard. As she did, a word she hadn't heard or spoken in over forty years suddenly shot right through lips. "Nooga!" Her peculiar cry reverberated around the eerily empty center of the campus. She clamped a hand over her mouth. Where had that come from?

Suddenly, Bao Yang and Lucero Fuentes burst through the doors, galloping past her. Charged with the very important task of fetching some envelopes in the office for Mrs. Penn, the two first grade girls carried their heads high as they broke a school rule. Bao, with the teacher's scrawled request on the Post-it note in her hand, shot ahead. Lucero's legs were shorter and she struggled to catch up. "You know," she panted, "you really should walk in the halls."

Deedee glanced around, worrying another adult would see her ignoring the girls or, worse, had heard her shout. Why had she suddenly felt so compelled to belt out what had once been her drill team's competitive expletive? Her own mother had made embarrassing random exclamations her whole life. Deedee had always sworn she wouldn't be anything like that woman. She sighed. She didn't want to deal with little girls running in the halls right before her eyes. She sure wouldn't want to deal with the ghost she'd brought forth—the ghost that she couldn't see—scurrying right along with them.

Chapter Twelve

Andy was waiting for Sienna just outside the terminal. He took her carry-on bag and kissed her. His black Prius purred in the background. A turbaned taxi driver tooted his horn once, but the noise was lost on them. Even after the honking became insistent, it took them both a moment to realize it was directed at them and another kiss before they could pull apart. Laughing, they climbed into Andy's car. He suggested heading straight to an early dinner and Sienna agreed. Neither of them had any intention or interest in going back out for a good long while once they reached Andy's house.

Andy drove her to the landmark restaurant where they'd eaten before, *The Old Eli Grill*. In the lobby, an antique sign advertised the oyster bar. The mermaid painted on it was much more seductive than Pilar's *Maritza*. Still, Sienna was struck by the synchronicity of encountering *una sirena* on the opposite side of the country. More mermaids, reclining bronze beauties, adorned the candle-lit sconces that illuminated the dark mahogany booth that the host led them to. Andy kissed her before they sat down. Although he'd thoughtfully mentioned preparing his guest room, the question about where Sienna would really sleep that evening flickered between them like a subtle flame as they sank onto sable velour.

Their attraction for each other was as palpable as the scent of whiskey in the air and as flammable as the static cling that nipped at Sienna's skirt. Yet, their conversation was mundane. Sienna explained how Matt's dad was traveling a lot less for work these days and was happy to spend time with their son while she was away. Andy mentioned a winter syllabus he was drafting and how there was never enough time to cover everything for pre-service teachers.

At the mention of how there was never enough time, Sienna blurted, "I think Moore is making me crazy." She hadn't intended to sound as sincere as she did and to her absolute dismay tears welled in her eyes.

As if her sanity was legitimately on the line, Andy nodded and took her hand.

The waiter arrived with a bottle of Syrah. "Jest sos you all know," he said as he poured the wine into crystal goblets, "I never be noticing which distinguished looking gentleman be with which beautiful lady. I make myself scarce during assignations." He backed away quickly.

With one hand still entwined with hers, Andy lifted his glass with the other. "To a sanity-saving assignation in our nation's Capital." They clinked glasses.

"There's a part of me that truly loves that phrase." Sienna said after the first sip.

"Sanity-saving assignation?"

"That's a good one, although I meant our nation's capital." The wine warmed her throat. "It makes me think D.C. is like America's brain. It's the place where people make the connections for the whole system to work."

"I think you are right." Andy winked. "Moore really is making you crazy."

She knew their first real in-the-flesh and face-to-face date wasn't the time to tell Andy about talking to the Swami or the Swami talking back, but he was an expert in the profession that was creating her mental decline. She took another sip of her Syrah and considered confessing to possibly hearing voices.

"You aren't crazy," Andy said gently. "The insanity around you just makes you feel like you are sometimes. Clearly, your nation's capital and its policies exhibit signs of schizophrenia."

Sienna sighed. "A failing public school is probably one of the best places to see the symptoms. Right?"

"Right," Andy agreed.

Sienna ran her hand over her plush seat. "It's so fancy in here."

"This is where members of Congress and the Senate hang out. I'll bring you back for breakfast and you'll see who's who."

It was lovely to sit there with a modest Syrah. It would be quite a treat to sit among people in thousand dollar suits and spend an hour enjoying double-digit priced plates of pancakes, drenched in Grade A maple syrup, instead of keeping hungry kids from running in the walking zone toward the free breakfast they only had five minutes to eat before the bell rang. She took another sip of wine, noticing the warm tingle in her lower back and legs, enjoying the urge to giggle. She imagined the next GOTCHA show beginning with Chase Haight asking his co-host, "Did you hear about the small town schoolteacher who got drunk in our Nation's Capital?"

"Speaking of, look to your right," Andy said. "That's Senator Panky."

"Who?"

"Dedicated union-basher, anti-immigrants."

Sienna felt a surge of dislike. "Panky is such an unfortunate name for a politician," she mused, glancing at the balding man. "Don't tell me his first name is Hank."

As Senator Panky's date stared at her cell phone, he turned his head to wink at Sienna.

Ugh! Taken aback, she opened her menu. "He's probably part of the reason Dulce has latched onto Esteban," she whispered to Andy from behind it.

"Who?"

"Dulce. A former student. Beautiful. Smart. Hard worker. She always said she wanted to be a teacher or librarian, but I don't know if she'll make it. I'm worried she'll just marry Esteban. He's the only Mexican boy in town with a job. Then the two of them can make, what do the politicians call them, anchor babies? Would Mr. Panky prefer that?"

"Do you think Dulce is conscious of what's she's doing?"

"Politically? No. Throwing her life away is completely personal. Esteban is super cute."

"You are super cute," Andy said. "When we were in college, I wanted to ask you out for coffee. I didn't though. I worried it would be inappropriate because we were both engaged to different people."

"You didn't think it was appropriate for us to talk?"

"Well, you were so beautiful."

"I *was*?"

"Still are," Andy said quickly. "You look just the same."

Sienna blushed. She'd been so busy securing her place in life back then, planning a wedding and preparing for a perfect life to be divided between a big house behind a little white picket fence and a classic brick elementary school surrounded by chain link.

"I'll always remember Dr. Chen's face when you asked why the curriculum was at odds with what child development experts told us."

"I'm still asking that," Sienna said. "I still get no satisfaction."

Meanwhile, midshipmen in uniform were on the prowl, leaning in too close to talk to women sitting on stools—the lot of them admiring their own moves as they stared at each other in the mirrored wall behind the bar. Senator Panky was basking in his own glory, too. His voice carried as he told his companion, "And so I was set for life. I had everything in place. I figured I might as well work for the government. You know, give back a little."

The hair on the back of Sienna's neck rose.

Andy smirked. "I wonder what that means coming from a key vote for a billion dollar national achievement test. Oh! Sorry! I didn't mean to bring that up...yet."

"A national achievement test? I thought guys like him were all about state's rights."

"They are. Senator Panky believes so strongly in state's rights, he's pushing for the national test to come a few weeks before each state's annual measure of student progress. That way it will help the kids warm up, making each state look better than the national average."

"Seriously?"

"You can read the brief. And guess what they're going to call it?"

Sienna shook her head. "I don't even want to try."

"Come on," he teased. "I'll give you a hint. They took a cue from your state's WASTE."

Sienna's mind whirled for a moment. "No way? Don't tell me they are going to call it the NASTE?"

"They can and they will, if Panky's bill passes."

"So all my English Learners will get the WELT, do the NASTE, and then fail the WASTE."

"That's right," Andy said grimly. "And, if Panky gets his way, your salary and retirement benefits will be tied to their scores."

Sienna felt a chill. "That's dangerous."

Andy lifted her hand to his lips and kissed the soft flesh of her fingers between her slightly inflamed joints. "Let's not think about it right now. Let's just think about us." Even though Panky was directly across the aisle, Sienna suddenly felt joyful. Neither the bitterness at Moore Elementary nor the fleeting thought of GOTCHA scandal-inciting news stories could detour her. She would risk, "Small Town Schoolteacher Makes Love in Our Nation's Capital."

Chapter Thirteen

Sienna followed Andy through the black wrought iron gate and the narrow front yard separating his row house from the busy city sidewalk. He ushered her up the brick steps and through a solid oak door. Once inside, he set her suitcase down on the uneven floor at the base of an aged oak staircase. She took in the intricate carving of a colonial newel post, the patina of the railing, and the Persian runner. The crow's feet pattern on the antique rug seemed to usher one directly up the steps and through the open door of what seemed to be a waiting bedroom.

"This is gorgeous," she told him, glad she'd decided against staying at a hotel.

"Yep," Andy was clearly pleased that she thought so. "This place is special."

He gestured for her to walk ahead past the staircase through the narrow hallway into the parlor. Once there, he bent to lay the back of his hand against a baseboard heater, reminding Sienna of when she took Matt's temperature. "I turned this up before I left for the airport," he said. "Sorry, it's still a bit cold in here. The glass in these windows is over two hundred years old."

Sienna left her coat on. "This place is charming," she said. "How did you ever end up here?" She meant the East Coast, Georgetown, the old home on an end lot. Although Andy's place was much smaller than hers, she guessed his mortgage was easily four times what she paid for her house on Teagan Hill.

"It was a total surprise when I inherited this from my great-uncle," he explained. "The family always expected him to donate the proceeds from selling this place to Public Radio. It never occurred to anyone, yours truly included, that he'd actually leave it to me along with a little money to do a fair bit of renovation."

Sienna couldn't help smiling. On her sixteenth birthday, just as soon she was old enough to drive, her own Uncle Ed had given her the red Volkswagen Beetle he'd meticulously maintained for over twenty years. "Were you his favorite?"

"I don't know about that. It was a counter-intuitive gift, given what happened to my wife." His mouth twisted as if he were probing an ulcerated gum with the tip of his tongue.

"What happened?"

Andy unconsciously raked his fingers through his hair. "She was electrocuted—by a hair dryer. She wasn't even using it. It fell into the sink while she was rinsing her toothbrush."

Sienna didn't doubt the truth of what he was telling her. Still, it was difficult to fathom. Dry hair. Brush teeth. She thought of how many times she did exactly the same thing every morning on auto-pilot with her mind on the multitude of tasks that she had to attend to during the day ahead.

"Our apartment building was better than most on the block," Andy said, "but it was barely more than a tenement home."

Sienna was confused. "I thought you left school for a high paying job."

"I only lasted two years at UPS, before I tweaked my knee delivering a treadmill to a third story apartment. I went back to school. My wife and I didn't want to pay for a car so we rented a place near campus. Something was wrong with the old knob and tube wiring in our building. Sometimes, you'd blow a fuse and smell the smoke." Andy swallowed hard, making a fist with his right hand, as if he trying to clamp down on any unnecessary details he might inadvertently spill. "The landlord said it was her own fault for not unplugging the cord before she ran the water, but by the time she died, the fire department had already cited that cheap bastard seven times. Not that that meant anything to the courts. I've accused and convicted him of negligent homicide over and over again in my mind in the middle of the night for years."

Sienna took his hand, and led him to the couch.

"The irony was," he added, sinking onto the leather sofa beside her, "she was studying to become a social worker. She was actually running late for a community meeting about substandard housing; asbestos in the ceilings, little kids eating lead paint. She never gave a thought to *our* wiring...and I just wasn't paying attention to it." He sighed, "I never used a hair dryer." He looked down at their clasped hands. "I never thought about it. In those days, I used disposable razors because they were so cheap." His voice cracked on the last word.

"Oh, "Sienna said softly, lifting her free hand to cradle his cheek, feeling the late afternoon stubble against her cupped palm. "You didn't feel guilty, did you?"

"I sure as hell did. I've been to counseling, though," Andy swallowed hard and cleared his throat twice, awkwardly. "I'm really sorry. I don't know why I felt so compelled to dump all that on you on our first evening together."

"No need to be sorry," Sienna said gently. "I wanted to know how she disappeared from your life." With her hand still on his face, she looked into his despairing eyes. She could tell that there was more—something else that he wasn't telling her, something else he needed to say, even if he didn't know that himself. She'd heard it in his voice and she dared to press him, even if the truth might put a damper on their time together. "Tell me," she said hesitantly, "about... cheap."

"Cheap?" He sounded angry. Dark emotions flittered across his face.

Sienna wondered if she'd made a mistake.

Andy leapt to his feet, striding to the window, pacing back and forth as if he were about to put a fist through the leaky glass. "Cheap? Cheap? The apartment was cheap. Cheap enough for graduate students, expecting their first baby." His nostrils flared as he stood facing her. Clearly, he'd cast himself in the same role that he'd given the careless landlord. In his own mind, his negligence was criminal too.

"Baby?"

"Yeah."

Sienna bit her bottom lip.

"It was cheap enough for a baby." Andy's eyelids fluttered. He believed he was responsible for the death of his wife and child. He waited for her to judge him.

Sienna rose slowly. She went to him cautiously and instead of opening her arms as Dulce had done for Esteban, she simply placed her hands, one on top of the other, upon Andy's heart. He closed his eyes, feeling the gentle pressure, feeling held, smelling her, cinnamon, jasmine, compassion.

"Thank you," he whispered. "I never remarried. I had a few long term girlfriends. It never worked out. They couldn't understand my drive—my passion for my work. They said I was a fanatic. Damn it! I don't think I ever fully understood why until just now."

"I'm so sorry," Sienna said. A tear ran down her cheek. "Good work that helps people and thoughtful books that try to improve your profession and your world do give Life meaning, but they aren't substitutes for lovers or children."

He pulled her close. They stood like that in silence, warming each other as night fell outside the timeworn windows. "Thank you," he said again. The streetlamps came on, casting contemporary light through age old frames.

***

Later, after a long kiss, as if something had been settled on his end, Andy asked, "So what about you? It must be hard to be divorced."

"I don't think of myself as divorced."

"You don't?" He took a step backwards. "Are you thinking you'll get back together?"

"No!" Sienna said. "It's not that. I just don't think a person should be identified by their marital status. I hate how people assume they know something about another person based on labels like single-mother."

"Or widower," Andy added, thinking of all the well-meaning invitations to family meals he got from colleagues who thought he'd enjoy listening to them schedule dental appointments around picking their children up from soccer or dance class.

"There's a teacher at school who invariably prefaces her take on a kid's learning problems with, 'Well, he has a single mom.' She never stops to consider that he might need more hands-on experience with base ten blocks."

"Shh," Andy traced her mouth, slowly, sensuously. "Let's not have any more relationship history or shop talk tonight." He slipped his palm behind her neck, cupping the base of her skull. Entwining his fingers in her hair, he took her lips between his. And after a long, sweet kiss that would have set off a chorus of taxi horns at Reagan International, Sienna felt herself melting. "Mmm," she moaned, wanting to love him.

He pressed into her. "Shall I put your bag in the guest room?"

"Your bedroom would be better."

***

The next morning, they held hands on the steps of the Capitol. Andy asked, "Did you see all the people here during President Obama's inauguration? They were packed tight, all the way past the Lincoln Memorial." He pointed over the long green stretch of mall to a white blur in the distance that Sienna couldn't have made out even if she had been wearing her rhinestone studded driving glasses.

"I didn't get to watch it," she said ruefully. "Deedee wouldn't allow us to have the televisions on in the classrooms."

"Why not?"

"She said she didn't want the children to see him get shot."

"What? "Andy grimaced. "That's messed up. Are you telling me that at Moore, a school with a fifty percent plus minority population, no one was allowed to watch the first black president in American history being sworn in?"

Sienna nodded grimly. "I was mad. I said the exercise and celebration of democracy were more important than teaching the children to get ready for developmentally inappropriate and unfair testing, but people just rolled their eyes at me."

"What a fantastic example of a hidden curriculum! May I use it in the class I teach next quarter?"

"Sure," Sienna said. "I was angry and depressed and I felt like a kid on restriction—like I was being punished for being a teacher, for being so tied to other people's children that I couldn't witness or participate in such an important event. I mean, if I were at home with my own child, I would have watched it. Matt and I would have watched it together."

Andy shook his head. "Moore is not Deedee's empire. It's an American public school! Did you say anything to her about it afterward?"

"No. I didn't have a T.V. in the portable anyway and the computer wasn't set up for streaming yet. I played it on the radio."

"The radio?"

"She didn't say we couldn't listen. The kids were so happy." She smiled at the memory of the faces gathered around her metallic blue boom box. "You should have seen them smile at me when President Obama mentioned teachers."

Andy nodded. His face was troubled.

"She apologized after she realized the staff and students at Teagan Hill got to watch it."

Andy shook his head. "But by then, everyone at Moore had learned the lesson."

Later, when they toured the national museums, Sienna was surprised to discover that there were no admission fees. She fervently wished she could bring her English learners to see them. The only museum in Purewater was the historical museum, open on Tuesdays and requiring a two dollar entry fee. In the Purewater repository, they could see a Native American stone bowl and knife and a dusty box of indigenous things excavated when they built the original Moore Grammar School. Mrs. Moore's old mink coat was encased in glass there, but it just wasn't quite the same as the authentic Lakota baby carrier embroidered with berry dyed porcupine quills in the National museum or President Abraham Lincoln's actual hat or chair.

For any of Sienna's students to see the real Star Spangled Banner or an original Ford from 1908, they would have to have several hundred dollars each for airfare and hundreds more per night to stay in a hotel and eat. They would each need far more than Miguel's grandma, a full-time worker at Burger Bling took home in a month. As Sienna stopped to gaze at Julia Childs' recreated kitchen, she said, "When *Reading Fare* doesn't work for the kids, Purewater will let me do what does, right?"

"Sure." Andy said. "Let's go for a walk." She thought he was trying to keep the subject of school at bay, but twenty minutes later, they stood before the United States Supreme Court. "The answer to your question was decided right here." He stepped behind her and wrapped his arm around her waist. He spoke softly into her ear. "In 1981 with Castaneda v. Pickard, the Fifth Circuit Court established a three part test to see if schools were complying with the Equal Educational Opportunity Act of 1974. First, the school must implement a program based on sound educational theory, or at a minimum, a legitimate experimental program design. Secondly, they must provide enough staff to carry it out, and lastly, if the children are not making progress, they must change course."

Sienna scoffed. "*Reading Fare* is not based on language acquisition and learning theory."

"I'm sure the marketing department at Pica sold it as being based on sound educational theory," Andy said. "Purewater officials are probably insisting their staff implement it precisely because they were assured that it was."

"I wish there was some kind of Supreme Court counseling program for kids and teachers on how to bear it while we wait for the third part of *Castaneda* to kick in." She gazed at the painstakingly sculpted pediment emblazoned with the words, *Equal Justice Under Law*. She wished the crystalline flecked white Georgia marble pillars in Washington, D.C. and the peeling metal posts in Purewater *could* be doing the same job, *could* be supporting institutions that championed justice and mercy.

Why couldn't she just do what she knew was right for the children? Sienna pondered the statutes flanking the entrance to the Supreme Court. On the right, there was a young man called Authority of Law. On the left, there was a much larger statue of a woman called Contemplation of Justice. As Sienna peered at her, she realized that a smaller version of Authority of Law sat on Contemplation of Justice's armrest, like a child receiving a lesson from his mother.

If Contemplation were to spring to life, to stand up, to shift her weight, re-cross a leg, or even swat a mosquito, little Authority of Law would topple right over. Their white marble robes reminded Sienna of the Swami back in *The Writers' Lair*. Of course, contemplation was the only sane option for a public institution.

And what of Pilar's *Maritza*? For Sienna, in the presence of Contemplation of Justice, on the steps of the United State Supreme Court, she became a symbol that all children, especially those like Pilar, needed teachers who can dive deep and stay down long enough for their eyes to adjust to what lies below the surface in a murky sea. Contemplation of Justice and what it reveals is bigger than the Authority of Law.

***

Sienna plucked books from the built-in walnut cases on either side of the stone hearth and curled up on the coach in front of the fire. Andy's private library was packed with many titles that she knew, and many more that she did not recognize. *The Secret Greed of American Schoolteachers* by Senator Panky and *Why the Teachers' Union must be Busted* by Chase Haight had come in a package for him to review.

Andy entered the room with a bottle of dessert wine and two fluted glasses. He bent, kissing Sienna on the forehead. "I could get very used to having you here. Are you sure you have to go home?"

There was no mistaking the longing in his question and it tugged at her heart. She nodded yes and exaggerated her frown.

He turned his eyes to the books piled around. "No time for love?" He picked up a book, *Data is the Answer*. "Got time for a trend line?"

Sienna rolled her eyes in response.

He chuckled, sinking onto the sofa, pulling her feet onto his lap so that she felt the swelling of his groin. "Come on, Baby," he said. "Haven't you ever had just a little bit of data envy?"

She pursed her lips primly, while her eyebrows danced. "You're sounding quite Freudian." She took the book from his hand. "Why does Nancy think recording Pilar's test score in a data base does any good, especially if we aren't giving her the foundation she needs to make progress? Can't she see how much the kids are suffering?"

"Start looking for allies." Andy's tone had switched from a playful lover to a protective commander-in-chief.

"Allies?"

"On the inside. There have to be at least a few in a school that size. If you are determined to bring attention to what's really going on, you will need a lot of support."

"I have support," Sienna said slowly, remembering it was only an imaginary consortium, one consisting of the Swami, *La Maritza*, and *La Mujer de Tierra*.

"Sienna," Andy stared into her eyes. "I'm serious about this. You are a poet in a very plebian world. Data envy aside, Freud is discarded, and there's absolutely no purchase order for anything related to Jung in today's public schools. Panky plays hard ball."

Sienna swallowed hard. Andy's expression softened. He sighed, sympathetically and said, "Enough for now. Let's give our relationship a chance. Let's do something fun. Let's plan a trip!"

Relieved to change the subject, Sienna eyed him over the rim of her glass. "Let's sneak away to where they make this yummy stuff."

Andy picked up the bottle and donned his reading glasses to read the label. "Sierras de Málaga. Andalusia." His blue eyes twinkled behind his lens. "Perfect! We'll bask in romance and beauty. The question is, could you go there and not practice your Spanish?"

She grinned. He looked adorable in his spectacles. "No *bésame, bésame*?"

He shook his head.

"*No hazme el amor?*"

"Absolutely not."

"Oh!" She pouted slightly. "What would we do instead?"

"Explore Moorish delights? Stretch out in the sun? Feed each other olives?"

"Learn Flamenco!"

"We can tour the legendary Alhambra."

She laughed, "We'll have plenty of time for all that since we won't be making love."

"Why not?"

"You said *No bésame*."She leaned in, kissing him on the lips.

"I'm a fool," Andy said comprehending. His hand slid beneath her sweater, gripping the bare skin of her waist. "What else did I accidently cross off the itinerary?"

Sienna wrapped a leg around him, subtly arching her pelvis to press against the increased swelling in his. She squeezed with her thigh, whispering, "*Hazme el amor.*"

Slowly, Andy peeled himself from her body, took her hand, and led Sienna toward the staircase. Grinning in anticipation, they embarked for his bedroom.

* * *

"Forget what I said earlier," Andy whispered. "Feel free to practice all the Spanish you want on our trip."

"I'm glad you've changed your mind, *mi cariño*!" Sienna said. Her voice sounded sultry.

He laughed softly. The tip of his nose was nestled in the tender skin beneath her ear lobe.

In his bed, her body hummed, simultaneously alive and deliciously languid. She wanted to stay with him. "I don't want to go back to Moore," she groaned. "I just want to run away. I want to go be a gypsy!"

"I bet we could find you a cart in Andalusia." He traced her naked clavicle with his finger.

"Oh!" she breathed eagerly. "Let it be red and decorated with roses."

"Okay," Andy said. "I'll put in for a Sabbatical." He touched her so gently, so reverently, so obviously enjoying how her flesh felt beneath his fingertips. He stroked her long silky hair as it snaked over her breasts. Curling a strand around his thumb, he asked, "What color is this? Red or brown?"

"On the artists' palette?"

He nodded.

"Sienna," she said, softly, "like my name."

If passion hadn't depleted him, Andy might have wondered if she'd really been born with enough hair on her head to inspire her mother to name her because of its color or he might have marveled at the suggestive power of a name to manifest such a match. At that moment, blissfully spent, he did not have the vigor left to consider those possibilities. "Beautiful!" was all he could whisper, before drifting off to sleep.

Sienna's mouth was dry and her throat was parched. When Andy began to snore softly, she slipped from his embrace out from beneath the sheets. She gathered her neatly folded pajamas from her suitcase and tip-toed, stark naked across the braided yarn rug in the hallway to the guest room. There she put them on for her foray into the still unfamiliar kitchen. She found a copper teakettle, a tin of loose-leaf chamomile and a strainer to make tea. Carefully balancing a steaming mug and a cool glass of water, she climbed back up the narrow and crooked bi-centurion staircase, trying to keep the old steps from creaking.

It was thrilling to think of how many people had climbed those very steps since the colonial era. They'd needed candles back then. Now, Andy had a Frank Lloyd Wright-inspired nightlight plugged into an outlet in the hall. The mirror at the end reflected its light, guiding her way through the still unfamiliar house. She remembered Edith Wharton had written, "There are two ways of spreading light. To be the candle or the mirror that reflects it." If she had only stared into Andy's mirror a little longer, she might have caught a glimpse of me following her, curiously tapping into her thoughts, accessing her feelings, but she didn't. Sienna's thoughts were on Andy and her body longed for sleep.

Andy's nakedness was too distracting for her to get any real rest so she turned back into the guest room. In blissful reverie, Sienna sipped her tea, remembering Andy's touch and his compliments. Of course, it was pure fantasy to think of traveling to Spain. She couldn't afford a trans-Atlantic trip. Maybe, they could go to Santa Fe, New Mexico instead. Maybe they could visit Gaul Santiago's supposed art gallery. No! She didn't want to know if *Arte para la Gente* wasn't real. She didn't want to find out *La Mujer de Tierra* had been mass produced by exploited factory workers. She really wanted her to be formed from the clay of Redención, dug up from the volcanic base of *La Madre Ardiendo*.

Sienna recalled all the colors in the multicultural colored pencil and crayons collection that she kept in *The Writers' Lair* and thought of *The Maritza*. She was used to students drawing her, representing their fascination with her lipstick by giving her oversized, heart-shaped, crimson lips. They often exaggerated her eyelashes, too, making them much longer and thicker than they were in real life. It really was an interesting twist to have a child create a mermaid with her features, especially her hair. When Sienna was Pilar's age, she hadn't liked it at all. She thought of her mother's palette, and all the paintbrushes she'd dipped in various shades of brown.

***

When Sienna was growing up, her mother rented a sunny apartment in an old Victorian house. One Saturday morning when Sienna was nine, she lay sprawled on the yellow chintz sofa stamped with pink roses the same size as her hands, surrounded by fairy tales from her school library. Nearby, in the turret with southern exposure, her mother sat at a folding table covered with blue surgical sheeting. Sienna watched Bridget apply acrylic to the bark of a tree she was painting on a wooden cupboard. "What color is that?"

"Burnt Sienna," Bridget had replied. "Like your hair."

Sienna frowned. Her hair wasn't burnt. Suddenly cranky, she

snapped. "That gives me a headache."

Bridget swirled her brush in a jar full of paint thinner and wiped her hands on the surgical rag lying across her lap. Its solid blue contrasted with the busyness of her calico artist's smock. "Maybe, you just have a headache," she said.

"From that color!" Sienna was adamant. "I hate it. I hate my hair."

Bridget sipped from a chipped coffee mug. "Sienna is beautiful."

"It is not!"

"Well, you can at least admit it's better than being bald. You didn't even have hair until you were almost three. You should be very grateful to have the hair you have now."

Sienna scowled. There really was an agonizing constriction around her temples.

Bridget seemed to be considering whether or not to reveal something. After a moment's hesitation, she said, "I'll tell you a secret. "I actually imagined you with sienna hair before you were born."

"Mama!" Sienna exclaimed in dismay. The stories spread all about her were full of women who had imagined their unborn children and then made very specific requests about their appearance. Skin as white as snow. Lips as red as blood. "Why didn't you ask for something different?"

"You were already going to be who you were going to be by the time I knew enough to ask for anything." Bridget said. "I couldn't have changed that and I wouldn't have wanted to. You're perfect the way you are. Would you like a damp compress for your headache?"

Bridget's faith in the healing powers of damp compresses annoyed Sienna. "No," she retorted. "I just want to know why you named me after an ugly color."

"Come here," Bridget drew her daughter into an arms' length embrace to hold her and consider the offending hue. "Sienna is very intense," Bridget mused. She picked up the end of the long French braid running down her daughter's back, holding it up in the sunlight so she could compare it to her palette. "Your hair is actually somewhere between raw and burnt."

Both of those options sounded terrible to her. Sienna squeezed her eyes shut. "I don't want to see it."

"Hmm." Bridget sounded perplexed. She placed the back of her hand across Sienna's forehead. "You don't have a fever."

"I'm not sick Mama. I just want stories and magic and I want to have beautiful hair."

"Ah!" Bridget said. "I see."

Sienna opened her eyes. What did her mother see?

Bridget handed Sienna a box of forbidden, because they were so messy, oil pastels. "Make your own stories and your own magic," she said, digging out a sienna crayon, "and most definitely use a tiny bit of this color, even if it does give you a headache."

"But why, Mama?" Using the full range of pastels was a treat— almost worth using the one she didn't like. "Why do I have to?"

"Making a little magic with something is always the best way to stop hating it."

Doubtfully, Sienna sprawled at her mother's feet and drew a small, red fairy house on burnt sienna wheels that could be pulled by a snow-white unicorn. She drew, exactly what she needed that morning. Drawing helped her forget what had happened when a classmate told her that smart people only read true books.

When she finished drawing the winding raw sienna path her little cart could follow into the mystery beyond the page, Bridget called her daughter to the window seat where they watched hummingbirds sip nectar from bright fuchsias in hanging baskets. Bridget asked Sienna if she'd like to hear a story about how she'd known what color her unborn daughter's hair would be before her birth. Sienna nodded eagerly.

An ambulance rushing toward Georgetown's emergency room woke Sienna up from a memory turning into a dream. She bolted upright, bewildered in the unfamiliar bed. Taking a deep breath to calm herself after startling, she returned to Andy's room to slip under his tangled sheets.

Sleepily, he shook the linen out so it settled over both of them like a cloud around the steamy peak of *La Madre Ardiendo*. They slept with the curve of her back supported by the slight paunch of his belly, fitting together like the handcrafted silver spoons that had nestled in the kitchen below them since the first American Revolution.

Chapter Fourteen

On Monday morning, Sienna watched students line up for the bus that would transfer them to Teagan Hill, all the while calculating how many more times she'd have bus duty before Andy came to speak at an educational conference in nearby Sinclair. As the steam rose from her mug, Sienna momentarily lost herself in the memory of Sunday morning love-making beneath the pulsating stream of an oversized stainless steel showerhead. Andy had driven her to the airport with her hair still damp. Too bad she'd have to wait almost a month to be with him again.

Fantasies about a lover were as out of place in a public elementary school as a Swami or *una muerta* haunting the hallways. A nine year old girl tugged on Sienna's sleeve. She smiled kindly at the child, masterfully masking her reluctance to get back to work.

Wearing a plush hoodie with a popular designer's name embroidered across the front, Laurali Hadley screwed up her pale, freckled nose, saying, "My dad says this school sucks. He knows because his mom is the boss of the school board. The teachers at Teagan Hill are better."

Sienna didn't feel like giving a tutorial in manners and since Laurali Hadley didn't attend Moore, she decided she really wasn't under any obligation to. Instead she asked, "Who is your teacher up there?"

"Mrs. Alcott."

"I know her." Sienna said warmly. "She's nice."

Lisa Alcott had been the lowest teacher on Moore's seniority list when Moore's failing status gave parents the option to transfer their kids to Teagan Hill as long as there was room up there. So many decided to make the switch that Teagan needed another teacher and Moore had to give one up. After spending the last two weeks of summer decorating her classroom, making copies, and organizing materials for third grade, Lisa was called at four-thirty p.m. on the Thursday before Labor Day and told to pack it all up, move, and get ready to teach fourth grade. Most of her preparation had been a waste of time.

Her husband took an extra day off of work to help her set up her new classroom as quickly as possible. Of course, they couldn't claim his lost wages as a charitable deduction on their income tax. Nonetheless, just by driving her second-hand Honda up Teagan Creek Road, Lisa became a substantially "better" teacher. Since the kids at Teagan Hill often came to kindergarten already almost reading, she would be able to relax and enjoy herself and her students a little more. In fact, the percentage of her students likely to pass the reading section on the WASTE tripled, before she ever got a chance to meet, let alone instruct, them.

Laurali said, "Plus, Mrs. Alcott is prettier than any teacher here."

Sienna bit her lip as Deedee approached wearing a silver power suit that complimented her upswept platinum ponytail. Deedee smiled as if she hadn't, only a few days before, accused Sienna of sabotaging their students' success, as if she'd never suggested that Sienna quit, or hinted that she might try to force leaving upon her. "How was your trip back east?"

"Great." Sienna had no desire to discuss her romantic assignation with someone who had also accused her of being too passionate. Her trip back east had definitely been that.

Laurali was bored because the wait for the shuttle bus was long. She snatched a book right from another waiting child's hand. Deedee turned sharply toward the ensuing argument and startled. Clutching a gray pillar, she gasped, "Are all of the children in that line going to Teagan Hill?"

"Yes." Sienna nodded.

"Those are the kind of kids who pass the WASTE! How can they leave us? How can they just walk out? We need them here now!"

Deedee was usually ensconced in her office, buried under paperwork, emails, and phone calls early each morning, long before Moore's students started coming and Teagan's going. Still, it was no secret that sixty kids had transfers. "Oh my God!" Deedee went on. "If this is the way it is, we're just going to keep falling behind Teagan Hill. The Mexicans here are just like…rabbits!"

Sienna couldn't turn her back on the children while the school buses were arriving. She shifted her body uneasily as if that could shield them from what Deedee might say next. "These are good kids," Sienna insisted. "They're trying to learn as fast as they can."

Alondra hurried past, pale and tense on her way to a free breakfast, clutching a well-worn Guatemalan worry doll in her clenched fist. "Deedee," Sienna said, "There's something terribly wrong with us having to depend on the test scores of these children to make our school look good."

"If they don't get their scores up," Deedee snapped, "our jobs are on the line."

"It's insane for us to have to depend on the test scores of children who don't even understand the language the test is written in to make us, highly-educated adults, look proficient."

"Well, that's just the way it is."

Deedee's shadowy threat was suddenly overwhelmed by a much more immediate danger. As Travis Hadley, Laurali's cousin, exited his bus waving the brand-new Play Blade his grandmother had given him, he tumbled from the top step. Struggling to his feet beneath the weight of his backpack and still shouting to friends on the sidewalk, Travis lurched forward as an incoming bus rushed into the parking stall where he staggered. Sienna ran, frantically waving her arm at the bus driver to brake, all the while pleasantly intoning, "Notice the bus. Travis. Notice the bus!"

Travis made it to the cluster of friends on the other side of the red unloading line in the nick of time. The new driver, a discharged corporal freshly returned from Afghanistan, drove the front wheels right over where the boy had fallen and then up onto the curb. Neither soldier nor student registered the near hit. Travis didn't even notice Laurali shouting his name and waving smugly as she boarded the shuttle. Travis had had a big breakfast at home. He had the same peanut butter alfalfa sprout pancakes every single day. He had no real excuse for being oblivious except that Jorge and Brandon wanted to spin his Play Blade before the bell rang.

With a pounding heart, Sienna returned to Deedee. "If Travis Hadley can't notice a bright yellow school bus about to bowl him over, just how is he supposed find the main idea, let alone all the supporting details in abstract and contextually-divorced academic material?"

Deedee chortled. "You are so funny!" She shook her head in amusement before adding. "His grandma firmly believes in basing teacher pay on WASTE scores."

After seeing the magnificence of the Capital Mall and Senator Panky's manifesto in Andy's living room, Sienna felt twelve tons of insurgence whoosh through her. "That's crazy! Who does it benefit if a teacher's ability to feed her own children or pay her mortgage depends on the performance of a kid who is clearly more interested in his new Play Blade than in a boring text selection about a physicist who lived sixty years ago?"

"Don't start in on *Reading Fare* again," Deedee said. "Fidelity to that program is the only way we're going to get our scores up. We're going to implement it down to crossing the last i and dotting every t."

In response to Sienna's confused expression, she added, "Soon kids will be riding the shuttle bus *to* Moore and they won't be so hoity-toity up there on Teagan Hill."

As Deedee rushed to her office, Sienna noticed a stray piece of black yarn on the concrete—a strand of worry doll hair. She put it in her pocket to give Alondra later. The doll would be bald before long.

***

After school, Sienna was pleasantly surprised when Jolie came to her portable until she realized it wasn't a social call. Something was wrong.

Jolie's face was ashen. "Did you hear?"

Sienna's heart began to race. "What?"

"Deedee wants me to move the library...before Thanksgiving Break."

Sienna was flabbergasted. "Why?"

Color returned to Jolie's face as tears sprang to her eyes. "She said she got an aha from talking with you this morning."

"About what?"

"Apparently, she looked up how the percentage of ELL kids has increased in our building over the past few years and how it is projected to increase. She said we need to create an ELL Center so we can get all the ELL kids across the district to come here and that the library is the only space big enough for that many kids. It's win-win, she says, because this way she can keep our enrollment up to replace all the white kids who are transferring out."

Sienna felt dizzy. If the families of the thirty or so other ELL kids scattered across town agreed to transfer to Moore, it would create scheduling chaos for her already overtaxed ELL program. It was easier to worry about Jolie's immediate concern. "And where would the library go?"

"In the old cafeteria!" Jolie grimaced. "I just looked in there. It's awful. It's full of mildewed curriculum. It will take at least a whole day just to haul all that stuff out of there and another whole day to clean it before the books can even be moved, let alone make it nice."

Sienna wrinkled her nose. "It really stinks in there." Even if the moldy books were taken away, it was against school district policy to use scents, potpourris, or essentials oils to cover the smell of rotten wood or the decaying carcasses of birds in the rafters.

Sienna remembered how Matt's first grade basketball team had practiced in there and how the whole time they played, the coach sounded as if he were directing them under water. "The acoustics are terrible."

"That's why she said you can't have the ELL Center in there. She thinks that since libraries are supposed to be quiet, acoustics don't matter to me."

"What? You're a library teacher. You are supposed to read aloud and teach research skills."

"Maybe I can get one of those amplifiers, you know, with a microphone."

"There are only two outlets in the whole place." Sienna remembered once trying to help Matt's coach rig up an electronic scoreboard.

"I'll need outlets for the computers," Jolie said, "and shelves. The current library was designed to be a library so the shelves are built-ins and can't be taken out."

"This is unreasonable." Sienna sighed. "I'll go talk to Deedee."

"You can't. She won't be back until next week. She's on her way to a conference and then going home to visit her family. She told Captain Swabby to round up some moving boxes and to start clearing the old cafeteria right away. She said we can cancel our classes next Wednesday so we can have the move all done by the school board walk-through the first of December."

"We'll have to work over Thanksgiving Break to get it done by then," Sienna said angrily. "I have family coming from out-of-state."

"And my daughter will be home from college."

Fuming, Sienna called the office to ask the secretary, Mrs. Donahue, for Deedee's cell phone number. Jolie paced the length of the portable anxiously while Sienna dialed.

Deedee was breathless when she answered. "I can't talk!" Sienna heard Deedee's heels clicking on the tile floor of an airport terminal. "I'm just about to board the plane. Aren't you thrilled about getting to create a great place for kids to learn English?"

"With *Reading Fare*?"

Deedee sighed with exasperation or, perhaps, exertion. "Well, you can do a little of whatever you do for ELL with them."

"Really?" Sienna's anger was replaced with a twinge of hope.

"Yes," Deedee said like a fairy godmother granting a wish. "As I told the Superintendent when I got approval for the move, we're supposed to be here for the kids, right?"

Sienna was pleased. "I don't need the library. I could stay out in the portable."

"Nope!" Deedee said. "If we are going to do this, we are going to do it right. I want a showcase ELL center, just like the one they have in Sinclair."

"Deedee, Sinclair has completely different demographics. It's a more affluent community. Many of the parents of the ELL students are executives, engineers, or doctors and the district spent a lot of time intentionally shaping their program to address the specific needs of that population."

"Now, don't do that, Sienna," Deedee scolded. "It's racist. Our poor kids should have the same opportunities as their rich kids."

Nonplused, Sienna pressed on, "It's very disruptive to move the library on such short notice. And poor Jolie! She just started here."

"We are here for the kids," Deedee said firmly. "If Jolie values her job, she'll have to do what's best for them."

Sienna's stomach clenched. Funding for librarians was just as precarious as funding for ELL teachers. Unfunded by the state, the positions were both usually left up to the unpopular district levies and administrative discretion. Their existence was always dicey.

"Is this really the only way?"

"Like I said, I've thought a lot about it, Sienna."

Sienna heard a flight attendant say, "Welcome aboard."

Then Deedee said to a fellow passenger, "Excuse me. Will you lift my carry-on up there for me? Thanks. Sienna? Where are we? Oh yeah! Once we have everything in place, it won't matter how hard it was or what we had to give up to get there." Sienna heard a masculine grunt of exertion, the slam of the overhead compartment. "Jolie just needs to relax," Deedee went on. "I know! Why don't you go into my office, get the bouquet some kid left on my desk, and give it to her. It's a little limp, but it should cheer her up. Oh! And tell her not to bother unpacking the fiction!"

"The fiction?"

"Yeah. I've been reading an article about the new national standards. It says reading for information is way more important than reading stories. We might as well set our library up accordingly."

Sienna bit her lip to stifle a scream.

"I've got to hang up now," Deedee told her. "The person who sat in this seat before me must have been really fat. I need both hands to tighten the belt."

The pilot said. "Welcome to Flight 446 to Palm Springs."

The phone went dead.

Jolie said, "The only good thing about being at Moore instead of at Teagan Hill is that there are only half as many library books here. That's less for me to pack and move." Then, she brightened. "That's it! Teagan Hill surplused all of their old freestanding library shelves just last year because the PTA bought new ones for their expansion. Whatever they sent to storage would probably be enough for Moore's collection." Jolie's face brightened as she asked, "Where would discarded furniture go? Let's call the D.O. and ask."

"Let's not get the district office involved," Sienna suggested. "They'll probably say something like it's too blatantly inequitable to send Teagan Hill's hand-me downs to Moore. They'd hem and haw about it." Angry about Deedee's condescending accusation that she was racist, she said, "They'd say it looks racist."

"It would look stupid to put all the books on the floor," Jolie fumed.

"Let's just ask Captain Swabby to hunt the bookcases down. He'll find them, the old pirate!"

"They're probably some funky color." Jolie said. "I bet they're eggplant or avocado green like a 1970's refrigerator."

"My mom had one of those."

"Mine too."

"Actually, Teagan's bookcases were orange." Sienna said, remembering library meetings up there. "Funky."

"Retro chic," Jolie heaved an enormous sigh. "Well, once the plywood comes off the outside of the windows, there should be some natural light in the old cafeteria." She glanced at the marigolds blooming beside *La Mujer de Tierra*, still pumping their spicy scent into the portable. "And if I brought some big plants in, that would clean up the air a little."

"And you could probably find a nice rug to cover the lines of the basketball court. That would warm it up."

"Or I could have them sit in the center for story time. You know, use what's there and make it kind of fun." Jolie was still overwhelmed, but she was beginning to rally. "Maybe there's a score board and we could record how many stories we've read on it."

Sienna nodded. She decided not to tell Jolie what Deedee said about the fiction or that she believed a second-hand flower arrangement would make all this okay. She looked around *The Writers' Lair.*

She'd have to move all her stuff, too. She thought of her dirty laundry at home still in the suitcase with the airline tag banded around the handle and the shriveled carrots and empty milk carton in her refrigerator. She needed to go to the market. She wanted to download and print some of her pictures from the nation's capital to share with her students. Instead, she grabbed a piece of paper from the recycling bin and made up a plan with Jolie so they could accommodate *la jefa.*

Chapter Fifteen

Nancy Albright decided that it would be a good service project for her students to help with the move. The students would help Sienna and Jolie and Sienna and Jolie could help her by supervising them while she got entering their *Reading Fare* test scores into the RIDE (Reforming Instruction through Data Entry) spreadsheet before her Thanksgiving Break deadline. Pilar and her classmates were excited about the move. Carrying boxes full of library books would be more fun for them than staring at a thick stack of *Reading Fare* worksheets could ever be.

Javier kept daring boys to be macho, to carry two, no three boxes at a time. Sienna was certain that most of their families had no medical insurance and suspected that Nancy's way of getting the data entry time she so desperately needed was violating some child labor law. "No way, Jose!" she shouted at the staggering boys, bending backwards beneath too much weight. "One box at a time—especially since it's pouring rain."

Jolie cringed at the posturing, worried that if a kid dropped a soggy cardboard box en route it would burst open. She imagined the library books sinking into one of the multiple, waterlogged potholes littering the parking lot. If they weren't damaged that way, she worried the titles would be completely mixed up and hundreds of books would end up in the wrong place. As she watched the first ragged line of jovial nine year olds stagger out of the old library, every box became a ship with an untried captain at the helm, sailing across a dangerous ocean, she actually felt seasick.

When Tammy Lewis discovered Nancy was getting her RIDE done before the holiday break, she sent her second graders to help. Even though it was raining, some wore black construction paper pilgrim hats. Others came in scissor-fringed, Native Americans vests crafted from 100% post-consumer fiber grocery bags.

Ahead of them, Sienna cleaned the scavenged bookshelves with her beloved Window Bright as fast as she could. Pilar waited nearby for one of those shelves to dry so she could unload her box.

"That stuff's not approved!" Captain Swabby barked.

"I don't care," Sienna retorted. "It smells bad enough in here without adding the stench of that institutional cleaner you use."

"Is that all the thanks I get?" Captain Swabby shook his head in mock disgust. "Where'd you get those paper towels?"

"Bonny Deals."

"They aren't issue."

"Yeah," she snorted. "No one seems to have any trouble with me buying and bringing tissue from there for the kids to blow their noses with."

"Hey! Facial tissue is not my jurisdiction, unless it's bloody."

Sienna grimaced. "You realize, don't you, that it takes three times as long and three times as many of your pathetic paper towels to clean up what I get with one of mine?"

"I know," he said. "It's job security."

Sienna sprayed more of the forbidden cleaning agent. "These shelves are filthy."

"But I got them for you, didn't I?"

She stopped her frenzied work to bat her eyelashes at him. "Thanks."

Jolie appeared behind a would-be Native American warrior who'd left his Thanksgiving re-enactment to become a mover. His brown paper vest sluffed onto the slippery former basketball court that was now the floor of the library. Jolie dropped a heavy box with a thud beside him. She stood rubbing the tight ropes of tension in her neck as water streamed from her raincoat, mixing with the remains of the boy's costume. "I don't know what we would have done if you hadn't tracked them down. Captain Swabby, you're our hero."

"Yeah, sure I am," Captain Swabby groaned. "Flattery will get you anywhere. I'm outta here!" He turned to go, stopping suddenly, to examine an unsightly gouge in the one of the plaster walls.

"Don't worry about that," Jolie said. "I'm going to cover it with bulletin board paper."

"You can't." he said automatically. "Fire code."

"I don't want you bringing any of that yucky gray paint in here. I hate that color."

"Well, you can buy your own paint," he said. "I won't tell."

Jolie snorted. "I can barely pay my own rent. Even if I could, it's not right to use my own money for facility maintenance."

"Okay. I still have a partial of saffron somewhere." Captain Swabby said. "It's yours, if you want to go gold." He gestured toward the other three walls. They were all red brick. The high windows were coated by raindrops.

"It will look fantastic!" Sienna said. "Red brick, yellow plaster, orange Formica. There was a piñata with those same colors at the swap meet." She turned toward Pilar. "*La biblioteca nueva will be bonita, verdad?*" Pilar was working on verbs conjugations so Sienna spoke in both languages.

Pilar knew enough English to answer. "Yes! I like red and yellow. Very much."

Captain Swabby gave the girl a thumbs up. "It would have been ideal," he said, rolling his eyes as if imagining more favorable conditions to work in would always be a fantasy, "if I'd had enough time to paint in here before you had to move all the books." He used the skull and crossbones bandana hanging from his back pocket to mop his forehead. "Sometimes, this place reminds me of the Titanic. I hope Deedee is enjoying her trip down south," he added, "while we grunts get this dump shipshape."

* * *

After school was dismissed for the long Thanksgiving weekend, Pilar went home to tell Lucia, Ramon, Esteban, and Dulce, who was always hanging around *Casita Rio* now, how her class got to help with the move. Just as she'd finished, the phone rang.

When Lucia hung up, she smiled at Pilar saying, "That was Ms. O'Mara. *Las maestras* are still working and they're getting hungry. Would you like to take their order to them?"

"I'll go with you!" Dulce offered, looking to Ramon and Lucia for permission, "and can we stay and help?"

"You can all go," Ramon said grandly, nodding at his wife. "I won't be too busy. Purewater people don't want Mexican tonight. They are home dressing up turkeys."

Lucia waved her hand toward the back door. "The turkeys out there aren't at home."

Ramon chuckled proudly at her use of the idiom. *"No problema, esposa. El bandido y yo.* We can feed *a todo el mundo."* The whole family laughed. Pilar thought it was funny how Lucia called people birds and Ramon spoke of a burrito as if it were his best friend. *Un amigo bueno!*

Since the robbery of the Bank of U.S., finding Baldwin's missing heist had become the hobby of many. *El Bandido* was a special meal deal Ramon created for folks who did not want to waste time sitting in the restaurant while the riverbank waited to be searched. Like Clemencian pilgrims prostrating themselves during the final approach to the shrine of *La Sirena,* the searching hordes combed the edges of the Purewater. Faith alone could not fill their bellies and no treasure-hunting dogma dictated that seekers fast.

El Bandido was meant to give them sustenance. Since the oversized burrito was most often eaten sitting on a log or leaning against river rock, *El Bandido* came wrapped in wax paper so that the *carne asada, cebollas,* and hot *ajo* would not fall out. Ramon told anyone who would listen that the *carne* was because rich people ate red meat every day. The onions were to trigger the diner's last tears for once someone found the money there would never be another need to cry. He added the jalapeno and garlic to create a wall of protection around the finder and his or her family so that they would never be taken advantage of after becoming wealthy. Ramon told the family that he'd got the idea about the garlic from a 1970's Dracula comic book Gaul had given him when they were boys back in Mexico. *El Bandido* came with value-added—a cup of coffee with condensed milk, cinnamon, and a pinch of chili to keep the searchers "hot on the trail." Ramon got that English idiom from an American television show.

And so, leaving him to stuff his tortillas while most of America crammed bread crumbs into the hollowed out guts of fowl, the others carried a takeout *fiesta* tray laden with *empanadas, sopas,* rice, and beans down First Street. Soon, Lucia was arranging stuffed animals and hanging posters in the new library while Esteban and Dulce began covering old plaster with gold paint. Matt O'Mara arrived after the Dojang closed for the holidays. He greeted everyone and began the second phase of the move, carrying boxes from the old portable to the old library which was now the Newcomers Center.

The police chief wasn't far behind him. When Wolf first entered the library, Esteban and Lucia grew nervous, exchanging sidelong glances, wondering if they should make their excuses and leave, but it wasn't long before they realized the policeman chief was really only there because he was smitten with Jolie and wanted to help. Jolie actually gave him an order, sending him away to help Matt. "I need to think," she told him with a twinkle in her brown eyes. "And you are distracting me."

Pilar thought of how Mrs. Albright vehemently disapproved of people distracting each other and kids always looked dejected when they were sent out into the hall. Captain Wolfgang looked oddly happy for someone being scolded and banished. Later that evening, Pilar found herself feeling comforted by his presence on campus as she left Lucia to scurry across the dark lot alone, fixating on the light in the windows of the Newcomers Center. When she arrived, she realized the first thing Sienna had done was to recreate the altar, setting *La Mujer de Tierra* upon the bookcase behind her desk and hanging *The Maritza* and *Meet Me at the Swami* over it.

"That will be a good place for kids to draw," Sienna said, pointing Pilar toward a table laden with a large moving box packed with crayons, markers, colored pencils, and various containers to organize them in.

While Pilar luxuriated in arranging and rearranging art materials, Sienna and Jolie conferred in the back corner of the empty old space to consider a framed picture on the wall. An indigenous woman reclined on an abstract wave while an indigenous man waved a rattle over her body. "This used to be the first thing you saw when you entered the library," Sienna remembered. "When we got the projector, the screen had to go where the picture used to be. Deedee wanted to trash it. I just asked the tech guy to rehang it—out of sight."

"It was really hidden when all the books were in here." Jolie said. "I've never taken the time to look at it before now. I like it."

"Me, too." Sienna said. "And it's perfect for a multicultural center."

"Maybe it should be in the library where the whole school will be able to enjoy it," Jolie said. "I mean, where *los gringos* can be exposed to it."

"What are you all talking about?" Wolf set the last box from Sienna's portable down on the ground and joined them.

Together, they all considered the picture. Pilar left her art supplies and imaginary studio to have a look and Lucia, having kept vigilant about Wolf's whereabouts all evening, trailed in at a discreet distance to hover behind the group.

"He's a Native American healer," Sienna explained.

"*Él es un curandero!*" Pilar exclaimed. "*Como las mujeres de Redención.*"

"Ay!" Lucia said softly. Even though her *madrina* was too far behind them to place a warning hand upon Pilar's shoulder, Pilar felt it. She realized that mentioning healers must be like not having papers, or like not revealing how many family members really lived in an apartment, or like pretending not to have known Gaul before she supposedly met him for the first time on All Saints Day. It was just another one of the things she was not supposed to share with *gringos*. But Sienna and Jolie just smiled as if they didn't share Lucia's worry about a girl who sometimes let what she was not supposed to have in her mind occasionally slip out through her mouth.

"Ay!" A man's oddly familiar voice echoed Lucia's

admonishment. However, his tone was filled with admiration as he added, "What a treasure."

Sienna whirled around to see Gaul Santiago and Ramon Vega coming up behind them. Gaul nodded at Sienna. "We meet again, *maestra*. Ramon said we were coming to a school. This…" his eyes swept over *La Mujer de Tierra,* front and center on her bookcase, "looks like an art gallery to me."

It occurred to Sienna, once again, that he could be a con and, if that were true, she'd be embarrassed for him to think she'd fallen for his sentimental story about the statue's origin. To test his authority on the subject matter, she gestured toward the shaman. "Do you know something about this type of painting?"

Gaul studied the small details, peering at the frog carved on the rattle in the healer's hand and at the raven soaring over his head. He pointed to the bottom right hand corner. "Do you see this icon where a signature should be? It's a mountain and a rock with a river."

"What does that mean?" Jolie asked.

"In the 1960's, there was a movement by a group of Native American artists to sign their work this way. The belief was that through using this icon, the artist split the work into a third party, away from himself and away from the spirit that inspired him."

"Why?" Sienna asked.

Gaul said. "I think I can explain this way. Several years ago, I acquired a raven rattle. A truly amazing piece. The handle is worn smooth from being used in the ritual of passing power from one elderly chief to the next in line for hundreds of years. Rich men would come in, asking the price, assuming that if they owned it, some sacred power would somehow just descend upon them. Over time, I've watched people interact with art. Though few would ever confess to it, many seem to think that if they can buy a sacred piece, the artist's powers or the magic of intention within can somehow transfer and accrue to them. The symbol on this painting was an attempt to remind those in the know of what can be bought and sold and what can never be."

"Hmm…" Sienna said, "I like that school of thought."

Jolie said, "And I love this piece. It sure seems out of place in this community."

"That's changing now," Sienna waved her hand toward the unpacked boxes. "That's why we're going through all this, right? We're going to celebrate different cultures now." Sienna felt a twinge of excitement travel up her tired spine. She would staple *The Writers' Lair* banner up before she went home.

"Is there an artistic community in Purewater?" Gaul asked.

Wolf rubbed his chin thoughtfully. "We have a crafts fair at Christmas." He must have felt Pilar scrutinizing his Roman nose just then because he looked down and smiled, kindly, as if he actually liked her. It seemed to her that he saw her as a real girl, not just one of the many Mexicans moving into his town. And, then he strode over to her mermaid picture, asking, "Who is the artist of this one?"

"Pilar," Sienna said. "It was one of her first pieces. Isn't it lovely?"

"Yes, it is," Wolf said. "What do you call it?"

"The *Maritza*," Pilar said shyly. Her whisper was barely audible.

"*Sí. Muy bueno,*" Gaul declared. His eyes twinkled as he turned to Sienna. "Is this the piece you said would cost me?" In all seriousness he said. "I'll take it and I'm prepared to pay."

For a moment Sienna was actually afraid Pilar would let him take it. "*La Maritza* is not for sale." She glanced at Pilar. "Is it?"

Pilar shook her head. "The *Maritza* is for Ms. O'Mara. I can make more."

"You do that," Gaul said encouragingly.

Sienna's stomach clenched at the memory of how Pilar's work on the picture and the vocabulary she was learning about her grandmother has been interrupted *on El Día de Los Muertos* by Deedee's demands and the *Reading Fare* test. The abrupt relocation hadn't allowed her any time to get back to it, either. "She'll have time to work on more soon."

Gaul's eyes flickered over to where *La Mujer de Tierra* stood, still flanked by vibrant marigolds. He met Sienna's eyes and nodded. And Pilar felt truly safe for the first time in America.

Chapter Sixteen

"Why would an art dealer from Santa Fe be making regular visits to Purewater?" Andy asked.

"He's a friend of Pilar's family," Sienna replied.

"Are you sure he's not a drug dealer?"

Sienna was taken aback. "That's not like you."

Andy cleared his throat. "I can't help wondering if he's tall, dark, and handsome."

Gaul was fairly dark and fairly handsome but he was only about two or three inches taller than she was. "He's not that tall."

"Great," Andy said wryly.

Sienna's entire body felt heavy from exhaustion. The dull headache she'd had all day was becoming sharper. Sugar would help. Her tongue was tingling with nutmeg and ginger. Luckily, Matt had been able to get to Purewater's bakery just minutes before they'd closed. Her family wouldn't care that she'd already dug into one of the pumpkin pies. "And so," she continued far too weary to address flirtation or jealously, "Gaul took the painting off the wall. On the back, there was a card explaining that when Mrs. Moore bequeathed the land to the school district way back in the 1920's, she stipulated that the painting be displayed on site for all perpetuity. I really want to keep it in the Newcomer Center. The thing is, more kids will get to see it if Jolie puts it in the library."

"How is the Newcomer Center?"

"Bizarre." She readjusted the laptop, angling so that she knew for certain that Andy couldn't see the dirty dishes littering the kitchen counter.

"How so?" he prompted.

"I feel like I'm in the belly of a whale in there. Surrounded by all those empty shelves."

She sprayed a huge spiraling dollop of whipped cream onto the tiny sliver of pie left on her plate.

"Just think about how lucky you are to have the space!" Andy was quite chipper. "It took the Supreme Court 146 years to get its own building. You have a Newcomer Center after just a few years in the outback."

"And I don't have a five minute hike to and from the bathroom anymore. There's actually one in my new space and it's completely private."

"What a perk!" he said.

Sienna nodded. Walking was good, yet in a world tied to the minute hand and governed by bells, the distance mattered. "I can make a lot a copies and correct a lot of paper in the time I'll save."

"It's probably best not to calculate to that degree of efficiency," Andy said. "Senator Panky has just introduced a bill to minimize recess. He just might add an amendment to dock teacher pay if they go to the bathroom."

Sienna felt angry at the idea of restricting recess and responded with sarcasm. "Either that or Pica will start marketing a standards-based, test-preparation chamber pot for the classroom."

Andy chuckled, "In all seriousness though, I am really glad Deedee has decided to let you carry on with *The Writers' Lair*."

"Thank you." Sienna didn't like being sarcastic and she was almost too tired to care about *The Writers' Lair*. "Hey," she said shifting the topic. "I'm really glad to have you in my life this Thanksgiving."

"I feel the same about you," Andy said. "I'm sorry if I'm pedantic about the Supreme Court. I wouldn't be if we were together." He sighed longingly. "I wish we were."

They blew kisses into their screens and logged off for the night.

Thinking about how hard it was to be so far from loved ones, Sienna realized she only had about twenty minutes to clean up the kitchen before her mother, Uncle Ed, and Aunt Susan arrived in the car they'd rented from the airport. Wishing she hadn't worked quite so late all week, she filled the sink with hot soapy water to soak the residue off the week's dirty plates and helped herself to another piece of pie.

* * *

"Teaching kids to write is good medicine," Susan said when they'd all finished the Thanksgiving dishes.

Bridget nodded. "Everybody knows what happens when a part of the population is shut-down, disenfranchised. You get graffiti, gang violence…slum city."

"It's a good thing your principal came around," Susan said. "I mean, really, imagine what a small town like Purewater would be like after ten years if half of all the students who go through Moore essentially end up illiterate, frustrated with schooling, and angry?"

Sienna pointed toward the silver roots at her temples. "*Reading Fare* is responsible for this. I started losing color right around the second week of implementation."

"Ah, honey," Bridget said. "That's easy enough to fix. Two hours in the beauty shop is all it takes."

"That is until you are ready to give yourself credit for your age," Aunt Susan said. "Every woman deserves to own her own life experience and display the wisdom she's gained."

"That's true," Bridget mused. "Maybe the best part of going gray is it helps women stop comparing themselves with each other and focus on real stuff. Still, save your color as long as you can. If you're too stressed at Moore, you should just go work at another school. Any school would be lucky to get you."

"I think it's okay now," Sienna said. "Soon the staff will realize how obfuscating *Reading Fare* is and how all the testing is hurting everyone."

"What do you mean by that?" Uncle Ed was at the back door,

130

panting, pressing Matt's basketball into his heaving chest.

"You don't really want to hear it," Sienna glanced at her uncle. "My boss says I'm too specific."

"No, tell me. Give it to me straight. I want to know what to say when my golf buddies start bashing teachers."

"I'll tell you quickly. Then I really need to stop talking about work." Sienna described a *Reading Fare* test question that required students to read a passage with advanced vocabulary. That particular vocabulary had not been taught during the unit the children were being tested on, nor had it ever appeared in any of the *Reading Fare* curriculum for any of the younger grades.

"So," Susan said, "the curriculum designers assume that kids have learned those words elsewhere."

"But where would ELL kids get to learn them if the system is determined to make even ELL teachers follow the *Reading Fare* curriculum from day one?" Bridget asked.

Ed furrowed his brow. "I don't know. Maybe I need Special Ed," he joked. "Get it? Special? Ed?"

The women groaned.

"I'm just trying to apply a little levity to the loony bin." He ruffled Sienna's graying hair just like he had when she was a little girl. "I'm really sorry it's so tough, sweetie." His eyes brightened with the certainty he knew how to make her happier. "I'll get Matt. It's time for a family game of Scrabble."

Chapter Seventeen

On the Monday right after Thanksgiving, Deedee announced, "We should require school uniforms at Moore."

Several teachers grimaced. It might have been at the suggestion or because they were eating Calories Counts. Controlled portions, masquerading as lunch, had gone on sale at Bonny Deals right alongside cans of whole cranberries and post-holiday bread crumbs.

"We need to form a committee."

"Can we make parents buy them?" Tammy Lewis wasn't eating at all. She stood on a chair, pinning tattered gold garland above the window overlooking the parking lot.

Sienna, standing by the microwave, reheating Bridget's traditional Day-After-Thanksgiving soup asked, "Do you mean something like everyone wears blue pants and a white shirt?"

"No." Deedee said. "I mean real uniforms."

Real uniforms would cost the Fuentes family or the Garcia clan a lot, Sienna mused—even if they only bought one per child. There would have to be a mid-week trip to the laundromat where just washing them would cost more than two or three outfits at the swap meet did. She almost said something, but she was wary. She didn't want Deedee yelling at her again, Instead, she said, "We should probably stay away from white."

"I was thinking black and blue." Deedee said.

Nancy's mind was racing. "Since we can't afford to fix the

drainage on the playground, maybe we should just go with earth tones to match the mud."

"How about bright colors?" Jolie said. "It's so gloomy around here in the winter."

Sienna was certain a staff that approved gray paint for the exterior of their school would never select neon clothing for their kids. "Let's go for hot pink, orange, and yellow."

"And electric blue," Jolie added.

"I like rainbow colors, too." Mavis Penn said.

Deedee snarled. "We aren't hippies. I want us to look classy. Like a private school."

"We aren't a private school," Tammy said.

Deedee scowled. "And," she added coldly, maliciously it seemed, "to set the tone, teachers will wear uniforms, too. Gray tweed. Slacks or a skirt. No! Jumpers!" Suddenly, she clapped her hands in delight. "Teachers will wear jumpers!" She beamed happily.

Sienna scanned the mostly distressed faces in the staff room. She couldn't tell if her colleagues were disturbed by Deedee's fashion sense or her mood swing.

A long-time union representative who was close to retirement, Mavis had seen a variety of administrators come and go. She swallowed her blood pressure medication with a sip of water and dabbed her mouth with a napkin. Primly, she said, "It will be even more upscale than a private school. We'll all be just like governesses."

"Yes. It's very *Jane Eyre*," Sienna adopted a playful tone, hoping Deedee would get the allusion before mandating an edict they'd all regret.

"Indeed it is," Jolie added, as if she were the queen of England.

"Jane who?" Deedee asked. "Air? Do they have a website?"

"You're joking, right?" Jolie gripped a white plastic butter knife. Her hand shook a little. She was still furious about being told not to unpack the fiction.

"No. I'm serious." Deedee said, "I love online shopping. It would be great if we could order online."

"There is a link," Jolie said, "to a school for the impoverished daughters of the clergy."

Nancy made an involuntary sound and, as if to stifle herself, snatched the last leftover segment of a sprinkled doughnut from the empty tray in the center of the table. She popped it into her mouth and chewed with her front teeth, like a rodent.

"We all need to be on the same page around here," Deedee insisted, "Literally in *Reading Fare* and in the spirit of achieving higher standards. I want you to be able to remember that every single time you see one of your colleagues. I want you to think common curriculum, common clothes. I want it to be your mantra."

"Well then," Nancy said slowly, "what color should we wear under the gray jumpers? Black? Blue?"

Deedee beamed at her. "That's where you get free choice! You get to decide that for yourself, Nancy. Pick whichever one you want. Black on Monday? Blue on Tuesday? I don't care. Mix it up. I'll support whatever you choose."

"I look better in blue," Nancy said. A green sprinkle was stuck between her front teeth. "Would it be okay if I wore blue all the time?"

"That would be just fine," Deedee said. "And look at you, Nancy! Look at how quickly you're adjusting to the idea. You are a model for embracing change. I hope all your colleagues will learn from your example!" Deedee took in the whole room with a gesture before giving her undivided attention to Nancy once more. "Would you like to chair the uniform committee?"

Nancy blanched. "Uh…well… my daughter is going to State and my son is starting basketball this week and I'm the team mom so I have to…."

Deedee nodded her head up and down vigorously.

Nancy joined in. "Well, okay. I 'll do it."

"Wait just a minute," Sienna said, "Our fourth graders need to learn how to write persuasive essays. Let's have them do research on school uniforms and write what they think about them. Maybe, they could have a debate. The whole school could come and watch. The kids could vote."

"We don't have time for all that research, writing, and

speaking!" Nancy gasped. "The fourth grade at Moore is already a whole *Reading Fare* unit behind every other school in town."

"This would be a personally meaningful project," Sienna said. "It's relevant to the children's lives. We could teach them every skill that *Reading Fare* claims to cover by leading them through this project. And, they'd get to experience being active, thinking citizens in a democracy."

"That is not the point of this," Deedee spoke through gritted teeth. She closed her eyes and drew a deep breath, lip-synching her count to ten. When she opened her eyes, she spoke with exaggerated calm. "I want uniforms to build team spirit and get rid of distractions so that kids and teachers can focus on our learning improvement plan. We have to get our reading scores up! I don't want to waste time thinking or talking about anything else."

"We teach in an American public school," Jolie said. "Who does it benefit when getting higher reading scores preempts participation in informed public discourse?"

"This is elementary school," Deedee hissed as if they'd all missed a memo. "Kids can't participate in public intercourse. They're too young. They don't know what's good for them. Frankly, some of you don't seem to know either."

With that, all the teachers began chattering about uniforms.

When Sienna heard the phrase "regulation hemline" from the table in the farthest corner of the room, she pulled a black beret from her coat pocket and positioned it over her hair. She took her soup out of the microwave, struggling to keep her hands from trembling and deliberately draining the emotion from her voice. She succeeded spectacularly, sounding unusually cold and aloof as she swept out the door, leaving a wake of steam behind her. "I've got to go," she said to no one in particular. "I'm binding grammar poems into chapbooks today."

Deedee watched her go and then glanced at the clock. "Oh shoot! I've got to go, too. I have a meeting at the district office about getting more ELL kids."

"Really?" Nancy wrinkled her nose. "Why would they send them here? That's only going to drive our test scores down more, especially since Sienna still isn't following *Reading Fare*. There's no grammar poem or chapbook in this week's scope or sequence."

"Don't worry," Deedee said in a low voice, loud enough to be overheard, "I'm working on getting the other ELL teacher in Purewater transferred here. Even though she's just got out of college, she has apparently figured out how to follow *Reading Fare's* pacing guide with her students." Deedee backed out the door adding, "Nancy, the Jane Air catalog might be a good place for your committee to start. Send me the link."

"I'll do it right now!" Ashley Whitfield waved her smartphone in the air. "I'll look Jane Air up right now and email the link to everyone."

"*Jane Eyre* is a novel," Mavis told her.

"Not necessarily," Ashley said. "It could be a clothing company with the same name."

"It's not." Jolie muttered.

Peering at her handheld, Ashley exclaimed, "It *is* a novel! With 328 pages! Wow! Who has time to read anything that long?"

Jolie widened her eyes at Mavis. "I'm going back to the library now" she said. "I feel a sudden need to unpack the fiction."

"Quite right," Mavis said, dabbing her mouth again.

In her office, Deedee drooped in her chair, just as her nine-year-old self had slumped in the backseat of the old Studebaker. How many times had she watched her mother from there? She'd peered through two panes of glass, the sedan's window and the entire east side of a Chattanooga coffee shop. While she ate the dry crusts of a peanut butter sandwiches left over in her Raggedy Ann lunch pail, her mother sat in the restaurant, drinking French Roast with cream— no sugar—smoking a Virginia Slim, scribbling in a stenographer's notepad, wearing a black beret.

Deedee wondered where Sienna had gotten that ridiculous hat. It looked just like the one her mother had donned during those long, boring hours. Was it a uniform for poets? Deedee could never be on that team. The laughter of her older sisters had made that clear the one time she'd tried on Edwina's beret in the car while they all waited for their mother to sweep through McPhee's with a wire basket full of discounted tuna and a bulk jar of mayonnaise in the crook of her arm.

Deedee snorted. Sienna was a decent ELL teacher, but she was as incomprehensible to Deedee as Edwina had always been. Her sisters, Marilyn and Maisie, had had their own secrets as well, constantly reminding Deedee of her exclusion from it with their impenetrable signals, the lift of a brow, the biting of a lip.

The glances her staff had exchanged over lunch reminded her of that and, damn it to hell, if they weren't sending her back to square one, after she'd finally cracked her sisters' code.

Yep. She'd done it. Just days ago on Thanksgiving, forty years to the day past her first hush-hush visit from Aunt Flo, in the same kitchen where she'd done her primary school homework, Deedee had finally realized that a head tilted to the side and a smidgen shrug meant, "See! Mama's crazier than a shithouse rat!" And then, like a young child finally mastering her short vowel sounds and applying them to Dr. Seuss, she realized widened eyes meant "Don't tell." The half-smile signified, "Keep her guessing." When Rosacea-flushed nostrils flared, her sisters meant. "We've got the upper hand now." Sometimes, all it took was tucking a strand of hair behind the ear. And once again, as she did after every visit back to her birthplace, Deedee remembered that she hadn't been allowed to get her ears pierced as long as she lived in her Mama's house because of the nasty infection Maisie suffered after her initiation into the world of gold studs.

The way Sienna had tucked her hair behind her ears when she'd donned that stupid hat in the staff room made Deedee angry. The way she'd wanted to question her idea about uniforms and then gone cold and become aloof was infuriating. She seemed to know something Deedee did not. Deedee hated feeling that way. She knew she'd only stumbled into understanding her sisters' secret language at this late date because she was, for the first time, its beneficiary. Her mother had leaned in asking, "Tell me, Deidre, darling. Do the children at your school read?"

Deedee had nodded enthusiastically. "We've just adopted a fantastic new program!"

"But do they read?"

Something about that question made Deedee nervous. She tucked a stand of her shoulder length hair behind her ear, so that it curled slightly, almost cupping one of the thick, 14 carat, gold hoops she sported. It was a magical act because, as if on cue, Marilyn jumped in to save her from having to answer. As if she were a fairy godmother waving a wand, Marilyn passed the butter dish to their mother and changed the subject. "Real butter is so much better than margarine."

Maisie said, "And I just love the centerpiece Mama."

"I got everything at McPhee's," Edwina whispered. It pained Edwina to buy flowers at the grocery store instead of the bona fide, but now defunct, florist's shop so she launched into a lament about small businesses going under downtown. As the conversation at her mother's lace-covered table eddied around her, swirling away from her school improvement plan, Deedee savored a flaky croissant with intense gratitude.

Her sisters had helped her deflect Edwina's difficult question. They'd protected her in a way, protected her from deeper reflection. She certainly didn't need to come back to her school to find her staff creating another private language around her right after she'd had the sweet taste of sisterhood for the first time ever back at home.

* * *

At the weekly faculty meeting that Thursday, Nancy passed a platter of peanut butter cookies around. "They are full of protein," she said, urging Mavis Penn to eat one.

"I have to watch my cholesterol," Mavis replied. "Doctor's orders."

Deedee held up her hand to refuse the one offered to her. She was anxious to launch into the implementation of uniforms. Still, she made it a point to ask, "Is there anything we need to discuss before moving onto my agenda item?"

"Yes," Mavis said, "I've got first graders who still don't know all their letters, let alone their sounds. I just can't keep up with the

Reading Fare pacing guide. Given the special needs of our population, I'm wondering why our school didn't get an intervention program. Can we still get one for Moore? Or can I get a copy of *Reading Fare's* Kindergarten program and use that?"

Ashley Whitfield spoke up. "If we just have high enough expectations for our students, they will rise to meet them."

Leaning against the cold metal back of her folding chair, Mavis smiled warmly at the much younger woman. "I agree with that to a point, Ashley, but not if we make them feel like failures from the get-go."

"They are feeling like failures." Tammy said.

And with that tiny bit of dissension, tension clouded the staffroom like a thunderhead forming over an outdoor wedding. The cluster of probationary teachers burst into frenzied chatter.

Tammy popped a homeopathic stress mint into her mouth as someone exclaimed, "Can you believe they're at the top of the salary scale?"

"I think it's time for someone to retire." Ashley muttered.

Mavis slid back in her chair and stood up. Her chest heaved as she surveyed the room. Her years of negotiating on behalf of teachers, mostly women, to improve their working conditions had given her plenty of experience facing short-term self-righteousness of political bickering and the long-term social betrayal of her colleagues and the children crammed into their classrooms. Mavis surveyed the room. Some women were picking chopped nuts out of a cookie. Others doodled in the margins of a notepad. One was trimming laminate from a poster of a puppy that said *Wag your tail for teamwork.* She knew most of them were exhausted after simultaneously pushing a developmentally inappropriate curriculum on children and then having to respond and contain the non-stop emotional and behavioral reactions to that—all day long—day after day.

Mavis said, "Thirty years ago, my sister adopted a nine-year old girl. The kid had spent her entire life, up to that point, in a playpen in front of a T.V. She spoke with the intonation of sitcom characters, always pausing between her sentences, as if waiting for canned laughter to come out of nowhere. Naturally, she was awkward in social situations, but she was so hungry for attention that she was gratified when people laughed. The social worker called her communicatively handicapped."

Several teachers glanced at the clock. Some of the mothers on staff frequently parked their very own children in front of electronic screens so they could grade tests for the RIDE. Some of them longed to be home holding babies cared for by others while they'd spent most of the day pouring their own energy, enthusiasm, and encouragement into strangers' children. Other mothers still had chauffeuring older children to activities and orthodontists to do before they made dinner for their families.

Mavis kept talking. "One day when my niece was about twelve, the family dog snatched one of her favorite shoes. She shook her fist, like a cartoon character, trying to make him drop it. My sister coached her to use a powerful voice, to tap into an authentic feeling. The girl couldn't do it. The dog ripped her shoe apart."

Deedee shook her head sadly, "What kind of shoe was it?"

Mavis ignored her and went on. "As she watched him tear it to pieces, the girl sunk into a catatonic state. My sister called me in a panic, asking for advice. I told her to hold the girl. I told her to hold her until she'd been held enough. My sister wouldn't do it." Mavis put her hand on her clavicle as if it hurt to breathe. "She said, 'This kid's too old to be coddled.' Guess what happened? The kid quit talking. She's said a few things in the last twenty odd years, always keeping it simple. Real simple. Yes. No. Maybe. I don't know, and I've never thought about it. She dropped out of school and now she lives on prescription pills in a group home. If I had to do it over again, I would have marched over to my sister's house, pulled that girl onto my lap, and held her myself."

"Mavis!" Deedee jumped to her feet, flushing beet red. "How can you say such a thing? You have a union background!"

"Yeah!" Someone shouted. "You know that we're not supposed to hug our students."

"I wouldn't even want to." Nancy wrinkled her nose. "Jonathan stinks!"

Mavis furrowed her brow. "I don't mean literally! I mean metaphorically. Don't you remember Sienna's poem?"

There was a collective gasp. Sienna froze in her seat like Pilar often did. No one at school ever mentioned her poem—last year's grand prize winner in *Poetry Now*. For some inexplicable reason, it seemed to be taboo.

Deedee responded loudly—angrily, "We are here to do what research says is best for the children, not what we, what you, think is best for them. *Reading Fare* is researched-based so we are using it. Mavis, you just need to push yourself and your students harder without a bunch of handholding. You may not use a different program or reach down into a lower level."

"I will not make children cry," Mavis said, "or let them give up on reading before they even get started. I want them to read because they love it."

Deedee thumped her hand against the breast pocket of her tailored blazer, beating out each word as if she could pound it into Mavis' head. "They don't have to *love* it, Mavis," she said. "They just have to *do* it."

As Mavis gripped the edge of the table apparently struck by a wave of dizziness, Deedee clapped her hands briskly. "And now for what's really good for the order. Let's discuss jumpers. They come in small, medium, and large."

Mavis was absent the next day. By morning recess, the staff had learned she'd been rushed to Purewater's emergency room around ten o'clock Thursday night due to arrhythmia. Her heart had suddenly begun to beat far too fast. While being airlifted to the University Medical Center in Sinclair, she had a heart attack. A long-term substitute was being interviewed to cover her class. Mavis would be on leave for at least three months, probably longer. Her medical team had, raised the possibility of her needing an artificial pacemaker for the rest of her life.

In the Newcomer Center, Sienna replaced the fading marigolds with pots of miniature roses. As she set the red and white blooms beside *La Mujer de Tierra*, she hoped Mavis would recover quickly and without complications. After the previous day's staff meeting, she'd been sure Mavis was going to be the ally Andy told her she'd need. She'd been planning to talk to Mavis at lunch. "Now she's gone," she murmured to *La Mujer de Tierra*.

La Mujer de Tierra seemed to whispered back. "Teachers are getting sick."

Then the Swami added. "Or going crazy."

Chapter Eighteen

The Writers' Lair was dwarfed in the hull of the old library. To save on the power bill, Sienna only used one light switch. As the children passed the "awka rock," their voices echoed off the dark shadows in the hollow space.

Belmaris practically whispered. "One night my grandpa was sleeping and he heard a noise."

Sienna cupped her hand behind her ear as if trying hard to hear it herself. "What kind of noise was it?"

Belmaris clutched at her heart, hunched her shoulders, and made a sorrowful noise.

"Oh!" Sienna said, impressed by the intensity. "That's a *moan.*"

Belmaris nodded, receiving the vocabulary, and getting on with the story. "First, my grandpa, he went to the bathroom. There was no one in there. Next, he went to the kitchen. The back door stayed open. But no one push it. My grandpa, he was getting some water. He heard the noise again. Finally, he went to the liquor store." Belmaris looked around at her fascinated audience of fellow authors. "And that's the story of how my grandpa heard a ghost."

Sienna wondered if the grandfather had gone to the liquor store first and heard the ghost later, but she would let the sequence in the little's girl's story stand separate from whatever realities might have inspired it. "Where was your grandpa's house?"

"By the river." Waving her hand dismissively, Belmaris added,

"In Mexico."

"Did your grandpa tell you anything more about the ghost by the river?" Sienna wondered.

Belmaris leaned forward studying Sienna's face in the dim light. "You think she real?"

All of the children leaned in, breathlessly waiting for her verdict.

Sienna inclined her head thoughtfully, "What did your grandpa say about that?"

"He say she after him all the time he a little boy and a man."

"Same ghost?"

Belmaris nodded.

Pilar shifted uneasily as she made some sense of the conversation.

"Did he ever see her? Did he ever say how she looked?" Sienna asked. "I want to make a mind movie of her."

Belmaris fluttered her fingers up in the air. "She nothing, and then," the girl broke off, grabbing the back of her own neck and hanging her head as if she were a kitten suspended by the scruff of her neck between her mother's teeth. She shuddered as if an amorphous spirit had actually seized her own solid flesh.

And in that moment, I, the silent omniscient, cold-hearted narrator of this tale suddenly wanted to be part of the conversation. I clasped the nape of Sienna's neck. She shuddered and I knew she felt a sudden and a real chill. She struggled to keep the panic she felt from showing on her face. She put her hand at the very base of her brain. With her touch, with her warm palm upon what had once been the back of my human hand, I began to wail, not as I did when trolling the rivers, but with relief—the relief of a lost child finally being found and the relief of finally being held. Centuries of grief and confusion poured out of me.

Pilar squeezed her eyes tight. She clamped her hands over her ears, shaking her head violently from side to side.

Valentin's eyes widened until they were enormous. He whispered, "*La Llorona!*"

"*La Llorona?*" Sienna asked him desperately, pressing my invisible hand downward toward her shoulder in an attempt to free herself from my chokehold. "*Que es esto*?"

"She cry." Valentin ducked his head and hunched his shoulders. "No stop."

"Was your grandpa's ghost sad?" Sienna asked Belmaris. "*Triste*?"

Touched by the teacher's urgency, Belmaris nodded, frowning to make the point.

"Oh!" Sienna said sympathetically. "She was very sad."

Somehow I had been heard. Now everyone in the room knew how I really felt. With a final shuddering sob, I let go of the teacher. Pilar uncovered her ears. Valentin sat up straight. Sienna got back to business writing a word on a Post-It note for Belmaris to stick in her ELL folder. "When you write your story," she said, "say the sound your grandfather heard was a *moan* and don't forget to explain that the ghost was very, very, sad."

With that, I felt something very unfamiliar. I know now it is called hope.

Relief washed over the faces of the children. Their fear of me passed. Belmaris wrote about her grandfather. As she wrote his story, mine began to come out, too. Just as the children had brought the Swami to *The Writers' Lair*, they made a place for me.

* * *

Meanwhile, in the library, Captain Swabby cleared a musty broom closet. "It's great you are taking that disgusting stuff away," Jolie said, wrinkling her nose at an industrial-grade garbage can with the matted clumps of ancient tangled gray mop hair drooping over its rim. "Maybe that's why it smells like something died in there. I don't need that space tonight. You can finish the rest tomorrow." Captain Swabby's shift was over. She knew the night custodian had already come on duty because he'd checked in with her, letting her know he had to skip vacuuming the library because someone had shoved a wad of paper towels down every toilet in the boys' bathroom.

"I can't finish in the morning!" Captain Swabby exhaled in

exasperation. "Deedee wants this closet cleared out and cleaned up by three o'clock today." With sweaty vengeance, he tossed an old fuse box and a broken yardstick in with the old mop.

"Why?"

"I don't know." Gasping, he swiped his forehead with a red bandana before positioning a rusty two-drawer metal file cabinet onto a hand truck. "I just do what I'm told."

"I suppose somebody has to." Jolie finished taping a new spine label onto a children's novel. She held it up for him to see. "It's fiction," she announced defiantly. "It's a story."

He was used to teachers telling him random things. He nodded agreeably. "That's just what I'd expect to find in a library." He slid a fresh new mop head onto the end of a new mop handle and began to swab the floor in the concrete closet.

Nancy called from the entrance. "Hey Jolie, my kids are writing non-fiction book reports this month. Please don't let any of them check out any fiction."

Jolie's smile was strained. "Actually, I always let kids pick two titles…"

"Good! So for this month, make sure they are both non-fiction books about the same topic. I'm not coming in, "she said with a little wave. "Sorry, my bladder is timed to the minute." She disappeared from the doorway.

Captain Swabby set up a box fan. "This should dry the floor more quickly and maybe even freshen the air. I'll be back in a few minutes." He pushed his junk laden hand cart out the door and careened around the corner, barely missing Sienna as she rushed into the library.

"Hey!" Jolie's eyes lit up when she saw her. "I found your poem. It was awesome. I can't believe I actually work with someone who won the *Poetry Now* prize! I hope you're still writing."

"I'm working on a little something," Sienna said intentionally vague. Jolie seemed very sincere, but she had become guarded about her poetry at Moore. It seemed to make people uncomfortable.

Jolie waived her hand toward two boxes barely visible behind the library counter. "Captain Swabby found those books shoved in

146

the back of the broom closet. They are full of brand-new multicultural books that have never been processed. Do you know anything about them?"

Sienna went to investigate.

"Be careful," Jolie cautioned as Sienna opened a box. "There are *stories* in there."

"Heaven forbid!" Sienna exclaimed in mock dismay. "Imagine having stories in an elementary school library! Leave it to Deedee to misinterpret the next new set of standards."

"Well, Nancy's on the same bandwagon, now. She's banned fiction for the month."

With a rug rolled under his arm, Captain Swabby wheeled the handcart back into the library with a teacher's desk upended upon its platform. Jolie gasped with pleasure. The only workspace she had was the library counter.

"Don't get any ideas," he barked. "It's not for you. You can't have it."

"I thought there weren't any extra desks around here."

"There aren't. "Captain Swabby unrolled the plush oriental rug that Sienna recognized from Deedee's office. He centered it in the broom closet. "Deedee said to get a desk in here immediately, so I grabbed the one from Mavis Penn's room. Her sub will just have to get by."

Captain Swabby was a political genius. Mavis's sub would surely be chagrined to lose the teacher's desk, yet she was probably so happy to have a long-term job that she wouldn't dare complain. She'd probably buy one from Goodwill with her own money and have her boyfriend haul it to school for her.

"Who's moving in here?" Sienna asked. An itinerant speech pathologist? An occupational therapist?

"Don't know," Captain Swabby said. Huffing and puffing, he bypassed the fan to position the desk on top of the rug inside the closet. He dashed out.

"Visiting dignitary?" Jolie proposed.

Sienna shrugged.

Captain Swabby rushed back in with the bouquet the school

secretary's husband had just sent to mark their twentieth wedding anniversary. A little water sloshed out of Mrs. Donahue's vase as he set the flowers on the corner of the desk. "Done!" he exclaimed with relief as he straightened a wayward purple aster. "I've gotta get outta here before she tells me to do one more thing. My grandson has basketball practice. See you ladies tomorrow." He sprinted out the door.

Jolie walked into the closet. "There's no ventilation in here." she surveyed the roughly plastered walls. She sank into the metal fold-out chair Swabby set at the desk, apparently the best seat he could procure. Her eyes narrowed. "Anyone who sits here with the door open will have a view of everything in the library. This is really creepy. I feel like I'm under surveillance."

"That's what you get for circulating fiction," Sienna said wryly.

"I guess so. This is the perfect spot for the library police."

"You are partial to cops, aren't you?"

"One of them, anyway." Jolie touched the petals of a rosy powderpuff tenderly. Then, she plucked the florist's card out of the arrangement of pink, purple, and white blooms. "Happy twentieth! I got a bouquet like this once."

"How long were you married?"

"Twenty-one years. Do you think Mrs. Donahue will miss these?"

"Maybe she donated them to the cause."

"What cause?"

Sienna shrugged. "The mission against fiction? I don't know. Right now, I'm looking for ghost stories from Mexico."

"There might be something in those boxes. Help yourself and feel free to put some spine labels on them, if you're so inclined." With that, Jolie pushed a heavy cart behind a book case and knelt on the floor to shelve a day's worth of returns. Sienna knelt behind the counter to search through the boxes.

They'd barely begun when they heard the click of Deedee's heels and then her voice. "I'll be sure to have Captain Swabby clear the reader board before he leaves tonight."

Sienna was about to stand, to make her presence known, but the woman with Deedee gushed, "Oh, Deedee. I'm so glad you understand why the school board just doesn't want to single out immigrants. Spanish signage on First Street sends the wrong message to the community."

"Oh Mimi!" Deedee echoed the other woman's effusion, "I'm so glad you are coming aboard."

"Thank you for such a warm welcome, Deedee. I can't tell you how much I appreciate it."

"With your help, I'm sure we'll get our reading scores up."

"Maybe," Mimi said. "Let me remind you that at this point I'm still only here to observe and, maybe, just maybe, offer a few teeny-weeny suggestions now and again."

Deedee's laugh ended with a snort. "I'd love to see the notes you've already taken."

"I don't have much yet."

Deedee cut in. "Here's your office!"

There was a moment of stunned silence. Mimi said, "Wow! Thanks for the flowers."

"You're welcome." Deedee said. "You'll love Jolie, our new librarian. She gave me a little lip at first about holding back the fiction. She just didn't get how important it is to get kids used to the idea that informational reading is the way of the future, but she came around. She did a nice job moving in here after our ELL teacher requested the old library for a Newcomer Center."

It wasn't clear which of them moved first. Jolie stepped out from behind the shelves and Sienna rose from behind the counter to see Deedee standing with a familiar woman—the blonde with the clipboard who'd she'd been conferring with in the hallway on Halloween. Now, the woman had a name—Mimi.

Slowly, it dawned on Deedee that the women she'd been discussing during this administrative briefing had been within earshot the whole time. "Oh! Speak of the Devil! Devils. They're both here." She crossed her arms across her chest and scowled, like a mother, deciding which of two grounded children should be beaten first for emerging from captivity without permission. Sienna watched a tug-of-war between the downturned corners of Deedee's mouth.

Would she pretend she hadn't been talking about them? Would she accept responsibility for it?

"Drat!" Deedee exclaimed. "Do you ever hear your mother's words just fly out of your mouth? I never speak of the Devil, but my mother sure did. Mostly she meant my father. I don't even have kids," she said, patting Mimi's forearm, "even so, sometimes I say the things my mother said and I feel my face getting all consorted like hers."

"Contorted?" Mimi asked.

"Yes. I remember how my Mother used to cake the make-up on. I remember freaking out once when I was little because her face looked like it was flaking off."

"As I explained to Brenda Hadley," Mimi interrupted, "I'm sure your staff will benefit from a little support and coaching while implementing a brand-new curriculum." She smiled warmly at Jolie and then at Sienna. "We have an opportunity to make a real difference now. Purewater School District is willing and eager to improve and we are poised to make some great changes here." She nodded sympathetically as if responding to unspoken disagreement. "I know change is hard, but I'm sure we can all agree that it is time for the system to align with itself and give students the education they deserve."

Sienna didn't speak. She wanted to ask if aligning the system with itself was the same as aligning it with the children but Deedee had just lied about her and she didn't feel safe. Asking a probing question didn't seem to be a good idea. Deedee didn't really like them.

Deedee led Mimi away, saying, "And please let Brenda know I am happy to save the district tons of money in translation services. I never thought we should send notices home in Spanish anyway. And Mimi, if you wouldn't mind, could you please check on how Brenda feels about school uniforms? Some of my teachers want the kids and staff to start wearing them. I'd love to hear her opinion." As the women disappeared from earshot, she added, "One of our go-getters, Miss Whitfield, has already found a supplier. Jane Air."

"Did you hear that?" Jolie hissed, striding up to the counter. "I gave her lip? What am I? Sixteen? I'm not her daughter. She's not my mother? Whatever happened to professional expertise? I have a Master's Degree in Reading Instruction and Library Science. And she said you, you *wanted* the Newcomer Center? You tried to talk her out of it."

"And she's the one who told the staff she wanted school uniforms."

"That's right," Jolie said. "That was her idea, too."

"Something is wrong with her." Sienna felt a pang of compassion. "Maybe she's ill like Mr. Rochester's first wife!" She racked her brain. Had there been a diagnosis in Austen's *Jane Eyre*?

"Then we ought to lock that lunatic in the attic." Jolie looked up, searching the ceiling. "Just as soon as we find the opening."

"Captain Swabby knows where it is."

"And I bet he'd be willing to help put her up there after this afternoon. Who is that Mimi person?"

"I don't know," Sienna said. "I saw her here once. It seems like she's from the district office or some kind of reading coach."

"Then she should help me defend fiction. Stories can change, even save, a person's life when all the articles, reports, and studies in the world can't."

"I know," Sienna said. She scanned Jolie's face. "Which story saved you?"

Jolie sighed. "Let's just say a short story about two cowboys on a mountain helped my ex-husband have a conversation with me that he should have had with someone when he was eighteen."

Sienna racked her brain, for character, setting, and plot. "Oh!"

Jolie was finished discussing her ex-husband's sexual preferences. Back to business, she asked, "Why didn't we interrupt Deedee and insist on accuracy?"

"You mean why didn't we correct our boss while she was obviously trying to make a good impression on someone hired to poke around and improve our failing school?"

Jolie nodded.

"Because you, my friend, don't even have a desk of your own."

The next day, Sienna was at her computer. She had Valentin's school registration paperwork with her and she searched for information about primary schools in Mexico. It took a long time to find a registry of schools in the state of Clemencia. Annoying pop-up ads seemed to be getting past the district firewall, but she didn't have the time to put a tech ticket in. The server was slow.

When she finally came across the correct website, the word *Cerrado* was printed in red beneath the town of Redención. Closed. She wondered how much schooling Pilar and Valentin had had before coming to the United States.

As Sienna clicked a link, hoping she could find out how long the school in Redención had been shut down, Deedee strolled into the Newcomer Center, smilingly. She sank into the chair next to Sienna that students used during editorial conferences. The painting of the shaman still hung on the far wall and he seemed to be shaking his rattle right over Deedee's head.

"I'm sorry to have to tell you this," she said. "The school board doesn't support having a Newcomer Center after all."

Sienna's heart sped up and her legs tensed as if preparing to bolt. The loading icon on her black computer screen continued to spin.

Deedee continued, waving her hand toward the empty book shelves. "You really don't need all this room."

"I know I don't need all this room." Sienna said evenly. Her heart continued to race. It was hard for her to speak without sounding as if she were running.

"Don't you worry," Deedee said. "I'm not moving you back to the portable, at least not yet. I can't. It's already full. Can you believe it? As soon as you moved out, people started dumping all their friggering old curriculum in there."

Sienna gasped for air.

"I know. Crazy, isn't it? Well that's not your concern. Back to what is. Apparently we are going to move in another direction altogether. We won't be having ELL anymore. You won't be taking kids out of their classrooms any longer. You can go in there and help them do whatever the teacher wants you to do with them."

Sienna wanted to suggest that would be fine if whatever was

happening in the classroom was more like what was happening in ELL, but Deedee did not give her the chance.

"That is to say, you will help them with *Reading Fare*. You won't really need your own teaching space at all anymore. So, for now, I'm going to have you move into the library with Jolie. We'll put a partition up and you can test and tutor kids behind it."

Sienna pressed against the base of her sternum with her fingertips. Her diaphragm felt like a vise. She tried rolling her shoulders back. The spasm continued.

"Don't you get along with Jolie?" Deedee asked and smiled, delighted with herself at being able to read Sienna's body language. She'd had such a break-though over Thanksgiving!

"I like Jolie."

"That's interesting." Deedee said doubtfully. "I bet you didn't know that Jolie came to me with a long list of complaints about the way you left things in the library."

"What?" Sienna asked. Moore had had a series of part-time librarians for the past few years. "How is that possible? I haven't worked in there for a long time."

"Well, don't worry." Deedee said. "Mimi will be in there with the two of you, at least part-time, so if you and Jolie have any problems she can help smooth things over."

"I don't understand what you are getting at," Sienna said. A wave of adrenaline washed through her. "Jolie and I are friends. Who is Mimi?"

"You met her yesterday! She's our brilliant new reading coach."

"Can I keep seeing my pull-out groups for the rest of this year?"

"I guess so."

"The kids need small groups because the classrooms are too crowded for me to let the ones who need to talk the most, talk. We're always being hushed. And when they're having lessons in the classroom, they get overwhelmed, intimidated, or interrupted by the native speakers' very legitimate needs to go faster than they can."

Deedee shrugged.

Sienna felt another, stronger burst of anxiety. Deedee didn't seem to get what she was saying. "It's crucial to be able to speak and to be listened to while learning a new language. The acoustics in the old cafeteria are atrocious."

"You mean the library." Deedee nodded her head up and down, signaling Sienna to accept the new reality.

"Can't I just have my groups in here until next year?"

"Nope." Deedee shook her head vehemently. "I know this is difficult, but you need to move in with Jolie before winter break."

"We just moved!" Sienna looked over Deedee's head and met the shaman's gaze. It dawned on her that if she were moving in with Jolie she could and would take him with her. She had quite the collection now, what with the *Maritza*, the Swami, *La Mujer de Tierra*, Lupe's drawing Meet Me at the Swap Meet and the shaman. Somehow it comforted her to know they could go wherever she went, but now irritation seeped into her anxiety.

She didn't want to repack, move, and set-up her stuff again. Andy was coming to spend Christmas with her. All she wanted to do in her spare time was daydream about spending time.

She drew a deep breath and, trying not to sound argumentative, asked, "What's this space going to be used for now?"

"Special Day!"

Sienna hadn't expected that. "This whole space is going to be used for five kids?"

"Six." Deedee grimaced. Confident that Sienna had accepted her orders, she explained. "Here's the real deal. They need a private bathroom where the kids in diapers, or whatever they wear, can be changed. As it is now, they have to use the regular kids' bathroom and the stalls are too narrow for all the wiping and such. Normal students keep walking in on them. Pee-Yoo! It's embarrassing all around. Some parents are making a stink. Pardon the pun." Deedee laughed appreciatively at her little joke. "Seriously, this is actually a major legal issue. If we dedicate this space for the Special Day kids and they are the only ones to use the bathroom, then they have the privacy they need. Problem solved. Plus, you know those kids are too loud. They throw chairs and cuss like sailors. We can't have that going on in the main hallway. Parent volunteers and community members go through there all the time."

Sienna gestured around the space that could easily accommodate seventy students and seven thousand books and would now be used for six kids, one teacher and two aides. "Wouldn't it be more practical to build a bathroom in their classroom so more people could use this space?"

"Then, we'd have to deal with codes and permits and contracts. The money for that sort of thing comes from a different fund." Deedee help up her hand, like a traffic cop. "No more discussion. Yes, your Newcomer idea was a good one, but we don't want to get sued by Special Ed parents."

"What about Lau v. Nichols?"

"The Chinese kid again?" Deedee scowled. "If he's still acting up, go ahead and send him to the office. I'll take care of him."

As the door shut behind Deedee, Sienna's computer finally loaded a State Department report on Clemencia.

Americans were advised to avoid the province due to drug wars, frequent kidnappings, torture, and violence, even and especially against women and children. She didn't want to think of Pilar and Valentin living in a place like that. It upset Sienna to imagine Esteban there. He was the same age as her own son. She knew something terrible had happened. The children from Clemencia were obviously traumatized.

Sienna stood up. "It's time for us to move again," she told *La Mujer de Tierra*. Something, beyond just wasting precious instructional time packing, unpacking, improvising, and adjusting to a new space disturbed Sienna. The casual disregard of the bond she could create with the children in a small group and the careless relocation of their special space bothered her.

Curiously, she pulled the *Reading Fare* Assessment book from the shelf beneath *La Mujer de Tierra* and flipped through it until she found the exam for the unit in which the prefix *re* as a meaningful unit of speech was covered. The test question for that particular word was, ironically enough, *Which word means move again*? She checked the answer key and found that, according to Pica, the correct answer was *remove*."

Should she teach that with fidelity? Should she teach the

students to say and write things like, "We have to *remove*. We have *remove* ourselves? They want us *removed*?"

Trying not to think about how removing *The Writers' Lair* felt in her gut, she returned to searching the Internet for pictures of Redención, but all she found was an image from a private art collection that was currently on display at the Museum of International Folk Art in Santa Fe, New Mexico. It was a mermaid fashioned from clay. The caption read, "Made from Clemencian clay."

"Hmm," she said to *La Maritza* and La *Mujer de Tierra*. "You've both got something in common with her." As Sienna turned back to her computer, the Swami materialized in the top edge of her computer screen as if he were the image of a colleague who'd sent her an email. He spoke sonorously, "Dive deep." With that, he was gone and in his place was the screensaver Andy had sent her from Washington, D.C. It was a picture of the statue outside the highest court of the land. The Contemplation of Justice seemed, just for a moment, to raise her eyebrow as if asking Sienna a question and expecting an answer.

***

Sienna needed to splash cold water on her face. She knew how to slow, what some would call, the muse down, how to stem the tide until four o'clock when she could go home and let the erupting poem flow. But Nancy blocked the faucet in the staff restroom.

"I keep forgetting to trim this," Nancy confided when she caught Sienna's reflection in the bathroom mirror. Nancy used her pinky finger to press an unruly, fast-growing hair back up into her nasal cavity. And then, as if allowing Sienna to witness her personal grooming allowed her access to Sienna's sex life, she asked. "How's Dr. Doll these days? Still dreamy?"

Sienna had an instant vision of Nancy in the staff lounge urging everyone to help themselves to a plate full of Butterscotch Blondies and all of Sienna's secret indulgences. She frowned.

"Oh!" Nancy clucked, pulling her finger out of her nose. "Not so good? Huh? Honeymoon period's already over? And you didn't even get married! Long distance relationships are hard to hold onto, especially since they are mostly delusional."

Sienna had just had a meeting with Deedee and talked to *La Maritza* and *La Mujer de Tierra*. The Swami had talked to her and now Contemplation of Justice seemed to want something. It just wasn't a good time for her to be called delusional. "I'm not going to tell you about my lover!" she snapped. "Not when the only passion in *your* life seems to be forcing me into fidelity to a sadistic curriculum."

Nancy's eyes widened and the hair, or a completely different one, popped right back out of her nose. "We have to do what's best for kids."

"Yeah?"

"Yeah!"

"Then we should be paying attention to all those poor dead little Reading Babies piled up like bones in a mass grave…"

Jolie dashed into the bathroom, slammed into the tension, and bounced back against the inside of the door as it swung shut behind her. Rain drops spackled her face like tears and her hair was wild and windblown. In her hand, she held an adult-sized pair of black-handled scissors—tip up, gleaming like a knife.

"Freeze!" Nancy hollered. Her barked order was as effective as a stun gun. "Don't you know how to walk with scissors?" Nancy bellowed. "Give them to me!"

Jolie relapsed, spinning back in time, to a brick building, to Room 4 in Portland, Oregon—Ms. Smith's class. Obediently, she laid the offending object in Nancy's outstretched hand.

Nancy stuck the tip up her nose and snipped. Then, she turned the scissors upside down, squeezing the point with her palm. "This is the proper way to carry scissors," she said. "I expect my students to carry them like this and I expect all of my colleagues to model doing things correctly, even if you are just a librarian and an ELL teacher." She waved her hand as if to shoo Jolie away from exit. As she left the restroom with the confiscated object, Nancy added, "You may have these back at the end of the day."

In her wake, Jolie's dropped jaw formed a soundless, well-enunciated. "Oh, My God!" Then, she said, "I just heard you're moving in with me!"

"Two derelicts in a pod!" Sienna said, relieved that if she had to share a teaching space, it was with Jolie. Then she remembered the bad news. "Along with Mimi!"

And so it was at twilight on an already dark, stormy evening in the library, Jolie defiantly finished unpacking the 398.1 section—fairy tales and myths. Sienna wrapped the shaman and his patient in an oversized garbage bag to protect them from the elements and waded across campus. A strong wind from the south crackled the black plastic, making her grip the frame more tightly, for fear it would be blown right out of her hands. The same singularly forceful gust jostled the horizontal rain gutter along the outside of the library so that a thin crack formed at the joint where two long sections of the drainage canal met. As rain fell, water began to seep through the schism and cascade, drip by drip, down the brick wall. Nancy left school in a hurry to drive her daughter to flag drill practice. She didn't have time to return the commandeered scissors to the library. She didn't even have time to just leave them in Jolie's mail box in the office.

The three teachers left school at three different times, rushing to their cars through driving rain. Slivers of sleet stung their cheeks. When they each fastened their safety belts inside of their own vehicles, they were as bedraggled as *La Llorona* has ever been in the nightmares of children, the hallucinations of drunks, or the cautionary tales of the grandmothers.

Chapter Nineteen

Sienna entered Ashley Whitfield's first grade with her mind on Andy. He was at her house, recovering from jet lag and his keynote presentation in Sinclair. He'd promised to help her finish moving into the library later in the day. Ashley glanced at Sienna. Clearly, the joy that lightened her step was not welcome in Ashley's classroom. She gestured toward the *Reading Fare* vocabulary words projected on the whiteboard. "Have them put each word in a sentence," she said as if Sienna were a subordinate instead of a highly-qualified, much more experienced colleague.

Dubiously, Sienna scanned the list and gathered some ink-smeared whiteboards and dried-out markers from a bin. Ashley called a small group of strong readers to her table, taking the only adult chair in the room for herself. Sienna's English learners stood in front of the words on the board, literally scratching their heads.

Pobrecitos. "Sit down, kiddos," Sienna said gently, gesturing for them to sink to the floor. "Your friends behind you can't see." Not that being able to see the words would have made a difference for any of them. Even the native speakers, the ones Ashley expected to accomplish the assignment independently, were at a loss, chewing on their pencils or picking the rubber erasers out of them.

"Okay, guys," Sienna said, sinking to her knees and selecting the potentially most meaningful word from the list to write on her small board. "This word is *basketball*." She searched the whiteboard ledge for an orange marker. There wasn't one there so she grabbed a red one instead.

"My cousin has one him house."

"I a team."

"My brother plays it."

Mimi strolled into the classroom with her pen poised over her clipboard.

Sienna thought about how much English this little band of *amigos* could learn and practice by talking and then writing about their personal experiences with basketball, but the assignment was not to write about personal experience. It was not even to write about basketball. It was to write a sentence containing the word *basketball* and then move on to write nine more completely different sentences about nine more completely unrelated things.

Sam didn't get that at all. He began telling a story, "I have a basketball! *Mi hermano y...*"

Feeling heartsick, Sienna stopped him. "Let's just make a complete sentence about basketball."

Although Mimi had pulled a short plastic chair close to Ashley to observe her with a small group, Sienna felt Mimi's gaze upon her. When Sienna looked over at Mimi, Mimi smiled, made a quick note, and turned her attention back to the classroom teacher.

"What else could we say about basketball?" Sienna asked her group.

Sam went on happily. "We do it by the cars. It do this." He pressed his hands together, making a whooshing noise.

"It went flat?" Sienna asked. She couldn't help giving him the word.

He nodded.

She groaned. Drawn in by her sympathy to Sam, Enrique volunteered, "I play béisbol." He waved his hand vaguely toward the door.

Sienna realized he didn't know the words he needed to communicate where. Did he mean on the school grounds, at the house across the street, or two blocks away at the park? In *The Writers' Lair*, she would have given him choices and asked which it was. Instead, in Miss Whitfield's room with great trepidation, she just wrote *I play baseball* on her whiteboard. "This is a good sentence," she said "because it gives us a clue. If someone does not know what a baseball is, this sentence lets them know that a baseball is something a person can play. They could think baseball is a toy or a game, right?" The boys nodded. Enrique beamed proudly.

"The problem is we are supposed to say and write something about a basketball to show we know what a basketball is. We could say *I play basketball*. We could also say *Sam's basketball is flat*."

She wrote the sentences fuming inwardly and quickly explaining that a flat ball has no air in it so it cannot bounce. She knew her words were somewhat meaningless to the boys whose basketball had never gone *whoosh* in the same way Sam meant it. She wondered about teaching *flat*. She could use a piece of paper, a two-dimensional plane. She looked around the room for something round to compare it with.

That's when she saw that the native English speakers at the table beyond her group had copied Sam's *I have a basketball* from her board and, eager to finish their work before recess, had moved on to the other words, independently writing *I have a blue. I have a big.* She glanced at Mimi. Couldn't she see how meaningless this all was? Mimi's expression was masked, clinical, as if now that she'd begun collecting data, human experience, expression, and interaction were forbidden.

Sienna reread the three sentences on her white board. The first time she framed each word between her thumb and finger so the boys could hear her say and see each individual word as separate entities. The second time, she moved her finger fluidly under each letter as she made its sound. The boys watched intently, moving their lips, always a sound or two behind her.

When she was done, Enrique patted her knee and beamed proudly. "You a good reader, Teacher. Nice job!"

"Thank you," she said, thinking. *Oh sweetie, you have no idea how far behind the pacing guide I am now.*

Enrique stood up, stretched his legs, and jutted his chin at her board. "We do a baseball one, now?"

Sienna was thrilled by Enrique's desire, but she could do nothing about it with Mimi monitoring her fidelity to *Reading Fare*. Regretfully, she said, "Baseball isn't on our list."

Completely bewildered, Enrique scanned Sienna's face. "*Pero*, I no like *basketball*."

One of the boys edged backwards, as if by scooting half an inch at a time, he could withdraw from the lesson without her noticing. She tried to explain. "Well, Miss Whitfield wants us to use these words because they are in a story you will read later."

Enrique chuckled. "But, teacher," he said affectionately, "you know I can't read."

And as the words he spoke filled his own ears, Sienna watched his awareness rise. He licked his lips nervously, swallowed hard. "I no English boy," he whispered. Fear flickered in his dark eyes.

Her heart ached for him. "You know what the word basketball looks like now. You can read that. Watch for it in the *Reading Fare* story, okay?"

He sighed raggedly. "I like *béisbol*."

"I know." Sienna felt very sympathetic. Learning to write was hard work. It would be easier and more engaging if he could do that difficult task about something he liked. He was just a little boy—like her own son had once been. Enrique's wrist was so small. She could encircle it with her thumb and the finger she'd used to frame the word basketball. She felt a surge of tenderness. It had been a long time since Matt was that little, and she would never have made him write about basketball if he wanted to write about baseball—not when he was just learning. Damn it! "Okay," she said in a low voice. "Let's just tell the truth here." She wrote. "*Enrique likes baseball,*" and read it to him.

"That's a good one!" He grinned as the bell rang for recess.

Relieved, the students hurried to line up. Once again, Sienna had failed at fidelity to *Reading Fare*.

Mimi caught up with her in the hall. "That was great!" She enthused.

"Do you think so?"

"Of course! I saw you making sentences with this week's

words."

"I don't understand how that's helpful," Sienna said. "I already know how to make sentences. The kids should be doing it."

"You're modeling," Mimi said. "That's exactly how an ELL teacher should support the curriculum. That's explicit instruction."

"Well, it may be explicit instruction," Sienna said, "but their minds aren't on it. The kids would learn faster if I supported them in making sentences with words they know and care about before I expect them to write sentences about words they don't know or care about."

"Forget it," Mimi said firmly. "They need to make sentences with this week's vocabulary words."

"They can't. They don't have enough language so then the teacher ends up doing all the work. What's the value in that?"

"It gives them *exposure* to grade level curriculum."

"The week's words aren't connected to each other in any meaningful way. The kids need to practice generating sentences that are meaningful to them."

"This just sounds like an excuse to do what you want to do, instead of what your job should be." Mimi said.

Sienna was angry. "Okay, just tell me *who* decided that this week's grade level vocabulary words are more important than the hundreds of other words and phrases these kids still don't know, like yard, playground, parking lot, or alley?"

Mimi sighed impatiently. "The curriculum designers picked the words."

"Why can't the children pick them?"

Mimi scribbled furiously on her clipboard and muttered under her breath, "I bet your mother was a hippie."

Sienna couldn't believe Mimi had just said that and Mimi snapped back to the administrative tone so quickly that Sienna could only wonder if she'd imagined the comment. "The *Reading Fare* designers probably had a very good reason for basketball instead of baseball."

"If they did, it should have been because basketball is more phonemically regular than baseball which requires paying attention

163

to the silent e."

"That's probably it," Mimi said.

"But, you realize, in this case, the word a kid wanted was actually more rigorous than the one the curriculum gave him. I could have introduced the silent *e*. Plus, he would have felt like reading and writing are truly relevant to him and he could have learned some vital vocabulary for communicating about his life."

"That sounds well and good, but you can't just go gallivanting off that way. You have to help him learn the material that will be tested at the end of the unit."

"Well, all I can say is that the boys did not learn this week's vocabulary. And I'm afraid that what they are learning is that school assignments don't make any sense. Enrique just realized he is already far short of what his teacher expects him to be and he also learned that there's no time or space for the literacy activity that he really wanted to engage with. He wanted to write and read about baseball."

Mimi checked her watch. "Don't worry about any of that. Stick with the systematic approach. It's just too hard to make sure required learning objectives are met while integrating subject matter with student interest."

"And it's too hard not to."

"I hear you," Mimi interrupted. "You are talking about where teaching becomes an art."

The knot in Sienna's heart loosened slightly. She nodded. "I can do art."

Mimi scoffed, rolling her eyes. "No one is paying you to be an artist. Just trust *Reading Fare*. Support the curriculum. Get the kids through each unit. The trouble with ELL and Special Education and every other supplemental program is that they pull kids away from what's happening in the mainstream classroom. Then, the kids who are floundering the most are being taught different things. If all our energies are focused on the same lessons, the same concepts, and the same skills at the same time, it will be much better for them. You should keep on doing exactly what you did with those first graders today."

Sienna began to protest, but Mimi interrupted her again. This time she smiled sweetly with warmth in her eyes. "First graders are so cute, aren't they? I just love their chubby little cheeks."

Down the hallway from where they stood, Pilar sat at a desk outside Nancy's classroom, holding a pencil in her hand. Her eyes were closed. With the side of one calf resting on her opposite knee, she flexed her bare foot and wiggled her big toe.

Mimi caught the motion in her peripheral vision. "Why isn't that little girl wearing shoes down there? What is she doing?"

"Praying."

Mimi frowned. "That's strange."

"No stranger than expecting her to take a reading test she can't read."

Mimi pulled her cell phone out. "I've got to run now. I'm late for an important meeting!" She smiled brightly and gave a little wave.

There are so many people, so many dramas, so many little stories, *cuentas*, in a school. I decided to follow Mimi for a change. As she strode across campus, bypassing kids jumping rope, she used her clipboard to protect her head from being hammered by stray four square balls sailing through the air. She had no idea that I was hovering just above her.

Chapter Twenty

When she reached her broom closet in the library, Mimi was startled to find a stranger sitting at her desk. His black hair was slightly rumpled and he hadn't shaved that morning. He wore tight black ski pants and a black turtleneck. At first glance, she thought he was a dad all set to pick up a child for an afternoon of skiing, but then she realized she'd seen him before at one of Pica's promotional conferences. He was dressed differently now. Still, he was as handsome leaning back in a folding metal chair as he had been in a three piece suit standing at the podium.

"Ms. Lang?" he asked, rising to his feet. "I'm Jules Holdaway, senior vice President at pica. I know you had an appointment with my sales rep today. Unfortunately, she couldn't make it. She cut herself."

The book club Mimi no longer had time for had just read a very dark novel about a psychotic cutter. "Oh, my God!" she exclaimed.

"It's not that serious," Jules said quickly. "Apparently, slicing a Yule Log and managing a conference call at the same time was just too much multi-tasking at once. I just happened to be visiting some old family friends in the area when I got word that the sales rep couldn't keep her appointment with you. I decided to ski half a day and fill in for her, so here I am."

Mimi extended her hand. "I really appreciate your visit Mr. Holdaway. My questions could have waited until she is better."

"I am glad I came. I've always known that Purewater is an

enthusiastic implementer of *Reading Fare,* but I didn't realize what a fantastic place Purewater Pass is for skiing. Have you been up yet this year?"

"I'm afraid I've had no time to ski." She tried to sound happy and upbeat as she confessed. "I've been absolutely swamped with work."

"I hope you get a little R&R over the holidays."

Mimi flipped through the assortment of clipboards, standing on end in a milk crate crammed under Mavis Penn's desk. She found the one she wanted and handed it to Jules.

"Nice printing." He was clearly impressed.

"I used to teach first grade."

"Sweet!" Jules eyed her closely, grinning at Mimi as if she were a lollipop wrapped in shiny cellophane. I could tell he thought first grade teachers were easy, happy to give out stickers, stars, and candy bars for very simple work. "Hey," he said leaning forward, "I'm starving. Is there anywhere to get some food around here?" He glanced at the clipboard again. "This looks like it will take us an hour or so. I'll focus better if we eat." He arched his brow, cockily. He was so sure that a former first grade teacher would be duly impressed by his willingness to take responsibility for paying attention to her.

"There's always something in the teacher's lounge." Mimi said. She knew for a fact that the snowmen stenciled on Tammy Lewis' decorative tablecloths were buried under an avalanche of Christmas cookies and holiday sweets. If she took Jules in there, they'd be constantly interrupted by exhausted teachers rushing in to pop rum balls in their mouths before hurrying onto another task that had to be finished before the Winter Break began. Mimi was becoming quite aware of how Jules' aftershave mingled with the musk of his early morning exertion. "We won't have any privacy." She imagined going to get some cookies and bringing them back to share in her office.

"How about I take you out to lunch?"

As sleep-deprived as Mimi was from staying up late to make her son finish his reading homework the night before, her body was tingling with attraction. She figured it was because of pheromones. She'd learned about them during her brief stint at medical school.

Jules may have been skiing hard all morning, but he smelled good.

"Can we get any good Mexican in this town?"

Her stomach answered with an embarrassing gurgle. It was lunchtime. Her blood sugar was plummeting. Mimi reminded herself that she wasn't a first grade teacher anymore. She didn't have any students to supervise and she wasn't actually tied to Moore Elementary School. They could just as easily discuss *Reading Fare* in a booth at *Casita Rio* as they could in a moldy closet or up at the district office. Besides, she could pick up a nice flan at *Casita Rio* for the party she and her husband were to attend that evening. It would be a treat to go out to lunch on a school day with a good-looking man. Not many women working in an elementary school got to do that. "There's a great little place just a few blocks away," she said.

"Would you like to walk?" he asked. "Or take my car?"

As Mimi gathered her purse, Andy wheeled an old T.V. cart laden with moving boxes through the library's entrance. The men scanned the other's faces as they crossed paths—as if they thought they knew each other and were trying to recollect how. Neither was in his hometown so it couldn't be that they worked out at the same gym. It couldn't be that they filled up at the same gas station nor could it be that they attended the same little league games to cheer for godsons or nephews. They exchanged polite nods as Jules and Mimi left.

"I know that guy." Andy moved the boxes from the cart onto a long table. "I can't place him. Who was she?"

"Mimi."

"Clipboard Mimi?"

Sienna nodded. They heard the jingle bells before Deedee rattled in.

"Well, well, Andy!" Deedee exclaimed. "It's so wonderful to see you again! Thanks for helping Sienna with this move."

"It's my pleasure," Andy said. "Though two moves in as many months is a bit much in the middle of the school year, don't you think?"

Deedee just grinned at him. After a moment, she asked, "Are you staying in Purewater? At Sienna's house?"

"It's great to see your school," he replied.

Deedee nodded. "I suppose it is a special treat for you to get out of the ivory tower once in a while. It's good for you to get a dose of what those of us in the trenches are really up against."

"Of course it is." Andy said. "It's also helpful for those in the trenches to come up to the tower once in a while to get a broader view."

"Ah, well," Deedee waved her hand dismissively. "No visionary can clean up those walls out there. Did you see all that graffiti? It just makes me sick. We've never had that kind of smut before."

Sienna hadn't seen the graffiti. She just knew and wanted to say it would only get worse if the children weren't allowed to express themselves—through writing, through drawing—in the places where teaching became an art, but she didn't bother. She just thought of Mimi's confident smile and muttered to herself. "You say basketball. I say baseball."

"It's so embarrassing!" Deedee practically wailed. "We have tons of parents coming today to help with holiday parties and whatnot. Captain Swabby had to go to Bonny Deals to buy a new paint brush with petty cash so he could cover it. God only knows how many people saw it before he got back. Chief Goodwin is looking for the culprits. I'd like to find them myself and bang their little heads against the brick they've just defaced. They've got to learn to stop and think about the long-term consequences of their actions."

Sienna stopped unpacking to stare at Deedee, who nodded at her as if they were colluding. Deedee went on sagely, "We need some kid to rat those hoodlums out, to give us a lead, to tell us who's been out there bragging about this on the street. Frankly, I'm a little worried about what will happen around here over the two week break. I've told Captain Swabby to keep his paint brush at the ready." Deedee pantomimed a broad swipe, her action besot with frenetic jingles. "What are you two up to for the holidays? I hope you aren't going to spend your precious time together hashing out school reform?"

"No," Sienna said curtly.

"You can stop worrying about what we're going to do with our

ELL kids because we've got Mimi now." To Andy, Deedee explained, "We are so fortunate to land Mimi Lang. She's such a cutting-edge reading coach. Totally up-to-date on the standards. She's got tons of experience implementing *Reading Fare* in Sinclair. They seem to win the Governor's School of Distinction Award every year."

Andy rubbed his chin as if pondering the news. "How have your teachers reacted to bringing Mimi on board?"

"Oh, we haven't told them yet," Deedee said. "The school board is still tweaking her contract, trying to get it just so. Where is Mimi anyway, Sienna?"

"She just left," Sienna answered. "I didn't ask her where she was going."

With tiny bells tied to their shoe laces, Bao Yang and Lucero Fuentes ran past the open door of the library, arm in arm. Deedee spun toward the sound of their pounding, jingling feet. "Stop!" She screeched, "Walk!"

Watching her run after the little girls with her wrists drawn up to her shoulders and her hands thrown back as if that would help her balance on the spiked heels of her own ringing red pumps, Andy asked, "Do you ever feel like a captive audience in her three-ring circus?"

"Sometimes," Sienna said. She realized she'd wanted him to stand up to Deedee for her—for her expertise, for her ideas, for democratic principles, for her humanity, for her heart.

Andy shifted uneasily, loosened his collar, and swallowed hard. He sighed, torn, clearly wanting to satisfy her unspoken longing. "It's just a job, honey," he said. "It's just a job."

***

At *Casita Rio*, the rich scent of mole wafted from the kitchen into the dining area as Ramon placed a basket of warm tortilla chips and a bowl of fresh salsa between Mimi and Jules. Esteban poured water into their glasses.

"I keep thinking I know that guy at your school," Jules said. "I've seen him before. What's his name?"

Mimi shrugged, smiling apologetically. "I haven't been on the job very long. I don't know all our teachers yet."

Jules dunked a chip in the salsa and bit into it. "Delicious!" he exclaimed. "Now tell me how I can I help you with *Reading Fare*."

"I'm wondering why in some cases the readability of what Pica has labeled ELL material is actually the same or harder than some of its mainstream selections."

Jules knit his brow. "That seems a little strange, doesn't it?"

Mimi nodded.

"I mean, you'd think it would be a little easier, you know, for kids still learning English."

Mimi nodded again. "I've got an ELL teacher who won't use *Reading Fare* and she's setting a really bad example for the rest of the staff."

"Well," Jules chewed thoughtfully. "I don't have an answer for you about that. I can assure you that we've hired experts in the field to help design this program. I'm positive there's a very good explanation for this and I'm sure they thought that through. I'm sorry it's not patently clear to your staff. Or to you. You know," he brightened, looking relieved, "we are hosting a big meeting in April for researchers, our curriculum designers, and assessment developers. And, of course, we always keep a few select slots open for administrators who are adopting the program. You should come." He nodded enthusiastically. "Oh!" He broke off, seemingly racking his brain for a vague memory, "Now that I think of it, I heard we were publishing a companion piece to the curriculum—sort of an idiot's guide." He chuckled apologetically. "Not really, of course. At Pica, we think teachers are actually quite intelligent." He whipped out his cell phone and began scrolling through old email. "Here's the memo. Apparently, we're calling it *Tollbooth to the Teacher's Manual*. He scowled. "I don't really like that title. I can't remember why they picked it."

"Yeah," Mimi said. "It sounds like you have to pay your fare— your Reading Fare—at a tollbooth. It's kind of muddled."

"It does seem a little discouraging." He frowned slightly, holding his phone at an angle to see it better, still reading the memo.

"It's supposed to be more like the *Cliff Notes*. Anyway, you should come to our conference."

"Maybe I should send a teacher instead."

"I don't know about that. Don't teachers just want to focus on their own classrooms? They don't really need to or want to understand how a whole program fits together, do they?"

"The ELL teacher I'm thinking about teaches kindergarten through fifth grade. She really does have a multi-year perspective. Where will the conference be?"

Ramon set *El Bandido* in front of Jules. Jules nodded approvingly, without saying a word to Ramon. Instead he told Mimi, "Santa Fe, New Mexico. Nice place to go in the spring."

Mimi gestured for him to start eating without waiting for her meal to arrive. "I went to Santa Fe once with my dad. He inherited an O'Keefe that he loaned to a museum there and he took me to see it on display. I was astonished that a desert could be so chilly." She'd always remembered the hot chocolate her father bought her after the exhibition. She'd been surprised and delighted by the little bit of chili pepper she'd tasted in it. She was remembering that special moment when she realized Jules was watching her closely. A little flustered, she asked, "How much would it cost to send a teacher?"

His eyes fell on the oversized diamond glittering atop her wedding ring. "How did someone like you end up in a place like Purewater?" He took a mouthful of *El Bandido* and his eyes widened with pleasure.

"I want to make a real difference," she said. "Purewater School District is willing and eager to improve and poised to make some great changes with...."

"The best curriculum," he said, chewing hungrily. "And the right leadership."

"I think so."

He swallowed. "So what fool stuck you in a broom closet?"

For a moment, Mimi was taken aback and then embarrassed. "The principal. She felt bad about it. The school is crowded. She's completely out of room. It's not ideal, but I don't want to complain. Poor woman! Her test scores are in the dumps. She's really stressed out."

"Educators make a lot of sacrifices."

Mimi scanned his eyes, searching for the condescension she often experienced and had come to expect from her dad and his associates who thought that because educators were willing to sacrifice luxuries and sometimes even a few of the simpler pleasures of life to eke out a modest living, they deserved to have less. She didn't see that pitying superiority. All she saw, in that moment, was his interest in her reality. Sitting with Jules, Mimi realized how overwhelmed she'd become in just the past few weeks, racing from school to school, meeting with school board members and administrators. They treated her like the Messiah and she was feeling a lot of pressure to save them from their fear of failing test scores. "Deedee was really sweet. She got me flowers!"

"I noticed them. I thought they might have been from your husband."

No, not from her husband. Mimi shook her head. He would have used the money for a sixty dollar bouquet to cover the monthly water bill. She looked down at her hands. Ever since she started commuting to Purewater, her fingernails and her moods at home had been as uneven and as ragged as her workdays. She was ashamed about how often she'd unloaded her stress by nitpicking at her family. There was no reason for her husband to want to send a bouquet or do anything else nice for her. Of course, Jules didn't know that. He didn't seem to notice how overdue for a manicure she was. He didn't seem to notice the zit, erupting on her chin. In fact, he seemed to be a man making an effort to conduct business while resisting an intense attraction to his client.

"Well, if you have to work there," Jules sounded resigned to an unpleasant fact, "the least she can do is keep a steady stream of flowers coming."

Mimi was intrigued. After all, she reminded herself, there is such little flirtation to be had in the field of elementary education. Hadn't she been the one to seize on what there was available, marrying the only male teacher at Sinclair Elementary twelve years earlier? And hadn't they started their romance in this very way, over a table, over a page full of questions about curriculum? Back then, they'd both been wearing jeans, sneakers, and matching sweatshirts with school mascots screen-printed on the front of them. Her husband had been wearing that exact same shirt that morning. Over the years, he'd accumulated a few dry erase slashes at the cuff and coffee stains on the sleeve, but he didn't want a new one. His sixth graders didn't care what he wore. Now, Mimi wore suits that cost more than she'd spent on her whole wardrobe during her first year of teaching,

Jules was still talking. "Let me know if they don't."

"Don't what?"

"Send more flowers."

Mimi hadn't shaved her legs properly in days and her kitchen sink was full of dishes. His attention was enough to make her blush. "One of our first grade teachers doesn't even have a desk. I really don't need more flowers."

"Yes, you do. It takes a ton of passion to bring about a turnaround. That's worth at least a few dozen roses."

"A few dozen?"

"At the very least."

"So," she said flirtatiously, "shall I send you an email if they don't keep up with the quota?"

"Absolutely," he said. "Just type WILTED in the subject line."

"Wow!" Mimi giggled. "You corporate types live large. I suppose you have a desk too?"

"Two or three of them," he said, scanning her face. "And a florist on retainer." He took another bite of *El Bandido*. "Look," he said when he swallowed, "I can tell by your questions that you're the real deal."

Mimi nodded. He was right. She was the real deal. *Summa cum laude* smart and her heart was in the right place. She really wanted the system to work for the kids *and* for the teachers.

"And, you know, it might be good for your mission if you do come to Santa Fe. Did you know that Pica is one of three finalists for the contract to write the NASTE?"

With that, Mimi felt a surge of excitement. So she had been right to commit herself to *Reading Fare*! If Pica got to write the NASTE, any student who had *Reading Fare* would score well on the national test. With her commitment to the curriculum she was truly poised to lead Purewater School District in the race to the top, to first place in the future.

"So come," Jules said. "Come meet the real movers and shakers. Forget about sending your ELL teacher. Come on your own. I've booked a block of rooms at a top notch hotel there and I'd be happy to take you back to the O'Keefe. Plus, there's a place nearby with some of the best Mexican hot cocoa I've ever had."

He leaned back in his seat as if giving her some space to consider, but before she could reply, he leaned in again. "Hey! I've got another great idea! Maybe as a successful implementer of *Reading Fare* you could speak at a NASTE retreat I'm planning in Southern California next year—if we get the contract, that is. I'm putting a series of retreats together. I'm calling it *On the Road for Reading.* Catchy, isn't it?"

"Yeah! It is." Mimi decided she wouldn't send Sienna. Fantasizing about two sun-soaked getaways, she didn't even notice Ramon at her side.

"Careful," he said, producing a plate of simmering mole. "Hot dish."

Chapter Twenty-One

Nancy stopped in the library, a sandwich in one hand and blackline masters to copy in the other. She smiled warmly at Sienna as if forgiving her psychotic outburst in the bathroom the other day. "Can you help a kid with writing this afternoon?"

"Who?" Sienna felt uneasy, as if this were a trap, as if Nancy would send an email of complaint to Deedee as soon as she agreed.

"Maria Guzman. She needs a lot of help. Why doesn't she go to ELL?"

Normally, Nancy acted as if ELL was a waste of everyone's time. "Maria passed the WELT at the end of second grade. Technically, she no long qualifies for service."

"How could she have passed?" Nancy asked. "She's stuck at a first grade level in everything."

"She might have had a few lucky guesses."

"I'm really worried about her. Mrs. Geiger spends a lot of time with her and she's still not making any progress."

Sienna had often noticed Mrs. Geiger, a teacher's aide, sitting by Maria. Some EL's hated needing extra help, so they lied about understanding material they didn't really comprehend. But some, like Maria, become addicted to having a personal assistant who, if they were lucky, ultimately fed them the answers in the final minutes leading up to recess. Mrs. Geiger often did that less out of sympathy for Maria and more out of fear that Nancy might report her as falling

176

short of her duties if Maria didn't finish her papers on time. Sienna was certain that even though she didn't technically qualify for ELL, Maria had become a supplemental support junkie.

Nancy scowled. "I'm thinking about referring her to Special Ed. She might even need Special Day! She thinks a paragraph is a hamburger!"

With that bit of information, Sienna made an instant diagnosis. "Have her come down at 2:45 this afternoon and I'll see what I can do."

"No! Wait!" Nancy frowned, "I don't want her to miss social studies. Can't you just come in and teach her how to write while I go on with the lesson?"

"She needs to focus on one thing at a time. What do you want her to write about?"

"Captain Cook."

"Captain Cook?" Sienna racked her memory for what she knew about him as a historical figure. "Hmm," she said cautiously, "an eighteenth century British explorer might be a little abstract for Maria."

Flustered, Nancy snapped, "It's part of *Reading Fare*. She has to write a summary of the selection about his life."

Sienna felt a flash of outrage. Who in their right mind would expect a struggling student to produce a written summary of a selection about a distant stranger that she couldn't even read? "Does it discuss his death?" She asked curiously.

Nancy narrowed her eyes.

Sienna went on, bitterness tinged her voice. "Does it describe how he was murdered by Hawaiians?"

Nancy's nostrils flared.

"Did you know that he and his men traded nails with the native men for sex with their wives?"

Nancy took a step back.

"Of course, the natives might have thought it was an honor when they thought Cook was a god, but once they realized he was just a man…"

"That's not in the curriculum!" Nancy snorted. "Will you please just help the kid write a decent paragraph?"

Sienna shrugged. "Of course, I'll help her. Don't you wonder how those women must have felt whenever they saw a nail afterwards? Like in a door frame?"

"I'm worried about you," Nancy said. "I mean really. Why would you even want to think about these things? Maybe, you should tap into our mental health benefits while we still have them."

Later when Maria came to the library, she explained, "I have to do something about a baker on a ship a long time ago."

"Do you mean, Captain Cook?" Sienna asked.

Jolie looked up from where she stood behind the library counter, covering second-hand books with protective plastic film.

"Yeah," Maria shook her head sadly. "Travis, in my class, he tell me Captain Cook die on Valentine's Day. In Hawaii." She clearly thought it was very tragic for him to pass over without getting to unwrap waxy chocolate in red foil or savor a single sugary conversation heart.

"They didn't have Valentine's Day in Hawaii back then." Sienna smiled reassuringly. "He didn't miss *that* party." Then, she flashed the black line drawing of a hamburger, she knew Maria's third grade teacher had used as a teaching aid. "Can you remember how many sentences a paragraph needs?"

Maria smiled shyly and shook her head. Sienna tapped each section of the hamburger; top bun, patty, lettuce, tomato, bottom bun. She tapped each one a second time, whispering, "One, two."

Maria counted the rest of the layers. "Five?"

"Usually. Good job. Do you remember the job of the sentences that go here?" She pointed to the buns.

"That's for the ketchup." Maria's lack of comprehension made the metaphorical comparison between the ingredients needed to build a sandwich with the functions of each sentence in a paragraph particularly obfuscating.

Jolie stifled a surprised cough and looked at Sienna, clearly curious about how she'd address this.

"Let's not do this," Sienna said quickly, setting the hamburger aside and sliding a box of magnetized photographs toward the girl.

"Your job is to sort these in any way that makes sense to you."

Maria's eyes lit up. Eagerly, she reached for the magnets, enjoying the slapping sound they made against the surface of the table. Quickly, she grouped pictures of people to her right. "These is the family." She put children displaying a variety of emotions in front of her. "And this is ways kids are."

"You mean these are the different ways kids can feel?"

"Yeah." Maria slid pictures of seat belts and bike helmets to her left. "And these are ways of being safe."

"Great," Sienna said. "Now, pick one group so we can write a paragraph about it."

Maria looked astounded. "I don't do that."

"You don't do what?"

"Write."

"I'll help you," Sienna said. She waved her hand over all the magnets. "Which group would you like to work with?"

Like a child extending an arm for a blood draw, Maria pointed to the family.

"Okay. So what can you say about this family?"

"It's a big family."

"That can be your main idea!" Sienna beamed. "If we were using the hamburger, which we're not, that would go in the top bun. We're just going to use plain paper today." Sienna picked up a pencil. "I'll do the writing. You just think about what you want to say about these pictures."

While Sienna worried that scribing for Maria would reinforce the child's over-dependency on school personnel, she also knew that if she didn't do the mechanical aspect of writing for her, Maria would never get *to the thinking*. She'd postpone that by pretending the lead on her pencil was too dull and needed sharpening. She would form letters sloppily and decide to erase them. She'd rub a hole in the paper that would need to be taped up or, maybe even the whole thing would have to be replaced. Then, she'd have to start over. The bell would ring and she'd be off the hook. "Before I write your main idea," Sienna said quickly, "Let's give this family a name. What do you want to name them? You can pick anything."

"Nah!" Maria sounded lazy. Sienna saw that she really lacked the self-confidence to make a suggestion.

"Let's use your last name. It's a great last name." Sienna wrote and then read aloud *The Guzman family is a big family.*" She pointed to the magnets again. "Now tell me everything you notice about these pictures."

Maria furrowed her brow, hesitating.

Sienna waited a full minute and tapped the sentence she'd written with the pencil, "If this is your main idea, you need some supporting details. You need to explain why you said this. How do know it's a big family?"

"There are nine people."

"There are!" Sienna said, writing. *There are nine people in the family.*

Maria smiled weakly and slumped. Clearly, she wanted Sienna to notice how exhausting this was.

"Remember," Sienna went on, "we need five or more sentences for a paragraph. We only have two. What else can you say about this family?"

Maria trained her eyes on the photos. The clock ticked loudly. Finally, she said, "There are a lot of men in the family."

"There are?"

"There's a grandpa, a brother, an uncle, a baby, and a father."

"That's good!" Sienna said. "The grandpa came first in the family so I'll put him first in the sentence."

Maria nodded. "And he the boss."

"Maybe. Is there anything else, you can say about the family?"

"No."

Jolie leaned forward to listen to the lesson.

"You mentioned the men." Sienna studied Maria's blank expression intently. "Can you say anything about the women?"

Maria shook her head, frowning.

Sienna said, "You could say there are a lot of women in the family. Then you could say that there is a grandmother and a mother and three little girls. That would be fair and give you two more sentences to support why you said the Guzman family is a large family. Do you want to do that?"

"Nah!" The girl shrugged, completely disinterested.

"Oh come on, Maria!" Jolie suddenly burst out. "Acknowledge fifty-one percent of the population."

"What?" Maria asked, turning around to look at Jolie.

"A little more than half of all the people in the world are girls," Jolie told her.

"So Ms. Fox thinks the girls should get at least half of the space in your paragraph," Sienna explained. "Listen to what we have." She read.

The Guzman family is a large family.
There are nine people in the family.
There are a lot of men in the family.
There is a grandfather, a father, a brother, a baby, and an uncle.

Sienna laid the pencil down, "Is this really how you want it to be?" She flexed and stretched her fingers. "Does this sound good to you?"

"Yep!" Maria seemed pleased.

"Shall we do another one?"

"No."

"Well, we are going to. I'll let you look at the rest of the magnets for a few minutes and then I'll be back." Sienna walked to the library counter, ostensibly for the economical district-issued tissue that felt like smooth sandpaper on a human nose. She'd have to pick up the better kind at Bonny Deals.

"I hope you realize how hard I'm biting my tongue," Jolie whispered. "So much for gender equity on the page."

"It disturbs me too," Sienna whispered, "but I can't teach English, sentence structure, paragraph formation, *and* raise consciousness in twenty minutes. No matter what I do Nancy is going to complain to Deedee or Mimi."

"What would it cost the kid just to *say* that there are women and girls in the family? For Heaven's Sake, you were doing the manual labor for her."

Mimi bustled into the library heading straight for her broom closet, clutching her clipboard and smelling of *El Bandido*. She

stopped abruptly, taking in what was plainly obvious to her—
teachers standing around, chit-chatting.

How could she go before the school board and vouch for
Moore's fidelity to *Reading Fare* when these women squandered
teaching time? Mimi knew it wasn't up to her to deal with personnel
issues. That was Deedee's department, but as her eyes fell on Maria,
she realized that the epitome of all that was wrong in public
education was playing out right before her eyes. Here was an at-risk
child, pulled out of her class and missing rigorous grade level
instruction to play with magnets while her supplemental teacher
talked to a friend. The girl was one of the children who, if Sienna
would just follow the curriculum and raise the school's test scores,
would surely get Mimi promoted up the ranks, out of the broom
closet, and perhaps to becoming a celebrated presenter at *On the Road
to Reading* where she could really have an impact on the world. As
Mimi surveyed the blatant infidelity to *Reading Fare* she gasped,
clenching the muscles in her jaw. Fury tightened her torso.

Sienna saw Mimi and sensed her rage. She returned to Maria
calmly. Maria pointed to a picture of a miserable boy and to a
grinning girl saying, "They are not the same. They're…uh…opos."

"Opposites? Opposite what?"

"Feelings."

"*Bueno*! So if you were going to write a paragraph about
opposite feelings what would your main idea be?"

"Feelings are opposite," Maria declared.

Sienna beamed. "You've got happy and sad. What's your next
detail?"

Maria seemed to lose her organizing principle as she pondered
the picture of a child sticking her tongue out. Sienna suspected the
girl didn't want to associate with someone as naughty as the child in
the photo. "It's okay, Sienna whispered. She's just being silly.
Chistosa con tus amigas."

The muscles across Sienna's shoulders constricted as Mimi
watched, but she pointed to the picture of a child playing chess.

"What about him? He looks serious. He can be the opposite of
the silly girl."

"No!" Suddenly, Maria pushed two other magnets together.

"Okay," Sienna said, examining Maria's choices. "How are angry and surprised opposites?"

"Well, someone could have a surprise party," Maria said, "and be angry because...."she floundered.

"Because they don't like surprises?"

"Yeah. They only like to know everything."

"So, that sounds like cause and effect to me," Sienna said. "Do you remember cause and effect from *Reading Fare* last week?"

Maria screwed up her lips, shaking her head as if Sienna had asked her if she remembered robbing the bank.

"Your main idea could be one feeling can cause another."

Maria nodded. "A kid could get angry because someone said she was stupid and feel dis...disa... because he got angry."

Sienna sensed a story. "Are you talking about two people? A he and a she? Or just one person? Who was angry? Who was disappointed?"

Through gritted teeth, a fuming Mimi finally spat, "This is not *Reading Fare*." She struggled to contain her impatience. "As I told you earlier today, you have got to accept that no one supports you teaching these kids to write. It's more important for you to focus on reading. From now on, any writing your students do should be directly related to a *Reading Fare* selection—as a response to something the students read."

"She tried that with Captain Cook!" Jolie said. "It doesn't work."

Mimi held up a staying hand toward her, continuing to scold Sienna. "Deedee told me you are a poet. Clearly, you are just making excuses here so you can be creative with students—so you can do whatever you want to with them."

"So that I can do whatever I want to with them?" Sienna repeated. "I am an ELL teacher. I want to help kids learn how use correct pronouns. I want to find out why a girl can't or won't acknowledge the women in her family so I can figure out if this language is too complicated for her or if she has built such a thick wall of cognitive disassociation and denial around gender that she can't even express if it was a *he* or *she* who was angry. I can't scale walls like that with people waving Pica's script at me to follow."

"I am absolutely sure *Reading Fare* covered pronouns," Mimi said.

"In the first week of third grade. Are you telling me that Maria has already missed her window of opportunity to get clear on them?"

"Remember, the only progress that counts is measureable." Mimi said. "If what you say is true about the third grade scope and sequence, pronouns aren't likely to be on her fourth grade test. Since they are not being tested, they are not being measured. You don't have to worry about teaching them right now. She'll pick them up later whenever the curriculum spirals back to them."

"How is she supposed to comprehend anything with pronouns until then?" Sienna asked. "And by the way, it never spirals back to them. It assumes she already knows them."

"Where's your fluency timer, Sienna?" Mimi asked as if she were a student who'd left her jacket out at recess for the tenth time.

"My what?"

"Are you telling me you don't know where it is? I would expect every teacher at a failing school like Moore to have one in her pocket at all time. You should have been timing and documenting how many words this girl can read per minute instead of trying to be so…um…creative with the curriculum."

Later that day, Sienna gave each of the students in *The Writers' Lair* a series of fluency tests. Each child read three different passages for one minute each. She didn't get to teach them English through writing. Instead, she used half of an hour to re-discover and document that they all read fewer words aloud per minute than what was expected of fourth graders.

***

That night in her bedroom, Sienna tossed her staff identification badge onto her dresser. It slid, falling between the wall and her bureau. She let it stay there.

"Sienna," Andy said soothingly. "You've done your job. You've advocated for the children and informed your supervisors of the problems with the tools they are requiring you to use. If they choose to ignore you and all the research that supports what you are trying to do with kids, that's their prerogative. It's out of your hands. You've done exactly what a good employee should do."

Sienna was exasperated. "But…"

"You're preaching to the choir, Baby." He wrapped his arms around her, pulling her close. She was angry and tense, ready to hop right out of the embrace.

"I don't want to squander our precious time together over this," she said, "but it's all so wrong."

"I know," he said softly. He pressed his lips into her hair and inhaled. "It's the system. You have to wait for the third part of *Castaneda* to kick in."

Sienna felt betrayed that he wouldn't get angry with her now. She'd seen him as equally impassioned about issues. Obviously all he wanted to do now was make love. "That's bullshit!" she cried, pulling away. Her eyes flashed.

"Come to Vandya," he coaxed, "next September when Matt goes to college. Just bide your time for another year. Don't rock the boat."

"This is ridiculous!" she cried. "I'm an excellent teacher and I've raised my son in this town. This is my home. Why do I have to move away just to do my best at my job?"

"I'm sorry." Andy took a step back. Sienna saw the hurt in his eyes and softened a little, wiggling back into his embrace.

With his arms around her, he said, "I want you to be able to do the work you love and be with me at the same time. It seems more likely that that can happen at Vandya."

Sienna sighed deeply, struggling to release her worries about work to focus on him. She let her hands slide down, pushing them into the back pockets of his jeans. Pulling his hips toward hers, she kissed him fully, pushing her tongue into his mouth, tasting Café Rio's *pico de gallo* and *cerveza* on his inner lip. "You are a very tempting man," she whispered, relaxing in the warmth of his pelvis. "And that's a very tempting offer. However, I honestly can't believe *you* just told *me* not to rock the boat."

"I want you to be free. Until then, I want you to be safe."

"I appreciate that," she kissed him softly. "But really? Don't rock the boat? That's so cliché, Andy. Surely you can come up with something better than that?"

His hands slid up beneath the hem of her sweater. "I'm not interested in linguistic prowess right now, Sienna." One hand traced the curve of her breast, the other moving to her waistband. "And, yes," he added, moving to unzip her jeans, "I can come up with something better." He knelt, using his tongue to trace a line from her bare belly button to the bikini waistband of her silky panties. Pulling the fabric down, he kissed the tops of her thighs. With one last insistent tug, denim and black lace crumbled around her ankles. She stepped out and he pushed the clothing aside with his foot.

Sienna shimmied out from beneath her sweater and let it fall to the ground as well. She lifted and pulled to hurry him out of his clothes, hungry to feel his flesh against hers. His evening stubble chafed the tender skin on her chin when they embraced for another long, hard kiss. As he pushed his tongue between her welcoming lips, he reached behind her back, unhooking her lacy black bra.

And when she listed onto the quilt, he sank with her. Everything institutional was easily forgotten in the inspirational grammar of sex. In the spectral whiteness of a fallen sheet, the primal beat of a headboard against the wall, and the echo of guttural utterances, she let go of the need to teach pronouns. She did not have to ensure that *he* and *she* are subjects with meaningful antecedents. There was no need to be concerned about direct objects like *him*, like *her* receiving the action of a noun. The possessive nature of *his* or of *hers* was clearly understood. Dr. Dahlstrom was just about to prove his non-verbal prowess for the third time when he was—when they were—interrupted by a startlingly insistent beeping sound.

"What's that?" he asked breathlessly, his body becoming still.

Cradled between his forearms, still undulating in the combined heat of their bodies, Sienna cringed. Weakly, she gestured toward the crumpled pile of clothing on the ground. "It's my fluency timer," she groaned. "I must have left it in my pocket."

"Oh my God!" Andy swore softly as the unrelenting sound

continued. "That was one hell of a minute."

Sienna laughed. "Honey, that was a lot longer than a minute. There's no telling what buttons got pushed when we started."

Andy slipped off of her.

She rolled to her side, reaching to the floor to dig the timer out of her pocket and shut it off. Andy's strong, still taut arms pulled her to him. In a side-lying embrace, they rested, legs entwined. "That damn timer is definitely a way to kill the love," he sighed—a long ragged sigh. "I guess we don't get to finish that last one."

"Don't worry, sweetie," she said soothingly. "Even the best ones rarely do." As the light layer of sweat on her bare skin dried, cooling her down, she snuggled even closer. "Anyway, we only count your middle score. And that one was way, way off the charts."

Chapter Twenty-Two

The next morning, *Gringo* lingered beside Sienna watching kids scramble down from the buses. Some wore furry red, white-trimmed Santa hats. Several staggered under weighty platters of cookies and various *postres* covered with aluminum foil. A few of them carried small wrapped boxes or beribboned bags for their teachers. Bao Yang and Lucero Fuentes shyly presented Sienna with gifts. Bao gave her a red rose, the rims of each petal blackened by frost. Lucero presented her with a box of candy from the Mexican grocery store and a prayer card commemorating the Mexican Holy Day of Obligation to celebrate the apparitions of Our Lady of Guadalupe.

Sienna examined the prayer card carefully. The downturned face of *La Madre de Dios* was framed by a midnight blue mantle strewn with stars. It was as if she had risen straight out the earth and the night sky had received her, like a mother crowns a toddler rising from the tub with a hooded towel. And like steam emanating from a child's body, a golden aura radiated around her. The story of her 1531 appearances to a peasant was printed on the back of the card and stamped with the slogan, "Protect the Unborn."

Sienna thanked the little girls for her gifts. As they skipped to the cafeteria, Sienna returned her attention to *Gringo*. She noticed the backpack at his feet was so full of overdue library books he couldn't zip it shut.

He peered up at her. "How you know what school you work at?"

"I know which school I work at because I can read the sign out front."

"I don't mean that," *Gringo* said. "I mean that." He pointed across the campus toward the old brick building where the library and ELL were now housed. "There are two addresses on the same place."

He was completely right. When she'd first arrived at Moore, Sienna had asked the administration about the two distinct plaques bearing different numbers over the same front door, but there had been no response.

He chortled. "That's so weird."

"Yeah. It is." Over time, the anomaly had become imperceptible to her. When she'd gotten no response from the administrative building, she'd just started using 2001 First Street, the address on an old publishers' invoice she'd found in a library cabinet. She'd completely forgotten all about the other option, 360 First. As the last bus pulled away and her duty ended, she invited Jonathan to bring his books to the library before school actually started, noting, "That backpack is too heavy to lug around until Mrs. Albright brings you to the library."

Clutching the prayer card protectively and careful to match *Gringo's* shorter pace, Sienna wondered how a public institution could have persisted in having two addresses over the same front door for so long. It really seemed like a problem for emergency personnel. Good thing Mavis hadn't had her heart attack at school in the library. What if Baldwin hadn't escaped down the river when he robbed the bank? What if he had run their way, panicked, and entered the school? What if there had been a real lockdown? Which address would the police dispatcher have been given? As for more mundane matters, having two addresses seemed like a problem for substitute teachers and UPS drivers. And then, because he was still at her house, at that very moment, Sienna had an image of Andy, younger, more buff, in a UPS uniform and then she thought of him, older and naked with a bottle of Andalusian wine in his hand. Quickly, with a smile tugging on the corners of her mouth, she banished that sexy phantom from her imagination.

The central office could ignore her request for clarity. *Gringo* wasn't about to be put off. "What if Santa Claus wanted to find you? How is he supposed to know which one is your address? Mrs. Albright says if kids don't know their address and parents' phone numbers by the time we come back from Christmas break, we have to stay in at recess and practice them. She says it's *vital*."

"She's right! Vital is a great word!"

Gringo scoffed. "That's the name of my Mom's shampoo."

"Oh! That's because the people who invented your mom's shampoo thought it was a great word, too. It really means lively, alive. It also means super important. That's how Mrs. Albright is using it. It is vital to know your address."

"Why?"

"So if you needed help, the ambulance or fire fighters can find you. And if you get lost when you aren't at home, the police can help you find your way back." She smiled at him. "Do you know your address?"

"932 WGM"

Sienna furrowed her brow. The Side Street Apartment complex units where she thought he lived weren't numbered that way. "Did you move?"

"Yep," *Gringo* nodded. "Into the car." He grinned proudly, "Wanna know how I learned our address?"

She nodded, feeling heartsick.

"932. I'm nine and my mom is thirty-two. W is we. G is gotta. M is move. We gotta move. I say it like this. We gotta mooooo, 'cause moo rhymes with two. 932 we gotta moo. But, we aren't really cows. Actually, I think Mrs. Albright should make kids learn their license plates too, in case they have to downsize." He struggled to keep from dragging his backpack on the ground. "Mom says the good thing about a down size is it helps kids find all their overdue library books."

"Yep," Sienna said. "And you can build up your muscles by bringing them back. You are being a very responsible library patron." She beamed at him, wishing again that they still had a school counselor to see what support was available for this little guy and his mom. Where would they use his mom's Vital shampoo? It was wintertime now. Their car must be freezing. "When did you move into the car?"

"Day after Halloween," he said.

"The day after Halloween! Mrs. Albright knows, right?"

"Nah!"

"She doesn't? Are you sure she doesn't?"

"Yeah. We made Christmas wreaths yesterday and she told me to give mine to my mom to hang on the front door of our house. So, that's how I can tell she thinks I still have one."

Sienna bit her lip. It would be easy for a frantically busy teacher to slip up that way, to forget, in the hustle of trying to squeeze a holiday art project into a jam-packed academic program, but Nancy didn't know. She really didn't know. If the students were given a chance to share what was happening in their lives and express themselves instead of being forced to write to the curriculum's fatally stilted and dull prompts, it sure wouldn't have taken a month and a half for someone at school to find out that this little boy was homeless. She remembered Mimi's directive from the previous day. Any writing you do should be directly related to a Reading Fare selection."

"So where have all these library books been since you moved into the car? The trunk?"

"Nope. That's where we keep the food. I was keeping these books in a locker at a gym. Our free trial is up so I have to bring them back."

Sienna imagined all the books shoved in the steamy locker room of a local gym.

"So what school do you live in?" *Gringo* asked. "2001 or 360?"

Live in? When their conversation began, he'd asked her which one she worked in. Very young children often think their teachers live at school, but Jonathan was old enough to know better. Maybe he's regressing, Sienna thought. Sometimes when children live through a traumatic event, like losing their home and moving into a car, they can block big chunks of information and experience from their memories. She had a feeling that Pilar and Valentin had done that. Sienna didn't have the heart to remind Jonathan that she had a house to live in and that she only worked at school.

"So which one is your address Ms. O'Mara?"

"360 First Street," she said. And suddenly, despite her concern for him, it was fun pretending she operated in a completely different dimension from the rest of Moore. "My address is *The Writers' Lair*."

After Johnathan turned his books in and went to class, Sienna read the prayer card Lucero had given her again more carefully. In 1531, Juan Diego was passing Tepeyac Hill in Mexico. He saw the Blessed Virgin Mary standing there bathed in mysterious light. She spoke to him in his indigenous language, telling him that she wanted a shrine built on that very spot so she could demonstrate her love and compassion for her people and offer them protection. For a native Indian to build on land colonized by Spain and the Catholic Church, Juan Diego needed permission from the Bishop in Mexico City. Bishop Zumarraga refused the request to build the shrine the first time Juan Diego asked, so Juan Diego returned to where he met the Holy Mother and told her of this rejection. She bade him try again. That time, the bishop asked for a sign so when Juan Diego next encountered the Blessed Virgin she told him where to find flowers to take to Zumarraga. Juan Diego wrapped the offering in his rough *tilma*, the poor peasant's cloak, and carried his bundle back into the city. When Juan Diego opened his cloak, beautiful red roses—miraculously blooming in the middle of the winter—rained down upon the bishop's feet. Additionally, to the men's amazement, there was also an exquisitely colored portrait of the Blessed Virgin standing on a snake on the inside of the cloak, crushing it. According to the card, "despite the more than twenty-two languages and almost fifty dialects spoken at that time, all were able to read and understand the symbolism contained in the sacred image. So it was in this manner that millions of natives were almost instantly converted to Roman Catholic Christianity."

Our Lady of Guadalupe's shrine was constructed right where the Spanish conquistadors had leveled an ancient temple dedicated to Tonantzin—to Mother Earth, to the Goddess of Sustenance, to the Honored Grandmother, to the Snake, the Bringer of Maize. As Sienna read, she had the sensation of wearing the serape Gaul had encouraged her to try on. It had been made from the same fiber as Juan Diego's and colored by crushing the feminine.

Deedee interrupted Sienna's thoughts, rushing in wild-eyed. "There's a huge line of parents dropping home baked treats off in the office! I need you to come over and tell them to take it all back! I don't understand what's happening. I sent notices home days ago to remind people that all party treats have to be store-bought. Can't they read? Jesus! I've got cookies and cakes and brownies coming out the ying-yang." She stopped for a moment to catch her breath. "And Brenda and Dr. Fray are dropping by any minute. Oh my God! It's a *board policy* NOT to have homemade treats in the building!"

"Apparently, it's also a board policy NOT to send notices home in Spanish," Sienna said, calmly placing the prayer card beside Bao's rose at the feet of *La Mujer de Tierra*.

"Just fix it!" Deedee screamed. Her body trembled. Her pupils dilated. And then as if she couldn't take another second of being in the light, she rushed into Mimi's dark, dank office and slammed the door behind her.

Mrs. Fuentes, the mother of Cassandra and Lucero, was in the main office. From what Sienna could gather from her, all the mothers who lived in the South Side apartment complex were under the impression that some store-bought cookies had been poisoned and that Mrs. Hayes had written to ask them to help protect *todos de los niños* by doing all the baking for the class parties. As Sienna faced the loving, protective mothers, who'd likely overspent their grocery budgets to buy sugar and margarine, she didn't have the heart to explain that the school board feared that theirs were the tainted offerings.

Mrs. Donahue looked up from the daily attendance report, carefully keeping her face neutral. Deadpan, she told Sienna, "Angela Hadley is here. She's in the copy room."

Sienna understood the unspoken suggestion. *"Un momento, por favor!"* She excused herself from the throng of moms as she rushed to consult with Travis Hadley's mom—the school board president's daughter-in-law, who according to her niece Laurali, took a lot of grief for not sending her son to the "better" school on Teagan Hill. Angela was quite willing to blame all the trouble on Brenda. Drawing on her own sketchy Spanish, she sent the parents and their platters home, explaining that Brenda Hadley did not trust them. As the parade of cupcakes wound its way across the back field to the apartment complex, Angela called her husband's Aunt Rebecca and Rebecca began to design the campaign signs for her next bid as the school board president. She spent the afternoon gleefully photoshopping a picture of Brenda dressed as Dr. Seuss's *The Grinch who Stole Christmas*.

Maria came back for more tutoring in the morning. She pulled the candy cane out of her mouth to show Sienna where the red stripes were dissolving. "This is all we got," she said. "No party. It's a rip-off. The kids are watching a movie while she puts our scores in the computer. I'm still a zero." Maria handed a sticky worksheet to Sienna. "I was supposed to read the fast facts and write a paragraph." In the top margin, Nancy had written a note. "Today's topic sentence should be: (The subject) had an interesting early life."

Sienna wished the assignment had been *Write about something interesting from your early life*. "What *is* an interesting early life?" she asked Maria.

Maria shrugged. Sienna urged her to read the first fast fact aloud. Thankfully, the girl could read that one fairly well. *John had to leave school at an early age because of his father's stand against slavery.*

"What do you think it means to leave school at an early age?"

"To go like my mom," Maria said. "She only did three years in Mexico, but she wants me to do all the grades."

Sienna remembered the hopeful face of the illiterate woman who'd brought a tray full of warm *churros* to school that morning and how her whole bearing had drooped when Angela turned her away. Maria, that hopeful woman's child was clearly so far behind the moving target of rising standards that statistically her chances of graduating from high school were almost nil. "That's a good text-to-life connection," Sienna said. "So, your mom and the man we are reading about both left school when they were very young. Now, do you know what slavery is?" Maria did not.

Sienna tried tapping into what early classroom teachers often covered in social studies. Harriet Tubman? The Underground Railroad? Either Maria hadn't heard of them or she couldn't remember what any of those words meant. Did she remember her own family's journey to America? Had it been anything like the Underground Railroad? Or had they simply boarded an airplane?

Despite Maria's ability to word-call the first sentence of the paragraph, it soon became clear that she did not comprehend it. She thought John had to stop going to school at an early age because his father was literally standing in the doorway, blocking his path so he couldn't leave the house. "My mom, she could not go, too. She told me her dad stand like this." The girl crossed her arms over her chest. "He say she have to stay home and help my grandma with the babies."

Sienna skimmed the rest of Maria's reading assignment quickly. It wasn't likely from Maria's background experience or the way the paragraph itself was written that the girl would ever be able to infer that the main character and his family lived in a pro-slavery community and John actually had a strong parental role model *for* actively bucking injustice.

So, Sienna just explained homeschooling and read the second fun fact for Maria because the child had never heard the words for what John studied at home. *At home John studied botany, zoology*, and *geology*. Even if Maria could have sounded them out, she had no idea how to pronounce the scientific words for the study of plants, animals, and the earth. Sienna told her, "He liked rocks and stuff."

Maria read the third fun fact. *John lost his arm in the Civil War*, but she thought that he broke it, so his sacrifice didn't have the same impact on her. *John became a professor of Geology.* Sienna defined Geology, but Maria didn't know what a professor was. *He developed a theory about the formation of the Grand Canyon.* Maria didn't know what a theory was or what formation meant. She had no idea what a Grand Canyon could be. Sienna glanced around the library for a book that might have a picture of the Grand Canyon.

All through the tutoring session, Jolie had been sitting at a card table she'd brought from home. Perched behind the computer balanced on a stack of thesauri, she said, "Do you realize the fun facts haven't actually told us which side he was fighting for? It's odd they don't say how it felt for him to lose a limb. They say nothing about how he coped with that?"

"We can't worry about any of that," Sienna said wryly. "Maria just has to get her assignment done."

After a tedious twenty minutes, Sienna had transcribed and Maria had read her own paragraph twice by the time Mimi bustled into the library. She stopped to listen as Sienna urged the girl to read her work for the third time, to see if she wanted to add anything at all.

Maria read, "John had an interesting early life. John learned about plants and animals at home. John learned about the earth. John grew up to be a teacher of rocks. John had a new idea about the Grand Canyon. There you have some fun facts about John."

Mimi glanced down at the *Reading Fare* Fun Facts worksheet and smiled. "This is great!" she exclaimed. "Just great!" She reached over to pat Sienna's arm. "You're figuring this out! I'm so glad you are using real grade level material! It's vital since standards are only going to get higher." Then, in her happiness, she seemed to float into the broom closet and, just as Deedee had done earlier that morning while hiding out waiting for the mothers to be sent home, shut the door completely.

Since there was no sense sending Maria back to class just a few minutes shy of recess, Jolie invited her to go sit on a bright orange beanbag chair in the middle of the old basketball court and look at some Christmas books. To Sienna, she said. "I really liked what you were doing with the magnets yesterday. Why do you have to use that crap?"

"I don't know." Sienna shook her head. "I've seen fourth graders write about things they know and care about and whatever they produce is always better and deeper than regurgitating facts they haven't been able to process."

Mimi stepped out of her office, her cell phone against her ear. "Jules? Jules? I have no bars. Jules? I can't get a signal." Frowning, Mimi shook her device. "Oh well. By the way," she said to Sienna, "I

196

do have just one teeny-tiny suggestion for you. Get a highlighter, a bright pink one for that girl. Girls just love pink, you know? And have her pick out and highlight the most important details in the text while she reads. Okay? Will you do that for me?"

Glumly, Sienna looked at Maria. The girl wasn't reading. She was only moving her lips pretending to be good, eager to please, desperate to be safe. Her Reading Baby would probably never be healthy and Maria might very well have a real, human baby of her own without ever developing the skills needed to support it. Lucero's prayer card had said, "Protect the Unborn."

Sienna turned away from Mimi, turning pleading eyes to the sacred image of Our Lady of Guadalupe, propped against *La Mujer de Tierra*. In truth, the artist had rendered *La Madre de Dios* on the prayer card to appear as miserable as Sienna felt. The holy mother's eyes were puffy. The skin over her cheekbones appeared bruised. One side of her upper lip was swollen as if she'd been punched in the mouth. Her neck was cocked to the side, at an angle, suggesting a painfully pinched nerve, a dislocation of backbone.

Sienna felt her vital energy draining as if all her blood were pooling out through the tips of her toes. She could not trust her facial expression or what she might say. She took the candy Lucero had given her from where she had lain it beside the prayer card. Mindlessly, she offered a piece to Mimi.

"Thank you!" Mimi said sweetly. "This will freshen my breath for the Superintendent. He and Brenda Hadley will be here soon to wish us all a very happy holiday!" She popped it into her mouth as Sienna unwrapped a piece for herself.

Mimi gasped. "H...h...hot!"

Sienna's dejection made her apathetic toward Mimi's discomfort. Sucking on her own candy, as if trying to draw heat from it, she watched Mimi's eyes water. "You know," she said, "I gave a fluency test in Ashley Whitfield's first grade this morning. The first sentence of the passage was *It was a hot day.* It took almost the whole minute before the little boy finally sounded out /h/ /o/ /t/. Then, he laid his cheek down on the table, completely exhausted. His eyes lolled back into his head and he asked me, "What's a hot?"

Normally pale, Mimi's complexion had gone bright pink. Her eyes darted about, obviously looking for water. She fixated on the fountain in the corner, but it had been shut off years earlier by the county health department. "What was his overall score?" she panted.

"Four."

"Per minute!"

Sienna nodded.

"And that's in the RIDE?" Mimi left her mouth open so the air in the under-heated library could cool her tongue. Evidently, she was imagining a dismal trend line on the progress-monitoring graph. "That's terrible! "Mimi spit the translucent red disc into the same trash can Pilar had vomited me up in to answer her cell phone. "Hi Jules! Oh my goodness! Yes! Dr. Fray will be here any minute. I'll meet you outside."

Mimi skipped out of the library. Maria ran to recess. They both passed Deedee who did not shout at either of them to walk. She carried a tape dispenser and a few papers pressed against her side. Moving like a child on Christmas Eve, stealing away with a handmade gift to wrap in secret, she seemed to believe that because she willed it to be so no one saw her and, in fact, that strategy often worked for Deedee Hayes.

***

After school was dismissed for Winter Break, Andy entered the library. Sienna was plucking tiles with individual letters on them from a plastic tub for the *Reading Fare* lesson required the first day back after break. Joyfully, she said, "I'm almost done plucking this goose and we can start our holiday as soon as I am." She glanced up. Andy didn't look happy. "What's wrong?"

Angrily, he asked, "Who hangs the reading material in the bathrooms around here?"

"Deedee."

"Have you seen this?" He thrust a paper with tape still stuck to the top of it at her.

Sienna shook her head. "I haven't had a chance to go to the

bathroom since school started." She only needed one more tile with the letter *a* on it before she could leave campus. "What does it say?"

Andy read an anonymous Internet story aloud. It was about a teacher receiving holiday gifts from her students. When he got to the last part, his voice shook. "The next gift was from the son of a liquor store owner. The teacher held the package over her head. It was leaking. She touched a drop of the leakage with her finger and put it to her tongue. 'Is it wine?' she asked.

"'No,' the boy replied with excitement. The teacher took one more taste before declaring, 'I give up, what is it?'

"With great glee, the boy replied, 'it's a puppy!'"

For a moment, against her will, Sienna visualized Nancy, or maybe Ashley, holding a cardboard box above her head, the damp bottom nearly collapsing beneath the weight of a snuffling, wiggling puppy as she tasted its pee. It was offensive. She was just too tired and too depressed to get fired up.

"Is this the kind of culture Deedee creates around here?" Andy asked sharply. "Is this how she communicates her belief that teachers are stupid? Does she really think that just because something is nicely package and tied up with a ribbon, they lose their sense of smell? This is disgusting! What kind of principal, what kind of person would tape this in the only place an exhausted, overwhelmed teacher might have a moment alone?"

Sienna was touched by his outrage. After all, she had wanted him to defend her the day before. "I guess she just thinks it's funny."

"And she's upset about the graffiti outside? What about what she's putting up inside? What's wrong with that woman?" He asked. "Why doesn't anyone call her on the culture she's creating here?"

Sienna shrugged, bitterly mimicking Mimi, "The only thing that counts is what you can measure." She hated the taste that hostility left on her tongue. "I guess no one wants to rock the boat."

Andy shook his head. "I'm so sorry, sweetie," he said. "I guess even I had to see this to believe this."

"So professor, may I be excused from fidelity to *Reading Fare*?"

As if Mimi really had been hired to maintain surveillance, she suddenly rushed into the library. She looked from Sienna to Andy, clearly still assuming he was a teacher in the building. *"Reading Fare* is not optional," she said, with a slight lilt of panic in her voice. Then, as if the corruption of such embedded, clandestine treason dawned on her, she snapped. "You two have no choice in the matter if you're going to work for Purewater." She smiled sweetly, beauty-queen style. "Forgot my laptop." She dashed back into her office, shutting the door behind her.

"Hey, do you have a map of this school?" Andy asked. "For reconnaissance."

Sienna gestured toward the plastic tub labeled GUEST TEACHER EMERGENCY PLANS stored under her desk.

Andy took a school map out and pecked her on the cheek. She didn't realize how panicked she must have looked about this PDA (Public Display of Affection) until he chuckled. He seized her lips then, pinning them between his for a sizzling kiss. "Finish up here quickly," he whispered. "Then, I'll spring you from the dungeon."

Like a knight, leaving the castle for battle, Andy left the library. Captain Swabby had spent the morning painting over graffiti. Now, Andy visited each bathroom stall in the building, including those in the children's wing, to tear down what the principal had posted about holiday gifts for teachers.

Chapter Twenty-Three

That evening to celebrate the beginning of the holiday break, Sienna and Andy met Jolie and Wolf at *Casita Rio*. A light snow was falling outside as they settled in at the alcove table where holiday lights twinkled in the store-front window. Dark red poinsettias bloomed on the sills. With their backs to the foursome, Esteban and Gaul sat at the counter, eating with their eyes cast down. Through the gap of empty space between them, Sienna glimpsed Gaul's stoneware plate piled high with Lucia's chicken mole and decided that's what she wanted as well.

After they ordered, Jolie said, "I looked up Maria's fun fact guy. The one with the interesting early life."

Sienna sighed. "I seriously don't want to talk shop."

"Just hear me out."

Sienna shrugged. She wanted to forget about Moore until Winter Break was over.

"He was an interesting guy," Jolie went on. "While he was out exploring the Grand Canyon, he got interested in and befriended the Native Americans. He collected the myths, tales, and vocabularies of several Southwest tribes. He helped Congress create the Smithsonian Bureau of Ethnology. Apparently, his passion for ethnography helped lay the groundwork for anthropology in the twentieth century. He was actually all about letting the people tell their stories and preserving them."

"Wow," Sienna said, dipping into the guacamole. "He's

probably rolling in his grave over what *Reading Fare*'s curriculum designers decided were the fun facts of his life."

"What are you two talking about?" Wolf asked. "I swear," he said to Andy, "these women have a secret language."

Andy chuckled. "Educationese," he said as the bells on the café door jingled.

Jolie said, "There's Mimi with her husband. I swear she *is* spying on us."

Sienna chose not to turn around.

Jolie waved enthusiastically. "Mimi! Mimi!"

Sienna glowered at her.

"Hello there!" Mimi said joyfully. "Imagine running into you two here. It's such a small world."

Sienna turned around in her chair. Her face was tight. She tried to smile convivially, knowing she probably wasn't managing it very well. She hoped she seemed pleasant enough.

Jolie said, "We were just talking about *Reading Fare's* Fun Facts."

"Great!" Mimi said. "You really did do a good job with it today, Sienna." She stepped aside so the man behind her could step up to their table as well. In that moment, Sienna thought they were holding hands, but then figured she was wrong because Mimi introduced him as Jules Holdaway, adding, "He is very interested in how we are using *Reading Fare*."

"Oh!" Jolie said. "He's not your husband?"

Jules and Andy stared at each, once again trying to identify the other.

"No! No!" Mimi blushed. "He's not."

Jolie said, "I was just now wondering why the curriculum leaves all the interesting details out of the fun facts. Maria was reading about John Wesley Powell today. It might have been good for her to learn that he formed a theory about the formation of Grand Canyon, but it might have been even better for her to learn that he also developed a lifelong passion for the languages and stories of the indigenous people who lived in the Southwest. I mean the guy actually formed the Smithsonian Bureau of Ethnology to help preserve native culture. Isn't that a fun fact, especially for at-risk minority students?"

Mimi blanched, unconsciously putting her arm in front of Jules like a driver slamming on her brakes attempts to keep her passenger from flying through a windshield. Her voice became quite clinical as she said, "It sounds like that Fun Facts activity was really focused on geology."

"Nope," Sienna said. "The focus was supposed to be on his interesting early life."

"That's why," Jules said, taking charge. "He studied Native Americans *later* in life. Do you get it? Later. Not earlier."

"The only thing interesting about his early life was that he was homeschooled because his father cared about human rights." Sienna said. "He got to choose what he studied, based on his own interests. He liked rocks, which led him to the Grand Canyon, which led him to the people. *Reading Fare* designers could have turned that into a beautiful cause and effect piece."

Jules looked at his watch. "I'll wait in the car, Mimi. I need to program the GPS."

When he ducked outside into the snow, Mimi confided, "We're meeting Dr. Fray for drinks! Mrs. Fray just loved the flan I brought to their cocktail party last night. Thank God because that made it worth my husband being mad that I decided to go over there instead of making it to his staff party in Sinclair. When I introduced Jules to Dr. Fray in the staff lounge today, Dr. Fray mentioned the flan and Jules said he wanted some and I said I'd get him some sometime. Of course, I never thought anything would come of it, but suddenly Dr. Fray invited us over for an intimate dinner while Jules is still in town! That means it's tonight. Whala!" Mimi glanced toward the counter. "I hope we can buy a whole flan on short notice."

Sienna and Jolie glanced at each. Were they supposed to congratulate her for any of this?

"I'm a strong believer in networking," Mimi said. "I'm formulating a theory that networking is actually more important for educational reform than teaching."

"That's very interesting," Andy said. "Do you think networking is more important than data?"

"Ha!" Mimi twittered. "You are a funny guy." She wiggled her way through the crowded restaurant up to the counter, leaned in between Gaul and Esteban, and asked Lucia for an entire flan.

Andy said, "I still can't place the guy she's with. Jules Holdaway? It's making me crazy."

"That's making you crazy?" Sienna took a swig of his beer. "What about what she said?"

"Yeah, but I have a feeling that guy is someone I should know." Andy let his voice trail off.

"You travel a lot." Jolie said. "Maybe you just saw him or someone who looks like him at the airport." She reached over to take Wolf's hand.

"Maybe he was on the cover of *Forbes*," Wolf said. "There's something shifty about him."

"Maybe you saw him in a tabloid," Sienna added. "Maybe he's a prince."

As if the reference to royalty reminded her, Jolie pulled a dirty dog-eared picture book out of her tote bag, "Look what was in Jonathan's overdue pile! *The Little Mermaid*. I'm going to try repairing it at home. I've got some fantastic old school book binding glue that is so toxic Captain Swabby would never let me use it at school. When it's all fixed up, I want to let Pilar check it out. What do you think?"

Sienna took the book. The bottom third of the cover was ripped away from the spine. The corners of the pages curled as if the book had been dipped in the sea and yellowed from drying in the sun. "It is all about a mermaid, which she loves, who is a beautiful princess from down under who is completely out of her element, like Pilar herself. But this little mermaid gives her voice up on a gamble on the off chance that she might please a prince who could never, ever really care for her."

"Yeah. It's a sad story. Hans Christian was a genius," Jolie said. "Maybe we should give Deedee and Mimi a copy of the *Emperor's New Clothes* to read, only we should call it the Emperor's New *Reading Fare*."

"That's a good one," Andy said. To Wolf, he added, "Librarian sarcasm."

Sienna nodded. "Hans was brilliant, but let's not give this story to Pilar. All she can do with it at this point is look at the pictures." She held the book up so they could all see the final illustration. A girl's lovely face, cracking with heartbreak and dismay, floated in a sheet of white foam. Her body had been erased by a murky sea.

Examining the illustration, Wolf grimaced. "I've seen too many real drownings on the Purewater. It is not a pretty sight in a picture book. It's horrible in reality." He sniffed audibly.

"Oh Wolf!" Sienna was touched and almost patted his arm, but when he sniffed again, she realized he wasn't choked up.

"This reeks of pot!" he said.

"That's the other reason I was taking it home," Jolie said. "To air it out."

"Jonathan's coat and backpack smell just like that," Sienna said.

"His mom is another sad story." Wolf handed the book back to Jolie. "Nice try, sweetheart."

Jolie nodded. "I've been racking my brain for a different book."

Sienna said, "She needs to write about the one she drew."

"I wish she could," Jolie said. "I wish everyone would just let you help her do it."

"Teach the kids to write, Sienna," Andy said, "Go ahead. Rock the boat in Purewater. Their stories matter, even if their facts aren't fun."

After handling the grubby book, Sienna reached into her purse for hand sanitizer, her fingers brushing over *La Mujer de Tierra* reclining inside, wrapped in extra soft brand name facial tissue. She hadn't left the statue at school. She was legitimately worried that someone would vandalize the library or as Jolie had joked, "Captain Swabby might paint her gray."

As Sienna felt the chill rubbing alcohol left behind when it evaporated from her skin, she said, "I'd love to know more about what's happening in Clemencia and *Redención*. If I knew what was going on down there, I might know how to help Pilar and Valentin." She dunked another chip into the guacamole and said, "Right now, I need a break from work."

Their plates came and they spent a pleasant hour eating and

talking before Wolf got a tagging-in-progress call and had to leave, hoping he could finally catch the town's newly prolific graffitists. He promised to text Jolie as soon as possible to let her know how long he'd be tied up. Sienna and Andy offered to drive her home if needed. The restaurant cleared and soon such a silence fell over the space that the distant music and crooning of *El Fuego* could be heard coming from the radio in the apartment upstairs where Pilar and Cassandra were having a sleep-over. Lucia strolled out of the kitchen to tempt them with flan. When she returned with their dessert, she had Ramon and Gaul in tow.

Gaul nodded to Jolie and Andy, but spoke directly to Sienna. "I couldn't help hearing you earlier. If you are interested, Lucia and Ramon would like to share a little with you about Redención. I can translate the difficult parts."

Sienna was well-fed and getting drowsy. The draft from the front door was a few degrees too cold on her legs and she wanted to go home. She wanted to have a long bath with lavender-scented Epsom salts and, possibly Andy. After all, Matt was with his father, so she'd have no compunction at about playing a siren and luring her lover into the depths of her tub.

Still, this was a precious opportunity to learn more and they had to wait to see if Wolf would be able to return for Jolie in a reasonable amount of time anyway. "Is it okay?" she asked. Jolie nodded. Andy was already pulling chairs over from the next table.

As Gaul sank into Wolf's emptied seat, Sienna introduced him to Andy.

Andy's eyes narrowed almost imperceptivity at Gaul. "I understand you know something about the painting in the library," he said, attempting to sound convivial, as if he'd never once worried that Sienna might have been attracted to him. "Of the shaman."

"Oh yes! It's a very interesting piece," Gaul replied, glancing from Sienna to Jolie and back again. "I've thought of it often, wondering what you decided to do with it?"

"We're sharing it now," Sienna said. "The problem was solved when I was relocated again."

Gaul nodded, though he was clearly confounded, wondering if

teachers normally had to move around like that in the middle of the school year. He shifted uneasily. "I fear I must confess to something."

Almost triumphantly, Andy sat back in his seat, washing his irrational jealously down with a swig of *cerveza*. He told himself that it was ridiculous for him to be concerned about Sienna and this man.

Gaul said, "I overhead you talking about ethnology, myth, Pilar, and her mermaid, and because of that, I know you are the ones—the ones with the *orejas*—to hear what someone in Purewater must hear to help the children in your school."

With that Andy's worries were appeased. Lucia, Ramon, and Gaul told what they could of biography, current events, and history though none of it would ever be included in *Reading Fare's* Fun Facts.

***

Lucia and Ramon were both born and grew up in the small village of Redención. Lucia's grandmother, Esperanza Cuevas, was famous there and throughout the state of Clemencia for the pottery her lineage made. As Gaul had told Sienna when he gave *La Mujer de Tierra* to her, the clay from Redención was very special. The Cuevas family claimed the rights to a special hot spring beneath *La Madre Ardiendo*. The clay moistened from that particular spring was called *matriz* and it was considered sacred.

When an object made of this clay was placed on an altar to call back *los muertos* or to request a blessing or a healing, petitioners usually received a sign that those prayers had been heard, if not answered, within three days. The source of the *matriz* was a well-guarded secret and for centuries, only a few chosen Cuevas women from each generation were permitted to know exactly where it was. The mates of these women were required to undergo an elaborate ritual to prepare them to stand guard whenever their wives went into the hills to retrieve it.

While this ancient tradition went on in rural Redención, other parts of Clemencia modernized. In the early 1960's, when Esperanza Cuevas was still a teenager, Gaul Santiago's grandfather ran for governor in the capital city. Just before he put his name on the ballot, his mother traveled to Redención and bought him a Cuevas pot. She instructed him to create a shrine to social justice in his home. He did. He placed the pot upon his altar, filling it with strips of paper on which he'd written his intentions and requests for blessings upon his work for the people.

After a grueling campaign, Santiago won the election. He'd worked hard, but he always believed that his victory had been granted because of the *matriz*. Because of his gratitude and reverence, he sent his adult son, Gaul's father, to Redención with the following instructions. Gaul's father was to find the source of the clay and to— very discretely—ensure that it was always guarded by the elder Santiago's new government. The clay was precious and powerful and the new governor did not want to rely upon poor peasants to protect it.

Gaul was a small child of three or four when he accompanied his father on the first mission to Redención. While his father negotiated with the Cuevas family, Gaul quickly befriended Raul Vega, the child of the Cuevas family's neighbor. The boys were just a few months apart in age. People made jokes about their names rhyming and teased them about being twins.

No one had expected Gaul's father to be absolutely enchanted by Redención and by the Cuevas family which embraced him and the protection he offered—with stipulations. They insisted that the guards he employed never know the precise location of the source of the clay. The Santiago soldiers were "permitted" to guard the Cuevas men who guarded the Cuevas women. Gaul's father adored Redención so much that he had a second home built in the village. The Santiago family spent a lot of time there so Gaul and Raul became lifelong friends.

When Raul's little brother, Ramon, was born, Gaul thought of him as his own brother. As the years went by, Gaul, Raul, and Ramon befriended Pablo Flores, who came to live in the village after spending his early life higher up on *La Madre Ardiendo*. Pablo was a gifted painter. When Governor Santiago sent his grandson Gaul to boarding school in the United States, Gaul took some of Pablo's art and a few pieces of Cuevas pottery from Redención to remind him of home. Coincidentally, Gaul's new roommate's parents were wealthy and well-connected art collectors. They were instantly intrigued by the pieces they discovered in their son's dorm room and thus Gaul's own career as an art dealer was born.

Meanwhile, back in Redención, Pablo married. He and his first wife had Esteban. Sadly, she died when Esteban was only eight years old. A year after her death, Pablo married the younger, Esperanza Luz, who had been named after the grandmother whose *matriz* had given Governor Santiago several consecutive political victories in Clemencia. Soon, Pilar was born to the artistic couple, Pablo and Esperanza Luz.

Ramon and Lucia were newlyweds and were thrilled to become her godparents, but before baby Pilar cut her first tooth, Gaul's grandfather became ill and died in the capital city of Clemencia. During the months of an interim government, a powerful drug cartel attempted to expand its presence in Clemencia. Since Grandfather Santiago's guards in Redención had been funded from his own discretionary funds, and no one knew about the secret deal, the soldiers were no longer paid for their clandestine protection. They left the village.

Pilar's godparents, Ramon and Lucia were quite young and decided to join Raul on a tourist visa to visit Gaul in the United States before starting their own family. Pablo and Esperanza Luz sent Raul, Ramon, and Lucia on their journey north with another van load of paintings and pots for Gaul to sell. While Lucia and the Vega brothers were having a wonderful time visiting him in Santa Fe, a shocking and brutal raid occurred in Redención. The Clemencian drug cartel came in, kidnapped several young people, and murdered the few who were brave or foolhardy enough to resist.

Pablo's paintings sold as soon as they hit the market in Santa Fe. Raul tried to telephone to share the good news. At first, he couldn't get through. He didn't worry right away, but after a few futile tries, all of them began dialing non-stop until they finally reached someone in Redención. It took two days before Lucia got through to her panicked mother, who was able to assure them that Raul's wife was safe. The Cuevas woman had taken her up onto *La Madre*

Ardiendo with them. Still, Lucia's mother was convinced that the government could no longer keep order in Clemencia. It broke her heart to banish her daughter, but she pleaded with Lucia not to come home. She insisted upon speaking to Ramon and begged him to keep her daughter in the United States. Since she was so upset and unclear on her geography, she forced him to promise to take Lucia as far north as they could possibly get before they got to Canada.

Afraid and excited about a new life in the United States, they applied for legal status and, with sponsorship and a small loan from Gaul, bought a taco truck, following migrant workers from the Southwest to California. Eventually, they worked their way north.

Raul returned to Clemencia on the next flight where he reunited with his wife and learned that Pablo and Esperanza had been safe the whole time. They'd taken Esteban and baby Pilar into the hills for a trip to the *matriz* the day before the cartel raided Redención. Finding his dear friends alive, Raul pleaded with Pablo to come with him, to move both of their families to Santa Fe.

Pablo and Esperanza Luz refused for two reasons. First of all, Esperanza was the only woman of her generation so far who had been initiated into the *matriz*. Pablo was the only man initiated into protecting her work with it. They did not feel they could leave. Even if Redención were threatened under the cartel or even if it were to modernize under a strong, future government, the Cuevas family's legacy there would always be their sacred responsibility.

Indeed, prayer and rituals involving the *matriz* appeared to be working. A new government, composed of many of Santiago's original cabinet, reorganized and successfully used the military to arrest members of the cartel. While increasing the military meant less money for many things like schools in Clemencia, it also meant it was probably safe to stay and create the sacred art Pablo and Esperanza Luz had been born to make.

Life did return to normal except that having had to imagine leaving it all behind seemed to inspire both Pablo and Esperanza Luz to produce more distinctly numinous work. Gaul was able to sell many pieces for very good prices. Resettled in Santa Fe, Raul got the license he needed and partnered with Gaul becoming an exporter, driving back and forth between Redención and Santa Fe several times a year.

Things went well for a few years until the previous summer. Gaul and Raul were set to visit Redención for a traditional festival. They couldn't travel together because Gaul had a friend's wedding to attend. Raul went a few days ahead of him. When Gaul reached Redención, the village was empty.

The people had disappeared. The art was gone, all except for *La Mujer de Tierra*. There had never really been cell service to speak of and Gaul realized the telephone wires in and out of the village had been cut. Horrified, he drove ten miles to the nearest town with a land line and called *Casita Rio* in Purewater. Had Ramon heard anything from Raul? Had Lucia heard anything from her mother? Had they heard from Pablo or Esperanza Luz?

Lucia was completely distraught. She told him Ramon was already on the road to meet a coyote who was smuggling Esteban and Pilar into the United States. A mysterious, terse midnight call from a stranger had directed him to pick the children up in San Diego, California. When Ramon returned to Purewater with them, Lucia could see that the children had *susto*, soul trauma, but at least," she said, with tears in her eyes, "they can still walk. They can still draw breath."

To this day, neither of the children had revealed what they had or hadn't seen in Redención. No one knew what had happened to them, to their parents, to Raul and his wife. For weeks, they'd feared the worst for all of the adults, but then received word from an immigrants' rights' volunteer that Raul was in a detention center in Arizona. That was a complete mystery because he'd always had the papers he'd needed to travel back and forth across the border.

* * *

"Please keep this close," Lucia implored Sienna. "There's too much we don't know."

"Of course," Sienna promised, humbled and touched by the family's ordeal. "I'm so sorry." She felt Gaul's dread at finding nothing left, except *La Mujer de Tierra*, and wondered if the statue had been a sign left behind for him to find. Had Esperanza Luz, in desperation, somehow managed to send her children to a foreign land in the care of a human smuggler? Had she cut the clay woman with an empty *rebozo* in half on purpose to signify her broken heart, her shattered home, and the absolute desecration of Redención?

"What about Valentin?" Sienna asked urgently. "Do you know about him? He seems to speak a dialect that Pilar knows and his papers say he is from Redención too."

Gaul and Lucia both looked down at the empty plates on the table. Sienna had a feeling that they wanted to tell her more, but were afraid. Carefully, Ramon said, "He has *susto,* too."

Sienna nodded. So many children needed more support. Meanwhile, data collection and test preparation were superseding any other priorities. Even dirty, little, blonde, blue-eyed *Gringo* had been homeless for weeks and no one had known until he told her.

Chapter Twenty-Four

The next day at the cabin they'd rented, Sienna and Andy went snowshoeing. Afterwards, Andy dragged the mattress from the bed to the fireplace. They made love before the crackling flames, smiling the entire time, and then Sienna took a long afternoon nap, nestled beneath a down comforter. She slept deeply for two hours, awaking to the enticing scent of basil and oregano simmering in a saucepot on the stove and sourdough bread, fresh from the oven. She stretched her full length beneath the covers, contentedly watching the snow fall outside the window. She thought of Matt snowboarding with his father and his family. She missed him a little, and she loved being on vacation.

Vacating. Running away. She'd fled Moore. But not like Pilar and Esteban escaping Redención. She shook her head, trying not to think about their tragedy or work as she pulled her jeans and sweater on and took her place at the table.

After filling their wine glasses, Andy looked at her seriously. "Do you ever want to talk about your divorce?"

"No," she said. "Do you want to talk about my divorce?"

"A little bit."

"Why?" she asked.

"I just wonder how it could have happened?"

"Because I seem so great?" She grinned at him. "Because I'm a fantastic lover and you just can't imagine how Matt's dad could let me go?"

"Basically, yes."

She shrugged nonchalantly, but couldn't hide the tears that came to her eyes.

"I want to know if you were hurt," he said. "If you are hurt?"

"I was," she nodded, "but we had a child between us to consider. Ultimately, we had to forgive each other for what didn't work in our relationship. Of course, I could forgive mistakes because he's always taken good care of Matt and of me too, so that I could be there for Matt whenever he needed me. Sure, I was sad, sorry for my son. When I realized there was no life left in my marriage, in our little family I felt like my heart split right down the middle. Like *La Mujer de Tierra*."

La Mujer de Tierra was still in her purse and Sienna dug her out. She set her on the table between their steaming plates of pasta, next to the bread basket and sighed. "My hurt was mostly about my fear that my child would feel pain and confusion. I never wanted him to feel abandoned or powerless over his life. I don't think he did. I don't know." Almost mindlessly, she broke the crust off her bread and laid it at the feet of the statue, just as she'd put guacamole there of the eve *El Día de Los Muertos*.

"Honey," Andy said gently, "you're feeding a doll."

"What if Pilar's parents were murdered? What if she saw it when it happened?"

He shook his head sadly. "I don't know." He reached out to stroke her hand. A moment later, he asked. "Would you ever remarry?"

"Maybe." Sienna blushed. "I want the trust and fidelity that people assume come with a wedding ring."

Andy leaned forward. "You do?"

"Except that Moore's interpretation of fidelity is ruining the word for me. I want a man to cherish my spirit."

"He'd have to have the eyes to see it to do that."

"He would. He'd also have to be able to show me his."

"You know what?" Andy said. "I could see how someone who got a glimpse of what you are calling your spirit might want to control it"

"In a relationship?"

"At work."

"That's not fair!"

"Especially since you chose a caring profession."

"I can't stand what's happening at Moore," Sienna said. "It's breaking my heart."

It's breaking her heart? I wondered how many times a human woman's heart could break? I was curious about that because when I was a woman, I didn't tolerate my heartbreak very well at all. Maybe Sienna and Matt's father had argued. Maybe she'd hurt her son's feelings, but she hadn't committed my crime. As I witnessed Sienna and Andy, I found myself wishing someone had been there to stop me. If someone had, I might have had another chance at love.

* * *

During the long, cold, rainy month of January, record amounts of snow fell in the mountains and it rained every day in Purewater. As the raindrops pelted their classroom windows, classroom teachers dutifully recorded what kids didn't know in RIDE. Sienna did what her colleagues wanted her to do in their classrooms, but in the pull-out groups that she knew she would lose the following year, she continued teaching English the best way she knew how. The stories that were produced, revised with vocabulary that was new to the children, and edited in *The Writers' Lair* were full of spirit, word play, and even heartfelt confession.

We took the ice cream to my room. My cousin, Nita, put her dresser in front of the door, but then I realized we forgot the spoons. We had to push the dresser away. Nita sent me to get the spoons, so I ran to get them. Luckily, my grandmother wasn't in the kitchen. She was still taking the garbage out, so I grabbed two spoons and ran back to my bedroom. We ate all of the delicious vanilla ice cream right out of the container! Then, our stomachs hurt horrible. I was so worried that my grandma would find out. She thinks kids should eat healthy food before they eat sweets.

***

215

One early Christmas morning when I was seven in my house my younger sister and I were awake and my parents were still sleeping. I was thirsty and I went to the cold kitchen to get a drink. Then I asked my sister to go see the Christmas presents under the tree. The tree was in my Uncle's room because he went to Mexico in a truck. My sister said, "Yes" We went into my uncle's room. The floor felt like ice on my bare feet and it was a little dark in the room. My sister felt scared. We saw a gold light coming through the window. A present was wrapped in shiny gold paper. My parents came and we opened it. It was a Wii.

***

I went to my cousins' house to celebrate Christmas. We ate posole and all the people that were there were talking about stuff. They talked funny stuff about their lives and they kept talking and laughing. The kids all went upstairs to play school. I was the teacher. First, I did attendance and then we did reading and the students were not listening to me. The students were talking and laughing. I told them, "Put your heads down." They did and I said, "You guys are too loud. You need to start acting like second graders. If you are ready, put your heads up and line up for recess." I didn't walk them out. I just walked in a circle and they followed me around and around. I said, "Here we are." They said, "Yeah!" They ran out. I went inside and made some work for the students to do. When I picked them up, I said, "You are going to take a test."

They said, "No!" I said, "When I call your name, you may come." Soon everybody got their test.

I made them finish their tests. Some kids took a long time, so I started to send them out into the hall, but, then we stopped playing. I said, "Let's go downstairs. I don't want to be the teacher anymore.

***

And then after listening to so many of her friends' stories, Pilar began to tell one of her own. In English and Spanish, with help from Cassandra and Lupe, she spoke haltingly and Sienna wrote.

I slept in the van. A man opened it. I woke up. We were at a church in America and the skinny mother of God was standing in the river over the door. She had no shoes on her brown feet. She had a white dress on and there was a white star shining over her head. I saw hills, like where my mother got

216

the matriz behind her. She was a star of the sea.

"What happened at the church?" Sienna asked.

"Ramon got us."

"And brought you to Purewater?" Gaul had told her about Ramon's trip to San Diego. There had been no Statue of Liberty to greet her in Southern California, but it seems Pilar had been welcomed by The Star of the Sea.

Sienna helped the children correct their grammar and Jolie created Xeroxed anthologies of the stories and gave a copy to each child. Sienna read them aloud like a proud parent to Andy over the phone or Skype.

"It's fantastic that Pilar is beginning to open up and express herself," he said. "Good work, Sienna!"

Jolie also read the children's stories to Wolf when he stopped in the library to say hello, which was often. The kids loved how much he seemed to enjoy their tales. He claimed all graffiti calls at Moore and those on the surrounding mailboxes and fences became his exclusive beat. The increase in graffiti wasn't good for the community, but it was good for his romance and the students learned to relax around him, even if their parents were afraid. In *The Writers' Lair* students read and listened to their own and each other's stories over and over again.

For the first time in their lives they experienced how it felt to read smoothly and fluently. Eagerly they read the words they knew, words they understood, words that represented their most precious memories, and their own inner selves. They began to ask questions about pronouns and conjunctions, adopt synonyms used by others, and look forward to writing their next pieces.

On the last school day in January, Pilar began sketching a woman. She was forming a clay pot.

"Who is that?" Sienna asked gently.

"My mom," Pilar said matter-of-factly, using an American term. "She makes these."

Sienna's heart caught in her throat. She certainly didn't want to push the child, to have her remember or reveal something that she might not have enough support to deal with, but if there were something that would be good for Pilar to share, perhaps a wonderful, tender memory, she wanted to give her the chance.

They were on the verge of a breakthrough, but when the first day of February rolled around, it was time for the annual WELT. Testing meant Sienna had to cancel her ELL classes to administer the four-part test to every single ELL student in the school. It took all month. As soon as that was finished, she had to assist classroom teachers in administering the P.P.T. (The Purewater Preparation Test) for the state WASTE. That took up the first two weeks of March.

She was finally able to resume *The Writers' Lair*, on St. Patrick's Day. She decided to have students write stories about what they would wish for if they encountered a leprechaun or other magical creature on the school playground.

Cassandra met an angel swinging on the swing set and wished to be whisked back to Mexico. Alonda met a glittery butterfly by the water fountain and asked for a puppy, and oh yes, a house too so she could keep him, since pets weren't allowed in the apartments. Miguel encountered a ninja under the cedar tree who would grant him speed in all things, especially in reading so Mrs. Albright would quit waving his fluency chart—with all its red bars well below the goal line—in his face. A talking monkey got Javier's attention by tossing chocolates at him from the top of the slide and hitting him in the head with a big truffle. *Truffle* was Ms. O'Mara's word. Javier asked the monkey to give all the kids a lot more time to write stories and do art in school.

Then Pilar spoke. Sienna wrote what she said.

School a desert. I see the puma black as night. I say Esteban needs a shirt for the quince de Dulce Saturday. I tell her tell me all the English. I tell her I want the present of the river. Where is my mom and dad and Puma, she say, "You ask too much little girl."

Sienna wanted Pilar to get her wishes. That night, with Matt's permission, she cleaned out her son's closet. On the way to Goodwill, she stopped by *La Casita Rio*, offering a nice formal button down shirt, a tie, slacks, and a pair of dress shoes to Lucia. Esteban got to wear the whole outfit to Dulce's *quinceanera*. She was happy that she and Matt could grant Pilar's first wish. She was working on the second, giving Pilar the English. She only hoped that the puma didn't get the final word.

***

Sienna visited Andy for Spring Break. Over lunch at the *Old Eli*, they discussed his upcoming plans to visit schools in Finland with colleagues at Vandya. Sienna shared how excited her students continued to be about reading each other's stories. "I wonder if I should try to balance out the magical creature fantasy with having them write about a time they didn't get what they wanted. I think it might help if we explored the theme of disappointment and generated some strategies for coping with it."

"That could be very powerful," Andy said, "but the consequences would probably be depressing, for you. Your staff would probably accuse you of dragging everyone down."

"In addition to dumbing it down." She laughed bitterly and then shook her head. "Make me stop. I want to have fun this week."

"Tell me about the weather in Purewater. That's always a good transitional topic."

Sienna rolled her eyes, pretending to yawn. "There was more snow than usual this year. The ski resorts expect to stay open for a few more weeks."

"Okay enough of that," Andy said. "Enough small talk. I have a proposal for you." He cleared his throat. Color rose on his neck. "It's a professional one."

"Oh!" She sighed. Was it with relief or regret? She wasn't sure. "Okay. What is it?"

"I'd like you to work with me to create a presentation and eventually even a full-blown conference on how writing with ELL students can be an extremely effective, efficient, and economical way of educating them in today's public schools. You can show how you address academic, language, and social-emotional needs through creating well-structured and intentional writing projects around their own life experiences. We can illustrate how your *Writers' Lair* is a means to an end in itself for protecting children's civil and human rights. You can show how vital it is for kids to..."

"Encode."

"*Sí!*" Andy answered in Spanish. "Will you? I think we'd make a great team and I'm just starting to set up next year's speaking circuit. Maybe you could write a book on the topic. If you did, I'd be honored to write your forward. You could offer a fresh perspective."

Sienna was excited, intrigued, and now she realized he'd actually been priming her for this with comments and reassuring praise over the past few months. She said, "Andy, what I'm trying to do with kids isn't really new. It just seems fresh because it's bucking the trend right now. Honestly, honey, I'm not interested in being political. I just want to teach. I want to help kids reach their potential. I would do what you're talking about only if it would help the pendulum swing back to the child-centered side a little sooner."

"Good," he said.

"I do have copies of all the student anthologies Jolie and I have made. They're good. I honestly believe a lot of the kids in my fourth grade group are close to passing the writing portion of this year's WASTE."

"That would be just the data that you need."

Sienna frowned at him. "Are you already working on the marketing?"

"I know you don't care about data, at least the way it's being bandied about," he said, "but having some will generate an audience."

"I do care about that in the sense that I want my kids to experience passing a high stakes test to build their faith in themselves. They can't quite handle the reading assessment yet, but with the writing, they have some control. They get to choose words they know to demonstrate what they know and what they think, instead of being quizzed on words they don't. If I could keep working with them, toggling back and forth between their writing and reading words written by others, I think they'll eventually become happy and competent readers."

"That's a fresh, subtle, back-door approach to reading instruction," Andy said.

"I've only gotten away with what I've done so far because they think I've accepted my fate for next year. And, my instructional year is already almost over. When I get back from this trip, Nancy, Deedee, and Mimi want me to print out sample WASTE selections and make the kids practice and practice and practice."

"What a waste of valuable instructional time and taxpayer's money!"

"I know," Sienna said, "and it's so unfair to the kids."

"And to you and your career." Andy leaned forward. "You need a chance to collect data to show how writing and reading work together this way. And if they won't let you do that, you should leave Moore."

The thought of having to spend all next year sitting on the floor in the corner of a classroom trying to force children to do *Reading Fare* worksheets made her want to jump right out of her skin. "Are you making a completely professional proposal?"

"There is a personal component." Andy knew her contract for the school year was almost up. He wanted to get things settled before she signed another one. They were distracted by a party being seated right across the aisle.

"Ah! Look!" Andy jutted his chin toward the opposite booth. "There's Senator Panky in for his lunch and a bourbon. He looks inordinately pleased with himself. Must have gotten an insider trading tip."

It was true Panky looked happy. He was grinning as if he'd just nabbed the woman of his dreams and had led her through a wedding party convened to toss cherry blossoms at them in celebration of their nuptials. Senator Panky's balding head and shoulders were dappled with the pink petals falling from the street's springtime trees. He was not with a bride. He was with three businessmen. One of them clapped him on the shoulder, calling loudly for champagne. "Give us a bottle of *Le Grande Dame*."

While a waiter responded to them, their waitress carried the restaurant's famous Senator Sandwiches to Andy and Sienna. With her apron-clad back to Senator Panky and his cohorts, she narrowed her eyes and tightened her jaw. "That bubbly is two hundred and twenty-five dollars a bottle," she hissed. "Two months of dancing lessons for my kid down that greedy-ass hatch in less than ten minutes. I can't believe it. They cut P.E. out of the school. Can't pay the teacher. They cut recess. Can't afford supervision and what they really need are some cops out there to keep the drug dealers away before and after school. I wanted her to take tap at the community center, but they closed that too. And, we wonder why there's an epidemic of obesity?"

Panky snapped his fingers. She whirled around showing him a friendly face. "Your plates are up next, Senator Panky."

Andy's phone vibrated. He glanced at it briefly, swearing under his breath. "What a nightmare!" He looked up at Sienna. His face was grim. "How is it that you happen to be here in our nation's capital on this historic day?"

Dread mixed with the rumbling in her empty belly. "What?"

"The NASTE has passed Congress and the Senate. And it looks like Pica got the contract, hands down."

"Ugh!" she groaned. "Jules Holdaway and Mimi will be delighted. Apparently, she's at a summit with Pica people in Santa Fe right now."

"Pica has meetings all over the country, but, the truth is, they're headquartered in Panky's home town." Andy inclined his head toward the party across the aisle. "Talk about pork belly legislation."

Slowly, things fell into place for Sienna.

"Do you know what this green stuff is?" Andy asked.

"Arugula. It's really good for you." Sienna took the greens he didn't want to replace the ham she'd removed from hers. "I heard my state spends something like thirty-five million dollars a year on testing. I suppose now they got the contract for the NASTE, Purewater's measly three hundred and fifty thousand for *Reading Fare* was just a drop in the bucket for Pica. A drop in the bucket that's drowning a lot of kids. And though no one is letting on, I think it's starting to make a lot of teachers really miserable. Is this Boursin cheese?"

"Yes," Andy said. "It's very rich."

"*Bon Appetite.*"

Although her first bite of the oversized Senator sandwich was truly delicious, Sienna couldn't keep herself from casting grim sideways glances at Senator Panky. How could he be in charge of so much and be so clueless?

The waitress returned. Sienna expected her to ask how everything tasted, but she surprised both of them by grimly saying, "Senator Panky would like to offer you two some champagne."

"What?" Sienna exclaimed, disgusted.

Panky himself stood and walked over. "I can tell you're curious about our little *fiesta* over here. We're celebrating a great step forward for America. I'm Senator Panky." He beamed with a gesture that included the companions behind him. "And these are my friends Chase Haight and Jack Holdaway. Please have a drink on us. Join us in toasting the passage of my NASTE bill."

In their stunned silence, he gestured for waitresses to hurry and fill their glasses. "Do you care about education, Miss?" he asked Sienna. "Do you have a heart for America's little public school children?"

Sickened, Sienna managed to say, "Yes. I do. I'm a teacher."

"Well," he took a step back. "What grade do you teach?"

"Elementary," she said. "ELL."

"What's that?"

"English Language Learners."

"Oh!" Panky stepped back a little further. It seemed to dawn on him that maybe the sideways glances she'd been giving him earlier might not actually have been an invitation for him to buy her a drink. Maybe, she hadn't been planning to dump the tweed blazer after dessert. Well, now that he'd gotten closer, he could see that this woman wasn't really quite as young as he liked them. "Of course," he said, "the NASTE will require you and your students to work harder than you are used to. It may require you to sacrifice a little more—to toe the line to meet rigorous national testing requirements to get federal funding, but I'm sure you'll ultimately agree that it what's best for kids."

Toe the line? Work harder? Images rushed into Sienna's mind—the black puma telling Pilar that she'd already asked for too much, Cassandra and her barefoot disciples, Dulce attaching herself to traumatized Esteban because she couldn't afford college if she could get in. Sienna stood up angrily. "Ultimately, I won't agree. You have no right to assume or insist that I will. Why should I ignore what I know because you have no clue about what teachers actually do for America's little public school children?"

"Amen, Sister!" their waitress cried. "Amen!" The other waitresses came closer, cheering, whistling, and stamping their feet. They would have clapped for Sienna too, if their hands weren't full of Panky's champagne.

The color rose in the senator's face. He masked his chagrin with bravado. Like a hero in an old-time Hollywood Western, he called to the bartender, "Get her a stronger drink. Whatever she wants." To Andy, he said, "My sympathies, Man. You got yourself a beautiful lady, but she's a pistol."

"You should go back to the House." Andy jabbed his thumb over his shoulder, pointing the way. "Read the writing on the wall. First floor. Roosevelt said it. 'Any oppression, any injustice, any hatred, is a wedge designed to attack our civilization.' Why are you and all your cronies attacking public school teachers and little children?"

"You guys are way too intense." Panky said. Lots of experts have agreed that the NASTE is a good move." He grinned at Sienna. "Teachers just have to learn there's really no such thing as a free lunch. Trust me. Go back to school and pledge allegiance to the NASTE." He picked up his bottle of champagne as if taunting them with it—as if he actually had the power to carry out his threat. "Or there might not be any federally-funded free breakfast any more either."

Chapter Twenty-Five

On the first day of May, Sienna placed a bouquet of hyacinths on her kidney table in the library. The past several weeks of trying to prepare her students for a high stakes reading comprehension test in English had been disheartening. She'd begun bringing flowers in on a regular basis. This coping technique wasn't great for her budget, but it was good for her spirits. She'd also taped an incentive chart on the corner of her desk. At the end of each class, when she gave her students stickers for submitting to the meaningless test practice, she stuck a small smiley face on her own personal chart. When she filled it up, she intended to call in sick and recuperate by reading for her own pleasure all day long. She'd also taken to listening to audiobooks on her phone on her way to work and even in the moments, like now, when she didn't have to interact with staff or students. Immersing herself in good literature kept her from thinking about how much time they were wasting on reading test preparation. When Jolie touched her arm, Sienna saw she looked upset. She pulled a plastic earbud from her ear. "What's the matter?"

"Deedee wants me to cancel the library this morning to cram with kids the classroom teachers think are in danger of failing the Reading WASTE." Jolie grimaced. "The kids on the list they sent me are mostly from your *Writers' Lair*."

Sienna breathed in the sweet fragrance of blue hyacinth. "The kids I've been coaching all month?"

"Yes. Apparently they still aren't up to snuff. The teachers gave everyone another practice test Friday afternoon and now Deedee is completely freaked out. She wants me to tutor them one last time before they start the exam."

"I'm so glad the WASTE starts today. I just want it to be over with!" Sienna pulled a cluster of tiny blue flowers from the vase and laid it at the feet of *La Mujer de Tierra*. She taped a sprig to the bottom of the Swami's frame.

Jolie ignored the odd little ritual and read Deedee's email aloud. "We know Sienna has tried, but since she wasted so much time focusing on writing this year, we think a different teacher might help the kids get ready for the all important reading portion of the WASTE right now. We will try to get Sienna more training on teaching reading to ELL kids and on how to work as a professional team player as soon as possible. Meanwhile, thank you for all your cooperation on this."

"I quit." Sienna said. "I quit." Then, she clapped her hand over her mouth. Teachers never said that in May—not when the fiscal director was grappling with staffing for the following year.

"Don't give up yet," Jolie said, beginning to type. She read her reply. "Sorry. Deedee. I have watched Sienna work with the children. No one else could have done any more or any better. If you insist, I will be happy to read with the children on your list. However, we also all know that cramming at the last minute is likely to be counterproductive and raise students' anxiety levels. If I work with them, I will ask comprehension questions about real books, not about practice test selections."

"Thank you," Sienna said. Andy had been right. It helped to have an ally at work. "I would go crazy here without you. I have an ethical responsibility to advocate for my students, but my boss won't listen to me. And she won't even look at Andy's books on the subject now because he's my lover. But, she should at least listen to the advice of other experts."

Sienna went to her bookshelf for what she called her ELL 101 textbook. "I'm going to the office to copy the chapter on how stress affects learning and performance and I'm going to stick it in her mailbox. I mean, if Deedee assumes that we are going to accept and forgive her poor decision-making because she's too stressed out to think more strategically, then why does she think stressing the kids out is going to make them perform better?"

Sienna reached for the book and her hand brushed against the edge of a piece of construction paper, lying across the tops of the spines. She pulled the paper out, studying the penciled outline of Pilar's missing mother, of Esperanza Luz, beginning to form a pot from sacred clay. Pilar had never finished the picture of her mother. She'd never finished the picture of her grandmother either. She'd never had enough time or help to write the stories that went with them. Her stories were being systematically erased before they ever had a chance to be remembered or written.

* * *

As Sienna hurried to the office, hoping there wouldn't be a long line at the copy machine or that it wouldn't be jammed, she felt an increasingly familiar fury rise within. As the thin soles of her Mary Janes pounded on unforgiving asphalt, her shins burned. Day after day, I hurry, she thought. We all hurry, hurry, hurry for nothing, or very little. The bones in her ankles were jammed. Her knees ached. Her hips locked. She felt the sting of sciatica. Anger scalded the lining of her heart and she wanted to scream to release the torrent of emotion. Weeping would be quieter. Even so, she had nowhere truly private to go. Sienna knew if she took refuge inside one of the bathroom stalls she'd have to look at pictures of gray tweed jumpers taped right over the toilet paper dispenser or read another anonymous intellectually insulting or artificially inspiring Internet story.

"Ms. O'Mara! Ms. O'Mara!" Frantic children's shouts broke through her despair. Her fourth graders stood in a cluster under the blooming dogwood tree near her old portable. "Come here! Ms. O'Mara, come here!" Cassandra called. Obviously, they wanted her to see something, probably some horrendous graffiti that Captain Swabby had missed on his morning rounds and would have to remove immediately. She'd have to hunt him down. He was probably in the cafeteria, helping with breakfast. She'd have to copy the research on stress and shame later. Damn it!

She took a deep breath as she hurried past a parked rumbling diesel truck, delivering its usual bleached-out bread to the nearby cafeteria. It belched exhaust and Sienna breathed in the black fumes—as foul smelling as her mood. As she reached the kids, Cassandra pointed back at the building she had just stomped out of. Sienna turned around to look.

Clumps of bright pink cherry blossoms lay like fallen snow banked against the base of the exterior. The dark shape of a woman was embedded in the brick. She stood directly below a crack in the center of the gutter. As if arising from within the solid wall, the shimmering outline of an elongated, oval aura surrounded her, radiating a pure, white light.

In a hushed, reverential tone, Miguel Pena asked Sienna, "Do you know Mary?"

"Mary?"

"*La Madre de Dios*," he whispered. The Mother of God.

Sienna nodded.

"It's her!" Cassandra declared.

With joy on their young faces, they studied Sienna's face. Would she believe in the miracle?

"It's *La Virgen de Guadalupe*," Lupe added as if to contribute to the teacher's comprehension.

Like drops of baptismal water, white dogwood blossoms fell from the branches onto their heads as Sienna continued to consider the woman's illuminated shape. All the colors of the rainbow undulated around her edges. A surge of what could only be called serenity settled over Sienna.

"You think so?" Pilar asked her, hopefully.

"Yes," Sienna said, blessing what the children obviously saw. "It is *our* Lady of the Brick Wall."

"She come to help us with the WASTE," Cassandra said confidently. "But, don't tell Mrs. Hayes. Or that lady with the clipboard. Don't tell Mrs. Albright too. *Ellas no entienden*."

"Don't worry," Sienna promised. "I would never tell them she came to help you."

And then Cassandra made a motion, rather like the traditional Catholic response to the word of the Gospel. With her thumb she made the sign of the Cross, on her forehead, on her heart, and then on each shoulder. The other children repeated the sequence and grinning, devoted and determined, they made the pilgrimage to the WASTE.

***

Nancy and Sienna stood in the front corner of Nancy's classroom, proctoring the Reading WASTE. Nancy had reminded the students several times to be completely quiet during the testing session. "In fact," she added ominously, "even a noise like coughing could create a testing irregularity."

"What if you have allergies?" *Gringo* asked, nervously. "I might have to sneeze."

"Don't." Nancy gestured for Sienna to move the box of tissues from the back shelf to *Gringo*'s desk.

"What if you have to throw up?" Travis Hadley asked in consternation. No one giggled. He was asking a serious question, one that several had on their minds, but were afraid to ask.

"Just don't do it on your test." Nancy gestured for Sienna to move the trash can next to Travis' desk. And with that, the WASTE began.

Nancy and Sienna watched students open the test booklets. They watched their eyes rolls back in their heads as they turned the first page.

"The print is too small," Sienna whispered, feeling the children's unease fluttering in her own stomach. "The passages are too long."

After the first few minutes, Nancy hissed, "Cassandra's too fidgety." Cassandra had slipped her foot out of a worn sneaker and was circling her ankle and wiggling her toes. She was also scratching at her solar plexus, as if hives were erupting on her torso. "I hope she's not getting the chicken pox or something."

"Nerves," Sienna said, feeling that something was very wrong in the room.

After a few more minutes, Nancy inclined her head toward Javier. "Could you check on him?" With tears welling up in her eyes, she choked, "I just can't take any of his shenanigans right now." For weeks, Nancy had told her class, "Take your time on the test," but now overwhelmed and anxious to be "done" with it, some kids were filling in their bubble sheets way too fast to have actually read any of the test selections. And to make it worse for her, Javier actually seemed quite amused by what he was doing.

With a sudden burst of sympathy for Nancy, Sienna strolled over and knelt beside Javier. "How's it going?" she whispered casually.

"It's funny." He was obviously surprised and delighted to discover how entertaining the WASTE really was.

"It's funny?"

He chortled. "Look!" Bursting into uncontrollable giggles, he pointed to a short answer he'd written. *It has a big boody.*

"Shh!!" She wanted him to quiet down, so he wouldn't make Nancy mad or make anyone laugh. His gleeful chortling was contagious under so much stress. Asking him to read would be the quickest way to sober him up so she said, "Can you read the question to me?" The question was about how an animal's body could serve it in its environment.

Proudly, Javier said, "I found my answer in the text, just like you and Mrs. Albright made us practice." He pointed to a line in the passage and guffawed, "See, it says the animal has a big boody."

Javier had read *body* as *boody* and thought that *boody* meant "booty" as in buttocks. He thought the test passage said the animal had a big butt. Remembering how the Swami came from the swap meet, Sienna realized that it could only be at a moment like this—when a child reveals such a misperception—would it ever occur to a teacher to teach the proper spelling and pronunciation of *booty* in contrast to *body*. Javier was going to miss the question because even though, in truth, the animal he was reading about did have a very large rear-end, he was not able to explain *how* a big butt helped it survive in the wild.

Meanwhile, Miguel, who had spent most of the test so far staring at the ceiling, began to hum. Within twelve minutes of starting the exam, he was alternating between rocking his chair and his desk back and forth or side to side. Sienna sauntered toward him. "What's up, Miguel?" she asked, looking him in the eye and then glancing down at his reading passage to show him where he was supposed to be looking without actually telling him to.

"I don't get it," he said, drumming the page of his test booklet. It was already so battered Sienna wondered if it could still be fed through the scanner to be scored upon its return to the state's central office. Miguel's head swayed back and forth with a beat only he could hear inside his head. His feet took up the rhythm, tapping on the tile floor. Cassandra scratched her shoulder desperately.

"Shh," Sienna said, reading the specific question for insight on what could be triggering this usually well-behaved boy's conniption fit. Miguel was stuck on the question that asked him to select which details from the text best supported the claim; *Doctor Jones was a generous man*. Sienna scanned the test passage. In the fourth paragraph, she read, *Dr. Jones was known for being altruistic. He volunteered at free clinics and organized fundraisers so children could attend summer camp.*

Sienna quickly analyzed what Miguel would have to do to get the points for this question. C—*He supported children getting fresh air and exercise*—was the best answer for supporting the claim that Doctor Jones was generous. A child would have to realize that organizing fundraisers for summer camp meant Dr. Jones supported children get fresh air and exercise. Miguel didn't know what fundraisers were and he had never even been to a day camp. He got fresh air and exercise in the small yard that his Grandma didn't want to be a safari.

But that wasn't the only layer of obfuscation. Miguel would have to know the meaning of the word *generous*, which she was certain he had encountered many times at Moore. He would have also had to know that *generous* is a synonym for *altruistic* and she didn't think he'd ever heard that word.

Even if he had encountered *altruistic,* the teacher who introduced it may have quite reasonably explained that an altruistic person is caring or giving. *Generous* and *altruistic* were certainly not part of Miguel's daily speaking vocabulary, so even if both of them had been covered in a previous vocabulary lesson, it would be hard for him to remember them. Plus, they weren't the sort of words that could be sounded out. So, it was very hard for Miguel to read them and then recall their individual meanings. Thus, even if Miguel knew both *generous* and *altruistic* meant the same thing, he'd still have to figure out that *volunteering at free clinics and organized fundraisers so children could attend summer camp* matched up with *supported children getting fresh air and exercise.*

Sienna snorted. Senator Panky had asked her, *Do you care about education, Miss? Do you have a heart for America's little public school children?* If Senator Panky had children, she was sure they'd been to very elite summer camps. Heck, they'd probably been on world-class safaris too, slumbering beneath canopies of mosquito netting. But, during the WASTE, Miguel was the mosquito. With the tip of a brand-new, extra sharp pencil, he dive-bombed his scantron sheet. Like a parasite with an eager proboscis, he ground the graphite into the circle beneath the *a.* "If I'm gonna be smashed by words, I'm gonna smash you," he muttered to his test booklet.

Nancy finally snapped at Cassandra, "Stop all that scratching! You're distracting everyone!"

All of the children glanced up at their teacher. Although they were used to her yelling once in a while, they appeared quite stricken. Pumping her stress into the classroom, their teacher's amygdala was like the bong Jonathan's mom kept under the driver's seat of her car. The children were getting second-hand stoned on her fear. Their test booklets were as rank with anxiety as the pages of *The Little Mermaid* had reeked of pot until Jolie buried it in Christmas potpourri—for two weeks straight. Sienna thought of Senator Panky's smug proclamation—lots of educational experts have agreed that the NASTE is a good move. Good for whom?

Afterwards, walking back to the library, Sienna saw Our Lady of the Brick Wall again. The apparition and the breeze ruffling her hair, helped lift a little of the WASTE misery off her shoulders. When she entered the library, Pilar was deeply immersed in her work on the image of her mother that Sienna had inadvertently left on the table. Pilar's newcomer status let her skip the reading portion of the WASTE, for this year only, and Jolie had been enlisted to supervise her while the rest of the fourth grade class endured the exam. Over the next few days, the state would still expect Pilar to write and solve a string of complex word problems on the math portion of the WASTE. Obviously, Jolie had set the *Reading Fare* packet Nancy had sent with Pilar aside and let the child resume the work of *The Writers' Lair*.

"Did she tell you anything about her mother?" Sienna whispered to Jolie.

Jolie shook her head. "Not a word. She got a little teary-eyed when she saw you left the picture out for her to finish, but she got right to work on it. How's the WASTE going?"

Sienna relayed what she had observed in Nancy's room.

"Maybe we should buy Nancy a bottle of really nice wine," Jolie remarked. "Maybe she'd give me my scissors back."

Sienna scanned the glossary in the back of a fourth grade *Reading Fare* textbook. *Generous* was not even listed. The word Pica put on the test wasn't even in the curriculum it sold to prepare children for the exam. She searched her regular dictionary and read aloud. "Generous characterized by noble or forbearing spirit, magnanimous, kindly, liberal in giving, openhanded, marked by abundance or ample proportions, full-flavored—as in a really nice wine. Altruistic is not even listed here in the regular dictionary."

She turned to *altruistic*. "As an adjective, it is listed under the noun *altruism*. That's another layer of language complexity and it's defined it as *unselfishness*."

"What?" Jolie remarked wryly. "Not *generous*?"

"And *unselfishness* in all its glory has a prefix *and* suffix. And *unselfishness* is not part of the definition for *generous* either. How could we expect ELL kids to link all this together while they are still trying to decode an unfamiliar text full of unfamiliar words?"

"This is so unfair," Jolie said. "To kids and teachers!"

"Especially when English Learners can be anywhere from 20,000 to 50,000 words behind their native speaking peers." Sienna said, thinking of Miguel grinding his pencil into his packet. "Nancy has drilled them on vocabulary lists all year long, but success on that one question hinges on a full analysis of just one of the thousands of words they haven't had time to learn and wasn't even included in the curriculum. Pica designed the WASTE and wrote *Reading Fare.* Even though Nancy practiced fidelity to *Reading Fare,* her students will still miss this one on the WASTE."

"Why would they even put *altruistic* on the fourth grade WASTE?" Jolie asked.

Mimi Lang shouted from her inside her office. "I can't believe my ears!" She stormed out, shaking with rage. "It is a violation of professional standards to discuss what it is on the WASTE. It is against the rules for a teacher to read the selection or the questions or look at the student responses. And here you are, Sienna. Not only have you done that, you are also revealing top secret information to someone who didn't even go through proctor training."

"Wait a minute!" Jolie said. "That's crazy. Why can't teachers read selections and questions?"

"To protect the integrity of the instrument," Mimi snapped. She scowled at Jolie as if she were an idiot.

"Actually," Sienna said, "I think it's so the testing company can get away with asking unfair and unreasonable questions. Otherwise, why don't we get to find out which specific questions kids missed when the test is over? Why do we just get a score and a ranking? Why are we being told to put all our trust into Pica? Pica's curriculum? Pica's test? Why are we being driven to waste valuable time blindly aiming for moving targets? Why are administrators like you hired to birddog teachers like us? Why does Pica get to rake in millions of tax dollars that we should be spending much more wisely and altruistically?"

Coldly, Mimi said, "I advise you to keep your questions to yourself. There's absolutely no excuse for you to know what's in the WASTE and you could be disciplined for revealing what you found out."

After Mimi's rebuke about not paying attention to what the children were being tested with, the familiar sign outside the testing area of their failing school seemed even more ominous to Sienna. It read "Authorized Personnel Only. No Media Allowed."

That afternoon, Sienna found herself, once again—not teaching—just proctoring the ELL students who hadn't finished the WASTE before lunch.

Belmaris clutched the hem of Sienna's cardigan "Teacher," she stared up at her, her dark brown eyes pleading, "I want to write." Sinking into a sea of children earnestly grasping at the print for something they could comprehend, Sienna knelt beside her. Belmaris's eyes widened. Absolutely frantic, she whispered. "I cannot make a mind-movie of this."

One week earlier, this same coffee-skinned little girl had sat in *The Writers' Lair* beaming, taping yet another page of notebook paper to the bottom margin of the last, generating a scroll that ran down the front of her desk and curled on the threadbare carpet. Her tale about encountering an elf on the playground was full of new English vocabulary. She read it to herself repeatedly while drafting and then again fluently to her delighted peers during "Author's Chair." Now, Belmaris trembled with self-doubt and fear. She whispered, "What's the office going to do to me?"

"Nothing, sweetie," Sienna said, thinking about how livid Mimi had been with her. She wondered, "What are they going to do to me?" but despite her own fear, like the ancient healers—the shamans—in some indigenous cultures, she stepped into the role of sin-eating and lied. "This test is to help your teachers know what you need."

Chapter Twenty-Six

The annual writing assessment was scheduled the day after the reading test. *The Writers' Lair* was very quiet. All that could be heard were the sounds of pencil lead skittering across the pages of barcoded pamphlets, the occasional erasure, and the periodic turning of dictionary pages. The air was thick with currents of creativity and concentration. Occasionally, kids looked up over cardboard tri-folds, otherwise known as "private offices" to look at Sienna. She scanned each face, questioning with her eyes. Each child grinned conspiratorially. *Conspiratorially.* In Spanish *con* means together. Conspiratorially. *Together in spirit.* As *la maestra* exchanged smiles with her students, they were conspirators, united in the celebration of burgeoning literacy.

Outside, a sign stamped with the state seal hung on the exterior door of the library. Just like during the reading portion of the WASTE, only authorized individuals were allowed to enter. No press. No laughter.

Inside *The Writers' Lair*, there was an occasional irregularity, the self-contained chuckle of a child discovering the Swami within. Sienna watched as the children, even under the pressure of the WASTE, generated and organized appropriate ideas using the best word choice given the words they did know. She watched them demonstrate sentence fluency appropriate for their development in grammar. Despite Mimi's admonitions that she not look, she glanced

236

at their work, gratified that they were remembering to start sentences with a capital letters and end them with periods. And Belmaris even dared to use quotation marks! Wow! Students were permitted to use conventionally published dictionaries on the writing WASTE. Sienna crossed her fingers, hoping they could figure out the first two or three letters of the words they needed, but couldn't spell, so they could find them in the fat alphabetized tomes. Compassion, sweet conspiracy, and pink hearts filled the room.

***

On the final day of the WASTE, Miguel opened the math portion, took a look at all the text, stood up and walked right out of the classroom.

"Come back here, Miguel!" Nancy called as he let the door swing shut behind him. Barely able to breathe, she dialed the office. "Irregularity! Irregularity!" she gasped, practically hyperventilating into the receiver.

When the call came, Sienna was standing at the file cabinet next to the secretary's desk, quickly reviewing the enrollment papers of another new student from Clemencia. Mrs. Donahue was helping the bus driver fill out a discipline report about the fight that had broken out in the back of the bus during a stop at the tracks for a long train. At first, the vet from Afghanistan wanted to make the offenders march straight off the bus and do push-ups in the median while the Amtrak commuter whisked by, but he'd been working for Purewater long enough to realize that no one could act on a decision until they'd filled out the paperwork to get permission from an administrator or a committee to move forward. Actually, driving a bus for a school district was a lot like being in the military, except there you didn't have to fill out paperwork before you assigned push-ups.

With an irritable glance at the retired lieutenant and secretary huddled over a carbon triplicate, Deedee stomped out of her office to snatch up Mrs. Donahue's phone. "Shit!" she hissed, slamming the handset down. "We've got another runner! Fourth grader named

Miguel. Smack in the middle of the WASTE!" She began to pace, muttering, "Damn! Damn! Damn! Last time a kid escaped he got all the way to the highway and it was on GOTCHA News Four." She snapped her fingers and pointed at the bus driver. "Is your bus here?"

"Yes, Ma'am."

"Let's get him before he gets too far!" Deedee grabbed her gold lamé rain jacket and gestured toward the back door where the school bus was parked behind the office. "You come too, Sienna."

Sienna exchanged an alarmed glance with the bus driver. She didn't know his name, just his bus number, 47. "Deedee," Sienna said in her most soothing voice, "I'm supposed to help proctor…"

"Come with me, now!" Deedee screamed, grabbing her umbrella, brandishing it at Sienna's feet. "I need you if the kid doesn't speak English."

"He spe…" Sienna began to explain.

Like a nipping sheepdog, Deedee herded her to the bus, shouting at Mrs. Donahue. "Call the cops!"

Afraid, she was about to be poked with the point of an umbrella, Sienna scrambled up the steps and quickly slid into the seat behind the driver as he started the diesel engine.

"Go! Go! Go!" Deedee yelled as Lieutenant 47 backed out of the parking stall. As he accelerated, Deedee stood clinging to the galvanized boarding pole. Her eyes gleamed with the thrill of the hunt as she craned her neck and scanned the sidewalk. "Take a right!" She shouted. She continued barking orders to turn left or right until they were several blocks away from campus. Finally, they ended up in the Bonny Deals' parking lot.

"I don't see a kid anywhere," Lieutenant 47 said over the rumbling engine. "Is this where you wanted to be, Ma'am?"

Deedee looked around somewhat dazed. "Yes," she finally said, fixating on the Starbuck's sign. "Let's go through the drive-up."

"The bus won't fit." Lieutenant 47 was very sure of that.

"No excuses," Deedee told him disdainfully. "You just have to try a little harder."

Suddenly, Mrs. Donahue's voice came out of Sienna's pocket.

She'd forgotten to put her bus-duty walkie-talkie back in the charger that morning. The secretary said, "Captain Wolf found Miguel. He's bringing him back in. I just called Grandma."

Just then, the dispatcher from bus barn radioed the driver, "Forty-Seven? I repeat, Forty-Seven. Why have you not docked yet?"

"I've been hijacked, Sir."

"What?"

"By the principal."

"Where are you?"

"At Starbucks."

"Get the hell out of there!" the operator ordered. "That place is off limits. GOTCHA News Four will be on our backs in no time."

"I am an administrator," Deedee said. "Let me out. I need an enormous espresso before I have to deal with that little stinker. My God! I bet his Grandma doesn't speak a lick of English."

***

Later, Deedee sat in her office with her steaming espresso cooling on her desk. She ignored the boy huddled on a plastic chair in the corner completely as she greeted Miguel's nervous grandma.

La abuela was obviously very tired and quite anxious. She'd worked late at Burger Bling the night before, alone with the skinny, pale, pimply kid who swore at her in English. After they'd finally closed the fast food joint, she'd gone straight to a tulip farm to trim and wrap freshly cut flowers in cellophane to ship to market. At least, this summons to school had come near the end of her shift. *El jefe* hadn't been happy about her leaving, but he was willing to let her go early, just this once, because she was a full crate of banded bouquets ahead of the other workers. Deedee made Sienna question Miguel about leaving campus.

"It was supposed to be math today," Miguel said, "but it was all reading, reading, reading. I'm sick of being smashed by words. I'm sick of being crushed, broken, and destroyed by them." He grinned at Sienna mischievously. "Those are cinnamons, aren't they, Ms. O'Mara? I looked them up in the thesaurus when I finished my story

239

yesterday."

She smiled. "They are synonyms. Good job, Miguel!"

"Oh, my God!" Deedee rolled her eyes. "Would you people just get serious?" She was shaking her head with dismay as Nancy and Mimi bustled in. Helplessly, she told Mimi, "I have no idea how to record this irregularity."

Miguel continued, "*Estoy* shattered and wrecked."

"Enough with the verbiage already," Deedee snapped.

Red-faced, Nancy nearly pushed her nose into Miguel's. "What's wrong with you Miguel? Why are you acting this way? You can never, never, ever just leave school! And right in the middle of the WASTE! Shame on you!"

Miguel's face suddenly hardened with fury. He clenched his fists.

"Stop it!" Sienna insisted. "Give him a break."

"He didn't do a single problem," Nancy snapped. "He doesn't need a break."

Mimi nodded vigorously. "We need to take this incident very, very seriously."

As if Mimi's words frightened her, Deedee suddenly tried interceding on the boy's behalf. "He did say he's being smashed by words—whatever that means."

"He just needs to build up his stamina," Mimi explained to Deedee. "A kid running away during the Math portion of the WASTE is a prime indicator that Moore's students, especially the EL's, need to read more story problems. Next year, we need to send a page of story problems home for homework every single night."

"You're right!" Deedee nodded vigorously. "That's a very good idea."

Nancy's jaw dropped. "I have been sending them home every single night," she said. "I really have."

Turning to Miguel's grandmother, Mimi almost wagged a finger at the woman. "You haven't been helping him, have you?"

Not understanding the preceding conversation or the question now being put to her, yet sensing the women had somehow resolved the whole problem, Miguel's grandmother shrugged meekly and relaxed a little.

While Deedee, Mimi, and Nancy conferred about how to mark the irregularity of running away after starting the test on the back of Miguel's test booklet, Sienna walked outside with the little family.

Miguel said, "I didn't leave school. Ms. O'Mara. I really didn't. The police will tell you that."

"Where did you go?" Sienna said gently.

"To Our Lady of the Brick Wall," he said with the ruefulness of a good boy accused of being bad. "Just to see her again."

Nancy swept out of the office, catching up to them. "Come on, Miguel," she said, grabbing his hand to lead back to where the properly designated, trained, and approved Mrs. Geiger was proctoring on Nancy's behalf so she could attend to the emergency.

His grandmother watched Miguel shake the teacher off and drag his feet as he followed her to the classroom. *"Tengo miedo, maestra."* She looked down at the muddy hem of her lavender swap-meet stretch pants, trying to hide her tears and the struggle to find the words she wanted. "He is a tulip," she said, brokenly. "We plant the bulb. We don't want the rats to eat him in the winter. The sun comes. He grows a little. He opens, but the rain drowns him. He cannot bloom."

Chapter Twenty-Seven

Dulce Gantala began volunteering in Moore's library as the WASTE wrapped up. It seemed odd for her to start the community service required for high school graduation at the tail end of her freshman year, but Sienna decided it was a good sign, that Dulce was still planning ahead, striving to get this credit out of the way so she'd be free to take more college prep classes later. Jolie welcomed the help.

Dulce started working during the school-wide book fair Jolie had to run. It was a great help to have Dulce there in the afternoons, selling paperbacks, feathery-tipped pencils, and posters of cute animals to the few kids who had actually had money to buy something at last recess.

They got a lot of first grade business, probably because Mavis Penn had returned from medical leave. She had a pacemaker and was missing a desk, but she sold her class on the joys of a book fair. Bao Yang and Lucero Fuentes and a few others came to the book fair every day and bought heart-shaped erasers or knock-off Play Blades with storybook characters painted on the side.

The end of the WASTE and the book fair happened to coincide with National Teacher Appreciation Week. On Friday, Superintendent Fray actually brought coffee and muffins to Moore and set them up in the staff lounge himself. He walked all the way over to the library to personally deliver some treats and a form letter of thanks from the school board to Sienna and Jolie. "Thank you for the work you do with our students," he said before walking back to confer with Deedee in her office, to resume the administrative huddle that somehow always excluded teachers.

"Wow!" Sienna said, sipping the latte. "This was nice of him. He knows how to step out of the big-wig bubble for a while."

"I think so," Jolie said. "Remember when he came at Christmas?"

Sienna nodded, but she didn't. That had been the chaotic day she'd sent all the mothers and their baked treats back home and then focused on packing and moving again as fast as she could to get out of there for Winter Break.

"His wife actually gave me a private donation to buy more books for our library. She was truly upset that we don't have nearly as many in here as they do at Teagan Hill."

"That was sweet of her," Sienna said, nibbling at the cinnamon crumb topping of her apple muffin. "I think he got these from the bakery. They're really delicious. No Bonny Deals on Teacher Appreciation Day!"

She went to face the cold hostility she always felt when she went into Ashley Whitfield's classroom. When she came back to her treat at recess, she sipped the cold coffee and watched Bao and Lucero Fuentes return to the book fair again. This time they bought two coloring books and two boxes of crayons. Hmm! They were big spenders. Mavis had really hyped them up.

Dulce was manning the cash box during the afternoon recess when the girls came back again. Valentin came too and they bought him a poster of a race car. When she was done with their sale, Dulce disappeared into the stacks, re-alphabetizing the picture books that the kindergarteners always left in disarray.

Deedee came in and asked Jolie and Sienna to sit with her at Sienna's kidney table. "I'm really sorry to have to tell you this," she said, her voice oozing sympathy while her blue eyes glittered like ice, "Dr. Fray has given me some bad news. With the projected budget cuts for next year, both of your jobs are on the line. Jolie, I think you should know that you very well may get a RIF notice next week."

The teachers were mute. As if Deedee thought they didn't understand English, she spoke slowly and loudly. "R...I...F means reduction in force."

Sienna shook her head slightly. It wasn't that they needed an explanation. Every teacher knew what RIF meant. It was the timing. On Teacher Appreciation Day?

Deedee continued, "Sienna, you have enough seniority. You'll probably be transferred to Teagan Hill to take Lisa Alcott's position. She'll be getting a RIF for sure. Now, Jolie, I don't want you to worry. I want you to be prepared. Dr. Fray is trying to figure out a way to keep everyone on board. He's even going to the swap meet tonight to promote a new levy the district is putting up for a special election. Unfortunately for the two of you, Brenda Hadley is equally determined to cut out what she calls nonessential instruction."

"Non-essential instruction?" Jolie repeated.

"Is that like English for kids who don't know it and the library for kids who don't have books at home?" Sienna asked.

"Exactly." Deedee nodded her head. "I didn't even know that we have a swap meet in Purewater? Did you? I guess its behind that Mexican place. Do you ever eat there?"

Sienna sighed. The swap meet had been rescheduled to Friday nights and relocated to the alley behind the row of businesses that included the Vega's restaurant because local sportsmen wanted the fairgrounds every weekend in May to trade guns and knives.

As the dismissal bell rang, Bao and Lucero came bounding back into the book fair, dripping wet. This time Dulce sold them neon pink and lime green spiral pens and matching miniature notebooks with glittery stars stamped all over the covers. She gave the girls plastic bags to protect their purchases from the downpour outside.

Sienna thought about not being at Moore Elementary anymore, about not getting to watch those little girls grow. As frustrated as she was there, she didn't really want to leave her English learners. She knew she could still choose between Teagan Hill or Vandya.

Jolie asked Deedee, "Can't you—as the principal—defend teaching English to ELL students and library skills for all the students at your school? Can't you advocate to the school board for what we do here?"

Deedee looked surprised. "Me? No. I mean I can try, but until the state funds us adequately, everyone just has to tighten their belts. We have to learn to stick to what's most important."

"Ms. O'Mara! Guess what?" Lucero called as she and Bao stopped by the table on their way to the exit.

"What?" Sienna was unable to suppress her smile in the face of their enthusiasm.

Shy, little Bao announced, "We bought stuff to write stories with."

"Great!" Sienna exclaimed, as if she still weren't in the middle of a completely demoralizing conversation with her boss. "I can't wait to read them!"

Bao said. "You come to the swap meet tonight. I show you."

"I don't think I can come," Sienna said. She could already feel the need to be alone to process what Deedee was telling her arising. "Bring your stories back to school on Monday for me. Okay?"

"Okay!" Lucero nodded eagerly. "I'm going to write about Our Lady of the Brick Wall!"

"Me too!" Bao said.

The girls skipped away.

"Wait!" Deedee called, bolting after them, grateful for a reason to flee. "You have to walk at school. You have to do the right thing, even if someone is looking."

"Even if no one is looking," Jolie shook her head. "Did she really say what I heard?"

"We're canned." Even though Sienna was dejected, she couldn't help hoping that the little girls really would go home and write in those shiny new notebooks. She wanted to see what they would have to say about the lady shimmering on the outside of the library wall.

"Shit!" Jolie said. "All I want to do is hurry home, crawl into bed, and cry, but I have to stay late tonight, greet parents, and run the book fair with a big, fat friendly grin on my face." As the ramifications of being unemployed sank in, she added. "Thank God, I'm only renting and I didn't buy a place that I couldn't possibly sell in this market. I've never been fired before."

"They can't fire you guys!" Dulce burst from behind the shelves. Clearly, she'd been crying while hiding, waiting for Deedee to go away. "All the kids love you," she cried passionately. "You are the best teachers ever!"

"Thank you, Dulce," Sienna said, trying to comfort the girl while her own mind was racing. Like Miguel, smashed by the WASTE, she suddenly wanted out of the situation. She wanted to run away—to Andy—but he was in Finland right now. She'd have to settle for her own neighborhood, for Teagan Hill.

**

Through heavy mist, Sienna hurried along the slick rural road trying to outdistance her anger, attempting to escape the frustration she felt flooding her whole body. She barely noticed the pale clumps of involuted tulips, shut down, and folding in on themselves against the dreariness of the day. At least, it was starting to stay light later. She'd have enough time to visit where Teagan Creek met the Purewater. Loggers used to float timber from that point, where they could watch the trees felled on the hill sail down the river. She had often taken Matt there to throw rocks. She probably needed to hurtle a few stones herself.

She traipsed on and on, listening to the full creek gush as it crisscrossed properties on the hill. Dogs ran to their fence lines, yipping and growling as she marched past and instead of talking to them kindly as she normally did, she glowered at them instead. She stomped past horses in their pastures and a neighbor's small private golf course, which when it was clear, had a fantastic view of Purewater Pass. Furiously, she passed an upscale mansion, the walls of which almost throbbed as a high-end sound system blasted the exact same cop-dusting song as the kid at the swap meet played before Gaul sent him away. That had been right before he had given her *La Mujer de Tierra*.

When she reached the gravel where the trail she wanted started, her cell phone vibrated. Checking to see if it was a text from Matt, she saw she'd received a picture instead. Our Lady of Guadalupe with Juan Diego kneeling at her feet filled the screen. The image was very similar to the one on the prayer card Lucero had given her way back at Christmas. The call back number read RESTRICTED.

Her phone vibrated again. A new text message read, *Never was it known that anyone who sought thy intercession was left unaided.* Who would have sent this to her? Jolie? Maybe, but her number wouldn't have been restricted. One of the ELL students? No. How would they get Sienna's number? It was unlisted. Andy? He had sent her posters of the Supreme Court's Contemplation of Justice and the Statue of Liberty, but he didn't even know about the apparition of the *Madre de Dios* at Moore Elementary School yet. Because of the time difference and his packed schedule in Finland, they hadn't had time to talk since the children first saw Our Lady of the Brick Wall. And they wouldn't talk until tomorrow night, at the earliest.

No matter who'd sent it to her, Sienna suddenly knew she was not alone in her fury and her grief. "Thank you," she whispered. Though the mysterious message comforted her, her body still screamed for activity. She was so intent on finding rocks or branches—anything to hurl into the water—she was surprised to look up and see a faded red van by the creek's edge.

Gaul Santiago sat on the threshold of the open side door with a bottle resting on his knee. He looked startled to see her—as if she were a ghost.

Perhaps the nearly cresting river was louder than her feet had been storming across the gravel. Sienna was perturbed by the stricken expression upon his face. "Mr. Santiago? Are you all right?"

"Ms. O'Mara," he said, regaining his composure. "It's a pleasure to see you again."

"And you." she replied. "Aren't you going to the swap meet tonight?"

"No." He shrugged. "I don't get much purchase in Purewater." He grinned wryly, as if he thought she'd understand exactly what he meant.

"Me neither," she said.

"So I've heard. Dulce Gantala has mothers and children in tears. Pilar is hysterical."

"Why?"

"Because you're leaving. But don't worry," he said, amusement and admiration playing on his lips, "Dulce has vowed to save your job. And the librarian's too. She's a pistol."

"Oh!" Sienna was touched. "That's very sweet of her! It's too soon to know how serious these RIF's are. They are always stressful and demoralizing. However, we get them often enough to keep them from being completely shocking."

Sheepishly, he indicated the bottle on his lap. "This is not my usual mode of operation. I am also feeling particularly defeated this evening. Would you like a drink?"

"What is it?" She didn't want to know what he was drinking because she wanted a swig. She wanted to know if he was drunk. He didn't seem dangerous in any way, but it would be good to know how far gone he might be.

"Irish Cream."

"Straight?" She only drank Irish cream in decaffeinated coffee after dinner between Thanksgiving and New Year's Day.

"I see." He laughed. "You belong to a wine-by-the month club?"

How could she explain that for her whiskey was a very hard spirit—that it made her sink straight into a hopeless view of the human condition?

"I don't usually drink it either," he said, "but there I was in Bonny Deals thinking about all the work Lucia and Ramon have done to help Pilar and how glad we all are that you are her teacher. I was standing in the store, realizing how crazy it was that we never considered you might move or leave before she got better. I was just standing there thinking this, scanning the wall of alcohol, and my eyes fell on this bottle. I thought it was appropriate tonight."

His reaction to her potential transfer seemed a little over the top. Still, Andy had told her that in Japan, elementary teachers gained celebrity status. In many of the Hispanic homes in Purewater she'd probably attained a lot of respect and affection. That was understandable. She, herself, had often been very emotionally invested in which teachers Matt got.

Gaul continued, "And then I just felt the urge to be by the river.

So, I drove up here. I laughed when I saw the sign back there. What's a more perfect place for drowning one's sorrows with Irish Cream than a place called Teagan Hill? Teagan is an Irish word, isn't it?"

"Yeah," she said. "It's old Irish for poet."

"Do you live up here?"

Cautiously, she nodded, "With my son. You might have seen him at Master In-Su's. He's a black belt. He might come along soon. He's into jogging."

Gaul knew who Matt was. He'd been paying close attention to everyone and everything connected with Sienna ever since their first meeting at the swap meet. He knew there was no way that the same red-blooded teenage boy he'd seen hanging out with his friends behind the dojang on a Friday night was about to be trailing after his mother. He held up the bottle.

"Care for some, anyway?"

Sienna hadn't had a drink since Spring break when she and Andy, savoring their Spanish wine, discussed dates for their fantasy trip to Andalusian vineyards. Now, here she was with a Mexican man offering her Irish whiskey.

And she did want some. It would be very tacky, almost unimaginable, to drink with him, but she found herself trying to remember just how much alcohol content was in Irish Cream. Same as a beer, right? She wondered what kind of message it would send for her to put her mouth where his had just been. She wanted the sweetness of cream on her tongue and the heat of whiskey to warm her heart. A little dulling of the brain wouldn't hurt right now, either. She was a lightweight when it came to drinking and would still have to walk home. She certainly couldn't let him drive her. She shivered involuntarily and she wrestled with temptation and indecision.

"Hold on a moment." Gaul said. He stood and ducked into his van. He returned with two clay coffee mugs and the red, black, and white serape. He gave her a cup half filled with the drink, set his down where he'd been sitting, and held the shawl up. "May I?" She nodded. He draped it across her shoulders.

The weight was comforting. "Did you say this was made from the same fiber as Juan Diego's cloak?" she asked.

He nodded.

"That's so interesting." She showed him the picture and text message she'd received as she approached the creek.

"That's really odd," Gaul said, showing her his phone. "I got the exact same thing just seconds before you showed up."

Sienna took a sip from the mug. Her first swallow made her feel warm and relaxed inside and she tried not to think of how what she was drinking had passed over the rim where Gaul's lips had been when he thought he'd be drinking from the bottle all alone. Her lips began to tingle.

"Someone must be on our side." Gaul observed, looking at the text once more before tossing his phone behind him into the van.

"Our side?"

"Trying to keeping these kids afloat. To turn them toward their human potential, instead of turning into drug dealers, gangbangers, and graffiti punks."

"Instead of drowning them in words and believing—or pretending— that we are being so very altruistic."

Gaul patted the floorboards, inviting her to sit beside him and she did, hesitantly. As they drank from the clay mugs, they watched Teagan Creek merge with the Purewater. A gentle breeze cleared the earlier mist away. Overhead, alders rustled, flashing the silver underbellies of their late spring leaves. A few vibrant blue Steller's Jays squawked and soared south along the river. Following the trajectory of the birds, down the hill, Sienna saw the tiny hot pink blurs of two children in the distance. The little ones seemed to have slipped out from beneath the green canopy of riverside trees. As they skipped along the bank, dread at seeing them so close to the water's edge, brushed over Sienna, but her protective impulses were inhibited both by drink and distance. There was nothing she could do about those faraway children and she ceased to worry when the dots of bright color merged with the bushes set farther back from the water.

Gaul poured more into his cup. "Do you know the story of *La Llorona*?"

"The ghost?"

He nodded.

Sienna hadn't eaten since she'd savored Dr. Fray's teacher appreciation muffin and she never did well drinking on an empty stomach. Still, in full awareness of all this, she held her mug up for more.

He poured.

"I don't know the story," she said, realizing he'd given her more than he had the first time. "I keep meaning to look her up, but I always run out of time or get rerouted."

"Well," Gaul said, "*La Llorona's* story is usually fairly short. Legend has it she was a very, very poor and very, very pretty *indio*. She used her beauty to lure a rich Spaniard into marrying her. They were happy for a while. Had some kids and then he cheated on her. And she lost it, went nuts. Drowned the children in the river."

Sienna frowned. "I don't get that at all. Why tell a story about a mother who would drown her own babies just because their father was unfaithful? Who would really do that? "

"*La Llorona*," Gaul said, solemnly. "She felt bad about it afterwards. She died of grief and to this day, her ghost haunts all bodies of water, especially rivers, constantly searching for her lost children. Parents tell their kids to be careful because *La Llorona* might mistake them for her own. The trouble is, they say, once she clutches onto an actual child, the only thing she knows how to do is drown the kid."

"That sounds just like Moore Elementary School," Sienna mused. "Every time a student gets lost, all we do is suffocate him or her with more tests and worksheets."

"I don't get that at all," Gaul said.

"Me neither." Sienna had no desire to discuss the educational system with him. She wanted a story. "Who told you about *La Llorona*?"

"Well, she was always just there in Redención when I was growing up." He refilled his cup. "Esperanza Luz, Pilar's mother, always told the story really well."

Watching the rapids crash over sharp slabs of granite river rock, Sienna remembered the day she'd found the awka rock. Esperanza

Luz was Esteban's stepmother, but when he was digging for Baldwin's lost money bag, he'd told Dulce that she never wanted Pilar, her daughter, to hear about any river ghost. Was it because she didn't want her daughter to know that a woman could do that to a child? Or was there another reason? "Can you tell me her version?" Sienna asked. "Can you remember it?"

"I can," he said, "and I am a good storyteller, but it looks like it might start to rain again. Do you have to go before the downpour?"

He was right. Drops were sliding off the leaves overhead, feeling like chilblains as they landed on Sienna's scalp and cheekbones. The sky seemed to burst into tears and weep into her cup. She was suddenly childishly miffed about everything. She wanted magic and a story and she didn't want her drink to be diluted one little bit.

"Is there room in your van?" she asked.

He seemed slightly alarmed and then intrigued at the prospect of the two of them squeezing in there. "It's tight quarters."

"That's okay,"

He narrowed his eyes, calculating something. "Do you realize that there's seventeen percent alcohol content in Irish Cream?"

"Is that a lot?" She stood up and swayed, clutched at the door to maintain her balance.

Gaul chuckled. "I guess I can't let you go wandering off right now. Welcome to my van, Ms. O'Mara. I've got an *El Bandito* that's still warm and some fine Mexican chocolate to offer you."

"Just as long as you don't have an Evil Eye in there. I can't handle any more of that," she broke off, aware that her words sounded a little peculiar although they seemed to make sense in this particular conversation.

The events of her evening were unfolding somewhat like the stories she'd assigned in the *Writers' Lair*. She wasn't meeting a ninja or a monkey tossing truffles in the school yard. An art dealer in the woods was far more interesting. And had she been asked by a magical creature to make three wishes, following the WASTE and the proposed pink slip on Teacher Appreciation Day, she would have requested exactly what she was getting—yes—a strong, sweet drink, a sturdy blanket, and a good story.

Wrapped in the serape, Sienna sat beside Gaul on a thick slab of shag carpet and leaned against a tall pile of Guatemalan blankets. Gaul poured more creamy sweetness into a mug molded with *matriz* and pulled a woven blanket from the top of the stack to cover their legs.

Their feet rested on the rubber edge of the van's side entrance. They had a bird's eye view of the Purewater valley below. In the gray twilight, the surrounding foothills were illuminated with pink as some of the day's descending sun broke through the dark cloud cover. As rain crystals speared white caps on the thrashing river, Gaul recalled Esperanza's wise face. He wanted to translate well for Sienna, if not word for word, then, please *La Madre de Dios*, he begged, then in the same spirit that Pilar's mother would have given the story to the woman her daughter would depend upon.

Of course, he had no idea what parts of the story he didn't know. He had no idea that I, who had inspired the ghost story of *La Llorona*, had been thinking about my life in *The Writers' Lair*. Esperanza Luz had always told my story better than anyone else ever had, but I didn't want anyone else to tell my story anymore. I wanted to do it and I wanted to see what Sienna would say to me and what she would ask me if she knew what really happened. If *The Writers' Lair* was to be erased, I needed to take this chance with Gaul. I begged *Los Muertos,* the ones who'd pushed me out into Purewater when Deedee demanded cruelty, to help me. I also begged *La Madre de Dios*, Our Lady of the Brick Wall, to intercede. I didn't deserve her help, but I dared to ask.

Chapter Twenty-Eight

Gaul said, "Once upon a time, a long time ago in Redención, a young couple named Jesus and Juanita were married. Soon afterwards, they decided it was time to have a baby. So, they lit the leftover stub of their nuptial candle and knelt on the dirt floor of their tiny hut to pray to the Virgin for a child."

I wanted to tell Sienna how the women in Redención make the request. They form tiny infants of clay and sprinkle blood-red portulaca petals over a simple altar of volcanic stone, taken from La Madre Ardiendo.

Gaul said, "Within the year, *una hija* with glistening brown skin was born. Her brown eyes opened immediately, ready to take in the world. The women cooed over the newborn as they swaddled her in bright cloth and passed her from one *abuela* to the next before they presented her to Jesus.

"'*Muy bonita!*' Jesus said softly, gently touching his daughter's hand.

Jesus was unsettled by the mess. Yes, he gently touched his daughter's hand and then he bent over Juanita, who lay exhausted upon straw mats still soaked with the fluids of birth. He gave her a squeamish kiss and then fled to the men.

"The baby was baptized," Gaul said. "They called her Maria Guadalupe. She was an answer to her parents' prayers, but some unseen darkness disturbed her. She squalled for hours on end. Baby Maria Guadalupe kept the whole village up at night. Her howls were louder than the coyotes. She made *los perros* bark, *los gatos* shriek. Everyone had advice for Juanita and she followed it. But it just didn't work to hold the baby upside down or tighten a sash around her tummy.

"Soon, whenever the baby whimpered, Juanita's arms stiffened, her whole body grew rigid and Jesus would hustle out to join *los hombres* for a smoke. Before long, everyone was gossiping about what a terrible mother Juanita was."

They said her milk was sour.

Sienna was indignant. "How was that helpful?"

"I'm just the storyteller here." Gaul smiled, begging indulgence. As if making amends for any shortcomings in his retelling of childbirth and baby care, he unwrapped a disc of stone ground Mexican chocolate and gave a piece to Sienna. "Late one afternoon when Maria Guadalupe had been crying for hours, Juanita had finally reached her limit. She snatched her daughter up from the water trough that was her crib and shook her hard. Then, Juanita ran. With the baby in her arms, she scattered the village chickens, practically flying toward the stagnant canal that the people mocked for daring to dream of ever becoming a real river."

"Both of them must have been absolutely exhausted," Sienna said, enjoying the unfamiliar grittiness of the chocolate dissolving on her tongue. "They were probably anemic."

Gaul went on. "Juanita held her baby over the mosquito-infested water and wailed. She had prayed to the Virgin for a child so she couldn't understand why the one she got was so difficult. She wondered why her infant had to disturb everyone around them?" The sad truth was she wasn't as upset about the child's pain as she was about how the baby's crying made people think she was a failure."

Sienna said, "So even more than wanting to *be* a good mother Juanita wanted people to *think* she was one."

Gaul nodded. "It makes sense. Juanita came from an ancestral line that believed a real *mujer*, one worthy of respect and admiration, could command a child's body, mind, and soul to do exactly what others expected by the sheer force of her will, the power of her manipulation, or her prayer. The village's techniques and Juanita's tireless efforts just didn't work with that baby, that body, but, Juanita's fear that she would be judged a failure rose up around her. As if she were a snake who bit her daughter, Juanita's fear and rage penetrated her daughter's tender organs as sharply as any fang. She shook her baby, again and again screaming. 'What's wrong with you? Why are you acting this way?' And then, she cursed her child. 'You should be like Donna Theresa's baby.'"

Gaul could not convey how much fear shot straight through that distraught little body. The pain of her mother's shaking and shaming was far worse than the colic that made her scream and writhe.

He said, "Sensing that Juanita was about to fling her into the murky water, Maria Guadalupe swallowed her screams. Her body became as still as stone. A coyote howled on a faraway ridge and when Juanita realized that what she heard was the cry of a distant beast and not the misery of her daughter, she did not drown the child."

"Oh!" Sienna said, surprised. "I thought Juanita was *La Llorona*."

Gaul shook his head.

She leaned in a little. He was a good storyteller and she felt the thrill of getting the *Redención* version. "Please go on."

Gaul offered her another piece of chocolate. She was about to refuse until she remembered that it was still Teacher Appreciation Day and her position was being riffed. She popped the rich coarse segment into her mouth.

"From that moment on," Gaul said, "Maria Guadalupe was a model child. She grew up to be the most beautiful and well-behaved *niña* the village had ever seen. There was never *un tiempo* when she'd failed to please. There was never a time, when she was not a success. She garnered little leniencies from the elders and praise from the people. When Donna Theresa's own daughter, the very child Juanita had more or less demanded Maria Guadalupe be like, asked, 'How is it that you are always so perfect?' she simply shrugged. She did not know how she'd become so perfect, but she was proud of herself, proud enough to be able ignore how often her stomach hurt.

"As she became a young woman, the young men in the village

hung around her, as young men will do. She enjoyed the attention, but she decided to wait for *un hombre rico* who could show her a larger world and give her nice things. One day, not long after her *quinceanera*, when she was helping Juanita pull *pan* from the *hornos*, Juan Gonzalez drove up to the oven. With his engine still idling, he admired Maria Guadalupe. She looked at his angular face, fiery black eyes, and broad shoulders and thought he was handsome. She thought that he must have very strong hands if he could control the shining steering wheel of his chrome-studded Citation. She told herself *El hombre estuvo muy rico.*"

"Wait!" Sienna said, shifting a little to lean back and peer at his face. "A Citation?"

In the dim light, she could see the smile playing on his lips. "It's what we have in our common experience. I first saw you at the swap meet when I was helping those guys load their Citation. You were looking at baby clothes."

"I thought this was an ancient legend," she said, a little surprised since she didn't think he had noticed her until he found her examining the serape in the tent.

"It is a very old story," Gaul said, "but in Redención storytellers make their stories relevant to the present day and to their listeners." For a moment his face betrayed worry about the present day reality of Pilar's mother, if she were still alive, but then he resumed the tale. "So when Juan saw Maria Guadalupe, he wanted her. They were enveloped in lust, a passion as hot as the steam rising off the rocks in the ovens they used to bake stone-ground tortillas."

Sienna realized that she and Gaul were almost touching. His body emanated warmth and it was comforting to her. She blushed. Fortunately, it was too dark for him to notice.

Gaul felt their closeness, too. He took a hasty sip from his cup and continued. "It wasn't long before they were married. Maria Guadalupe was very proud of landing such a wonderful husband and attaining such promising prospects. During the wedding preparations, she had spoken endlessly of her plans for *la vida perfecta*. Naturally, she had every expectation that they would be fulfilled. The people in the village were happy for her, of course, but carrying the burden of envy is heavy work and they all felt little relieved to watch her go. They watched her long veil, fluttering from the window of the Citation as the newlyweds careened over the desert and traveled to a larger town many, many kilometers away.

"Their *hacienda* was fancy and the surrounding land was pleasant. After rare desert rains, a gentle river would form and drain out into the sea not far from their home. *En la casa nueva*, Maria Guadalupe enjoyed many choices. The market offered many different and more plentiful foods and fabric than what her village had. Things were good, but it wasn't long before Maria Guadalupe discovered an unpleasant truth. Her rich husband had cruel friends. Before long, she began to suspect that shaking down the people, blackmailing, and accepting bribes financed her cozy existence. Sometimes, she felt sick to her stomach about it, but what could she do? Juan took care of her and within a few years, they had two beautiful children. She was a good mother. She did everything right. The children were healthy and active, talkative, and affectionate. People nodded approvingly when they met in the *plaza*. It was plain to see, Maria Guadalupe was a fine person, a good woman. No matter what wrongdoings her husband was guilty of, she was doing everything right.

"Then, one night Juan told Maria Guadalupe that he would not be attending the evening Mass and the party at a neighbor's house afterwards with her. 'Go alone,' he said. 'Take the children.'

"Maria Guadalupe felt a pain in her lower abdomen as surely as if he had stabbed her with a knife. '*Por que?*' she asked.

"Juan said, '*Por que* I saw Donna Theresa's daughter when I took tobacco to your father last week.

"The mention of Donna Theresa's daughter seemed to twist the knife his coldness had already thrust into Maria Guadalupe's gut.

"Juan said, 'Her husband is dead and I am leaving you for her. tonight. I am leaving you now.'" Gaul paused.

Sienna felt acid, searing the lining of her own stomach. With another spurt, thunder rumbled over Purewater Pass. Lightning struck, splitting the valley below them in half for a fraction of a second. Hail began to pound the roof of Gaul's van.

Gaul resumed the tale with a trace of irony in his voice since the poor weather outside was coinciding with events in his story. "As Juan threw some clothes into his *maleta*, thunder boomed outside. Lightning struck the desert, and the rain began to fall with an intensity that was unusual in that part of Clemencia."

"Wait!" Sienna interrupted. "Were they really in Clemencia?" She'd thought *La Llorona* was generic myth for a generic place.

"Of course. They were in Clemencia. Maria Guadalupe begged Juan to stay, to reconsider her heart, their vows, and the children."

Sienna's sympathy for Maria Guadalupe's desperation and shame filled her as thunder crashed so loudly overhead the shock waves rattled the van. She wasn't frightened by the weather. She began to shiver involuntarily when Gaul's tone hardened.

"Maria Guadalupe's husband told her. 'You aren't good enough. You don't deserve what I give you.' He tossed a few coins her way. 'Use this to buy a little food for the children, but this is all you will ever get from me. You'll have to find a way to manage on your own.' When he said that, Maria Guadalupe heard a voice hissing in her ear. The voice said, *'You should be like Donna Theresa's daughter.'* As Juan turned away, it seemed as if he'd withdrawn the knife and was walking away, pleased to see her blood on the blade. Maria felt an explosion of shame in her belly. She really wasn't good enough. Everyone knew that she hadn't even been a good baby. This would be the talk of the city and the countryside, and most definitely of the backwater village that she and Donna Theresa's daughter both came from. Anger, shame and a pride, as twisted as any colicky lower intestine could ever be, swelled up and engulfed Maria Guadalupe."

"Why was *she* ashamed?" Sienna asked Gaul. "Her husband was the one with the cruel heart?"

Sienna asked a question. Her mind rapidly supplied the answer. Maria Guadalupe came from an ancestral line that believed a *mujer*, worthy of respect and admiration, could somehow force everyone else to do exactly what "society" expected no matter what the cost to herself. She remembered Nancy standing at the front of the room watching her students take the WASTE, wafting fear that she wouldn't be able to make them do what her supervisors wanted her to make them do.

Deedee, Nancy, and Mimi had shamed Miguel the day he ran away from the WASTE to petition the Lady of the Brick Wall. They were full of the same panic Juanita felt when she realized her efforts didn't work with baby Maria Guadalupe. They were also filled with the panic Maria Guadalupe felt when she grew up and realized her efforts weren't enough to keep Juan doing what was needed to care for the family. Suddenly, Juanita and Maria Guadalupe's fear and rage merged with the fear and rage Sienna had sensed and seen at Moore Elementary School. The burning in the pit of her stomach ignited and erupted, flooding her body and mind—all of her senses.

From a long distance, she heard Gaul calling her name and shaking her. She almost rallied, almost heard Chase Haight broadcasting on Gaul's dismantled radio, "American Schoolteacher Celebrates Appreciation Day by binging with Mexican Storyteller," but she lost consciousness.

The mind movie, Gaul had started with his painstaking translation continued to reel in Sienna's dreamlike state. Now, somehow linked to Maria Guadalupe, as if she were a ghost tailing her instead of how it had been since I entered Moore, she watched Juan enter his office to gather up his accounts. She followed as Maria Guadalupe stormed into the kitchen where her adorable children, with brown eyes shining with love, looked up at her adoringly; admiring how beautiful she looked dressed for the evening's festivities.

Maria Guadalupe grabbed the girl who looked just like Pilar and the boy who looked just like Valentin by the hands. She dragged them out the back door, splashing through ankle-deep, lukewarm puddles. Sienna followed the hunched, muttering mother and the bewildered children through a wrought iron gate in the adobe wall that separated Juan's compound from the surrounding desert.

Twisted cactus seemed determined to spear them as they moved toward the edge of the black plateau. Shockingly sudden shards of electricity *en el cielo del noche* illuminated the moonless night. Wide-eyed and rigid, the children resisted moving forward.

"Mama!" the girl cried. "Why are we here?"

The boy asked, *"Adónde vamos?"* Where are we going?

Instantly, Sienna knew the answer. She knew what Maria Guadalupe was thinking. She felt what Maria Guadalupe was feeling. Maria Guadalupe was furious. Furious at Juan. Furious at her children for being so scared, so powerless, and so dependent on her while she was forced to be dependent on a man who did not care about her—did not really care about them. He had used her and now he was finished. She had nothing to give the children now, nor would she ever be able to get anything more to give them later. Their very presence, their weakness, their neediness ruined her chances of looking good to the tongue-waggers, to those who did not know how to contemplate justice, who had no compassion for those crushed by the very culture they created and sustained. Without Juan's love, or at least, financial support, Maria Guadalupe knew the children would always be a liability to her. It would only get worse as they got older. Before long, they'd be a walking testimony to the absolute failure of her will, manipulation, and prayers. She could give them all her life energy, but they would still be hungry, still wear tattered clothes. They would still walk about with the stunned longing for a parent with the resources to care for them and, better yet, for a village that understood criticizing and shaming a mother, is both a lazy and a malicious way to overlook the carelessness and cruelty of a father.

Nearly wrenching their arms out of socket, Maria Guadalupe rushed them off the eroding mesa, dragging them downhill to the river's rapidly blurring edge. Sienna followed. Something brushed against her calf and caught on the hem of her jeans. A scorpion in the swift, rising current swirled between her ankles.

Lightning struck again. Sienna felt sharp pain crackling through her entire being. As if she were Maria Guadalupe, she felt Maria Guadalupe squeeze, breaking a fine bone in her daughter's fragile hand. Between her own fingers, Sienna felt the child's collapse. Maria Guadalupe yanked the children forward.

Just behind them, Sienna screamed, "Stop it!" She flung herself against the transparent wall between the living and *Los Muertos*, grasping for the hem of Maria Guadalupe's white dress. Rain was the only thing that passed through her inflamed fingers. "Stop it!"

"I don't know what to do with you!" Maria Guadalupe told her children.

Sienna jockeyed to Maria Guadalupe's side, but she could not quite penetrate the veil.

"I don't know how to help you!" Maria Guadalupe shrieked. As Sienna watched, the ghost's profile took on Nancy's features, then Tammy's, then Mimi's and finally Deedee's. Each time the face transformed, the woman's voice changed, taking on it's into own distinctive tone. "I don't know what to do with you. I don't know what to do with you. I don't know what to do with you. I don't know what to do with you."

"You do know!" Sienna cried frantically. "You know."

As Maria Guadalupe's face returned, she shook the children violently. Sienna lunged toward them. "They'll forgive you," she said. "If you stop the insanity. They will forgive you, if you stop it this time."

"Stop it, Mama!" the children cried. "Stop!"

"Listen to them," Sienna pleaded. "Just listen to what they say. They will tell you what they need."

Maria Guadalupe froze. Lightning flashed upon her crazed face. Then, her proclamation filled the canyon, overriding the crashing sounds of river and storm. Coldly she said, "There's no excuse for knowing what's in the WASTE."

Maria Guadalupe swung the children over the abyss and let go. They fell a short distance and hit the deep river. Sienna watched them submerge and recoil, gasping. Groping unsuccessfully for each other, they spiraled around and around, as they were washed away, disappearing downriver.

Maria Guadalupe looked grim as the current caught the hem of her white dress and swirled around her legs. When she turned away from the cresting river's edge, she tripped over a tangled mess of tumbleweed and the skull of a cow that had whirled up from the desert floor. She fell toward Sienna, grasping for balance. Sienna reached out to steady her, but neither could reach through the veil between them. As Maria Guadalupe fell, mud splattered all over her and the agony within racked her body.

Sienna watched as Maria Guadalupe realized what she'd done to her very own children. In horrified disbelief, Maria Guadalupe gasped and moaned. "I've killed all the joy in my life." She scrambled up, and ran alongside the river toward the ocean, calling for her children—weeping. It was plain to see, that it was too late. They were lost. Sienna watched Maria Guadalupe's white form disappear among the cedar trees.

The cedar trees? There were no cedar trees in the desert where I destroyed my children. Suddenly, I realized that I had watched Sienna watch Maria Guadalupe run away. How could I watch Sienna watch me run away through evergreen trees? If I were watching her, watching me, then I wasn't the one running. If I weren't the one running, then somehow she'd pulled me out of my story by going into it with me. I was free. Did this mean I could just quit being La Llorona? Could I just quit?

Slowly, Sienna realized Gaul was still telling the story, while she remained standing knee-deep in water, peering through the cedar trees. "The people say Maria Guadalupe never got over what happened. She never stopped crying. Esperanza Luz says if only there had been one strong, wise woman in Juanita's village, this might have never happened. If someone had been there to teach the people that handling a difficult baby isn't about will, manipulation, or prayer the whole story would have been different. If someone taught the people how to remove the disturbing elements from a child's diet and to allow little ones to move to release what causes pain, Maria Guadalupe would have known how it felt to be cared for. She would have found a way to care for her children, even when she was wronged and desperate. Maria Guadalupe weeps to this day."

Sienna registered Gaul's arm around her, his body supporting her. She felt hot raindrops or tears streaming down her chilled cheeks. She remained where she was, feeling the rise and fall of Gaul's warm chest, smelling the hint of whiskey on his breath, the sandalwood scent of his armpit. The bottoms of her jeans were soaked. All she could see were the dark backs of her closed eyelids.

Gaul said, "She's never stopped looking for her lost children.

The people call her *La Llorona*, the Weeping Woman. They say she haunts all rivers, continually reliving and recreating her story. She is a sad, sad ghost."

Sienna scrambled up. "I just saw her." Her voice was hoarse, as if she had really been screaming.

Gaul peered into her eyes, as if searching for an imprint of *La Llorona* on her pupils like Juan Diego had seen the image of Our Lady of Guadalupe on the tilma he presented to Bishop Zumarraga. "*La Llorona* is in Purewater," Sienna said, as if waking from a bad dream. "Her spirit is the one that makes Deedee and Mimi and teachers like Nancy grasp the hands of frightened children and hold them down, drowning them with assignments and suffocating assessments. They are stuck in the same fear of being judged and cast out. *La Llorona* is here. I didn't understand that until now."

Gaul rubbed his face in his hands and looked up, awestruck and slightly aghast. "I didn't know *una limpia* could happen this way."

"*Una limpia*?" Sienna asked.

"It's a type of cleansing," Gaul said, grasping for an explanation. "*Una limpia* allows a traumatized soul to be healed, to reintegrate with spirit."

Suddenly, shouts and frantic cries traveled up, cutting through the cacophony of the river and creek. Gaul pointed down river toward the town of Purewater. Sienna struggled to focus her eyes. Was there a child flailing on the rapids? A small head bobbed up and down. Whitecaps swirled around it, like the child was being choked by the fluttering hem of *La Llorona's* dress.

Gaul leapt from the van. "Call for help!" he shouted. The way was rutted and rocky. He would never make it in time, but he took off at a gallop. Sienna pulled out her phone. There was no signal. As she followed Gaul through the woods that *La Llorona* had disappeared into, Sienna was aware of every real physical detail. Moss hung overhead. Bleached fungi swelled from crevices in cedar bark. Blackberry runners scratched her as she ran—still in the grip of a nightmare, feeling as if she'd witnessed two murders. As they rushed toward Purewater, Sienna felt she was leaving one trauma and journeying into another. With her finger on the emergency button, hoping to get a signal, she found herself pleading for intercession, "Oh, Lady of the Brick Wall, help us."

Chapter Twenty-Nine

Ramon and Lucia were stunned when Dulce announced that Ms. O'Mara and Ms. Fox were being sent away from Moore. Gaul had been right when he said that it had never occurred to any them that their beloved ELL teacher could be eliminated — especially when so many children needed her help to learn English. Unfortunately, the only control the Vegas felt they had over anything in Purewater was what happened in *Casita Rio*.

"We will pray about this later," Lucia told all of the upset neighborhood children milling around outside the back door of the kitchen hoping for the last of the day-old tortillas she would not serve to paying customers. "For now, play and be happy." She gestured toward all the people setting their tables up in the alley for the evening's swap meet. "Go browse."

"And listen to mariachi," Ramon added by way of offering comfort. "We got a real band tonight. No boom box."

"Yuck!" Dulce rolled her eyes in the most Americanized way possible.

Lucia thought she was already acting like a daughter in their house. Lucia glanced at Esteban at the cutting board, dicing *cebollas*. Lucia loved Esteban and Pilar dearly and wondered if they would ever be reunited with their parents. She smiled at Ramon. Maybe it was time for them to try again, to have a baby of their own, but would she really want her child to go to a school that would send a teacher like Ms. O'Mara away? She grimaced at the thought.

"What's the matter?" Ramon asked her. "You don't like mariachi anymore either?"

"I love mariachi," Lucia said, "and I love you." She thought of the altars back at home, where women rolled their requests for infants into clay and laid *matriz* babies at the feet of *La Sirena*. Suddenly, she had advice for the disheartened children. "Go back to our Lady!" she said. "Go back to the brick wall and ask *La Madre de Dios* to let Ms. O'Mara and Ms. Fox stay."

Pilar, Cassandra and her little sister Lucero, Lupe, Belmaris, Alondra, Javier, Miguel and Valentin quickly formed a procession. On the way back to the school, they stopped beside Grandma Yang's flower stall where the gray sky overhead made the huge bunches of vibrant yellow, orange, and red tulips all the more brilliant. Grandma Yang's English was poor, but she was attuned to the acute timbre of sadness. When Lucero explained the mission to Bao, Grandma Yang urged every child to choose one flower to take to the brick wall, as an offering to the lady.

The bigger kids had longer legs and a more elevated sense of urgency. Soon, they left the little ones trailing a full half block behind. Bao and Lucero stopped, still struggling to comprehend the issue.

Bao said, "They have to go away because the school have no money?"

Lucero nodded.

Bao said, "We have money. We can pay for them."

"Want to?" Lucero asked.

About twenty minutes later, they rejoined the rest of the elementary petitioners at Moore. The fourth graders sat cross-legged on the asphalt outside the library, gazing up at the apparition on the brick wall. Grandma Yang's bright tulips and some dark purple irises, borrowed along the way from the dentist's office, had been arranged on top of the pink litter of cherry blossoms at her feet.

"We can save the teachers!" Lucero announced. Gratified to be the answer to their prayers, she reached into her *El Fuego* hoodie and pulled out a hundred-dollar bill.

"Whoo Hoo!" Javier whistled. "Where did you get that?"

Lucero shrugged. "Is it enough?"

"I don't know." Alondra furrowed her brow, thinking hard, thinking about Mrs. Albright's story problems. Teachers need rent, gas, and groceries. "No," she decided. "We need a little more."

"Can you show us where you got all that?" Belmaris asked kindly. Kids like them never had cash. She only hoped the little ones hadn't done something that was going to get them all in trouble.

Lucero and Bao exchanged a look. This was a serious Math problem. They needed help from the fourth graders to solve it. Bao waved her hand back the way they'd come, saying. "Let's go."

All the kids retraced their steps, traipsing back through the swap meet in time to hear Dr. Fray begin his speech about the importance of passing a local levy because the state wasn't funding the district. All that was meaningless babble to them. They hurried past the card table that served as his podium and were hiking north by the time Brenda Hadley stepped forward, as a sitting school board president, to heckle the superintendent about using hard-pressed local people's money for non-essential frills like P.E. and music teachers, recess monitors, school librarians, and, for Heaven's sake, English Language teachers—in America, of all places. Enjoying the sensation of being in the lead, Bao and Lucero led the group beyond the city limits.

Set back in the woods just a short distance from the river was a double-wide trailer. The narrow porch was swept and bedecked with several planter boxes full of well-tended black-faced yellow pansies. The surrounding property was strewn with dismantled car parts and ditched vehicles in various states of disrepair. A No Trespassing sign propped on the front bumper of a 1957 Chevy pick-up truck indicated that the junkyard was someone's private domain.

The property actually belonged to the Hadley family. Indeed, Pilar recognized her classmate, Travis Hadley, kneeling on the seat inside the old truck, turning the wheel, pretending to drive. There was no telling what color the truck had been when it was new, back in the year when Brenda Hadley had been born. Her father had bought it as a personal reward for enduring the long months of his wife's odd cravings and the trauma of listening to her curse him during labor. His pride and joy was faded now. Its shell was like a hard-boiled egg chipped and dipped in watered-down purple dye. An antique by American standards, the Chevy was exactly like what the few people who had cars in Clemencia now drove. And so, like folks in Clemencia when someone they know has a car, all the kids simply clambered in. They discovered Jonathan the *Gringo* was on the seat beside Travis. The boys were having a sleepover and chose to have it in the truck since Jonathan was used to sleeping in cars and Travis had always wanted to try it.

"Ms. O'Mara can't go to Teagan Hill," Jonathan said when he heard the news. "She has to do bus duty."

Travis looked down at his grimy hands, resting on the iron steering wheel. He didn't really know the Spanish kids' teacher. He remembered how kindly she'd smiled at him when he thought he was going to be sick during the WASTE. She'd been really nice about it when Mrs. Albright ordered her to put the trash can next to his desk. She obviously hadn't thought he was faking his terrible bellyache. "I want her to stay too. She's a good one, but," he added knowingly, "it takes a lot of money to buy a teacher. My mom says it would be a bargain at twice the price for a good one, but my uncle and my grandma say teachers cost way too much because you have to pay for them to go to the doctor if they get sick from all the germs at school and you have to give them money for when they are too old and tired to take care of all the kids."

"We can afford it," Cassandra told him, grinning proudly. Ms. O'Mara had taught the word *treasure* when they wrote their stories about encountering magical creatures in the woods and getting three wishes. Now she could use the vocabulary in her real life. "My sister and Bao have found… a treasure."

Lucero pointed. "Over there."

She pointed toward a Chevy Citation in a low lying part of the property. Since it had been raining for months, water lapped at its underside. Blackberry vines with dark pink blooms trailed across its rust-spackled roof.

Travis laughed. "My mom wouldn't call that a treasure."

"Let's go!" Cassandra said. "We have to save Ms. O'Mara."

With water up to their ankles, the kids approached the Citation.

"It's getting dark," Travis observed. Gallantly, he opened the driver's side door and switched on the dome light. It did not illuminate the interior, but one headlight and one brake light came on outside. Bao opened the hatchback to reveal an old engine behind the back seat. The desiccated petals of a few marigold blooms powdered the surface between the dirty cylinders.

"I 'member this car," Pilar said, recalling how Gaul had helped make the engine fit inside on *El Día de los Muertos*. She remembered how the two men stuck flowers in the metallic tubes. Lucero reached in to where Grandma Yang's bouquets had been and pulled out a large Zip-lock bag full of rolled up cash.

"Whoo Hoo!" Javier whistled again.

"There a lot more," Bao said with a gesture that included a variety of junked vehicles scattered across the Hadley place.

"How did you find it?" Jonathan asked, impressed, wondering if his mom could find some cash in a similar way.

"We came by here one day," Lucero said, "and Bao saw her grandma's bouquet sticking up in the window."

"It was a rip off of good flowers," Bao said. "If the man not use them, we get them back."

"Why didn't your dad give them to your mom?" Cassandra scowled at Travis.

Travis shrugged. "He forgets to give her lots of things. Flowers, the rent."

"Yep. I know how that goes," Jonathan said. "My dad forgets to give my mom things too. That's why it's very lucky we don't have a car payment." He scanned the interior as if imagining how it would be to move into a Citation.

"We took the flowers to school so the principal could be happy." Lucero said. "We heard Mrs. Hayes yelling at the flag pole."

"She's like that." Miguel said.

"It's gonna take a lot more than flowers to make her happy," Jonathan noted.

Lucero shrugged, acknowledging that the flowers had been not particularly effective.

Miguel nodded. "That principal is a rip off."

"Yeah, man." Travis patted Miguel's back. "I wanted to walk out on the WASTE with you. I just didn't think a kid could do that, you know? I bet everyone wanted to run away."

"I didn't run away," Miguel said, "I just went to see…" Then, he stopped. The Lady of the Brick Wall was not something to confess to *gringos*. Ms. O'Mara didn't count.

"We found this money," Bao said, swinging the bag of cash before them "when we got the flowers out." She gave the money to Pilar, certain that the nearest fourth grader would be able to count it better than she or Lucero could.

Lucero could see that Cassandra was about to scold her for stealing. "We only spent a little bit," she insisted. "At the book fair. Mrs. Penn, she say, we can't have book fairs at our school if people don't shop."

"She say she be so sad if we don't have a book fair," Bao explained. "We came back here to get a little money to buy stuff at the book fair. We can't let Mrs. Penn be so sad. She have a broken heart already."

"Well," Cassandra said, clearly appeased. "Who do we give the money to when we pay for Ms. O'Mara and Ms. Fox? Should we give it to Mrs. Hayes?"

The contemplation of this dilemma was shattered by Laurali Hadley. Stomping through the saturated field toward them, she shouted, "Just what do you all think you are doing here? This is private property! Didn't you read the sign?" She waved her arms back toward the no trespassing sign on the Chevy. She stopped, knee-deep in water with her hands on her hips and glowered. "Oh right!" she said, recognizing the kids. "You can't read. You go to Moore. All you ever do is tax and spend!" Laurali's eyes widened as she also recognized what was in the bag Pilar held, "And now you're even stealing the car part stash!"

"Car part stash!" Suddenly, Travis understood. If his dad and uncle didn't hide their money out here, his mom and aunt would spend it on rent, food, and clothes. He frowned at Laurali. "What do you care, Laurali? You don't give a rip about car parts."

"I'm a good girl," she said primly. "I report crimes when I see them. Now I know for sure that Daddy and Grandma are right when they say your school sucks!"

"Our school doesn't suck," Miguel said angrily, swallowing hard. In truth, he'd suspected something was wrong for a long time. Did the school suck because they were all so dumb? But, then the writing portion of the WASTE had gone so well for all of them. They weren't *that* dumb, were they? He was truly confused.

"Moore is a terrible school!" Laurali stomped closer, shrill and splashing mud with every squish of her boots, corralling them with cruel words, "It sucks. It really, really does. It sucks!"

"She's my grandma's favorite," Travis told Jonathan.

"Obviously," Jonathan said.

Laurali continued to rant. "Just look at your reading scores. Pathetic! Absolutely Pathetic! You are all way, way behind the rest of the schools in Purewater and all the research shows if you don't make standard by fourth grade, you'll just end up in jail!"

"I AM not going to jail!" Jonathan screamed. She'd clearly hit a nerve with him.

Pilar did not want to go to jail either. She did not want to fight over a bag of money. She threw it at Laurali and fled, away from the screaming, away from the fear rising within her. Valentin followed, both of them moving as quickly as possible across the spongy ground.

Laurali Hadley might have been a fluent reader. She might have met standard on the WASTE and even finished it early, but she could not shift her footing fast enough to catch the bag. It fell with a plop a few inches beyond her where it was promptly snagged by the creek's undercurrent and began to race toward the river. Muttering about "wetbacks," Laurali tromped after it, pulling her boots up by the straps each time they got mired in the mud.

Meanwhile, beside the open hatchback of the Citation, Lucero grasped Cassandra's hand, whimpering. "We're going down."

"We aren't going down," Cassandra said reassuringly. "The police chief loves Ms. Fox. He won't be mad at us for trying to save her job."

Lucero shrieked, "No! The water is going up!" It was true, the river was rising. Her boots were filling with cold water. Her pants were soaked. The water was at the hem of her second- hand coat. Chortling and shouting at this amusing turn of events, all the kids climbed on top of the Citation, just like Pilar's goat in Redención had climbed on top of her school.

Meanwhile, Laurali made a final lunge for the bag of cash and tripped over the submerged chassis her uncle had long since forgotten was there. The rising water cushioned her belly-flop. She never hit the ground. As the full river mingled with Teagan creek, the overflow of their meeting flooded the Hadley land. Hidden currents swirled beneath the surface. As what had been Teagan Creek pushed Laurali closer to the money, what had been the Purewater pulled it away. She craned her neck to keep her face out of the muck. When she stretched her full length, reaching for the elusive treasure, the Purewater seized her.

Cassandra seated on the Citation—like the solemn marble Contemplation of Justice outside the Supreme Court—suddenly became animated. Pointing her finger, she declared, "It's *La Llorona*."

All the kids on the car beside her followed the arc of her finger and saw Laurali slipping away. They began to scream, shout, and wail. "*La Llorona*! It's *La Llorona*!"

Pilar and Valentin had reached the river trail by then. They weren't far from the edge of town where the backsides of the First Street businesses began. Pilar strained to hear what the others were shouting behind them. *La Llorona*! There were no good choices for them now. Jail or *La Llorona*—both were the stuff of nightmares!

Out of the corner of his eye, Valentin caught a flash of white as Laurali swirled alongside them. *La Llorona* had *her*? He'd only thought she went after Mexicans.

"Help! Help me!" Laurali called hoarsely.

Valetin recognized the terror mirrored in her eyes. She tried to reach for him, but *La Llorona* spun the girl around. Laurali made a terrible sound as her back was flung against a boulder in the middle of the river. She tried to grab hold of it, but it was too wet and too slick. *La Llorona* pushed her head under.

"How do we stop *La Llorona*?" Valentin cried.

"No one stops her." Pilar gasped. "No one can."

"But what if they could?"

Pilar stared at him hopelessly.

"Ms. O'Mara says make what you need." Valentin reached into his pocket and pulled out the awka rock.

Pilar stared at it. Was the awka familiar because it was part of sharing in Ms. O'Mara's class or had she seen rocks like it before? Yes, she had. Twice. In a very different place. She and Esteban had been fleeing, heading for the foothills. Her father had practically been carrying grandma. And the goat, *Diablo*, he'd helped somehow. And Mamá? Where was she? Her mother was bending beside the water. There wasn't time to stop. There wasn't time not to. Her father had been begging her to hurry. Hurry! *Apurate!*

The kids on the Citation shouted some more. Pilar looked up and saw a man racing toward them, running down the hill as fast as he could. He was a little heavy, a little clumsy, but obviously coming to help. Although he was too far away to identify, everything about him felt like Gaul. With that familiarity, she automatically knelt at the cresting river's edge and scooped some of the cold water into the little bowl of the awka.

Meanwhile, despite the weight of the crowd on top of it, the mud released its impounding quality upon the Citation. The river grasped and tugged. The car began to float. If *La Llorona* weren't involved, the children huddled on board might have found the ride exciting, but now they sailed into the currents of the nightmare too. Completely terrified, they continued to scream, "*La Llorona! La Llorona!*" As the car moved along, they clutched at one another, yelling at full throttle.

Downstream, Esteban didn't understand everything Brenda Hadley was saying to Dr. Fray. He knew it wasn't good. When he saw the hostility in the faces of those who applauded her and the downcast eyes of those she'd directed her diatribe toward, he sensed danger in the air. He heard his father's voice whisper in his inner ear. "Help your sister." Esteban broke away from Dulce and the crowd at *Casita Rio* and ran north along the river, following the path he'd noticed the children taking when Dr. Fray began his speech.

The Citation continued to drift off the Hadley property. As it approached the main flow of the river, just a little upstream of where Laurali struggled, its single working headlight connected with the awka rock in Pilar's hand. The high beam refracted off the water in its concave surface. To Gaul, approaching from the north, and Esteban, coming from the south, it appeared as if a mermaid were poised upon a large stone directing her light to illuminate a child caught in *La Llorona's* frenzy.

Laurali surfaced, continuing to spin, barely-conscious and turning blue. Esteban leapt into the water. As he caught her in his arms, they were slammed into a rock. Gaul dove in. When, he reached them, he thrust them against the rock island in the center of the river. Grasping at a jutting pieces of granite and finding a break in the stone in which to wedge his feet, he formed a cross with his body and anchored them in safety as if he alone could withstand the forces of the river and the rage of a ghost. Gaul heard the other children screaming, but he could not turn, could not look to see why. All he heard was the rushing water and all he felt was his heart pounding, against Esteban, against the girl.

Only when Esteban shouted, "Pilar is the one with the light," did Gaul actually realize he'd been desperately afraid that the floundering child was Pilar. Slowly, he realized that the child they'd saved belonged to someone else. The girl they'd just saved did not belong to his Pablo and Esperanza Luz. Laurali was not from his "family." She was not one of the children he'd smuggled into the safety of Purewater along with the precious art of Redención.

Sienna had followed Gaul, screaming directions into her cell phone, and was slightly more aware of the Citation than he was, but she hadn't really registered that it was drifting. The light reflecting from the awka let Captain Goodwin, the Fire Chief, and Matt motoring up in an emergency rescue boat see where to stop. Gaul handed Laurali aboard. Still in their white Doboks, they pulled Esteban up.

Sienna reached Pilar and stood, panting a step behind her. Pilar stood too close to the edge to risk startling her out of her trance.

Fascinated, Sienna watched Gaul board the rescue boat, through the bright clear light emanating from the awka rock. As Sienna she realized the children were still screeching. She turned toward them.

The Citation was traveling swiftly through the high water now. In the beam of light streaming between the car and the awka rock, Sienna saw that it was about to merge with the river completely. There was no possible way all the children clustered upon it could all be rescued if it capsized in the Purewater. As the vehicle shimmied, skidding slightly on unseen currents, the hysterical children froze, suddenly as silent as colicky little Maria Guadalupe had been when her mother dangled her over the canal, threatening to drop her in. Sienna's students were as rigid as *La Llorona's* children had been when she pushed them into the depths.

Sienna stepped forward, wrapped her arms around Pilar and holding her tight against her chest, yelled. "Jump! Get off now! Get off while you still can."

Caught in *La Llorona's* spell, the kids didn't seem to understand. Sienna screamed, struggling in her panic to remember Spanish. "*Atrás! Tienen Saltar!*" Was that right? Did it matter what she shouted? Even the white kids, even the *gringos* who should have understood her English were in *La Llorona's* thrall. Why hadn't it occurred to any of them to jump? Why were they just going along on the ride that would kill them?

"Get off!" Sienna yelled. "Now!"

Pilar trembled violently. Water sloshed out of the awka, slipping back into the river like a fish reclaiming its breath. With that sloshing movement, the kids on the car threw themselves overboard, taking their chances. With the equal and opposite thrust of each leap of faith, the car shimmied, bogging down just enough between ancient tree roots to slow its motion. Sienna waded to help pull the children up, urging them to scurry to higher and more stable ground.

As Pilar and Valentin reached out to help their friends too, people from the swap meet swarmed upriver. Parents and grandparents, aunts, uncles, friends, strangers, Jolie and Superintendent Fray embraced the children, wrapping them in dry sweatshirts and jackets pulled from their own bodies. Mrs. Hadley sobbed when the paramedics strapped Laurali to a gurney and she rode to the hospital with her precious granddaughter in the ambulance. As the siren started up, the riverbank finally gave and there was no longer any distinction between Teagan Creek, the Purewater, and the lowlands.

It wasn't long before the rumor started that the ELL teacher was *una curandera*—a healer. She had interrupted *La Llorona* in action and frightened her away. One story held that *La Llorona* had been so scared she'd hijacked Ian Hadley's Chevy Citation and driven out to sea. Another held that Our Lady of the Brick Wall had orchestrated it all to teach Brenda Hadley to count her blessings, each and every one, including the Mexican teenager and the swap meet vendor who saved her favorite.

Chapter Thirty

When the Hadley family heard from Travis how the near tragedy had been caused and the school board and the central office had been briefed, the Hadley daughters-in-law opened individual bank accounts for themselves and made their husbands build a fence around the junk that they were able to salvage after the water receded. Talk of RIFs mysteriously ceased. No one knew why.

Then, in the middle of June, Sienna, Jolie, and Nancy were asked to meet with Deedee. To their surprise, Mimi and Dr. Fray accompanied her into the library. The air was rife with tension as they took seats around Sienna's kidney table. Nancy trembled visibly.

Dr. Fray cleared his throat and began gravely. "We seem to have a number of irregularities on this year's WASTE."

Nancy blurted, "But Miguel sat through the entire test after we chased him down."

"I said *a number* of irregularities." Dr. Fray held up his hand. "It is very unusual for the state to have identified them this early in the scoring process."

"What kind of irregularities were there?" Sienna asked.

"Well, the first one," Dr. Fray said, "is that almost every fourth grader in your ELL writing group passed. This is quite startling. ELL students normally don't pass the writing portion. They certainly don't surpass their English speaking peers and some of yours did just that."

"Oh!" Sienna was overcome with giddy joy. "That's wonderful! I'd really hoped they'd pull it off." She beamed happily at everyone around the table, but Mimi and Deedee were stone-faced. Dr. Fray looked uncomfortable.

Nancy snarled, "They took that part of the WASTE in here with her."

"So?" Jolie asked. "I was in here the whole time. There was no cheating."

"It's difficult for kids to cheat on the writing portion," Dr. Fray observed. "But we will need your word on that, Jolie. Would you be prepared to sign an affidavit attesting to the that?"

Jolie glanced uneasily at Sienna. "Of course, but this whole inquiry is ridiculous."

"Well, there's another irregularity," Deedee said, "and it's much more important because it has to do with reading. Apparently, all of the ELL fourth graders in Nancy's class had the exact same scores on the reading component."

"Did they pass?" Sienna asked, confused.

"We aren't accusing you of anything yet," Mimi said to Sienna. "However, we do know that you take issue with *Reading Fare*, which is our program for preparing the children for the WASTE." She paused, leaving Sienna more flustered, to look from Nancy to Jolie. "So, we were just wondering if any of you might be able to shed some light on this situation for us."

"You need to tell the truth about what happened here," Deedee hissed. "It's your professional obligation."

"Did they pass?" Sienna asked.

"No!" Deedee snapped. "We're still a failing school—worse than ever—and now, we're a cheating school." She shrieked, "We're even failing at cheating! GOTCHA News 4 is gonna have a field day. Now, I'm never, ever, going to be the toast of the realtor's luncheon." She laid her face down on the table and covered her head with her arms, sobbing.

Dr. Fray shifted uneasily in his seat and cleared his throat.

Sienna stared evenly at Nancy daring her to disagree. "I was in

Nancy's classroom with her during the reading test. I was with her the whole time."

Nancy stammered. "Nothing happened. I mean Sienna just passed out tissue and barf bags. She might have read a few questions over kids' shoulders, but she didn't give anyone answers. The only strange thing that happened in there during the reading section was that Cassandra Fuentes couldn't sit still to save her life."

"Did you inform the test coordinator of that?" Mimi asked.

"And who was that?" Dr. Fray asked, opening a notebook. "Who was the test coordinator at Moore?"

Mimi said, "Deedee."

Deedee raised her tear-streaked face. "I thought it was you."

"It could have been me," Mimi said. "I think we had joint responsibility."

"I don't remember the meeting when we decided that." Deedee said.

"I might have some notes in my office," Mimi said. "Or maybe they're in my laptop."

"I'd say it's irregular not to know who the test coordinator is," Jolie remarked.

Sienna explained, "It used to be the school counselor, but since we don't have one any more."

"What happened to her?" Mimi asked.

"Budget cuts," Sienna said. "Last year."

Dr. Fray's pen was still poised. "Did you inform either test coordinator?" he asked Nancy.

"About what?" Nancy asked.

"The irregularity," Dr. Fray said.

"Which irregularity?" Nancy asked.

"I forget," Dr. Fray said.

"The itchy kid," Jolie said.

Nancy shook her head. "Cassandra is an ELL kid. If there was a problem, it would have been Sienna's responsibility to report it."

Everyone around the table stared expectantly at Sienna. She glanced around *The Writers' Lair*. At the Swami, *La Mujer de Tierra*, The Maritza, The Shaman, and Lupe's "Meet Me at the Swap Meet."

She looked at the anthologies of her students' stories beautifully illustrated and displayed on the whiteboard ledge. She remembered the story Pilar had written after the night with *La Llorona*.

The Awka Rock

One time my mother say a girl needs the awka rock if La Llorona comes around. She say if La Llorona really looks in it, she would stop taking kids. In my country, La Llorona was not after me. The bad people with big guns came. They take kids. We run. My mother—she was stopping and filling awka rocks with water. She make them all by Canal Luto. Awka rocks are the homes of mermaids. They come big. They come little. When bad people are coming, the mermaids hide inside. Bad people never see the mermaids. The water on top of the awka makes a mirror. The bad people check the mirror to see how they look. The bad people never see the mermaids. I pray to Our Lady of the Brick Wall that my mother and my father and my grandmother got into the stones with the mermaids.

Of course! Suddenly the whole inquisition made sense to Sienna. Cassandra had been praying to Our Lady of the Brick Wall during the WASTE. The little girl who'd been an angel on Halloween hadn't been getting a rash during the WASTE; she'd been trying to help her friends, the best way she knew how. She'd made the sign of the cross with her thumb on her forehead if the answer to the test question was A, on her solar plexus if it was B, on her left shoulder for C and her right shoulder for D. She had tried to be blessing, to be *generous*, to be *altruistic*, to ease the fear pulsating in the room, to tide them over until they could get back to *The Writers' Lair*. The children had watched her exaggerated signs and recorded the answers, according to what Cassandra's feet channeled. *Mary, Jesus,* and *Joseph.*

Deedee tapped her sandaled foot on the linoleum, as if waiting for a confession of wrongdoing, a lapse in duty.

Mimi spoke to Dr. Fray. "Sienna did not inform me of an irregularity."

"She didn't say a word," Deedee added.

"The DFA doesn't require us to report a child's skin condition,"

Sienna said.

"DFA?" Dr. Fray asked.

"Directions for Administration," Nancy snapped smugly. "I mean," she blushed, "for the administration of the test. Not for running the school district. I meant no offense."

Dr. Fray, batted Nancy's apology away as if it were a mosquito. "Why didn't you bring this girl to anyone else's attention, Sienna?"

"I talked to all of them about Cassandra before," Sienna said. "I told them that *Reading Fare* is too frustrating for her and the other English Learners. I told Deedee that Cassandra has been coping with the curriculum through prayer."

Deedee scoffed. "So she was praying during the WASTE?"

"She wasn't praying. She was…" Nancy broke off, resorting to mimicking Cassandra's motions.

"Is she Pentecostal?" Deedee asked.

Dr. Fray cleared his throat again. "She was probably just fidgeting. She sounds like a sweet kid who just cares about doing well."

"Oh, she does, Dr. Fray." Sienna continued, "They are all really sweet and they all really care about doing well. But, the Reading WASTE is so unfair to them. When they write their own stories they already know what they want to convey. That lets them focus on the English they need to learn to say what they already comprehend. When they write, they get to practice reading what they and their friends have written and they learn more words through revision. Once they have success with that, they will be able to read and understand what other authors have written. Right now, when they work with *Reading Fare,* they say their Reading Babies are dead. They say they are being smashed or drowned by words."

"How poetic," he said. "They seem creative too."

"They are!" Sienna wanted to show him the students' stories, but worried she'd be proving her infidelity to *Reading Fare* if she did.

"Being poetic and creative has nothing to do with our scores on the WASTE," Mimi said. "Or on the new NASTE. It also has nothing to do with *Reading Fare* which is the curriculum we bought to get our reading scores where we want them to be."

"They passed the writing!" Jolie broke in. "Isn't that where we want to be? We should celebrate! Sienna is onto something here. We should help her help the kids."

Dr. Fray nodded. "Sienna's work sounds very promising. The writing WASTE scores are something to be proud of."

"Well," Deedee said firmly, "Sienna just needs to get over herself and stop bragging about writing. We are judged on reading and math. This is a perfect example of why I'm so keen on uniforms for our staff. We have to be a team. I run Moore just like a family. If one sister gets too high up on her high horse, the others just have to cut her down. It's for everyone's own good."

Dr. Fray furrowed his brow.

Deedee spoke louder and a little slower. "I agree that Sienna is a good teacher, but she should focus on moving kids through the *Reading Fare* program. She shouldn't be wasting her skills on," Deedee waved her hand at the banner, "The *Writers' Lair*. No one cares about whether or not these kids can write about what happened to them in Mexico or wherever. It's time to blue-pencil this program. Delete, erase, and snuff it out. Working with kids who can't read to write stories is a waste of time."

"Dr. Fray," Sienna said urgently, "Do you believe that?"

He cleared his throat and stood stiffly. "Congratulations on your work with the children, Sienna," he said. "I wish you well, but this is out of my hands."

Horrified at his blank face, Sienna cried, "Whose hands is it in?"

"Shh," Mimi held a finger to her lips. "Don't ask questions like that."

"Dr. Fray?" Sienna insisted. "Tell me, please. Please!"

The superintendent looked at Deedee. He thought of all the district administrators and the elected local school board. Then, he thought of the state legislature, the federal government, taxpayers in general, publishers and their curriculum designers, and for-profit testing companies. He thought of parents and, finally, of teachers. His eyes widened. "Well, I suppose it's in everyone's hands."

The awka rock and the pile of stories about what happened the night *La Llorona*'s old tale changed were all there on the table right in front of them, but Sienna knew that Jolie was the only person in the room who could see them for what they were. She looked away to hide her tears of frustration. *The Maritza*, the Shaman, The Statue of Liberty, and Contemplation of Justice all seemed to nod at her.

Sienna's gaze fell upon Esperanza's *La Mujer de Tierra* and her eerily hollow *rebozo*. Somewhere along a frantic, fearful path, the child had fallen out, gotten lost, was left behind. The woman who'd cared for a little one, stood immobile in front of the makeshift classroom—split and divided within her Self. Sienna looked from Jolie, to Nancy, to Mimi, to Deedee, and finally back at Dr. Fray. Sadly, she said, "If that decision is in everyone's hands, then it's really in no one's."

Was it all a waste of time?

I used to be a weeping woman, but now I know more. Am I just an illusion? What about Our Lady of the Brick Wall? In a place where only that which is measurable counts, it is very difficult to tell. But you—you have been told. In *The Writers' Lair*, we make what we need. I'll meet you at the Swami.

Acknowledgments

Thank you to the children and teachers who inspired me to write this story. Thank you to Sharyn, Halline, John, Annie, Victoire, and Lisa for your careful reading and thoughtful discussion. I deeply appreciate the many people who supported moving this project to publication. You are angels.

25744880R00185

Made in the USA
Middletown, DE
09 November 2015